Mrs. Osborne

Memorials of the Life and Character of Lady Osborne

And some of her Friends - Vol. II

Mrs. Osborne

Memorials of the Life and Character of Lady Osborne
And some of her Friends - Vol. II

ISBN/EAN: 9783337107512

Printed in Europe, USA, Canada, Australia, Japan

Cover: Foto ©Raphael Reischuk / pixelio.de

More available books at **www.hansebooks.com**

The Slope, Newtown-Anner.

W. D. HEMPHILL, M.D., Photo

MEMORIALS

OF

LADY OSBORNE.

VOL. II.

Lady Osborne's Summer House.

1870.

MEMORIALS

OF

THE LIFE AND CHARACTER

OF

LADY OSBORNE

AND SOME OF HER FRIENDS:

EDITED BY HER DAUGHTER,

MRS. OSBORNE.

"Gather up the fragments that remain, that nothing be lost."—John vi. 12.

IN TWO VOLUMES.

VOL. II.

DUBLIN:
HODGES, FOSTER & CO., GRAFTON STREET,
PUBLISHERS TO THE UNIVERSITY.
—
1870.

INDEX TO AUTOGRAPH LETTERS.

	PAGE.
Mrs. Stanley,	7
Miss M. R. Warde,	20
Mrs. Warde,	22
Dr. Poole,	26
Rev. Henry Woodward,	45
Mrs. Riall,	68
Mrs. Hill,	78
Anonymous,	97
Dr. Arnott,	103
Professor W. A. Butler,	105
Father Mathew,	108
Mrs. Walker,	109
Lord Bexley,	110
James Walker (Bishop of Edinburgh),	113
Anonymous,	117
Edward Stanley, D.D. (Bishop of Norwich),	121
Samuel Hinds, D.D. (Bishop of Norwich),	122
Rev. Dr. Hanna,	123
Rev. Dr. Chalmers,	124
Lord Sydenham (Poulett Thomson),	126
Monsieur J. C. L. de Sismondi,	142
Rev. James Dunn,	168
Stephen Sandes, D.D. (Bishop of Cashel),	192
Marquis of Lansdowne,	193
Lord Ebrington,	194
Lord Lytton,	195
Charles Dickinson, D.D. (Bishop of Meath),	197
Rev. F. B. Woodward,	200
Richard Whately, D.D. (Archbishop of Dublin)	206

LIST OF ILLUSTRATIONS.

VOL. I.

FRONTISPIECE—VIEW FROM DINING-ROOM, NEWTOWN ANNER.
From a Photograph by W. D. HEMPHILL, M.D.

VIGNETTE ON TITLE—VIEW FROM DARK WALK, NEWTOWN ANNER.
From a Photograph by W. D. HEMPHILL, M.D.

VOL. II.

FRONTISPIECE—THE SLOPE, NEWTOWN ANNER.
From a Photograph by W. D. HEMPHILL, M.D.

VIGNETTE ON TITLE—LADY OSBORNE'S SUMMER HOUSE.
From a Photograph by W. D. HEMPHILL, M.D.

PORTRAIT OF REV. HENRY WOODWARD . . . . PAGE 45

PORTRAIT OF ARCHBISHOP WHATELY . . . . PAGE 207

PREFACE TO THE AUTOGRAPH LETTERS.

LETTERS stand in the same relation to biography that politics do to history. The events of a great character's life are made known by a mere biography, as history shews forth in the framed pictures left on the scaffolding of politics; but letters manifest the tone of mind as politics do the springs that guide the master hands accomplishing historical results.

The following written remains of the friends of Lady Osborne are all either of intrinsic interest in the judgment of the Editor, or of value on account of the (for the greater part) illustrious individuals who penned them for anything characteristic of such, has a charm belonging to it, and, if genuine, it must be characteristic.

In Lady Osborne's letters the Editor was struck by the still, unsettled, yet enduring interest of many of the subjects treated therein. In those, on the other hand, alluded to by

Mons. de Sismondi, though in their nature final, they come under the category of the study for which he was most famous—history; a qualification which, though chief, was only one of many others; for, in his life, he was celebrated for his enlightened and truly liberal views on contemporaneous matters; likewise for being the centre of the most brilliant society that passed through Geneva, the gangway of the South of Europe. The pick and choice of all who travelled thither were to be met with at his soirées.

In those days the Editor was too young to understand the remarkable plot of social ground upon which Fortune had assigned her first view of the world in its company sense. A person finding themselves, suddenly, for the first time, at the foot of lofty mountains, would hardly take in all their altitude. Still it was impossible for her, even, not to reverence the gracious host and hostess, and to wonder at all the well-filled book-shelves that had been the products of M. de Sismondi's brain, and to listen with interest to the recital of his travels in the company of Madame de Stael, on whom all the " beaux esprits " of the day waited at various stopping places, as upon a sovereign who makes a progress. There was to be seen the Marquis de St. Marsan, with fingers frozen in Napoleon's Moscow expedition, and accompanied by his lovely daughter, a model of grace and beauty. Remarkable instances of failure and success, were to be met side by side, as re-arded the past and future. On the one hand, the ex-Minister of Charles the Tenth, Baron d'Haussez, representing as he did ' individual will ' or despotism ' pur et simple;' and on the other, a personage who, in the condition of an exiled prince, the sagacious and far-seeing Mons. de Sismondi discerned a power that would be felt as one of the greatest in the world—the present ruler of the destinies of France. Queen Hortense, who, if she had been born in private life, would have been a most noteworthy person on account of her graces and gifts. She was an instance of the combination of a talent for music and painting; for, while well known as the composer of some beautiful " romances," including the present French national air (composed, too, when quite a child), she would graciously shew albums of portraits done by herself, which indicated her facility in the sister art. Foreigners of all countries and shades of opinion found a ready admission to that small but very remarkable salon.

It may not be deemed unworthy of mention that M. de Sismondi's sisters both married men conspicuous in different ways—Sir James Mackintosh and Mr. Wedgewood.

That brilliant assemblage has long since vanished, as do all the dissolving views of this life. Many of the letters are from those eminent for their lives bearing upon the great hereafter rather than as actors upon the stage of this life, with one or two exceptions, though to reach that last plunge they had still to perform their parts in this life, but with their minds fixed upon that state which, though so vague to the living philosopher, is revealed to every dead barbarian.

Here the Editor has assembled a group on the plan of Chênes, and she only hopes that they will meet with the genial reception they would have experienced at the hands of her on whose memory they wait as the central figure.

It will be seen that the hostile opinions on other subjects of the minds of the various writers did not hinder them from being unanimous as to the charming character of their correspondent.

The wonderful foresight of M. de Sismondi regarding the French Emperor likewise appears in his notice of the Oxford party.

MEMORIALS

OF

THE LIFE AND CHARACTER

OF

LADY OSBORNE.

" The following letters were written by the friend referred to in Lady Osborne's communications to her English relations as such a joy and resource in her solitude. They mark the great power she had of attaching others to her, though, indeed, the time came when extreme jealousy on the part of the writer put them asunder."

November 14th.

Your Holyhead letter, my dearest friend, relieves me from great anxiety. There had been such a succession of storms, that had I not trusted to your fears for detaining you on shore whilst there was one threatening cloud in the sky, I must have felt very miserable. Thank God you are safely over the only perilous part of your way, and so far I am happier than I was. Although I can never experience a more grateful feeling than in preventing, if I might, your wishes, yet I have not been solicitous to forestal your arrival at Yalding; a quieter hour will better suit the receipt

of my letter—an hour when, though all may be joyful, you
can spare a few moments of thought to one whose affections
and regrets have pursued every step of your progress.
Aspirants after a medium in all things may dogmatize to the
end of the chapter, but of that school I shall never be a disciple. It is no modified sadness that I feel at heart, and I
believe I must be content to endure it. I cannot be talked
into thinking our separation a trivial thing, or that when I
could never, without reluctance, part from you for one hour.
I am to consider several months as a mere point of time,
hardly calling for regret, and indisputably not challenging
any emotion allied to grief. My beloved friend, I bear you
no feeling to which such calm spirits as my well-meaning
lectures can apply their calculations. I lament you, and
that most deeply! Precious to me in every imaginable
sense—companion, associate, and friend, you are identified
with all objects of taste, feeling, fancy, and reason. I perpetually want to refer to you for participation or approval;
to look to you as a motive; to pride in your influence, and
to glory in that sweet intelligence which, once at least,
seemed to unite us in heart, thought, and attainment here,
and promised to shape the same course for us hereafter. I
have seen Newtown once since we parted, but I believe I
must wait for a more settled state of mind before I repeat
my visit. I had a notion that to see a spot so dearly loved
would be soothing. I was mistaken, however. The change
was too decided, and the recollections too fresh for such an
effect. Everything looked as deserted and forlorn as I felt
myself. The scattered furniture and disordered rooms so
unlike your home; the garden and shrubbery, lonely and
silent, had so little the character of those cheerful haunts
familiar to me, and all bore such striking marks of being
far removed from any preparation for your return, that I
felt it a relief to get away. Some time hence, perhaps, I

may regard those objects with different emotions, when
acute regret has subsided into a mournful tenderness that
can take comfort from dwelling upon every scene and circumstance that has relation to you. With Newtown will
begin and end my sum of indulgence. Their memory can
beguile many an hour for me; but, fancy (so far as she
might traffic with the future), I am not very desirous of
enlisting as an auxiliary. Seasons do not stand still because
we either sorrow or rejoice. The month of March will come
in due course; but, oh! my beloved friend, can it restore us
to each other—what has been? This is a question only pre-
science could answer.

I must not write further without thanking you for the
beautiful eye-glass which I got this morning; but do not
think me ungrateful for confessing that a memorial of no
intrinsic value, which had actually belonged to you, which
had been in your possession, and used by you, would be still
more precious than this glittering appendant; however,
doubt not that I shall always wear it, inanimate though it
be! always love it. I met the workman to be employed in
the alteration of your study at Newtown, and settled what
was to be done. The window is to be considerably enlarged,
and the door will correspond with it. For a new window
and door (of the latter, three parts will be glass), shutters,
pulleys, hinges, &c., &c., you pay ten guineas; the glazing
will cost between three and four pounds; the mason work
(for a great part of the heavy pier must be removed) two
pounds; so that, for about twenty guineas, painting included,
the room will be made as comfortable as you can desire. A
plain neat paper is not likely to be a material addition to the
foregoing estimate, in which I think I have not exceeded
your instructions. The grate may stand as it is. Tell me if
you are satisfied with the whole arrangement. Ryan and the
carpenter, promised to complete their part of the work

within a month. From time to time I will see how they get
on, and when they have finished, I will try if I can prevail
with Quin to lay out the ground before the windows, according to what I think would be your taste. J—— P—— has
been with Eben, to state that when he last saw you at Newtown, you consented to refer the valuation of his farms to
his friends, Fitzpatrick and Charles Riall. I hope you have
not bound yourself by any such promise; for Fitzpatrick
tells Eben that he will not value some part of the land at
more than five shillings per acre. C. Riall could easily be
overruled, and you would have to sustain a material loss
and endless vexation. P—— said he intended writing to
you for the purpose of obtaining a more formal assent to
his scheme, but Eben entreats that you will decline the
measure altogether, allowing him to make the necessary
arrangements, and referring P—— to him for particulars;
so much for business. I am advancing rapidly with your
cabinet, and I am grateful for such an occupation, since I
can no longer work near you; the next best thing is to be
employed for you; besides I think this piece of furniture
will greatly please you, and that solitary anticipation none
need envy me. The chairs I will repair and complete, and
if there be any other matter in which I can gratify you, or
be of use to you or yours, indicate your wish, and I shall
derive my truest comfort from observing it. I hope I have
not said so much of myself as to weary you; but this first
time of communicating with you I found it impossible
altogether to restrain the expression of my feelings and
regrets; for my affection, my most dear friend, I can find
" no " expression. Well may you say that in suffering or in
danger, not for myself, but for you, would be my thought.
With you is my tenderest love; for you is my warmest
prayer. Long before you receive this, I trust a letter will
be on its way to me, not hurried or concise, but one that

may really soothe me.   Letters are poor substitutes for
the look, the tone, the character ; affection, makes not,
however, the little less!   Kiss your darling for me, and tell
my sweet William that no " gage d'amitié " was ever more
prized, or worn with more devotion, than his ring. Mention
your own health whenever you write, and promise me to
have recourse to medicine if you should continue to be
annoyed by headache or the uneasiness of which latterly you
frequently complained.   In all things take care of yourself;
you are the sun to many hearts.   Strother is well, and says
he is comfortable; yet he expresses a strong wish to see *you*
again.   He dined with me yesterday, and promises to see me
very often.   Assure yourself that I shall always see him
with affectionate interest.   He got his watch, and I have
locked up Mrs. Smith's. If it be not to travel with Thomas,
how am I to dispose of it? Your medals I shall send by
him.   William is going on well; his appetite, strength, and
spirits are improving.   I hope Miss Warde continues to
amend.   Distribute regards from me just as they may be
acceptable, to Anna.   The girls send their most affectionate
love.   I had intended to cross the whole of this letter, but I
perceive that if I did it would be illegible. Do not disappoint me, my beloved friend, whether you had written
before or not.   Write to me on receipt of this; and do not
continue to enclose your letters to Deakins; it occasions a
delay which is very unwelcome to one so impatient to hear
from you.   Hardly do I know how to conclude; but were I
to fill sheets or volumes, would not half what is in my heart
find utterance.

God bless you, my best loved and most precious friend;
think me yours, and only yours, FOR EVER !

MARY STANLEY.

" The burning of the O'Sheas, mentioned in the following
letter, was one of those events that made so great a sensation in
the neighbourhood that, (as is often the case) in that locality,
it occasions surprise, that by the country at large it should not
be remembered like some great historical event. A farm-
house containing eighteen human beings, young and old, and
situated at the foot of the celebrated mountain "Slievenamon,"
was one night, in the year 1821, set on fire and surrounded
by fellow creatures armed with pikes, who with these weapons
thrust back into the burning house those who sought escape.
The Woodward family saw the flames the night of the crimi-
nal occurrence. The Editor perceives from this letter that the
deed was the result of a private feud. She remembers hearing an incident of the tragedy. A mother plunged a little
child into a pail of water to assuage its prospective sufferings,
but they were thus only rendered more lingering."

1821, Dec. 7th.

I do not lose a moment in replying to your letter, my
dearest friend. Owing to contrary winds often prevalent
during the winter months, I only received it this evening,
and having thanked you for its general kindness, most
gratefully soothing to me, I will not waste another word
upon myself, but proceed to give you the fullest information
in my power as to the actual state of the country ; my
intelligence, I trust, will go some way towards tranquillizing
your uneasiness, and arming you to meet the alarmists on
your side of the channel. If they report on newspaper
authority they must detail falsehood without measure, for
rumours of every description and shade of exaggeration find
their way to the Dublin papers, and are thence copied into the
English journals, nor is it difficult to conjecture how this
happens. We have alarmists here also, men to whom turbulent times or *the fear* of them would give both office and

emolument. To that part of the country for which you are most interested I have the happiness to tell you no disturbance extends, and the conduct of your tenantry affords a proof not only of their peaceable disposition, but of personal attachment to you, and of anxiety to secure your favor, and shew their sense of your kindness. Whilst absentees are railing, and clamouring, and petitioning about unpaid rents, and tumultuary dependents, your tenantry are quietly and voluntarily bringing in their rents, and uniting in one enquiry—" Will she not come back to be over us again." To this many-times-repeated question it will not be out of place to add a remark of Robert Grubb's who knows something of all men and all motives. " Lady Osborne," said he, " has nothing to fear ; the worst of those fellows will take care not to move a finger that might disturb her; her people feel that she will do them good, and so far from wanting to vex her, they would go through fire and water to have her amongst them." No part of the County Tipperary has been materially disquieted ; even the destruction of the O'Sheas, though an act of unparalleled and ruthless atrocity, was the fruit of a private feud, and wholly unconnected with that system which distracts the County Limerick, and districts of the counties of Cork and Kerry ; but wheresoever it may have extended its evil influence, it presents some features which not only distinguish it from every former infraction of the laws, but which must greatly facilitate the means used to restore order. None but the very lowest of the population are engaged ; they have neither leaders or favourers amongst the better classes; and no hostility against government, either political or religious, is a motive with them : it is a crusade against evils which undoubtedly pressed heavily upon them in many cases, a desperate venture between starving and hanging ; and it will be arrested whenever strong coercion and exemplary punishment shall be the order of the day. In the

County Limerick where the fire first blazed the great landed proprietors are almost to a man absentees. I instance but a few when I name Lords Courtney, Clare, Limerick, Mr. Fitzgibbon, &c., &c.: their estates are let at rack rent, and their tenantry are a miserable, oppressed, neglected, and demoralized race, reckless of consequences and desperate in mischief, the more so because a temporary impunity has attended their outrages, a circumstance much to be lamented, for when the spirit of insubordination was first manifested it could easily have been checked, but the resident magistracy were not numerous, and they were supine ; nor was the government prompt to supply the deficiency, indeed we are given to understand that coercive measures were long suspended with a view to stimulate into action those noble land holders, who, drawing from the soil more than its miserable cultivators could yield without starvation, are to be found in London, or in Paris, or anywhere but on the spot to which duty and interest should have bound them. Having so far given the dark side of the picture let me now present that which I trust every day will brighten.

Lord Talbot is a well-meaning man, but the present crisis demands something more, and Lord Talbot yields the Viceroyalty to the Marquis of Wellesley, whose character is firm and decided, therefore we may look for steady measures ; and union of council which it was understood did not subsist in the Viceregal Cabinet. Lord T. and Mr. Gregory it is surmised did not coincide in opinion with Mr. Grant, with whom it lay to take cognizance of our evils and apply the fitting remedies, and Mr. Grant, though a person of considerable talent, an orator, a statesman, etc., is not adapted either to turbulent times or embarrassing emergencies; thus you will perceive that we may expect a different application of our resources, and we have another and a more immediate hope from the special commission, which will sit in Limerick on the 15th of this month, for a trial of a long list of criminals. A special commission is an expedient recommended by experience, it once and speedily tranquillized this country when a far worse flame than the present had burst forth. Now my dearest friend I have endeavoured to trace the past, describe the more recent, and account for still existing outrages which disgrace poor Ireland. If I have not given you a sufficiently clear view, you must excuse me; I have not time to methodize my matter, it is now past twelve at night and not to lose the post, my letter must be in the office at ten to-morrow morning; a post I would not allow to pass, because I know your anxiety to hear from a quarter where you have so much at stake.

From public I must descend to private affairs, to one in particular, which I think of great importance to your interests I mean the line of road from Glenpatrick to the Suir, there are few things I have so much at heart as the seeing that plan in progress, and I have had a discusssion upon it both with Eben and Robert Grubb; the former I can perceive is rather desirous that it should lie by for the present; the truth I imagine may be that he has a holy horror of your venturing to expend one guinea (beyond what it makes) upon the quarry, and he calculates that to smooth your way by the new road would set you to work at once. I hope it would, and I also hope that the road will be in forwardness next spring. R. Grubb and I agree perfectly in opinions and views, and he tells me that some preliminary steps must be taken at the January Sessions, otherwise the presentment cannot be put in at the Spring Assizes. Would it not be well to write to him upon the subject, asking him to communicate with Captain Power, and to call upon Eben, whom perhaps you had better address upon the same topic, and urge to take the necessary steps. Thus stimulated he must give up his precious caution, and do what is needful. I believe I have told you all, and certainly all of importance that has been done in the way of business since you left Newtown.

The Kilmore heroes hold their ground, and I think with you that a compromise will be prudent; Eben made repeated attempts upon their Castle, but on each occasion his myrmidons abandoned him to his fate, which considering the times it is wonderful did not meet him in the shape of a bullet. Military he would not employ without a magistrate, and no magistrate could be persuaded to attend him; some interests have been paid, Capt. —— and Mrs. Osborne's.

Though the fiery elements which enter into the composition of our poor peasantry, are so innocuous to you, the natural elements visit you more roughly; we have had some tremendous gales within the last fortnight, and in one of them I grieve to tell you that the fine elm tree near the house of Newtown suffered severely, its right limb was lopped off, the left as you remember had separated from the trunk none knew wherefore. The windows of the rooms formerly Johnson's, were blown in and shattered, a quantity of lead stripped from the roof, one of the small domes over the corridor carried off, and dispersed in innumerable fragments, and to conclude the list of casualties, one end of the peach house much damaged; but the green house is unhurt. Whilst I was detailing affairs connected with the estate, I should have told you that Eben is now endeavouring to arrange with ——, but he I suspect will hold off till your return frightens him into equitable terms, to which he seems little disposed. I am sorry the library windows could not be constructed as you desire, I had thought of your plan before, but on consulting the workmen, found it impracticable. It would have shaken the old wall too much; however, I believe you will be pleased with what is doing. I shall attend to all your directions with respect to planting in the high field; I shall see Quin to-morrow, and then ascertain if this be the best time for the purpose. I will if possible have the plate engraved, but in Clonmel I fear there is no artist equal to the undertaking. There are very few of your books here, and those few carefully locked up. I have done with business; and now my dearest friend let me tell you that I do believe you will cheerfully return to your post, and in so doing, and sedulously cherishing your attachments to this country, and your views for the improvement of your dependents you will rank with the few whom Ireland can call her truly noble. Many a fond vision have I woven of your future distinction; not the adventitious distinction of rank or fortune, but that of an exalted character, applying power and influence to purposes of kindness; this indeed is your sphere of action and usefulness; the talent committed to your keeping, and with your principles and capacities, ten thousand fold will it increase in your hands. Of myself I do not wish to say more than that your "wishes," your "views," and your "gratifications" are dearer to me than my own; that your interest is my first thought, and that in promoting all that bears upon your welfare, I shall ever find a happiness that no other object in life can afford to me. I am grateful to you for saying that writing to me soothed your discomposure; thus it should be, and thus on all occasions and subjects it may be for the time to come; never more will you trace aught of those sensitive feelings which sometimes repressed your confidence. Mr. —— is as you say a self-sufficient boy, not worth your perturbation. I do not like to think of your being assailed, but heed it not, you shall yet boast, and proudly too of Ireland. Be assured of my punctuality in writing, and of my minute attention to the detail of every fact that can interest you. Tell me if in this letter I have passed over any subject upon which you desired information. William is not, I think, so well as when I last mentioned him,

yet not I trust materially worse. The weather which precludes
his taking exercise is against his improvement. Mary and
Kate go on well. With Mary's French I take such indefatiga-
ble pains, that I should hope her progress may be considerable.
I feel peculiar interest in doing so because you seemed to
desire it. Kate's English Grammar goes on too, but she will
never be the fore-horse of the team in literary pursuits. I
have written enough to weary you, but I could not well be
more concise. Kiss your sweet children for me. Remember me
to Johnson, and to whom else you please; and believe that
whilst I live, I shall obey your charge and continue to love
you. God bless you my dearest friend.

MARY STANLEY.

" Being anxious to preserve some of the " own words " of
two relations, both well beloved, and who both took their
departure for Heaven under Lady Osborne's roof, the
Editor gives the following letter addressed to her on the turning point of her life ; and an extract afterwards from a
letter written by an aunt, who was like a second mother to
her."

MY DEAREST CATHERINE,—The day after Jane wrote to
you, my father received a letter from Mr. Riall to offer to
take charge of one of us to Ireland in case he was not
obliged to go by Scotland on business; we did not hear again
until to-day, and as we find he goes by Bristol, my father has
consented to Jane's accompanying him. She goes to town
to-morrow, to set off for Bristol on Tuesday morning ; and
Mr. Riall intends sailing by the steam packet from thence on
Wednesday, so that I imagine they will be in Dublin by
Thursday, God willing. We do not know whether he intends to stay in Dublin, but I should think not. If Jane
finds he does, she will add a line to this letter in town, and

you can send some one to meet her there ; but I rather think he would proceed immediately to Clonmel.

My father was so decided in his objections to my going, that nothing I could have urged would have weighed with him. He fancies that I am ill, and that the journey would be too much for me, and therefore I am obliged to yield, although on many accounts I wished to have gone to you. I should have been less missed at home, and being older than Jane, melancholy scenes are more my province.

If her society yields you any consolation, my dear cousin, we shall be repaid for the sacrifice of her company at home; and I hope and trust that you will permit it to be so, for *her* sake, for your mother, for your little girl's, and for all those interested for you (and no person I believe in affliction ever excited more), do not, my dear cousin, *cherish* those feelings, those gloomy miserable feelings, which cannot be right in the sight of heaven. They will intrude, I know, and it will be a hard and long lesson for you to forget that such things were, and were most pleasant, but I think you may *prevent* yourself from dwelling on circumstances that can only agonize you, and tend to no good purpose. You are fond of Jane, and I think her good sense and good feeling will be of service to you. Do not reject her good offices, my dearest cousin, and remember it is only the idea that her society will be comforting to you that could induce her to take so long a journey by herself, and a separation from all her own family. You will, I am sure, my dearest cousin, consider this, and not let her experience the mortification of feeling that her efforts are unavailing, by seeing you refuse all consolation. I hope you will be able to come to England early in the autumn—change of place may *then* do something for you ; and, at any rate, you may be sure of meeting with sympathising friends.

It is a great mortification to me not to be able to be with

you and my aunt now, and I don't think myself that the
journey would have been of any disservice to me, but my
father seemed so determined to think that it would, that I
saw from the first he would not permit me to go. I am only
low and nervous, and the best remedy for that will be, learning that you, my dear Catherine, are restored to some degree of tranquillity; to that peace of mind which passeth
understanding ; that lasting peace which the world can
neither give nor take away. Religious enthusiasm cannot
last: it may elevate your feelings for the time, but it is like
the effects of ether, renders you more wretched after it has
evaporated.

Adieu! my dear cousin; console all your friends, absent
and present, by returning in some degree to your former
self; and, be assured, the spirit of your departed darling
will be best pleased by viewing you resigned and patient.

Ever, my dear Catherine,

Your affectionate cousin,

M. R. Warde.

"This extract points out that the writer, though a very
strong Protestant, believed that Popery was progressing and
would do so even more, and thus are evidenced the sobriety
and clear sightedness of her views.

Besides the fact that the Romanist exercises the right of
private judgment in as responsible, though in a lazier·
manner, by deciding upon the infallibility of the Church, it
has always appeared wonderful to the Editor, that Romanists
who believe that the powers of the Apostles were transmitted
fully by the apostolical succession theory ever go to a doctor.
In the days of the Apostles such persons were taken to them
or handkerchiefs brought from their bodies, gave health.
That they should go without money is not surprising, re-
membering the case of Simon Magus; but we read of no

failure as to a cure in the Acts of the Apostles. It has been said "miracles were not always wrought by the Apostles," but in the Romish Church the greatest of all miracles, Transubstantiation, is held to be unfailing.

Now Transubstantiation lacks the essential characteristic of a miracle which is to make a supernatural fact apparent to the lookers on. Regeneration has been instanced as contrary to this definition, but this example the Editor refutes by the words, "the wind bloweth where it listeth, and thou *hearest* the sound thereof, but canst not tell whence it cometh and whither it goeth, so is every one that is born of the Spirit!" Nothing is more evident to beholders than a change of character, however gradually it may be manifested. Moreover, Mr. Ffoulkes in his able pamphlet called "The Church's Creed or the Crown's Creed," points out that in the Church of Rome care is taken that the Pope should not be poisoned in receiving the Sacrament, as if Christ's sacred body could convey effectual poison!—that body so full of virtue, that in touching the hem of the garment in contact with it, the poor woman, of whom we read in the New Testament, was cured of her disease!

June 6th, 1827.

MY DEAR CATHERINE,—Being again disappointed of a frank from Lord Barham to whom I wrote for one, but having since heard he was still in town, or at Brighton, I cannot now expect it; I must put you again to the expense of postage, a thing I had hoped to have avoided, for when one has nothing very fresh to communicate one feels a little diffident of the value of their epistolary intelligence, when it is to travel far and cost much; yet I think if mine be of value any where, it is in that quarter to which I am now sending this messenger of friendship and goodwill to be received in the same spirit in which I send it. As a proof of the affection I feel for all the members of

the family who will read this, and be pleased to find that all
is well with me and mine, at least as far as a breaking up
constitution at the grand climacteric will allow me to be, for
I have frequent returns of my complaint—whatever that may
be—at present it is nameless; I can hardly define it. But
I suspect that in time it will take a more decided character,
and then I shall judge better what to expect from it; in the
meantime I must endeavour to draw the best advantage I
can from it, by turning my thoughts there, where only true
joys are to be found, and from the passing scenes of a world
where the changes and chances of things and of men and of
women are more against than for me . . .

As to my interest in the reformation of Ireland of which
you wrote so sanguinely, can you doubt that I should be
delighted to hear of the whole world worshipping our Creator
and Saviour in the purest form of religion which is known,
and divested of all the errors tacked to it by Popery; it is
my nightly and daily prayer, that our Established Church
may become a truly Apostolic Church, at which all nations
may congregate and worship in all the simplicity delivered
to us by its Divine founder; more especially do I pray that
the true light may shine on these United Kingdoms, and
much do I rejoice when I read of converts from Papistry to
our simple faith; but sad is the drawback on the pleasure I
derive from this, when, in the next page, I see Protestants
become apostates and new converts returning to their former
errors; this it is which has checked me from offering my
congratulations to you on those promises of reformation
which are so frequently held forth in the papers. The more
I examine Popery by the only criterion we have (the Holy
Scriptures) the more surprised I am that any rational being
can renounce our mode of worship for that of the Roman
heathenish form. I can believe that those brought up Papists
may continue so from the force of habit, and a wilful shutting

of the eyes to the light of reason; but how those born to a purer faith can lower their reason to the belief in the puerilities—the mummeries of Popery, I may say its blasphemies, is past my comprehension. It must be its pomp and pageantry, its absolving from sin, assumed as that Divine Power is by its priest, which draws them over to its standard. The Almighty suffers these delusions to continue for a time, and times, and half a time, and when he thinks fit He will overthrow them all, and the Saviour shine forth in the fulness of His glory; so be it. I have been lately reading a very excellent work—a history of the Reformation—which, in its introduction, carries you back to the earliest period of Christianity and proves the false claims to antiquity of the Roman Church. Since then errors seem to have crept in in comparatively modern times. I cannot recollect the author's name, but you have doubtless heard of and read it before this time; it is a very good addition to Milner's History of the same period, and if you have not read it, I recommend you to get it. It is in two quarto volumes and will make a good library book.

We have not had such a spring this year as the last; everything is nearly three weeks backwarder than in the last year. I hope you have been accommodated with the same showery weather we have had, for the good of the "*pratie*" grounds, which abundance is so necessary to the welfare of your poor Irish, who, if they have been forward with their crops, may soon be saved from starvation. I trust that they have shewn a little more foresight than usual in putting them into the ground. You may, if you please, distribute the three pounds to the poor creatures from us, as we have taken it on ourselves with ———. I wish we had something better worth sending, but you know how little we have at our command.

Your affectionate aunt,
S. Warde.

Sunday night, 6th June, 1824.

My dear Lady Osborne,—I have taken up my pen for
the purpose of fulfilling my promise to reply to your letter
of the 4th instant, and I have selected this evening to do so,
in the hope that I may not be interrupted in my intention.
I have given what I conceive to be the serious and most important parts of your letter all the consideration my time and
ability would allow, and I mean to communicate the results
without reserve, relying on your kind indulgence and patience " that you will bear with me to the end."

The separation by death from the object most beloved by
us, of all things on earth chills the soul with horror, and
frequently hurries the unsubdued mind to charge the God
of all mercy with injustice, and the attempts made by
friends to offer consolation to the afflicted sufferer on such
occasions, may in general be properly answered in the words
of Job, " Miserable comforters are ye all;" and the reason
why no comfort by them, whom natural affection and other
kind motives urge to offer their condolence on such occasions is, because they themselves know not Him from whom,
under the deepest shades of affliction, a ray of mercy shines
to cheer His suffering people, and who has told them that
he afflictions of this life are but momentary and light, compared with the unclouded happiness and everlasting joys
which await them in those regions where the redeemed shall
ever be with the Lord.   See 17th verse of the 4th chapter of
1st Thessalonians; also 14th John, 3rd verse.

There is a sweet reflection connected with the departure
of children, " That they are taken out of a world of sorrow,
and translated to a kingdom of eternal glory ;" and the Bible
tells us (5th Job, 7th verse), " Man is born to trouble as the
sparks fly upwards," meaning that trouble must be man's lot
on earth, as certainly as the laws of nature are true to them-

selves. We may as reasonably expect to see these reversed, as to meet with a human being whose earthly cup is not mixed with sorrow. Our own experience confirms this truth, so does all that we know of those around; and were we to devote our whole lives to searching for one individual who could say he knew no sorrow, the search would be fruitless. Suppose then the dear child, of whom you have been so lately bereaved, to have enjoyed that greatest of all blessings, good health; suppose him to have realized all your fondest expectations, formed on the extraodinary capacity of mind he displayed; suppose all your views concerning his prospects in life, on his attaining the age of manhood, to have been realized, still he would have been subject to trouble and sorrow. Rank, fortune, talents, genius, philosophy, nothing could have exempted him from that which God has said is the certain portion of man. But he is taken away from trouble to come. He is now beyond the reach of sorrow; and whilst you grieve for him, he rests in happiness upon that ineffable love which beams around the throne of God, and partakes of joys that are as boundless as eternal. But you wait to be assured that he is happy. It would appear that God in mercy to bereaved parents, perhaps, has revealed in the Scriptures that the souls of departed children are happy in eternity as the justified made perfect. This may be gathered from a consideration of the following passages of Scripture:—1st Kings, 14th chapter, 1st to 14th verses, that the good things (therein alluded to) which the Lord sees in the child, cannot for a moment be supposed to have tended only to the circumstances of his death. In the 18th chapter of Matthew's Gospel there are two remarkable passages respecting the love of the Lord Jesus for little children, which occur in the 3rd and 10th verses. The latter part of the 10th verse seems to me to be almost conclusive with respect to the salvation of children. If then this assurance is given on the authority of God's word that these (children's) angels always behold His face, you may reject every doubt as to the happiness of your child. But surely there is another inducement to you to look without one moment's delay to the ground of your one hope before God, lest it should be His will to take you out of this world. Another and more awful separation may take place between you and him, whose memory you now treasure in your heart. That such an eternal separation will take place, the word of God explicitly states in the 25th chapter of Matthew, 31st verse, to the end of the chapter.

I write to you, my dear friend, unreservedly, and to adopt any other mode would be, instead of kindness, dealing deceitfully on a subject of all others the most important to every human being. To be assured of a joyful meeting, never again to be separated from the object of your affection, holds out a prospect more bright and cheering than any else could afford. And if the unerring standard of God's revealed truth be appealed to, it will tell us in simple, plain, and intelligible language, that such an assurance may be attained. By what means? you will be disposed to ask. The word of God points out the way, and I have already referred you to portions of that word, which more at large set before us what the Saviour Himself says so emphatically in the 6th verse of the 14th chapter of John's Gospel. The whole of that chapter, rightly understood, abounds with comforts, and is replete with promises to the believers in the Lord Jesus Christ. But I may be adopting expressions which, perhaps, may be deemed by you as the effusions of enthusiasm, and therefore must be *plain*. The *way* to heaven, and if the Bible be true, the *one* and the *only* way to heaven, is through faith in the all-atoning blood of the beloved Son of God, shed for sinners on the cross, in which shedding of blood there is the fountain opened for sin and uncleanness spoken of by the Prophet Zechariah, in the 1st verse of the 13th chapter, in which all who are washed are cleansed from *all* sin. This is plainly stated by the Apostle John in his 1st Epistle, 1st chapter and 7th verse, to believe that the record which God has given of His Son is eternal life, read the 10th and 11th verses of the 5th chapter of the same Epistle; and whilst the Scriptures are full of assurances of eternal happiness to them who believe in the Lord Jesus, they denounce the wrath of God against all who reject the Saviour. See 18th and 19th and 36th verses of the 3rd chapter of John's Gospel, and 16th chapter of Mark, 15th and 16th verses.

I find I have allowed my pen to run to an unreasonable length, and I almost fear I have exhausted your patience. I shall conclude; but before I do so, allow me once more to revert to the great freedom in which I have expressed my sentiments on the present as well as former occasions, and to entreat your forbearance. Believe me to be sincere when I assure you that I have not been led to do so from any supposed or fancied superiority of character or judgment. On the contrary, an humble and anxious concern for your welfare and peace of mind has been my only motive; and one of the greatest comforts I could experience would be to know you had obtained that peace of mind which God's word declares this world can neither give or take away. Shortly after I had the honour of your acquaintance, I formed my opinion of your character and disposition, which early excited in my breast a strong and lively interest, not only in respect to yourself, but also to the dear object of all your care and anxiety. The affliction and severe trial you have since experienced the effects produced on your mind, have tended to increase my concern and interest in every matter connected with your welfare, and will, I hope and trust, plead my apology, for I can offer nothing else in extenuation of any seeming error in words or deed I may have been guilty of. And with great respect and every sincere and anxious wish for your health and happiness,

> Believe me to be,
> My dear Lady Osborne,
> Your friend and faithful servant,
> M. POOLE.

12 o'clock, night.

Sunday Morning.

Hackett has just handed me your letter, which I have read with great interest; there are several matters alluded to by you which I could wish to have replied to; but as I find from Hackett, that she intends to return home to-day by the two o'clock car, I shall only observe that there is no view you can give, or sentiment express, relative to what you describe to be your now altered state of mind, which could or can lessen for one moment the anxiety and warm interest I feel in every matter connected with your welfare; and notwithstanding the exceeding weight of affliction which seems to depress and overcloud your hopes and prospects of happiness, still I look forward to the period, and that not a distant one, I trust, when I shall hear of your rejoicing in the truth as it is in Christ, and joining in the Apostle's declaration as expressed in Rom. viii. 37, 38, 39.

I should wish very much for your sake to be introduced to Mr. Woodward, that I might have an opportunity of knowing his sentiments on religious matters; and my present intention is to pay you a visit on Sunday next. I shall set out by the early coach so as to be at Newtown to breakfast. I hope you may have it in your power to favour me with your company (private) without interruption, as I shall be obliged to return early the following morning. I am therefore most desirous to engross as much of your time and conversation as circumstances will admit; pray let me.

26 June, 1824.

My dear Lady Osborne,—I cannot avoid observing that at no period since the commencement of our correspondence have I experienced more deep and heartfelt grief and disappointment than the perusal of your letter of the 23rd instant has caused.   I cannot express the concern and interest I feel in your behalf.   Though sorrow may be allowable under a sense of sin and involved in troubles and afflictions, yet we must beware of an extreme; and sorrow indeed becomes sinful and excessive when it leads us to slight the mercies of God.   We ought to consider that we are under the direction of a wise and merciful Being; that he permits no evil to come upon us without a gracious design; that he can make our afflictions sources of spiritual advantage; that he might have afflicted us in a far greater degree; that though he has taken some yet he has left us many other comforts; that he has given so many promises of relief and support in the Bible, and that the time is coming when he will wipe away all tears, and give to them that love him a crown of glory that fadeth not away.   See 1 Peter v. 4; 2 Tim. iv. 8.   I regret my time at present will not admit of me entering more particularly into the subject of self-righteousness, but I hope to be able to do so shortly.   Pray read the enclosed little work, it is well written, and its author appears to be a *Christian indeed.*   I have not yet finally decided on going to Dublin ; perhaps I may be able to avoid doing so for sometime ; and if so, I hope to have it in my power to pay you a visit some day next week, which I am for many, very many reasons, most anxious to accomplish; in the meantime I cease not to give thanks for you in my prayers.   That the God of our Lord Jesus Christ, &c.   See Ephesians i. 16, 17.

I shall call at Ball's respecting Chalmer's work. I do not
recollect the book your mother alludes to, perhaps it was
Ringham Gilhaize, or a history of the Scotch Cameronians.
My eyes continue to mend. With best wishes for your wel-
fare and happiness, Believe me to be with greatest respect,
My dear Lady Osborne,

Yours most sincerely and faithfully,

MATTHEW POOLE.

Excuse this short and hurried letter. I have been engaged
all the morning and it is now almost two o'clock, and I am
afraid to lose this opportunity of sending it by the last car.

Sunday Evening, 27 June, 1824.

MY DEAR LADY OSBORNE,—I have suffered a good deal of
uneasiness of mind since I despatched my short epistle of
yesterday's date, fearing lest from the hurried manner in
which it was written, you may have been inclined to think
that I have become careless or indifferent to the grief and
anguish of mind you are suffering under, or perhaps from
the state of my feelings at the time I might have expressed
myself in a way which you may have deemed to be inap-
plicable to the peculiar circumstances of your situation. If I
have been the cause of pain in the slightest degree, even for
a moment, either by word or deed, I shall be most unhappy;
my head and not my heart has been the offender. Inten-
tionally, to add one pang more to a mind so deeply afflicted,
as I believe yours to be at the present moment would be
unpardonable, and to me a source of great disquietude. On
matters connected with your peace of mind and eternal welfare I confess I am warmly and most anxiously interested.
I cannot feel lukewarm or indifferent on subjects of this
kind where you are concerned; I must therefore be plain
and explicit: any other line of conduct would be trifling,

deceiving you on subjects of all others the most important, and I should be acting the part of a flatterer, nay, worse— " unfaithful," to the character I " have professed, a friend." In my last letter I said I was greatly grieved and disappointed on reading your letter of the 23rd instant—grieved to think you have received no alleviation from affliction of mind, or comfort from reading the Scriptures, and that the dark and gloomy cloud of sorrow and despondency still continues to shut out the bright sunshine of consolation, &c. as declared in the Gospel to the afflicted of God, and I felt disappointed to find that the gleam of hope which I had so fondly cherished from some sentiments expressed in one or two of your last letters,—" that all things were working for your good"—had not been realized to the extent I could have wished. But the Lord's hand is not shortened that it cannot save, neither his ear heavy that it cannot hear. See Isaiah lvii. 15. The invitations of the Lord to the weary and troubled in mind are beautifully expressed by the same Prophet in the 55th chapter, 1st to 5th verses. See also the words of the Saviour, Matt. xi. 28 to the end.

> " Eternal life thy words impart,
> On these our fainting spirit lives ;
> Here sweeter comfort cheers the heart,
> Than all the stores of nature gives."

It is most humbling to the pride of the human heart to be told that it is deceitful above all things, and desperately wicked, Jer. xvii. 9th verse, and that it cannot of itself do anything to please God. The word of God declares such to be the condition of every being that is born into the world. That all have sinned and come short of the glory of God every man's conscience must allow; the Gospel is the good news of glad tidings to sinners, showing them how a man may be justified with God, not of works lest any should boast, but through faith in the atoning blood of the Lord Jesus

Christ to all and upon all who believe the record which
God has given of his beloved Son. Sin, whether that
of commission, omission, thoughtlessness or otherwise, is
sin in the sight of the Almighty, with him there is no distinction. The sinner who has been brought to a knowledge
of this truth as it is in Christ, becomes acquainted with the
iniquity and crookedness of his heart. He sees in himself
nothing to boast of, no good, nothing to give him a claim to
the mercy of God, but the work of the Saviour on which he
rests his sole hope and dependence for acceptance and for-
giveness in the day of judgment, and it is a deep sense of
duty and love to the Lord Jesus Christ which influences
his whole life and conduct, and not from anything in himself
better than others; all self-righteousness is at an end, now he
is persuaded, and knows that when he has done all those
things which are commanded him, he will say I am an un-
profitable servant, I have only done that which was my duty
to do, Luke xvii. 10th verse, and you, my dear friend, when
you really and truly know and believe the truths of the
Gospel, will acknowledge *these things*, and will experience
the force and truth of the apostles expression, see 3rd chap.
Ephesians, 7th and 9th verses. Continue to give a portion
of your time daily to the consideration and contemplation of
the Scriptures, you have the kind and gracious invitation of
the Saviour for your encouragement, see St. Luke, xi. 9, 10,
11, 12 and 13th verses; and may the Lord strengthen and
support you in so doing. Connected with the Gospel hopes,
is its influence on the heart—it produces joy, peace of mind,
and submission under the trials and afflictions we are subject
to in this world, and gives the assurance of a blessed immor-
tality. To say that we know Christ is able to save, and
derive no comfort or satisfaction from it, is but deceiving
ourselves with a name to live by. May the Lord of his infinite goodness and mercy direct you my dear friend to

drink of that living water which is described in the Gospel of John, chap. iv. 14th and 15th verses, and prepare you to meet in the region of eternal bliss, the spirit of him whose absence you now so deeply grieve and lament, is my most fervent prayer. I could say much more on this subject, but I really find my eyes so weak and dazzling that I can scarcely see the letters I am writing. But I cannot conclude without cautioning you against indulging in " Young's Night Thoughts;" he is a dark and gloomy writer, and I have strong doubts if he was acquainted with the comfort of the Gospel at the time he wrote the work.

> "Though to our lot temptations fall,
> Though pain and want, and cares annoy,
> The precious Gospel sweetens all,
> And yields us medicine, food and joy.

Good night, my dear Lady Osborne, and believe me to be,
Yours, faithfully and respectfully,
M. Poole.

Monday morning, 6 o'clock.

For the present I have given up the idea of going to Dublin. I hope to have it in my power to pay you a visit about Thursday or Friday next, of which I shall apprize you to send for your mother's perusal, a very interesting work, M'Crie's Life of John Knox.

Ringham Gilhaize is a novel, I have been promised the loan of it, and shall retain it for your mother's reading if she wishes for it. Pray continue your correspondence; you see what trouble you have brought upon yourself by listening to my importunities, you will say I am never to be satisfied; in reply, if I am unreasonable tell me so.

Yours, very faithfully,
M. Poole.
c 2

15th July, 1824.

My dear Lady Osborne,—The Apostle Paul in his second epistle to Timothy, third chapter, after mentioning the persecutions, afflictions, &c., which he had endured at Antioch and other places, expresses himself in the following striking manner:—In the 12th verse, " Yea, and all that would live godly in Christ Jesus shall suffer persecution;" and the Saviour repeatedly warned his disciples and followers to expect from the world opposition and reproach for His name's sake. "For in this world ye shall have trouble," John xvi. 33; and in Matthew x. He tells them, "A man's foes shall be they of his own household;" and again, "He that taketh not his cross and followeth after Me, is not worthy of Me," verses 37, 38. Indeed the whole chapter is worthy of your attention. See also Luke vi. 22, 26; also John xv. 18–21. The Saviour when on earth held out no worldly inducement to those who wished to become His disciples. He declared "that His kingdom was not of this world," and upon a certain occasion when one said unto Him, "Lord I will follow Thee whithersoever Thou goest," He replied "The foxes have holes, and the birds of the air have nests, but the Son of Man hath not where to lay His head," Luke ix. 5–7 to the end of the chapter, and although a period of 1800 years and more have elapsed since the Saviour appeared in the world, yet the same spirit of opposition to His doctrines and followers which existed in His day continues, only under different circumstances, to exist at the present day. "But the natural man receiveth not the things of the Spirit of God; for they are foolishness unto him; neither can he know them, because they are spiritually discerned." 1 Cor. ii. 14. The doctrines of the gospel and all who are influenced by them, ever have been and ever will be despised by the great bulk of mankind—even by those who call themselves Christians;

so my, dear friend, you must expect to meet with reproach;
but recollect the emphatic words of that Master you profess
to serve, in Matthew x. 38 and Luke xiv. 27. You must
lay your account to lose all your gay friends, &c. Your
society will be no longer sought after by that description of
persons, for *the world* loveth *its own*, but I trust you will
not be forsaken by Him who has declared "My sheep hear
My voice, and I know them, and they follow Me ; and I give
unto them eternal life ; and they shall never perish, neither
shall any man pluck them out of My hand," see John x. 27–
30. The friendship of the world is not worth a moment's
consideration, and be assured it is impossible to please God
and the world, and those who think to do so will but deceive
themselves in the end. There is a very awful denunciation
against despisers of the gospel in 2 Thess. i. 6–10, which I
beg your attention to, as also the other portions of Scripture
which I have referred to. You say you are going to read
H. More's Life of St. Paul ; I approve of her writings
generally—at least such as I have read of them—and I must
freely admit and acknowledge her very superior talent and
intellectual powers, and believe me no one can admire and
acknowledge the superiority of the mind of women on most
subjects more than I do; I have always considered that there
are few subjects indeed to which women have given their
attention, that they do not excel in.

In your present frame of mind perhaps it would be better
that you do not enter upon matters of business, but although
I say so at the present time, I would by no means wish you
to encourage the idea that *a Christian in the strictest sense*
of the word, is not to engage in worldly affairs, the
Scriptures say otherwise; and, besides, there is no situation
in life in which there are not duties of this kind to perform,
but on this subject I will at some future period enter more
at large into . . . I fear it will not be in my power to

accept of your kind invitation until the week after next, as
I am under the necessity of going to Dublin. I purpose
setting off on Sunday evening. Pray let me know if there
is anything I can do for you there. Perhaps on Sunday
week next I may, please God, pay you a visit; I mention
that day as I am desirous of hearing Mr. Woodward preach
again, but you shall hear from me on this subject after my
return from Dublin.

With every sincere wish for your welfare and happiness,
believe me to be, my dear Lady Osborne,

Yours very respectfully and faithfully,

MATTHEW POOLE.

27th July, 1824.

MY DEAR LADY OSBORNE,—On my return from Dublin
yesterday, I found your letter, but I regret to say in such an
injured and discoloured state from having been put up in
the basket with the vegetables, as to be illegible; and I have
only been able to make out an unconnected sentence here
and there. I cannot tell you how much I have been annoyed
by the circumstance; perhaps you will have the kindness,
when you favour me with another letter, to say whether it
contained anything of importance which you wish me to be
acquainted with.

I take the liberty to enclose, for my dear little friend
Catherine, a few story books, which I selected for her when
in Dublin, and which I beg you will allow her to accept. I
have several more by the same authors, but I think of a
superior denomination; and should you approve of Catherine
reading such works I shall have great pleasure in sending
them. Indeed, I consider many of them of a description not
only to amuse but even to instruct persons of a more advanced stage of life. I have read some of them with pleasure,
and I think with improvement. They are in general well

written, and most of them on highly interesting subjects, perhaps you would wish to look over them. They are at your service—nearly all of Mrs. Sherwood's works bound up together. In consequence of having been obliged to postpone my journey to Dublin to last Thursday, I find it will not be in my power to pay you a visit to-morrow, as I had intended; but I hope to have it in my power to do so in the course of the ensuing week. I would rather prefer a Sunday to any other day, that I might have the opportunity of hearing Mr. Woodward preach; and I rejoice to find that he occupies so high a place in your estimation, which is a further inducement on my part to desire to be acquainted with so worthy and excellent a man. I fancy I have discovered in your last letter, something alluding to sectarianism as connected with my religious principles; believe me, I have no such views either in respect to myself or anyone else I may feel interested about. The peculiar forms of religion, I trust, have no influence over my opinions; and I dislike the idea of proselytizing to any sect; besides, I have always considered the doctrines of the Establishment to be strictly scriptural, and, as to church government, as unexceptionable; perhaps more so than any other church or sect I know of. Such are my present views on the subject; and, if you have been told otherwise you have been informed wrong. You have therefore nothing to fear on *that score* from any intimacy you may be pleased to favour me with. I trust I shall always act a fair and honest part in this, as in any other matter which I may be engaged in with you. I have no object or desire to prejudice your mind against the Establishment, I only regret that the clergymen of the Establishment are not all like Mr. Woodward, for if such was the case there would be but few dissenters. The man I esteem most in this world as a friend is a sectarian, yet I have never been influenced by his opinions or conduct in those matters, which you must allow is a strong proof of my attachment to the Establishment; but I could give you a still stronger proof of my sincerity in this respect, which I will do when I have the pleasure of seeing you. I have and can say a great deal more on *this* subject, but I find it is near the time of the car going off, so I shall for the present conclude.

With every sincere wish for your welfare and happiness, and with the greatest respect, believe me to be, my dear Lady Osborne,

Most truly and faithfully yours,

M. POOLE.

Monday morning, 2nd September, 1824.

MY DEAR LADY OSBORNE,—To be favoured with your unreserved opinions on the important subject of religion, is a privilege which I esteem and value more than I have words to express, and however unworthy I may appear to be (as I know I really am) as a correspondent, still you must allow me to request and hope that you will continue to communicate freely your sentiments and ideas on this *subject* as they arise in your mind, and which will be to me highly and peculiarly gratifying to receive. I have to regret that my time is so very frequently broken in upon, as often to prevent me from replying to your communications in that full and ample manner they deserve, and which would at all times be my anxious wish to do to the extent of my abilities; but as I have so frequently experienced your indulgence and forbearance on similar occasions, and as I have had many convincing proofs of your partiality towards me, I shall not attempt to apologize, but shall hope that when I appear to be deficient in these matters, that you will not attribute it to the want of inclination, but to my inability.

In all matters of a speculative nature connected with the belief of the Gospel, I honestly confess I am not only jealous, but afraid to allow the power or warmth of imagination to be too much indulged in, particularly in very sensitive dispositions, as I think it is apt to lead such persons as give way to the feelings and fancies of the brain so produced, to wander from, or, I should rather say, to lose sight of the only true foundation which can give hope, comfort, joy, and happiness in time or eternity. "The love and mercy of God as revealed in the sacrifice of the Lord Jesus Christ and the Scriptures, inform us that believers shall be raised up at the day of judgment a spiritual body, and shall be as the angels in heaven. I therefore infer that all ideas and feelings as connected with, or relating to, the things of this life will be done away with and absorbed in the *one object*—"Love to the Lord Jesus Christ;" and I am warranted from the Scriptures to suppose that all the happiness and joy of believers in eternity will result from that source alone, and also that all their thoughts and desires will originate and proceed from love and praise of the Lamb of God, who has washed and redeemed them with his blood, and presented them spotless before the throne of the Almighty, to His honor and glory through all eternity (see Rev. vii. chap., 9th verse, to the end of the chapter; also chap. xxi. 1st to the 5th verse, and chap. xxii. 1st to the 6th verse.) The knowledge, therefore, which I conceive believers will have of each other in eternity must be of a spiritual nature, and not in any manner or degree connected with the sinful and corrupt ideas of this life. Such are my opinions on this highly interesting subject; for I cannot for a moment allow myself to suppose that any idea, feeling, or otherwise as connected with this world, can ever enter into the minds or thoughts of the blessed in eternity; but I shall most willingly give up this opinion, if you can from the Bible produce a single passage or sentence in support of the contrary being the case. The parable of the rich man and Lazarus does not, in my humble

opinion, bear at all on the point in question. The object the
Saviour had in view appears to have been to direct the Jews,
to whom the parable was immediately addressed, and all
mankind to read and search the Scriptures as the only true
source of Divine information; and the knowledge which,
Dives appeared to have was merely that of the happiness of
Lazarus, and of his own eternal misery. I can very well
conceive the trying situation you were placed in when
exposed to the *full* force of Lady ——'s artillery; but you
must expect such things from the world if you continue
faithful in the service of your Saviour. The sayings of our
Saviour, and the writings of His Apostles, distinctly inform
us of the enmity of the world to the children of God in
Christ, and they also point out the trials which believers are
to expect and meet with in this life, even from their nearest
and dearest friends. I agree with you that ridicule is, of all
the ways of Satan, the most difficult to combat; still I hope
and trust that your faith in Him who is all-sufficient will
enable you to withstand these trials, and bring you off more
than conqueror. Do not suppose that Lady —— is more
opposed to a Christian character than others. No; it is her
candour in openly expressing to yourself what she thinks on
the subject. Very few persons would dare to do, whatever
they might, behind your back, insinuate; so far, therefore,
I like her Ladyship's conduct. She is, no doubt, a clear,
sensible, and experienced woman in worldly affairs, and
certainly a most agreeable companion; of course the more
dangerous. Her attack or insinuations on the character of
the Archbishop of Tuam is, I dare say, nothing more than
the ill-natured remarks of the world, and, I have no doubt,
without the least foundation of truth. Strange it is to say,
that so great is the dislike and enmity of the people of the
world to such characters as the Archbishop, that the slightest
error of judgment or conduct in them is immediately blazed

forth to the whole world with all the malignity possible to conceive, when the laws of morality are shamelessly and openly violated by others are passed over merely as trifling matters. Could my Lady —— expose in the same spirit the sins of a neighbouring prelate, and hold him up as a hypocrite, &c.? I dare say she would not; and, why? Because he lays no claim to the practice and character of that Master he professes to serve and honour. But are the crimes of such characters the less guilty in the sight of a holy and just God? Certainly not. I find I must or ought not to pursue this subject further. It is the bounden duty of Christians to avoid giving offence; to forgive injuries; to pray to God for an increase of faith; and to have an humble opinion of their best works. The children of God are not free from sinful dispositions and inclinations in this life.

The Apostle says, Rom. vii. 18, " For I know that in me dwelleth no good thing; for to will is present with me; but how to perform that which is good I find not." And in the 24th and 25th verse of same chapter, " Oh, wretched man that I am," &c. But they know they have " an Advocate in heaven who ever liveth to make intercession for them, who was delivered for their offences, and was raised again for their justification." And it is this glorious hope and promise which gives them peace in this world, and the hopes of eternal life in the world to come, and not from any goodness or supposed righteousness, or anything else in themselves. I find my time will not allow me to proceed much farther. I must, therefore, postpone the consideration of the other subjects of your letter to another occasion.

I am concerned to say that I have scarcely a hope of being able to pay you a visit for some two or three weeks to come. Whenever I feel myself *at liberty* to enjoy the happiness of spending a day in your society I shall acquaint you. Every day I regret more and more my inability to see you,

and most anxiously wish and desire to live in your neighbourhood, if I could with prudence do so. On the subject
of the Quarry scheme I have not by any means relinquished
the idea; but the difficulty with me is, how I should be able
to procure a trustworthy person as a resident to carry on the
works, as, from the *nature* of the thing, I need only give it
an occasional visit. I should require some business more
extensive to induce me to quit Waterford and give up my
professional pursuits; but more on this subject another time.
I send you a little book, which I beg you will read, and
return to me after you have done so. Pray do not allow it
to go into any other hands but your own, for reasons which
I shall hereafter explain. I thank you for sending me the
Trials of Margaret Lindsay; when I have read it I will give
give you my opinion of its merits. Pray write often. You
cannot believe how much I am pleased and gratified when I
receive a letter from you. I wish I was a better hand at my
pen than I am, that I might have it in my power to express
and convey all I think and wish on the various subjects of
our correspondence. With the greatest respect,

Believe me to be,

My dear Lady Osborne,

Yours faithfully and sincerely,

MATTHEW POOLE.

" The Rev. Henry Woodward was the son of the Bishop of
Cloyne. He was a man of whom no perusal of his writings,
beautiful as they are, could give a just idea, his life and
conversation were so very remarkable; but fortunately essays
and sermons, and 'The Shunamite,' or a few smaller
works, remain in the world of literature to testify in a slight
degree to the ethereal nature of himself. At one time, when
he preached in Dublin, crowds like those who went to hear
Chalmers used to follow him; but for many years before his

death, from choice, he lived in great retirement, though always active in the service of his duties. He lived to be eighty-eight, preserving his faculties to the last, and used to say "his latest years were his happiest."

The Editor takes occasion to mention here one of the effects of the Church Spoliation Bill with reference to the scene of professional exertion on the part of his son, the Dean of Down. Together with a large proportion contributed by himself, he collected and expended on the Cathedral of Downpatrick for its restoration the sum of £3000. In 1871, not being a Parish Church, the building is to be put up for sale, unless the Church Body are able to undertake the expense of keeping it up."

MY DEAR LADY OSBORNE,—I feel, I hope truly, grateful to God for the account you give of your dear child, and of the relief which you have received from your anxieties. I trust you will find in the end that they have been quite unwarranted by the nature of Catherine's complaint; such is my belief. I hope, please God, to see you in the morning, and shall be able, while your mind continues unsettled, to devote as much of my time to you as you wish. Independently of strong inclination, I think it now my first duty.

May God peculiarly bless you, ever, my dear friend,

Yours most affectionately,

H. WOODWARD.

" The difficulties alluded to in the next and others of Mr. Woodward's letters point out, by the perfect absence of all these subsequently to the arrangements entered into, that the landlords should pay the tithes, how utterly uncalled for is the present confiscation bill."

January 18th, 1832.

MY DEAR LADY OSBORNE,—I had the happiness of receiving your letter of the 7th on Friday. I was absent at the time at . . . or should have had it sooner. Only that my mind has been so occupied and my time so engaged, that often as my thoughts were with you, my dearest friend, I thought it better to put off writing. Indeed, anxious as I am that you should keep to your kind promise of writing once a fortnight, I do not feel that I have any stated time for answering, at least any one agreed on. It may interest you to have some specimen of the state of things here. I had a letter from Sir William Gosset saying that Major Miller was instructed to protect my drivers where I drive for the tithe composition. Armed with such a set, I thought it would be well to summon a meeting of the Popish farmers to lay this communication from the Castle before them. Monday last was the day appointed, and forty-four notices were issued. Mr. Barton, —— and —— agreed to be present as my friends. On Sunday Mr. —— preached on the subject. He told them not to go; he told them not to pay tithe; but (bursting into tears) to let the last cow or blanket be taken. The effect was that, though my three friends appeared, not *one* farmer came. A young man, whose family Miss Darby had been of service to in sickness, met her the other day; she spoke about the tithe. His answer was, that his clergy had forbidden him to pay, and added that they considered their clergy *could not* desire them to do anything wrong. This he repeated with great calmness over and over again. The remarkable thing is, that the young man is a person of the most excellent character, mild and amiable in his disposition. You ask me as to the Orange business. It seems, as far as anything worldly can be, a bright exhibition of what is elevated and conservative in society, arrayed against all that is foul and base. The six leading names arc refreshing to the eye, and seem (contrasted at least with their opponents) as if the list were formed by the Angel who is to gather God's elect together, or by the one who keeps the register of the Book of Life. I am afraid that no effort can now save the country; the frown of God seems to be upon it. The horrid coalition of Popery with infidelity and radicalism seems as if the nation were given up. I am doubtful, but, even though a clergyman, I think I shall sign the Protestant petition. Never, doubtless, did Protestantism appear so comparatively bright.

Please to tell Jonathan that I hope to write to him tomorrow or next day; but he is in my debt. Frank presses me to withdraw his allowance, and I have written to George to recommend his maintaining himself by pupils. I beg you will have the great kindness of writing regularly. God Almighty bless you.

Ever, dearest friend,
Most affectionately yours,
H. Woodward.

January 28th, 1832.

My dear Lady Osborne,—I think there must be some unaccountable delay in the course of my letters. I am much obliged to you, however, for the anxiety you show at not having got my last. I feel your correspondence too necessary to my comfort to trifle with it by remissness on my part. I trust, my dearest friend, that the indisposition you speak of will quickly wear off. Everything of local interest here merges in the awful event of Mr. Whitty's death. Before this reaches you, you will in all probability have seen it in the papers. On Wednesday last he left his home to call on some parishioners. Not being at home by six o'clock, Mrs. W. became alarmed, and sent to the Peelers stationed

near. They went out, and after a long search brought word
that they had traced Mr. W. to Mr. Robbins, of Suir Castle,
about two miles off; that he left that place on foot at three;
but that further they could not trace him. A more general
search then commenced, and within a quarter of a mile of
his own house, in a field, was found this meek and quiet
pastor weltering in his blood, quite insensible, but still
breathing.   He was taken home to his wife and four
daughters (his only son being in Dublin), and at half-past
six the next morning went to Abraham's bosom. The proxi-
mate cause of this horrid murder (which I should have told
you was by *stoning*) was, that at the late sessions of Cashel
Mr. W. presumed to process for tithe. Believe me, my
dearest friend, that your advice as to driving for tithe would
be under all circumstances most objectionable; it would be
a movement, upon a great scale, that could effect nothing
but complicated mischief.   Mr. Roe breakfasted here on
Thursday, and was thanking God *he* had never done it. The
fact is, that even if the cattle were driven without effusion
of human blood, no one would levy the distress, or could do
it, without imminent risk of life and property. It is remarkable that a lady told me some time ago she thought Mr.
Whitty's life in peculiar danger.

He certainly, though a very heavenly-minded man, contrived (I believe from a conscientious scruple about compromising what he thought *sacred rights*) to entangle himself
constantly with his parishioners. This is *entre nous*, but it
may be satisfactory to my friends to think that there was
something in Mr. Whitty's case which distinguished it from
mine. I shall send an article to the " Evening Mail " on
the subject of Mr. W. I am not sure they will put it in;
perhaps thinking a newspaper not the proper place. I have
formed actually an affection for E—— H—— which I could
hardly describe. I feel to him as if I might humbly hope

that he is my spiritual child. May God be his defence amidst the dangers which surrounds his soul! George Gough is also inexpressibly dear to me, and so is Willy Pennefather. We had at Mrs. Hill's, on Tuesday last, a most satisfactory meeting. Mr. Butler dined there afterwards, and brought a brother, a young officer, much to be liked. We had Edward Hutchinson and Miss H. also.

The lecture in the morning was attended by thirty-five, almost all gentry. Shall I ever have the happiness of lecturing at Newtown again? At all events, I trust that nothing will prevent my meeting you in a better and happier world. May God prepare us for it!

Ever, my dearest friend,

Affectionately yours,

H. Woodward.

April 8th, 1832.

My dear Lady Osborne,—I felt somewhat uneasy at your delaying to write longer than the usual time, and therefore, your kind letter was more than usually welcome. I am quite prepared for many of my friends thinking that it was injudicious to print the letter to Mr. Stanley at the time I did; but with every respect for them I must see the matter in another light. I do not see why the Church should be collectively insensible to that call which says, " Seek ye first the kingdom of God and His righteousness, and all these things shall be added unto you." I consider the Establishment as a means, not an end, and as a means we can judge of her by that rule, " Ye shall know them by the fruits." Now certain it is that the Establishment has not worked successfully for the last century; her enemies have multiplied and strengthened, her children have deserted her, her hedges are broken down, so that all that pass by pluck off her grapes. You my dear friend are in the midst of the Protestant Camp, and therefore, the comparative strength of the cause seems greater than it really is. Besides you have Gordon who would shout victory while half his head was above water. My opinion is that the times call for much seriousness, and much prayer, and that if the Lord has it in His intention to save the existing institutions of the country, (which I much doubt) He will raise up a spirit of devotedness amongst us far less alloyed with secondary motives, and far less conformed to the mind and temper of the world, than that which volunteers to fight what it considers the battle of the Lord. My dearest friend I perceive that circumstances as well as other causes lead us to take curiously different views of the matters which are passsing before our eyes. Perhaps if I ever have the happiness of taking a ride or walk with you again, it may entertain us to talk some of them over. Your account of poor —— is most affecting. It is remarkable that just before I received your letter containing the same words I said "I fear that poor man dies and makes no sign." To see a tender heart cased up in steel against all that could console or comfort it is melancholy indeed. It will, whether you succeed or not in doing him good, be a pleasing reflection to yourself that you so often turned aside from pressing calls and exciting circumstances, to visit that poor disconsolate young man; if he be still alive I say, may he be called in even at the eleventh hour and find rest to his soul.

. . . . . . How remarkably he is dealt with, and how mercifully if he could or would but feel it. Only think of the —— hounds being out on the fast day. You will much oblige me by telling me how Mr. —— goes on. Has he made any movement towards Irving? We had a very good Clerical meeting yesterday; Mr. Cavendish is really becoming a serious Clergyman. Think of our having seven Clergymen at Mr. Hill's last Lecture ; besides Mr. Hill and myself, we had Mr. Mansell, Mr. Dixon of Dungarvan, Robert Bell, Mr. Cavendish and Henry Perry. You will have heard ere this reaches you, of the death of poor Major Fancourt, poor Mrs. F. is in wonderful affliction; Giles told me yesterday a trait of him. They travelled to Limerick in the coach, and a dangerous accident occurred, from which they were providentially preserved. Giles afterwards joked about it, and applied to the circumstances they were in the words of some old song ; Major F. then with great politeness and seriousness, represented to Giles how inconsistent it was just after God had so mercifully saved them, to turn the mind to a jest. Mr. Giles added to me that he never was so surprised by anything in his life as by that mild rebuke. God bless you my dearest friend.

Ever, most affectionately yours,

H. WOODWARD.

April 18th, 1832.

MY DEAR LADY OSBORNE,—This post has brought the intelligence of the severe trial to which you have all been exposed in the death of Mrs. Warde, an event in which I am sure you will believe that I take a deep and lively interest. I have often heard you describe the many valuable and amiable qualities of your aunt. Her own letters also, which you have sometimes given me the privilege of reading, bear ample testimony to that head and heart which it is my fervent hope will be raised again, the one to reason without any cloud of error, the other to feel without any mixture of pain or sorrow. You will very much oblige me by even a few lines to say that the effects of this most sudden shock have not affected your health and spirits more than what is in such case unavoidable ; and to tell also how your mother has been supported, and how the Wardes bear up under the unspeak-

D 2

able loss, for such, I am sure, it has been to them. I need not suggest to your well-furnished mind consolations which the Gospel holds out to those that travail and are heavy laden. The first lesson we learn in the school of Christ is the utter vanity of expecting any settled rest or stable peace in any thing but God. Hard as it is to learn, we must be taught this practically by losses, afflictions, and disappointments, sent in mercy and dealt out gently as we are able to bear them, and though no chastening seemeth for the present joyous but grievous, nevertheless you, my dearest friend, will know it yieldeth the peaceable fruit of righteousness to them that are exercised thereby. If, indeed, you had felt the affection for poor F—— that you did for Mrs. Warde, the separation might be gloomy indeed ; but you have described her to me as one for whom friends cannot sorrow as those that have no hope. You have, I trust, a solid ground of expectation that your next meeting with her will be in glory. I really think among other motives of consolation that the state of the world should be taken into account. What are the prospects which present themselves to a lover of good order and established institutions such as Mrs. Warde was ? and particularly to one so far advanced in life and so little prepared to adapt herself to a new order of things ? I am afraid I can have done nothing by this letter, but shown my good will. You are so well acquainted with all that I could suggest on the present subject that I feel it useless to write much upon it, and I do not like introducing ordinary topics at such a moment, still less do I wish to introduce myself ; nevertheless I cannot help saying a word even on that worthless subject. I have been somewhat tempted to think, particularly from the late irregularity of your correspondence, that your friendship for me is not what it was. This I say not in the way of blame ; I have not one thought of the kind ; I say it because I should be glad and obliged if you would with

Christian openness mention if there are any specified grounds
for such a movement in your mind. My own belief is that
such grounds are erroneous and could be explained away,
because I cannot conceive *what they are*, and this of itself I
think argues that they cannot be solid. I can hardly think
that any fancied difference about merely political matters
(for indeed they are but fancied), could effect a change in
so old a friend. I certainly do not think that the heated
atmosphere in which such a mind as Mr. G—— lives is
friendly to true piety, but this is no political opinion. One
comfort I have, which is, that there is an Almighty Friend
who never can change, and whose nature, I trust, I know
more and more. And now be assured, if indeed you value
the assurance, that my friendship and affection for you is
unchanged and unchangeable.

Ever most affectionately yours,

H. WOODWARD.

July 4th, 1832.

MY DEAR LADY OSBORNE,—I feel deterred when I would
sit down to write to you by your not having pointed out any
mode of sending my letters free; and really in point of any
thing they communicate I fear they are purchased too dearly
at the price of postage. You will have heard long before
this reaches you of poor Lord Donoughmore's death ; Miss
Hutchinson will, I understand, remain, at least for some
time, with her sister. This is, in many respects I trust a good
arrangement. . . . I know not how to feel about Jonathan's suggestion of the Lock chapel. In all human probability it will not be offered to me, and that will settle the
point; if it is, no doubt any call to England at such a junc-
ture of affairs in Ireland looks providential. But then my
time of life is oddly suited to such a transition as that from
Fethard to the Lock. Frank tells me that the Chapel is

very large, and this daunts me. I can always preach most at my case in a room about the size of the Dublin Asylum. I wish I knew the precise dimensions of the Lock Chapel. Dean Bernard is now here, and tells me that he was, he believes, made a governor of the Lock in 1814, having made a donation of £50 at the time to the institution. If this does not constitute a governor, he would wish now to become so. Might I beg of your Ladyship (as you can do it through many channels) to have an enquiry made whether Dean B.'s name is on the books, and if not, what should be done or paid to make him a governor. I should feel reluctant to give you this trouble, but I know your real desire to oblige a friend, and you will perceive that Dean B.'s wishes of being connected with the Lock are on my account.

Please to give an answer as soon as convenient to this. I went last week to Affane, in the County of Waterford, to hold a lecture; and, literally, the numbers were so great that the carriages had exactly the appearance of the breaking up of a great Dublin Congregation.

They have now a very pious and highly gifted young minister at Lismore, which is a great change. The cholera is now at Clonmel; may we be prepared to meet it if it comes here. God bless you, my dear friend,

Your most affectionate,
H. WOODWARD.

July 6th, 1832.

MY DEAR LADY OSBORNE,—I received your most kind letter, enclosed in Catherine's to Louisa, for which I return you many thanks. It would indeed be delightful to visit the scenes you describe in Regent's Park, and to see the dear friends I have in London, and to enjoy the happiness of your conversation and society, but at this moment I must put such thoughts out of my head. These are no times for leaving glebe-houses. It is a great mercy to be allowed even to remain in them and to be supplied with food and raiment. In the midst of all the apparent trials of the times, however, I thank God that my own mind has been kept in more than usual peace. The unspeakable blessing of religion, and the madness of preferring broken cisterns to the streams of living water seem clearer, and are more habitually present to my mind than ever. I am also more and more convinced that Christianity is a present salvation, and that almost all our unhappinesses are brought upon ourselves. I say almost all, because I think there are trials and sufferings in life which would have been felt to have been such by the humanity of Christ. But the sufferings are comparatively of rare occurrence. In most cases, I believe unhappiness to be the working of unhappy tempers. It seems to me very important to observe the following distinctions with mental as with bodily pain; the cause may either be inward or outward; in the former case it is a disease, in the latter a mere accident. A man may lie on a bed or couch and be in pain, if the pain is from within, when he rises he will carry it with him, but if the pain arise from something in the bed that hurts him, he has only to leave the bed to be at ease; so it is with different kinds of trial. If our distress arises really from things that in themselves are grievous to innocent human nature, then our unhappiness betrays no want of mental health, and we want nothing but change of circumstances to make us happy; but I believe very few have such a case to show, and therefore in most instances unhappiness and unholiness are the same. I find one symptom of age creeping on me though I am very watchful against it; it is that of repeating the same thing to the same person. Did I use the comparison of a man lying on a bed in pain, in a letter to you before? Alas! I find it is too true you are not returning to the country; I do not however blame you for it, nor do I blame you being unwilling to mention it where you thought it might occasion pain. It is a great comfort to me to hear regularly from you. I met a poor woman the other day begging, who told me that her husband was, nine months ago, blown in pieces by the blasting of a rock at the slate quarry ; there was something odd but so interesting about her that I gave her something (a thing very uncommon with me now). Before I heard her story, she told me that she and her husband were Protestants, though she appeared very ignorant; also that she brought a child to me to christen about six months ago (of which I have a vague recollection). I know that you have no part in working the slate quarry, nevertheless, considering that the woman is a Protestant and that she has children to bring up as such, I thought it right to mention the thing. Mr. Smith could doubtless get you information. The Pallisers are expected in a few days. Poor Miss O'Meara is dead; much regretted by many who knew her real worth which was very great. I am sorry to say there are by no means comfortable accounts of George G.'s health. Lady G. told me yesterday that they had written for him to come home. I feel unwilling to direct through Lord D. as you do not do so; shall I in future? God bless you my dearest friend.

Most affectionately yours,
H. Woodward.

" The man of the name of Connors mentioned in the next letter, was the same person who was murdered by Mrs. Manning, and from his extraordinary mode of transmitting a sovereign through the post, that wretched woman would seem warranted in the term she applied to him when making her ghastly joke that " she had cooked her goose."

Fethard, Tipperary, Sept. 20th, 1832.

My dear Lady Osborne,— . . . . Things are going on in this country just as usual; nothing yet has been done by Government towards collecting the incomes of the Clergy in this neighbourhood, and no Papist thinks of paying tithe; in the meantime I thank God that I feel no want. We had at a Lecture at Mr. Cooper's last Friday, a Mr. —— who five months ago was a Popish priest, but is now a Clergyman, (and I hear a very zealous one) of the Established Church. One lady says that he is preaching such sermons at Tipperary that he is driving them all full gallop to hell. I hope you will not think that I have taken a great liberty in desiring a man of the name of Connors to call on you for a pound which I will pay punctually to Mr. Smith. It was the only way I could think of to transmit so small a sum, and the case is so interesting that it will I think fully plead my excuse with you. The man is a convert from Popery; he was driven from this Parish by the terror of persecution; he went to London in a state of beggary, and on his going I lent him the above sum. It has pleased God to take him up in his distress, and he has been put into a comfortable situation. Such is his honesty that he sent me a sovereign made up in the seal of his letter, and on my delaying to acknowledge the receipt, he was so afraid that I might by any accident of the post lose the money, that he actually sent a second pound, thus paying the debt twice over. In his letter he says that he is now above want, and that "It will be the pride of his soul throughout eternity that he encountered misery and poverty for his Saviour's sake;" may God send us many such converts as this. You will much oblige me by mentioning if Bulbridge is in the country, I could send it by him. I should imagine that Mr. Gordon will not stand for the College by what I see in the papers respecting him. If I have a vote I know no one that better deserves it. I take it for granted that he does not oppose Mr. Lefroy, or any one of his principles. I see by the papers that Mr. —— has got a living; who ordained him? I hear that

Miss Hutchinson is likely to be at your house in London; Jonathan is my authority. I know that you always liked her, and I think that you would now like her better than ever. The . . . are all that could be wished, indeed there is a growing seriousness in this country. Mr. Lloyd who has lately returned to it after an absence of more than three years, is greatly struck with the general improvement. What do you thing of Lord H——'s Society for Church Reformation; whether their plan be wise or not in my judgment some reformation is much wanted. Though you are to be so long absent, there is some comfort in thinking that Mr. —— is not to be the proprietor of Newtown. Poor Mrs. Fitzgerald has followed her sons! God bless and preserve you.

Yours most affectionately,

H. WOODWARD.

Fethard, April 8, 1834.

MY DEAR LADY OSBORNE,—I will not trouble you with apologies for not writing, though I could say much about my waiting to ascertain from your brother where my letter might be sure to find you, and the odd delays arising from that and other causes; but you may be assured that, whatever my silence was owing to, it neither did or could proceed from any want of deep and unchangeable affection and attachment. Things are going on as usual. I have lately spent about three weeks in Dublin, where I find everything indeed to cheer me in my ministry, even at this eleventh hour, so much so, that I am, please God, going again there to-morrow. I find a home at the Scott's, which makes me feel quite comfortable. On Friday I am to address the clergy assembled at the Rotunda, before the Church Missionary Meeting, and I have engaged to preach two Charity Sermons. It appears odd for me to leave home so much, but my desire is to go where Providence leads. I left Louisa with Mrs. Scott, and hope with God's blessing to join her again. Your brother, I find, is going to be married to Miss Riall. I pray God that it may be for the happiness of both parties. I feel it distressing to leave the country just at this moment, as Letitia Lloyd seems drawing near her close, but having engaged myself I cannot be off. She is just in the same heavenly state as her dear mother was. Mrs. Hill is now here. You have no one in this country who loves, esteems, and values you more than she does. I don't know whether you knew Mr. ——, son of Mr. —— of K——, when you were in the neighbourhood, he has really become one of the most genuinely and truly religious men I ever knew : it is a remarkable change, because he was a most frivolous character before.

Mr. Palliser's loss has been, as you may conceive, great indeed to his family; he was the great mover and mainspring of the machine, and the whole system seems paralyzed. None but the ladies are at Derryluskan, from which they go in about a fortnight, not to return, at all events not for months. The other families of the country much in *statu quo*. Mr. Barton's health just as it was. Mr. Perry, they say, is going to be married to a Miss Townsend ; this is odd gossiping for me, for indeed I am no meddler in other people's affairs. The state of this country is very interesting; our Church rapidly improving under all its trials, and Popery spreading wide its branches while withering at the root.

—— is as infatuated as ever, but nothing can quench the *vital spark* which seems to animate the breast of so many of the inferior clergy, and laity of both sexes. May I beg a letter, and that you will not delay because I from accidental hindrances have done so. I heard that you

were coming to London to complete the purchase of Newtown. If you write, which pray do soon, direct to No. 3,
Merrion-square, South, Dublin.

I send this to Mr. Smith. May I beg to be most kindly
remembered to Mr. and Miss Smith, and that you will give
my love to Catherine. May God preserve and bless you.

Ever, my dearest friend,
Most affectionately yours,
H. WOODWARD.

Fethard, July 22nd, 1834.

MY DEAR LADY OSBORNE,—I have been prevented from
writing by my ignorance of your direction, which I have at
last heard through Dora Pennefather. Mrs. Hill told me
the contents of your letter as far as it respected me only the
day before yesterday at Dungarvan. I can most truly assure
you that on my part no diminution of esteem or affection has
taken place. You are pleased to speak, both in your letter
to Mrs. Hill and in your late one to me, in terms which I
allude to only to say that I feel the use of such terms much
more applicable to myself than to you. If I could suffer
myself to take pride in anything, be assured that I know
nothing which would so much tempt me to it as having been
so much prized by such a person as I consider you. This is
language remember which has been drawn out by the expressions of your two letters, and in such a connection it
could alone be rightly understood, but it is most sincere.
You may indeed most truly reckon on in me a friend unchanged
and unchangeable; my whole nature must be taken to pieces
before the deposit you have made in my mind could be got
out. I am very sorry to learn, as I did yesterday, that we
shall lose the Hills at Knocklofty. Dr. Tuckey of Clogheen
is dead ; and Henry Perry has got the living. Possibly the
Hills may come into Clonmel, but of course to sad incon-

venience to themselves. The Pallisers, I hear, return in September. Mr. Barton of Grove has lately had a very dangerous fit of the apoplectic kind which he is slowly getting over, but a repetition is much to be apprehended. The Sam Bartons, Hills, Hugh Goughs, and others from this neighbourhood are at Dungarvan. I have taken lodgings also there for George, Tom, and Louisa, for whom sea-bathing would, I am sure, be very useful. This will keep me backwards and forwards, which I find very useful in a ministerial way. We have large congregations at Dungarvan. I preach also at Cahir where, I am happy to say, Mr. Cavendish has become a very decided character. Another of the Miss Butlers has become a Protestant. The Pennefathers are now in the country. Willy has been delicate in body, but in full health of soul. Letitia Lloyd is fast hastening to join her blessed mother. I fear the congregations at Killaloan are sadly reduced, but your return will, I trust, revive matters there. Lady Glengall is coming over, and there. are great threatenings of private theatricals, &c., but her ladyship will, I think, find things much altered in that neighbourhood,— Mr. Cavendish will, I am sure, do his duty firmly. I shall be much obliged to you for a line in answer to this. I should be glad to hear your observations on the state of religion, and how far Socinianism is advancing or receding. I suppose you are in the midst of delightful scenery. I beg my kindest love to Catherine, and remain, my dearest friend,

Ever most affectionately yours,

H. WOODWARD.

March 17, 1835.

MY DEAR LADY OSBORNE,—I must reserve to an early opportunity, please God, the pleasure of writing more fully. I am now preparing to go off to Waterford to preach for the

Church Missionary Society. There are two passages, one in Romans v. 8, and the other, 1 John, iii. 17, which appear to me the most convincing possible. I will in a future letter submit to you why I think so, but could not now. The sight of Newtown the other day recalled to my mind many endearing associations—but I must conclude.

Ever, my dearest friend,

Yours most affectionately,

H. WOODWARD.

My DEAR LADY OSBORNE,—Though my last letter remains unanswered I cannot let this go without a few lines. It gave me great pleasure to hear from Louisa that your dear Catherine was pleased and gratified by the letter she received from me some time ago. I do indeed most sincerely pray to God that she may devote the " ten talents" which the Lord has committed to her trust; that she may at last hear that sentence which outweighs the whole value of this world, " well done, good and faithful servant!" I hope soon to write to herself. I received your liberal subscription to our Church Missionary Society from Mr. Smith, for which, in the name of the institution, I return many thanks. Things go on here much as usual. I shall tell you nothing about elections, because Mr. Smith will do all that. I rejoice to hear that wherever you go you keep up your connection with religious people and religious exercises, and trust also my dearest friend, that you cleave in heart to the gracious fountain of salvation and of happiness; yes, I trust and pray that none shall ever pluck you out of your heavenly Father's hand, and I trust that if I have the happiness of meeting you again on this side the grave, we may both rejoice in the thought that we have been enabled, in the midst of infirmities and sins, still to fight the good fight and to keep the faith. I must conclude; just going to Wednesday's prayers. Ever, with unchangeable friendship and affection,

> Yours truly attached,
> H. WOODWARD.

Crossboyne, Claremorris, September 12, 1839.

MY DEAR LADY OSBORNE,—I feel extremely thankful to you for your kind anxiety, and with much gratitude to God can say that I have been much benefited by change of air. Whether it was principally in my own feelings, or whether the real state of the case justified it I know not; but I certainly had some serious impressions that God was about to remove me from this sphere of action; but I now begin to think that it may be His pleasure to leave me here some short time longer. Believe that I am very little disposed to sit in judgment upon others; I feel too deeply my own utter unworthiness and sinfulness to do so, and am much more inclined to lean severely upon myself than upon my neighbours. The grand test to put everything to is this: "How will it appear to me at the hour of death?" This I am sure you will allow, is the only safe rule; instead of judging or condemning you, my prayer is that God may guide you through the snares of life. My return is still uncertain, but I should hope that in about a fortnight I may be at Fethard. Louisa is, I thank God, quite recovered; and is gone this morning to see Connemara, and for that purpose to pass two or three days at Mr. Martin's; Tom and Mr. Crofton go with her. Sincerely praying that God may guide and bless you, I remain, my dearest Lady Osborne,

> Most affectionately yours,
> H. WOODWARD.

September 25th, 1833.

MY DEAR LADY OSBORNE,—We hope, please God, to hold a Church Missionary meeting in Fethard on Wednesday, the

12th of October, and look with confidence to the support and co-operation which you have never withheld on such occasions. Amongst other speakers Mr. Roe has already promised to attend. You would much oblige me by circulating a few notices which I shall take the liberty of sending around you. I have twice missed the pleasure of finding you at home when I called at Newtown; on one occasion I called unexpectedly, and perhaps you never heard it, as I came no farther than the lodge; on the other you were obliged to be absent. Nevertheless, my friendship for you is of such a nature that the root and substance of it I believe are imperishable. What falls in with the religious history of the mind is recorded there for ever. God bless you, my dear Lady Osborne,

Ever, most affectionately yours,

H. WOODWARD.

" In revising it plainly appears from the dates on the letters mistakes have been made in arrangement, but the errors do not affect their complete meaning."

April 24th, 1844.

MY DEAR LADY OSBORNE,—I thank you for your two most kind letters, which nothing but a press of more business than I can well manage would have prevented my answering at once. I send by this post another copy of my paper on the Attorney-General's duel. I wish I knew what you and some of your friends think of it. In my letter in the Dublin Post Office I begged of your ladyship to send me anything that gave in a compressed shape, an account of the machinery of the National Education system. My objection to the plan was not as you suppose, because the Priests have a share in it, but because I do not like joint education in the abstract. This prevented my ever examining the details of the system, but this was what I felt to be a peculiar view of my own, best to be kept to myself, as scarcely any, as I know would agree with me. The great body of the Clergy, however, declare themselves anxious for joint education, and really, I think, are offering a very senseless opposition to the National Board, and are running their (stupid) heads against Government, they know not why, but because others who know not why either, are running on before them; I really am tempted to write something on the subject—to contribute my mite to prevent the Church from running foul of the State, and from the same cause which occasions such accidents at sea, that the wits of the former at least are in a fog. Now that Sir Robert Peel is said to declare that he will withhold patronage from the opposers of the National Board would be my time, who could and would preface my observations by saying that I would take no preferment. I beg of you to keep what I have said on this subject a secret, they are the confidential breathings of my mind, and I may think quite differently by-and-bye, as the subject is quite new to me.

Ever, your truly affectionate and much obliged,

H. WOODWARD.

Fethard, Tipperary, December 24, 1846.

MY DEAR LADY OSBORNE,—As all our subscriptions to the Church Missionary Society must be forwarded by the 1st of January, it is my part as Treasurer to remind you of this; and also Mrs. Osborne, to whom I beg you will mention it with my love, and save her thereby the trouble of receiving a separate note.

I have been more of an invalid for more than a fortnight than for a long time before; and at my time of life particularly, such interruptions should lead to much solemn thought. The times are truly serious, and seem as if Providence were about to interpose in some remarkable way.

For my own part I cannot conjecture what, short of a miracle, is to save the country; there may be plans, which, if agreed upon and put into execution, might at least mitigate the evil; but what is the use of plans if they emanate from no centre of authority, which turns speculation into practice. The game is next to desperate, and it is badly played. One thing at least I am sure of, namely, that we should individually commit these matters to God in prayer, and as to temporal prospects prepare for the worst.

Yours most affectionately,

H. Woodward.

My dear Lady Osborne,—You will not, I am sure, think it a liberty in me to suggest that it would be desirable for you to send a line to the Editor of the *Daily News*, to contradict the report of your having left the country from fear. If you dated your letter, as of course you would, Newtown Anner, Clonmel, you could simply refer to that date in proof that you had not left the country.

I am delighted to hear such good accounts of Mrs. Osborne and the baby. Believe me, my dear Lady Osborne,

Most affectionately yours,

H. Woodward.

Mullingar, July 30, 1853.

My dear Lady Osborne,—I thank you most sincerely for your kind letter which found me at this place; I hope I feel grateful to a merciful providence for the degree of convalescence which I experience, though, as yet, it is far short of perfect health. I felt quite sure at one time that I was about, through the mercies of my Saviour, to enter those calm abodes where the weary are at rest. I felt that at my time of life to put on again the harness and drag at this life's load was not what a kind Providence was so likely to intend for me as rest from my labour; but it seems, perhaps, that God has still something for me to do; and I must say, that if I would at times sadden at the thought of being a mere cumberer of the ground, such letters as yours are a great cheer to me, for I feel that sermons, which a taste like yours can so approve, may be useful and influential in quarters from which I hear no report. Tom is very comfortably settled here with a nice little wife, and good congregation. We hope, please God, to be at Fethard on Thursday next, where Frank proposes to meet us. I beg my best love to Mrs. Osborne, and remain with much affection,

Very faithfully yours,
H. WOODWARD.

April 26, 1856.

MY DEAR LADY OSBORNE,—I felt very much obliged, as well as gratified, by your kind note from Newtown. Your passage to Holyhead was, I fear, a rough one; but it is now over, and I trust that the rest of your journey has been pleasant, and that change of air and scene will quite set you up. You cannot be better than I most truly and sincerely wish you, both in body and soul,

Being ever most affectionately yours,
H. WOODWARD.

I beg my love to Mrs. Osborne, with many thanks for her kind mention of me; I somtimes feel that she has mistaken somebody else for me, or me for somebody else, but hope she will not visit it on me when she discovers her mistake.

" The writer of the next letter was a direct descendant of the celebrated Bishop Berkeley.

The Editor has observed in all the letters to Lady Osborne

that those of the earliest date, from people who became subsequently strongly under the influence of religion, all had a
tendency thereto in their nature. She remembered the text,
' These were more noble than those in Thessalonica, in that
they received the word with all readiness of mind, and
searched the Scriptures daily whether these things were
so. The truth was, the ' more noble' always fraternized with
her.

The Penal Laws against religion are so often flourished in
the face of Irish Protestants, that it is a comfort in this
letter to see allusion made to the most effectual hindrance to
social progress in Ireland in past times. The causes named
were, though less morally horrible, practically worse for
natural developement, and while so much is said against Penal
Laws—defended by none—let us, Protestants, not forget
the horrors, the bodily tortures, and murders of the Inquisition, sanctioned by the Romish religion, as well as in some
instances, murder outside its immediate pale, and these without reference to general massacres. Onesidedness is the
folly of the day."

Clonmel, February 27th, 1822.

MY DEAR LADY OSBORNE,—I received a sincere and heartfelt pleasure on reading your letter, which I wished much
should arrive, though I did not *ask* for it, and have therefore
a *double* obligation to you; and I shall with earnestness
endeavour to meet your kind feelings, which if I do not
express as well as you, it must be because they are too
many for me to choose amongst. You must always find or
make friends while you follow your own kind and ingenuous
disposition, and I am happy that you think we resemble each
other in any point of disposition, but how often do various
circumstances combine in this " working day world " to make
us appear differently from our true selves, and as Rosalind

says, "if we step out of the beaten path we get so many burrs to our petticoats that we can scarcely shake them off," but how tedious is that same beaten path of life, and what a weary load it is. My spirits begin to tire sadly, and are not sufficient to bear me out in anything but the common trodden road of existence. How enviable that feeling which you recal to my mind, and that time when merely to live, to breathe was joy and happiness that belong exclusively to youth (though neither you nor myself can yet be classed among the ancient of days).

I passed that happy time in a most romantic country place, where I literally lived in the trees like a bird; being a spoiled *pet* I did as I chose at all times, and had a friend of my own age, who really resembled an angel in disposition as well as appearance, and who I doubt not is now one. Oh! what a change, to calculating the price of a sack of potatoes, or seeing a piece of beef cut up with the thousand odious etceteras attendant on a narrow income and strict system of economy. You see, that living in the solitude I do, I must either be an egotist or be silent, but your descriptions of your happy family circle called forth these animadversions. May you always experience the same, or a greater degree of happiness, and for myself I say, the will of God be done. I was much struck to-day on reading the Psalms by that beautiful and poetic verse: "He that now goeth on his way weeping, and beareth forth good seed, shall doubtless come again and bring his sheaves with him."

You mention Miss Godfrey. I have frequently seen her when she was with Lady Kingston, as she has often been at my uncle's at Bowenscourt, and I have been at Mitchelstown (Lady K.'s), but I can hardly say I am acquainted with her, as I had not then even begun *to go out*, being not more than sixteen years old. Of course I did not *venture* to *approach* a person so much older than myself, but I heard every one call her a sensible, agreeable person, and if I mistake not, I have a cousin, Miss Berkeley, who knows and likes her, and whose (word torn out) is, I believe, a relative of Miss Godfrey. Mrs. Perry of course recollects her perfectly. I remember Miss Smith (now Mrs. Barthy, the actress) was there also, a protégée of Lady Kingston's, who used to bring her everywhere she went herself, and she made herself very agreeable by reading and reciting.

What shall I say to you "au sujet d' Irlande?" It would not be generous in me when you have with such generosity and good feeling, for my country, entered the lists in defence of her fair fame to attack yours, and retaliate upon her the injuries, the poverty and misery that drove this ill-fated country, to commit those frantic acts that are called rebellion. But when you recollect *who* it is, that, exulting in the pride of riches, comes for the purpose of breaking her thriving infant manufactories, that they should not interfere with her own, thus snatching bread from the mouths of thousands, and sending them forth in idleness; who it is that has taken the *jewels* from her crown to set them in her own; you cannot be at a loss to set forth the cause of all this mischief, and tell those, who exclaim at it, that they are those who made it all. Without hyperbole, as far as I can gather, the extreme of poverty is the cause of this state of things; and (but let us not *whisper* it even to the passing air), within the last week there have been great outrages committed in the county of Cork, my own dear birth-place. The mail coach was stopped, three of the horses shot dead, coachman and guard severely wounded, and the coach turned topsy turvy into a bog-hole, with all its wheels in the air, the passengers having first been delivered at a birth from the inside. Believe me, I am not so unfeeling as *really* to jest upon the many cruel occurrences that have taken place, whereby so many have been deprived of their dearest relatives by the wanton acts of these unfortunate people. I fear we shall hear of more such, and worse.

Poor Mrs. Perry has by no means recovered her spirits; and most unfortunately an event has just occurred at Wood-roofe, which does not tend to make them better, the sudden death of Mrs. Barton's maid while there. This is indeed a world of calamity; it is not wonderful that the spirits should sink with increasing years, as "all are doomed alike to groan, the *feeling* for another's woe, the selfish for their own." I am sorry to say I feel an increasing dislike to *society*, to go any where from home is an exertion which I really do not feel equal to.

We have refused invitations to the Pallisers, Grove, Woodroofe, in any case, however, I would not leave mamma alone during the winter. I was indeed much grieved I was not able to go to the Cox's while Aunt Bowen and Martha Prittie were there, the same reason prevented me, as I have, I hope, learned to prefer duty to inclination. Do not suppose that I murmur at our reverse of fortune; far from it. I thank God for it. Adversity is like the dervise's ointment in the Arabian Nights, which closing your eyes to this world shews you the incomparable riches of another and a better. Uninterrupted prosperity is, I am sure, the most dangerous state for frail humanity to experience.

I have been amusing myself taking lessons from an Italian drawing master, who paints fruit and flowers in a peculiar style, and very beautifully. He regretted your not being in the country, as he reckoned on you as a pupil. Hayes is going to give up his shop, and dispose of his stock by a lottery of ten shillings a ticket. He has some very pretty things; I am sorry he did not succeed. How happy I shall be to see you again, my dear Lady Osborne. Let us indeed efface all traces of a coolness so unfounded, and which could never have existed had we looked in each others faces;

but when people are separated, every " trifle is, though light as air, confirmation strong."

I am sure you must be tired of me. You do not mention the dear children, so I conclude they are well; nor your own health, which I hope is also good. Make my compliments acceptable to Mrs. Smith and Miss Warde, and believe me to be always your sincere and

Affectionate friend,

A. RIALL.

I have not once seen your brother, and I really thought it would only annoy him to attempt to draw him out of his retreat without any prior acquaintance. Colonel Bagwell has purchased Oaklands. The family are to take a house in this town for a year.

" These letters of Mrs. Riall show the writer only under one aspect, as a member of what was at the time styled ' the religious world,' but she was a most accomplished person, and one of the most agreeable conversers possible. It must be remembered that in that day parties were more divided than they are now; and that then, if religion were a subject of interest at all, it was a matter of course, that the subjects and practices permitted or prohibited by the person who awoke the vibration of that cord, should be adopted by the instrument acted on, as thoroughly, though not coercively, as under the Papal spiritual domination, but no one was more sparkling in social intercourse than Mrs. Riall. The editor has seen much of both irreligious and religious people, and she takes this opportunity of affirming, that even if there were to be no Hereafter, the latter are in this world much the pleasantest, provided they are intellectual, or at least, sensible people."

August 1, 1829.

MY DEAR LADY OSBORNE,—Expecting to hear by Mr. Smith, I deferred writing to you till his arrival, and now thank you for your two dear kind letters. How fully my heart replies to such kind expressions of Christian love from so beloved a friend as you, I need not attempt to explain. What a precious thing is a Christian friend! How often my wonder is excited at the blindness, the extraordinary delusion, of the world in rejecting happiness in its highest sense, even here below, that it may feed on husks from the swines' trough. And what happiness, then, is a Christian's heart! My dearest friend, is not it the truth of all the tales of those magic wands we used to read of? Possessed of "the secret of the Lord," we are invulnerable to unkindness, above insult, safe from harm of every sort, if not wholly at least in a degree, which, a worldly mind, would not, could not, credit, even though it may increase our suffering at the sight of a world which is enmity against God. In all society in which I was accustomed to the happiness of meeting you, I feel an indescribable void, and lately at Derryluskan, it amounted to a feeling of deep depression. I felt a sense of isolation, a loneliness, particularly when Mr. Woodward was there, which brought back all my old feelings of dread of his *not understanding me,* which I was just beginning to conquer a little.

Of the success of the first Bible meeting at Fethard, and the fine speaking, I am sure Mr. W. has told you, so I will not. We have been for a few days at ——— lately, and through the mercy of God we narrowly escaped having another scene of woe there. S——— had a bad fall from his horse lighting on a small heap of stones, exactly over the heart, which must have received a violent shock from the effects. Though he had no apparent injury he suffered much from pain and weakness, but was going on quietly, of course in bed, and having a physician. It happened on Saturday; and about 3 o'clock that night we and the whole house were aroused from sleep by a cry of such deep despair and agony, which rung through the house, followed by another, and then all was silence and darkness that I never, never shall lose the recollection of it. It proceeded from poor Mrs. —— on being told by the physician that —— was dying; and it appears that no one could have been nearer death that did not expire, for the heart was already collapsed, and quantities of wine alone was the means of restoring circulation. You may imagine the scene we then had, everyone rushing to the stairs, no one knowing the truth, but of course supposing him dead—all this in the hours of darkness.

Arthur went down to the room, and found him with every appearance of death—a deep faint, cold as ice. He is now able to leave his room. May God grant some good effect from this warning; but, alas! I doubt that such will be. It is most awful that, after the many recalls to God they have had, they are still wholly devoid of the only foundation; and both Mr. and Mrs. —— are but like the branch when separated from the tree, which, while a little sap remains, may appear fresh, but has no root. He has a sort of sentimental religion ; but apply that never-failing touchstone, ask a confession that we are wholly sinners, wholly saved by the merits of Christ, and they recoil. Still he is incessantly talking of the Bible, but seems to understand everything the wrong way. His mind is like a bad mirror, which reflects nothing correctly, but as it appears to be at work we must hope some good may result.

The two little boys are the finest creatures I ever saw, so altered and improved as to make you doubt their identity, only for an occasional glimpse of the original habits. The

youngest fell on his knees, and prayed aloud for ———,
when in that state calling aloud on his father to join him;
he, poor man, was quite distracted. I thought of Scripture
—" At midnight there was a great cry;" it made me think
of the coming of our Lord as a thief in the night, or in the
words of the hymn, " While a guilty world are sleeping."
Mr. —— was warmly defending duelling at dinner the day
before, also worldly amusements.

There is a clergyman in this neighbourhood who is much
interested in their state, and appears to be a sweet creature
and a true Christian, but I fear is almost too yielding and
too indulgent for their case. I lament with you the establishment of a theatre in Clonmel; it makes us pray more
fervently for the coming of the Lord. It seems that nothing
else will do, for the whole world lieth in wickedness.

I am your most attached friend,

A. RIALL.

August 25, 1829.

My dearest Lady Osborne,—Your most kind and gratifying expressions lead me to think I may, without being
troublesome to you, again so soon have the comfort of communion with you, from the midst of the melancholy and
dispiriting scenes of this present state of things. I allude to
the very sudden and awful death of poor Mrs. P—— in
particular. It makes me low and nervous; and I confess there
are even of those I love none that I can turn to without a
feeling of disappointment, which I suppose must be so, until
in " unfettered union " spirit can mingle with spirit without
the obstacle of this material body.

The Sunday before last Mrs. —— was at church, and on
Thursday night after she died. It appears to me to have
been merely the sudden breaking of a thread which had gradually worn away, and worn away from the suffering which

is always attendant on the having chosen this world as a portion, and of course finding in it but constant disappointment. . . . How everything adds to our desire of the coming of that Lord who will " restore all things." Everything seems in confusion; and I cannot conceive that Popery has even yet a shake, or that anything short of the Second Advent can destroy it. Surely a few converts are as nothing towards its subversion. Have you been carried along the stream of the general interest in prophecy, which penetrates into even the most retired places in, I think, quite an extraordinary manner, as if sent by a single movement. What a curious division of opinions seems to exist on that as well as every other subject. There seems to be no standard, until the Lord shall set up an " ensign in Zion."

Mr. Woodward called here the day before yesterday for a few moments, on his way home from Doneraile, to inquire about the ———'s. He found Mr. Jonathan Woodward and Susan and Dora Pennefather here, who had just rode over from Darling Hill. Of course, as you know, all my ideas fade before Mr. Woodward's, and I become very nearly an idiot. What is the cause of it, I wonder? You only, like the eagle, can gaze unmoved at the sun. I am sure it will appear to you very like thinking too highly of myself, and not at all flattering to you, to say that you are almost the only person with whom my intercourse and communion is without those feelings of disappointment which I continually feel with others, even thinking most highly of, and loving them as most dear Christian friends; but go beyond a certain point, and you find perhaps energy enough, but not depth of feeling, or deep feeling, without energy enough to support even conversation, or perhaps so much of both that you are afraid to give an opinion, lest it might come in painful contact. This must proceed from the encumbrance of this vile sinful body, which will not allow us to show what we feel in many cases. Oh! what delight it would be to have them changed, and glorified and spiritual bodies. I often ponder on the mystery of sin, to think that after all I have known and felt, I can still go on sinning against such an unspeakably merciful Saviour, who has given me so much in delivering my soul from the " net of the fowler "—delivering it from the world. Who hath made thee to differ? we may well say.

Did you get a " Free Press "? Mr. Smith wished me to send it to you. Did you ever see such insolence as the account of the Clonmel meeting?

I went to see poor Mrs. —— during Mrs. ——'s short illness. Passing through Fethard, I found myself in the midst of a funeral, with such a number of gigantic priests dressed up with such quantities of white linen, that they were really like something spectral as they stalked about. My heart grew sick. The people were only collecting for it, and everyone had white linen on them, so that literally the town seemed peopled with spectres. I cannot describe the effect of the appearance, it was very depressing. The dear Pennefathers are also much depressed. I think they were at —— one day, and had a melancholy scene with the girls before Mrs. ——'s death. I saw her in her room for an hour, with the melancholy group that were round her bed; she lay insensible nearly the whole time. It was something of apoplexy. She looked quite beautiful. There was no opportunity for any preparation for the great change, as she was insensible throughout. She was a devoted wife and mother. Tell dear Catherine I was very much obliged for her nice letter, which I will soon answer. I fear my letters to you of late have been so full of gloomy events, that you will think of me as a bird of ill omen. But I hope and trust in the goodness of our God that the present cloud will soon pass away, and the " Sun of Righteousness appear with healing on His wings" to every mourner and to every sinner; and may we meet in light and joy. God bless you, my dearest friend.

Ever your most sincerely attached,

A. RIALL.

" Mrs. Hill in speaking of Lady Osborne used to say, " To no one so much as her" can be applied the term used to Nathanael, " Behold an Israelite indeed in whom there is no guile !"

Mrs. Hill, the wife of a clergyman in the County of Tipperary, was one of those people gifted with great mental and moral superiority, who, having no career in the world save that of quiet domesticity—made no noise out of their own circle but who within that are honoured—if not as prophets, at least as much valued intellects and bright examples. Mrs. Hill collated the edition of Bacon edited by Archbishop Whately. The ensuing scrap is an analysis of hers."

The kind of double action of mind cannot be better exemplified than in a story Georgina tells of a man who said " The pig did not weigh so much as I expected, but somehow *I never thought* it would."

5, Graham Terrace, Queenstown.

My DEAR LADY OSBORNE,—I am encouraged to hope that a renewal of long suspended intercourse between us may be rendered acceptable to you by one of the enclosures I send being from *the* Archbishop for you, as you will perceive by his autograph; the other I forward to you from myself, wishing to know what you think of the tone and spirit of the criticism. It was sent to me anonymously in an envelope bearing a Cumberland post mark; I must own it made me not a little angry. Was it that you were angry with me for

my last letter that made you allow it to be the last to pass
between us for so long a time? I was so glad to hear that
that you had recovered the severe attack you had of illness,
and I trust you are by this time quite restored to your usual
health and that your Christmas is a happy one with those
dearest to you, around you. I am passing the Christmas
away from home. My dear Frances has been suffering
severely with Neuralgia, and I thought a change would be of
use to her besides taking us both away from some sad associations, which a recent bereavement within this year connects
with a home circle, more peculiarly at this season ; you
have, and dear Mrs. Osborne too, my warmest wishes that
this anniversary may bring to you as happy recollections as
earth can give, and those bright hopes which nothing earthly
can dim.

When you see Mrs. Phipps pray give her my love and
warm Christmas greeting. Believe me, dear Lady Osborne,

Ever yours affectionately,

ALICIA HILL.

5, Graham's Terrace, Queenstown, January 2, 1856.

MY DEAR LADY OSBORNE,—I must not, by delay in telling
you, lessen your amusement in hearing that the criticism
which I sent you was written by the Archbishop himself.
While it is fresh in your memory you will better appreciate
the accurate knowledge he there displays of the charges
usually brought against him of egotism and dogmatism. He
got it copied by a friend of his in Cumberland and sent to
me through the post just as I sent it to you. I was completely taken in, as was everyone else in the house, a few
hours after he arrived at Blackrock; it was during his late
visit to Cork, and he kept up the joke admirably till a short
time before he left, he pleaded guilty to having concocted
the whole. I thought of trying whether you would be taken

in and he caught eagerly at the idea, and begged me to send
it to you. Does not what seemed to us virulent abuse assume
a totally different character of real wit, now that we know
it to be his own criticism on his own works? He will be
delighted to hear you were taken in as I was. [A fragment
of a letter.]

MY DEAR LADY OSBORNE,—Miss Hutchinson and I, on our
return, communicated to each other our mutual anxiety as
to your state of health, and we both blamed ourselves for
not having pressed upon you the absolute necessity of your
allowing yourself more rest than you do, and determined to
speak to you the first opportunity, but I am now induced
not to wait for one, as I am furnished with too good a text
not to preach upon it. I write from bed, where nothing but
complete exhaustion has placed me; while I was with you
I was suffering so much from headache and pain in my side
that it was quite an effort for me to speak, and instead of
yielding to my weakness, I absurdly persisted, on my return
home, in getting up at five as usual, and this morning when
I had been up about an hour, my five senses chose to take
leave of me and I only recovered them to find myself again
in bed; this I can ascribe only to my having for the last ten
or twelve days got but four hours' sleep. I am now quite
well again, and only mention it to you as an excuse for what
you may perhaps deem officious, in one known to you for so
short a time; and yet I do not think you will, for you must
perceive that you have excited in me a more than ordinary
affection; you are more to me than any woman has ever
been, for I can honour your character as well as love it.
Why is it that I can write this to you, while not one word of
affection escapes my lips while with you? But it was not of
myself I wanted to speak, I will not tell you that your life is
valuable, this is nothing; but I will say that I am deeply

persuaded that your dear child's eternal happiness is, humanly speaking, bound up with your being spared to her; you know how varied her temptations will be—spare yourself then to be her earthly guide till her eyes are opened to recognize and trust her heavenly Guardian. ——— has, with grateful emotion, told me of your kindness to her; the Friend of him who hath no friend will bless you for it.

Your affectionate,
ALICIA HILL.

"As this book is a memorial of Lady Osborne and her friends, a very few letters, not addressed to herself, but to the Editor, are inserted as showing the characters of those who were her chosen companions. Possessed of every other moral quality, gratitude was not omitted in Mrs. Hill's character, and she dedicated the noble intellect with which God had gifted her to His service."

Tuesday, December 17, 1839.

MY DEAR CATHERINE,—I send you part of the "Heroine," but I am sorry to say the first volume somebody has borrowed, and not returned; but if I can see you, as I hope, to-morrow, I shall endeavour to put you at least into possession of the "dramatis personæ." I am inclined to believe that you will think it too broad farce, and not like it. The four little tracts (I know you like that word), translated from Krummacher, await your acceptance, as I have taken the liberty of writing your name. I like the encampment of Judah best; will you think it too imaginative? And yet I do not believe you have decided that imagination—that falcon of the mind—is to be hooded when religion is in the field. Fancy, at least, in embellishing solid themes by analogies, is a sweet minister. Take that appeal in Romans v. 7, 8, where reason seems called upon to weigh the superiority of the love of Christ above all human love, and has not imagination here much to do? Must it not with its magic pencil lay before reason, so that it can take it in at one view, not only the portrait of the austerely just man whose character may command esteem, but scarcely more affection to the sacrifice of life; but that also of the good man, whom the heart springs forth with all its sympathies to meet, and for whom it could even dare to pour out its best blood, and in the picture must also enter the contrast to all that is just and good in the sinners for whom Christ died. Imagination paints all, and then reason is called upon to decide whether God did not indeed "commend His love towards us."

But however it may be in religion, I cannot but think that reason, when in her sobriety she rails at imagination, is but proving herself an ungrateful mistress to a faithful servant. I question whether any proposition has been submitted to her in which imagination has not lent her aid, unknown it may be to ourselves, to place before the judge. Nay, when the awful majesty that lies in the simplicity of pure reason sometimes strikes me, "Could I be thus struck without imagination"? To me it seems the very retina of the mind's eye. Then stay with me still, sweet angel! You will laugh at my flight, but even in this wild flight I am sober enough to remember that there are times when this angel may seem to trouble the waters of the mind, and seem to trouble it for healing, when it may be excited, aye, and religiously excited, and yet the soul left in its idolatry. Could I forget what I have experienced, a religionism without faith, without grace, without unction, a piety of the imagination that was indeed a morning dew, that passed away before the first beam of sun, of that world which nothing but faith can overcome!

It is my deep conviction that to be a Christian is a great

and a serious thing, and that imagination and every high
thought must be brought into captivity to the obedience of
Christ. I once had a friend who used to say, " Some Christians
do unchristianize me." What a pang it would be to me
to think that any levity of speech, any inconsistency of mine
would yet stand before you in array with that religious
world with which you are so disgusted. Do you know that
I have made out a little consolation for myself for your
going away. I have taken up an idea that this religious
world does not exist on the Continent, at least in that tangible
systematic form which must always more or less disappoint
and repel the mind that has formed to itself a higher
standard than aught human can ever reach. But after all I
know not whether these inconsistencies be not to my mind
a proof of genuineness. Do you remember Mme. de Stael's
" Les caracterès vrais sout tojours inconséquens;" and if the
individuals composing this body were not severally endeavouring
to act up to a standard presented by their own
consciences, were they bound hand and foot to a system
merely of man's devising, as they are accused of being,
would they not present an unvarying front, an unbroken
line, that would defy attack?

I know a person fully impressed with the necessity of
keeping up the decencies of public worship, but who is
equally impressed with the conviction that no sermon can be
worth listening to; that person, from complete abstraction,
I have seen present an aspect of deep uninterrupted attention,
while one seated near, anxious to hear, betrays by the
very effort to recal his thoughts at times, that they have
been wandering. You will think this a strange illustration,
but after all it is all idle. " By my words," says our Lord,.
not by any man's interpretation of them, "ye shall be judged."
Paul and Barnabas quarrelled, but what of that? Is Christ
divided? Was Paul crucified for you? And surely in a

point, the very essence of which lies in the giving of the affections, would any plead, "Lord, I would have loved Thee more, had not others loved Thee so little"! Could we see a gracious master, wounded in the house of his friends, and the heart not swell with more devoted loyalty, with more uncompromising fidelity?

My coming to the end of my sheet reminds me how I have run on. You will not, I think, suspect me of intending to preach. If I know myself I never will volunteer a sermon. I know that the truest friend to a cause may prejudice the mind of another. Philip even, in the joy of his heart at finding Jesus, says in mistaken statement, "Jesus of Nazareth;" and Nathanael asks, "Can any good thing come out of Nazareth"? Were it my last word I would use it to beg of you to let neither the open enemy to the cause of God, nor its professed ally, nor its real friend, come between your soul and your God. We but waste time in asking, "What shall this man do"? His command is, "Follow thou Me."

I did not intend to care about anyone again, in the way of forming a new attachment, and here I am actually finding myself young enough for it still. Is it not odd that I think of you as two separate beings. I found a little note of yours to-day, written, I should think, when you were about eleven. May God bless you.

Ever yours,

ALICIA HILL.

Mary Street, Cork.

MY DEAR MRS. OSBORNE,—I cannot resist sending you a few lines I have just met. We have so often liked the same things, that I feel almost sure you will be pleased with them, but this time I want your little Edith to like them, as I thought of her immediately on finding that my little grand

child enjoyed them, at least parts of them. I have in copying the lines taken the liberty with them of substituting
'Edith' for the 'Gerald' of the original. I saw lately the
"Child's Christian Year" edited by Keble, and was so much
disappointed in it. The "Christian Year" is so exquisitely
beautiful that I expected something, at least approaching to
it in anything published by him. There is not such a collection of sacred poetry as it is; there is I should think more
or less of rapture in all praise, in all adoration of God, and
therefore we have so few hymns at all worthy of the name,
for "rapture is born dumb." Have you seen Keble's version
of the Psalms? It is much closer to the original, at least as
we can judge of it by our Bible translation, than the version
sung in the Churches, which in so many places spoils the
passage; it would be a pity to lose some of the old Psalm
tunes which another version might not suit, unless where
doctrinal error is involved, change might not be improvement. I am quite enjoying the idea of THE Archbishop
coming to Cork. He is to hold his visitation here on the
30th, and I shall be able to see him. It would be such deep
pleasure to me even to see him for one moment, I could not
tell you the continual proof of his unmeasured kindness I
am receiving, and how he seems to watch every opening for
literary employment for me. He writes to me so kindly on
every topic he thinks might interest me. I owe to him and
Mrs. Whately the success my son has met in Australia; in
short the very sight of the handwriting of either of them is
like sunshine to me. I have been employed selecting some
of the apophthegms in which his works abound, for instance,
"Honesty is the best policy, but he who acts on this principle is not an honest man." "Persecution is not wrong
because it is cruel, but cruel because it is wrong." And
again, It is one thing to wish to have truth on our side, and
another thing to wish *to be on the side of truth.*" I can

never help smiling when I think of Mr. Osborne having first heard of me in connection with the story he tells of his first visit to Newtown. I heard of Lady Osborne soon after her return from Bath and trust she continues well; her bath must be somewhat more tempting to her now than it could have been in those terrible winter mornings, indeed the heat these three last days has been so excessive that I could almost live in cold water. I ought to write both to her and Mrs. Phipps, but I have not been in such spirits as would be good natured in me to inflict on my friends, so all my writing is for business, and such as the Frenchman describes:—

" Au peu d'esprit que le bon homme ait, l'esprit d'autrui par supplément servait-il compilait, compilait, compilait." With kindest regards from Frances. Believe me

Ever affectionately yours,

ALICIA HILL.

My dear Mrs. Osborne,—I cannot thank you as I feel for your kind invitation, but I have made it morally impossible that I could avail myself of it. Truly you are very good-natured to forgive, or very unsuspicious not to impute to me a most insidious way of offering myself to you. I like the *last* best, and to believe that you have been exercising the " charity that thinketh no evil." Had I known that the Archbishop was to be with you it might indeed have been a strong temptation for me to have said, " Will you let me go to you?" for I long for an opportunity to say one little word of the gratitude and reverence I feel, but that would have been honest and open, as it is, even to meet him, and if you but knew how much is in that *even*, you would know how much I prize the honesty and straightforwardness, that when I remember my letter to you and your answer, I only wonder you could give me ever again credit for, I did not think of his Clonmel visitation, and literally obeyed an impulse in sending you off the little poem. It is singular that I thought it rather abrupt on my part to commence a correspondence in this way, but checked myself in offering an apology as likely to make too much of a trifle. I feel so much your kind desire to give me this *great* pleasure, yet I am sure you will quite understand why I could not possibly accept your invitation. You must not however be disappointed *for* me as I trust I shall see him in Cork.

Ever yours most affectionately,
A. HILL.

What is better in a railway accident than presence of mind?

The blood rushes to my face when I remember some expressions in my letter. I hope Lady Osborne is with you to enjoy the pleasure of meeting his Grace.

April 15th, 1834.

MY DEAR LADY OSBORNE,—I was indeed glad to receive your last affectionate letter, though I have not told you so; but I cannot now let Mr. Smith go to you without a few lines. I need scarcely say that I forwarded your letter to Mr. Woodward immediately, and I know you do not require an assurance that any you wish to send through me I shall be happy to receive and forward. He told me it was a " delightful" letter, and I can well believe it. Had you only expressed half the wish to return home that you did to me, that alone would be pleasure to his unalterable friendship for you. Mr. Hill and I have been staying a few days with him, previous to his leaving this for Dublin, where, I believe, he will remain a month at least. I think I can be unselfish enough to say I am glad he is gone there, for his last visit was a great cheer to him; and there is, in this country, so

little of the materials upon which he is fitted to work that
we can scarce wonder that leaving it for a little should give
a spring to his mind, in the hope of elsewhere finding a more
congenial soil.   I have been told that nothing could equal
the enthusiasm excited by his preaching in Dublin.   He was
followed by crowds; and I do not wonder, his style is so
peculiarly his own that there is nothing at all like it; and I
believe that his powers were never in fuller vigour than at
this moment.   Immediately after Mrs. ———'s death, the
suddenness of which seemed to have shaken his nerves considerably, there seemed something like a failure in his sermons,
but he soon rallied, and is now himself again in mental power;
while in every christian grace I think he has made progress
that does me good to see.   Religion seems now to be to him
at once excitement and repose.   Perhaps the true test of
religious feeling is whether it has indeed filled up the void,
and satisfied the craving of the human heart for an object.
I often ask myself whether it has done this for me, and I
thank God, I am of late enabled to give a happier answer
than at no very distant period I could do.   Were it possible
to cease to feel interested in Mr. Woodward upon any other
ground, yet as a mere specimen rare and most singular
and difficult to be solved, he must be interesting to those
curious in the study of character.   I almost think I know
him now.   It seems indeed most cold-hearted in me that I
have not before this expressed my sympathy in the delight
you must feel at the change in ———'s feelings.   One is
not half grateful for such events as these.

Till we know even as also we are known, till we can
estimate the priceless sacrifice of the Lord of Glory, we shall
never feel the full value of an immortal soul; never rejoice
as we ought on its return to happiness in God!   How I shall
like to see ——— again.   You talk with pleasure of your
return to Newtown and the society of this country.   Is it

that distance has on retrospect the same effect it has on the prospect in advance of us:

> " Lending enchantment to the view ;
> Robing the mountain in its azure hue.

It is not many days since I, with a friend of yours, made in imagination the circuit of the land " from Dan to Beersheba," and with the exception of a very few flowers indeed, found all barren. But it may be the fault was in the eyes that looked and not in the objects themselves. It ought to be so, since you can think of all here with such pleasure.

Mme. De Stael's maxim would tell exactly against our jaundiced view—" tout comprendre rend trés indulgent et sentir profondément inspire une grande bouté."

The change at . . . I feel lamentably. I believe I have never said a word to you of ———. She is what is generally known by the name of a most good-natured person, except that this sometimes implies a failure in shrewdness, which she has to a remarkable degree; a Tory in politics, highly attached to the Tory Church of England as by law established (how long the last clause will continue to designate it is just now somewhat problematical)—so highly attached that she saw in Mr. Woodward's lectures in our room, an attack upon it more dangerous than ever Guy Fawkes' success could have proved. Liberal to the poor, and capable, I am persuaded, of being a steady friend wherever she attaches herself, and good-tempered and good-humoured enough to make you sometimes forget her want of refinement and mental cultivation.

You must know that she has a great antipathy to blue stockings, and will not allow them the immunity Byron did when he said he cared not how blue a woman's stockings were, provided her petticoats were long enough to cover them; for when Mr. Butler pleaded in favour of one of the cerulean sisterhood, not me, for I do not know whether she even suspects me of belonging to the race—that " she never obtruded her information," she said, " oh I that's nothing, when once I know that a woman is a blue, I live in constant fear of a deluge." Only conceive when in dear ————'s day literature was the current coin of the realm. Mr. Butler's defence of the poor blue reminds me of a compliment paid to me which E—— told me of yesterday. It can scarcely be surpassed even in that happy land of happy phrases and elegantly turned phrases, in which you are. An eulogium on my talents and information (praise I never coveted) was bound up with " but what is best of all you would never find it out." E's gravity, gave way before such a tribute as this, and she hailed it with one of her shouts of laughter. You will say I am in a cynical humour to day. I hope not, for certainly cynicism is not Christianity. Buchanan in his " Christian Researches," mentions that eminent Christians in the Syrian Churches, were known by the name " men of the beatitudes." Is it not a beautiful title? a Christian should be a man of the beatitudes, walking in the gentleness of his Lord's example, in the benignity of his spirit. Richard —— has just been married, and came here for a few days immediately after his marriage. I have had a proof of how little there is after all in celebrity. I discovered, that till I told her, his wife had not the most distant idea that his name had ever been heard beyond his native city, or the town of Bangor, where he met her. Anyone so devoted to another as he is to her I never saw. He has just now all the energy that happiness gives, and preached a splendid sermon on Good Friday, in our little church. Did you hear a report that Doctor —— has evinced such a leaning towards Protestantism as to raise the jealous suspicion of his own party, and two Jesuits have been sent down to watch him? What a stamp this (if true) sets upon his honesty of character hitherto. I shall long to hear more of him; such a thing as this must interest any one. I often speculate with deep interest upon the possibility of finding you changed—not in principle—but in that openness which left—was it only the outer court of your mind or your imagination accessible to all who looked to it with a wish to find it so. If I find myself changed in aught (and perhaps this letter is a proof of how completely I have continued to run the same round) it is in this particular. Time was when if I could not throw open the inner shrine, the outer court was fast closed too; but I have now found out that the outer court may be thrown open without any less strict guard on the sanctuary, and that civility to an acquaintance does not necessarily involve treason to a friend. Are you as much devoted to study as ever? For the last year and a-half I have done little or nothing, and I catch myself ofton repeating " cui bono," which I used to call the watchword of dulness and insipidity.

You thank me for not believing some reports. I should have shown very little knowledge of your character could I have credited them for one instant. . . .

Is constancy an element of happiness in such a world as this! I do believe it is. Give her my love. Did you ever meet or I should rather say, do you know any one, male or female, whose character in some traits of it are precisely hit off by the following description.

Son défaut selon moi, c'est de ne jamais mettre complète-ment á l'aise ceux même qui lui sont chers, un grand fonds de bouté, une disposition secrète a la mélancholie rassurent ceux qui l'aiment et donnent le besoin de mériter son estime. Des mots fins et delicats font entrevoir son caracterè; il semble qu'il comprend, qu'il partage même tout bas, la sensi-bilité des autres et que dans le secret de son cœur il répond a l'émotion qu' on lui exprime mais tout ce qu' il éprouve en ce genre vous apparait comme derièré un nuage, et l'imagination des personnes vives n'est jamais avec lui ni totalement découragée ni entièrement satisfaite."

When you write to me, and I do hope you will do so soon, try and remember to tell me if you have an original for this portrait. I am suffering just now from rheumatism in the head, and have been for some time. I trust you suffer less from headache than I have heard you do. Before I close this I want to tell you a thought which occurred to me the other day for the first time, as removing the apparent want of connexion between the 16, 17, 18, and 19th verses of the 16th Luke. It occurs to me that the mention of John the Baptist brings to our Lord's mind his violent death; whence the transition was natural to the cause of that death. Herod's adultery—and then as if the mind of the Saviour were led to the thought—" the poor shall not alway be forgotten, the patient abiding of the meek shall not perish for ever." He relates the parable of the rich man and Lazarus as illustration of future retribution. I should not think this worth sending you so many miles, but that Mr. Woodward seemed quite struck with it as a discovery and a solution of a difficulty which as such had never been presented to my mind. My first thought was wondering that I had never before taken notice of the apparent want of connection. It is time to say " Good bye."

Ever your affectionate,
ALICIA HILL.

Did I tell you anything of my little girl; I should say too much of her. She is my heart's darling. I am sure you would like her.

MY DEAR LADY OSBORNE,—I am too glad to hear from you not to write, though it be only to tell you so. I find your letter took from Monday to Wednesday to arrive at Rochestown, so that I have some fear that you will have left Fethard while this is making its way to you. I should like to hear Mr. Woodward's ground of objection to chess, the one which I felt strong enough to make me give it up was the obvious one, that it appeared to me a waste of mental energies which in my case it drew out to the utmost—it seemed laborious trifling. The vivid pleasure with which I found Mr. Woodward expressing the same sentiments and occupied with the same subject, made me feel what the secret of charm, the rest of it might be to many minds; the thought of an infallible, unchangeable human centre. I quite enjoy the thought of your being at the Glebe; it must be so happy for you. Do you know I am not quite easy about your cold bath; I cannot but think it would be better for you to have it within doors; I wish you would think about this.

I am reading some sermons of Mr. Newman's, there are some beautiful thoughts and his power of educing the whole character from some slight indication, some little touch of Scripture, reminds me so much of Mr. Woodward. There is a beautiful sermon on the "Individuality of the Soul," and another on the "Greatness and Littleness of Human Life," another too on the "Hidden Life of Christ;" if you have not read these I trust you will like to do so. You will be glad to hear that in an Adelaide paper I received to-day, there are most encouraging reports of projected railroads and public works, which seem to hold out good prospects for my son; I think I can venture to say that his ability will be recognized if he gets but opportunity to test it; we could not yet hear of his arrival. Mr. ——— most kindly brought me a Danish Bible from Dublin, but could not get a Danish Dictionary, so that I have not yet been able to do much with Grant's books, and I am afraid I have already kept them too long. It will be worth my while to study it, as if I succeed in getting any book to translate I am not so likely to have

competitors as in the other languages; this is the more
important to me as I have nothing original in me, whatever
imagination I have is rather reproductive than creative; the
motive, too, being altogether pecuniary, though situated as
I am a most legitimate one, is calculated rather to induce
industry and perseverance, than to excite the higher faculties
of the mind.   I am not quite sure that such a motive would
be as legitimate in religious works, otherwise theology would
meet better the bent of my mind.   I think I have given you
quite enough of "I by itself," that piece of egotism of a
language.   We are reading Macaulay again with ———, she
desires me give you her kindest regards.   Frances begs me
to thank you for your kind remembrance of her.   I cannot
tell you the pleasure this renewed intercourse is to us; we
must not let it again be interrupted.

Ever yours most affectionately,
A. HILL.

MY DEAR LADY OSBORNE,—I have been suffering from the
effects of a fall which hurt me very severely in the back and
head, and the first day I got your letter I was not able to
write; the next I made an effort to get for you a fuller
statement of his Grace's views, but not succeeding I must
try to tell you as much about them as a head somewhat out
out of order will let me.   He thinks the quarter from which
the real danger is to be dreaded is the Tractites, and depre-
cates strongly the alarm and indignation of the people of
England taking a wrong direction and being vented in any
such manifestations, as in 1780, which would, he thinks,
cause a strong re-action towards Romanism.   He dwells upon
the inconsistency of the alarm and surprise at that which has
been so quietly borne with by the English so long as it only
affected Ireland, while from the circumstances of the latter
country the influence of Popery was more to be dreaded.

The appointment of the Bishops he regards as render-
ing them more independent of the Pope than the Vicars
Apostolic removeable at his pleasure. "There is something
wrong and something new in the Papal proceedings; but the
new is not wrong, and the wrong is not new." He fully
sympathizes with you in your indignation against the Tract-
arians; as to me, while considering (and what I am about to
say is like an *Irishwoman*) them one and the same with
Popery, I have long thought them far worse, and my only objection to classing —— and —— with Cardinal Wiseman and
his Bishops is that I think the latter too good company for
them; as for —— he is below contempt. I am sure amid all
your indignation and excitement you do not contemplate
any coercive measure being brought forward by the government, or if brought, being attended with any success. I have
been told that the principal Irish Romanists think this
measure of the Pope's a most injudicious one, and that it
has thrown back Romanism a century. I trust it may not
be a recoil, only for a fresh and greater spring. I cannot
tell you how I rejoice that you so abjure the Puseyites;
Popery itself has not more trammels for the mind. I heard
a discussion of half an hour between two clergymen as to the
admissibility of allowing a pocket handkerchief to rest on
the *table* during the reading of the Commandments; as he
had not gone quite the length of calling it the altar, it struck
me as absolutely ludicrous. You must excuse this hurried
scrawl, as I am not at all well. It gratifies me to think you
wish to have me near you sometimes; truly I often wish that
it could be so ordered for my own sake; as far as giving you
any interchange of thought, I fear you would find out soon
that I am not good for anything or anybody now; I wish so
much you would tell me what Mr. Woodward thinks of all
the excitement. How often have words of his acted like oil
upon the waves! I never hear from him now, but when I

want to be quieted I go to the Shunamite—it is like breathing another atmosphere.

My dear Frances is well, and much gratified by your remembrance of her; my little grandchildren are very nice and very good, " of course," you will say. I trust you can give a good report of yours as to health. Pray give my kindest regards to Mrs. Osborne. What an intensely interesting session of Parliament will the next be! The Archbishop has a seat this time; I could not tell you half his kindness or half the trouble he takes about me—I should like a coinage for him, " Master Heart," only that it implies too much of command for so gentle an influence as his kindness.

Ever yours affectionately,
A. HILL.

Mrs. Hill used to say that if she were to be put in prison and allowed to choose only one book besides the Bible, she would select Mr. Woodward's " Shunamite."

Part of a letter from Mrs. Hill.

Look at the *Quarterly Review* for January, 1821, and you will find a review of Miss Austen's novels. It is written by the Archbishop and you will like it. He sent it to me while in Cork. It is singular that almost the last thing the Archbishop said here as he went away was a vivid picture of a father's manifestation of delight at the arrival of his children, from whom he had been separated; and one of the last conversations with Mr. Woodward was his pressing the duty of restraining the expression of such feelings in meeting after absence.

You would have been amused if you had heard his description of my handwriting. Dr. Hinds* says people write

---

* Author of an admirable work that ought to be reprinted, " The Three Temples."

illegibly out of annoyance. It is virtually saying, "My letters are worth getting any way." I intend to reform if I can and be humble, but I am writing in a great hurry. With affectionate love,

Ever, yours affectionately,
ALICIA HILL.

" The Editor is not at liberty to put a name to the writer of the three following letters, but it is one that carries with it weight for distinguished intellect and goodness, and these qualities are, moreover, represented by a family and not merely by the writer himself."

Kenmare Arms Club Hotel,
Killarney, July 26th, 1831.

MY DEAR FRIEND,—Now that I am at a distance from you, the remembrance of your kind hospitality to myself and friends is so pleasant, that I cannot deny myself the satisfaction of expressing to you the obligation which both they and myself feel to you for your kindness during our abode at Newtown. It not being always a safe thing to trust one's self with the " viva voce " expression of an obligation such as I feel, I did not venture to give utterance to all I could have said, and therefore may have appeared from my silence to have left you in a much colder manner than the occasion might seem to warrant. I will not, however, do you the injustice to suppose that much assuring is necessary to cause you to believe that I shall always consider the circumstances which brought me under your roof as among those most calculated to contribute to my happiest recollections, and that my residence with you will be ever more regarded much in the same manner as a traveller regards an oasis in the desert.

Having thus placed my feelings upon record, I should, perhaps, do well to close this communication, but a kind of promise I gave you respecting the Arian Controversy, makes me rather feel the difficulty. On reflection, I seem to have undertaken more than a *traveller* ought to have encountered, since I fear that the constant movement to which I shall be subject, will not leave me sufficiently at leisure to bring together in a condensed form such matter as may serve to silence the objection or doubts of persons who may hesitate to admit the Supreme Godhead in the person of the man Christ Jesus.

To enter on an undertaking of this nature in a hurried manner, or under unfavourable circumstances, might expose me to the fearful responsibility of injuring the cause I intended to serve, and therefore I should like to defer the fulfilling of my promise to you on this matter until my travels have been brought to a close. In the meantime, nevertheless, I can be reading the Scriptures with a view to the subject in question, and shall be very glad to be supplied by your reading with texts which bear upon the following points, viz.:—

1. The predictions respecting the divine nature of the future Messiah (Isaiah ix. 6).

2. Texts which describe the attributes of the Jehovah, " I the Lord change not."

3. These texts of Scripture which attribute to the man Christ Jesus the same perfections as are ascribed to Jehovah, " Jesus Christ the same yesterday, to-day, and for ever."

By this means the supreme attributes of the divine nature, having been shown to be those with which the Messiah that was to come was to be invested, mankind in looking out for the Christ will be constrained to pass by all claimants to that high office in whom the divine attributes do not reside; and Jesus of Nazareth having at the same time been proved to possess the perfections of omnipotence, all men will be constrained to acknowledge Him as " God over all, blessed for evermore."

I have thus supplied you with occupation for those hours which are usually devoted by you to devotional exercises, and shall take no little pleasure in knowing that you are, though far distant, still present with me in the investigation of that part of truth which lies at the foundation of our hopes of eternal life. I may add, that you will find great assistance from a little tract "On the Trinity," by Jones Nayland. In this tract, texts of Scripture of the kind above-mentioned are collected and put in a logical form, and from its size and character it would, I think, altogether answer your purposes if reprinted in a cheap form, much better than any compilation of texts which I could arrange. This sentence, I assure you, is not penned in mock-modesty, but in sober earnestness, as you will at once be convinced by referring to the tract. The only alteration that it occurs to me might be made would be a revision of Jones's preface. And now having written you a theological dissertation, I will commit its defects to your forbearance, with the full assurance that I may do so with safety, having everything to hope from your friendship.

May the honour of that Divine Saviour, whom we profess to serve, be ever precious in our estimation, so that whilst we read the Scriptures for the confirmation of our faith in the divine character, our lives may show forth for His praise.

Believe me your much attached friend,

———.

We purpose leaving Killarney on Friday afternoon, so that my address for a fortnight will be Sir Edward O'Brien, Dromoland, near Newmarket, Clare.

Pray give our united regards to the happy circle at Newtown Anner, and say we all wish ourselves back again among you.

April 15th, 1832.

MY VERY DEAR FRIEND,—Although I had made arrangements before the receipt of your letter to leave Cambridge
for town on the 16th (to-morrow) I have written to postpone
my visit till the 23rd, as one of the main purposes of my
visit to London would be defeated by your being unavoid-
ably absent. How much I sympathize with you in your
distress, you can yourself judge if you have been called
upon ever to condole with a much loved friend in affliction.
I can understand, too, from experience those feelings of
regret—hopeless regret which are excited by the recollections
that cross the heart when it reproaches itself for having
omitted to minister to the wishes of a deceased relative, so
fully as it imagines it might have done. Let me comfort
you, however, by the thought that you can now be certain
that through that Almighty Saviour who overcame death,
your deceased relative is enjoying a far more exalted satisfaction than she ever could have derived here from your
affectionate attentions to her, how long soever she might
have lived in the daily enjoyment of them. Look forward,
too, to the period when it may be permitted you to renew
with her, before the throne of God and the Lamb, an affection,
which, the more deeply it may have been seated in the soul,
the more proportionably was it incapable of ever approaching
perfection here ; deeply also as you may deplore your
bereavement, remember that a compassionate Father in
Jesus Christ takes beloved relatives and friends from us, in
order to free us one by one from those many ties by which
our hearts are attached to earth, or rather by taking all we
love to Himself. Is it not His blessed will, thus by holding
out to us a prospect of meeting them again, to draw our
affections more earnestly to that better world. These considerations will doubtless have already and often occurred to

you, my dear friend; and my prayer is that they may be realized to your consolation. May the God and Father of our Lord Jesus Christ support and strengthen you.

Ever your devoted and attached,

46, Clarendon-square, Leamington, December 8th, 1834.

That unhappy country (Ireland) seems to be destined to be the field in which the battle now pending between God and Antichrist, in all its forms, should be fought, if one may judge from appearances.

I need not inform you how restless the spirit of Popery is, nor advertise you of its intolerance. I think, however, both that restlessness and intolerance has assumed a more definite form of late; encouraged, as Popery has been, by His Majesty's late Government. I do not think sufficiently ill of those to whom the Government of Ireland has been immediately committed, as to suppose that with full purpose of heart they have desired to depress the Protestant religion, and to raise Popery in the exclusion of God's word, but the result of their measures tend to this effect. We could scarcely have expected that in these days of affected liberality (for it must be affected) any government would have been prepared to consign the education of several millions of its subjects to a system in which the word of God is proscribed; but such is the fact as regards Ireland, and if a child is taught to read by the *Government* it must agree that its soul shall never be visited by the light of life. By this means Popery must increase for a time, yet if one says a word in discountenance of the system one has to bear the reproach of objecting, merely because one disapproves of the party in power. That speculative ungodly men should try to conciliate a body of men, whose subjection to a secret and turbulent agency, seems to set laws at defiance, is not to be wondered at; but it is surprising there should be such an utter absence of common observation in politicians, as that they should not have discovered that it is hopeless to attempt conciliation as respects a religion which the history of the Christian world in general, and Ireland in particular shows, will be satisfied with nothing short of domination, and has been a matter of surprise too to me that the Irish Landlords, as a body, have manifested such apathy on this subject, in which they are infinitely more interested than the Protestant Clergy, now undergoing a process of starvation. As a member of the clerical body, I have often felt most acutely the little sympathy which my Irish brethren have received from the proprietors of the soil, who ought at once to have undertaken the payment of tithes on their respective estates until the question has been settled. Yet if it had been lawful, I could have enjoyed all the secret gratification which a malevolent spirit could deduce from a conviction, that, if things be long permitted to take the course they have taken for the last two years, the day is very near when no Protestant landlord will receive more rent than a lawless faction thinks fit to accord them. Lately, however, the Protestant gentry have opened their eyes to their future prospects, and a great many proprietors, by taking the payment of tithes into their own hands, have completely overthrown the Popish agitators, and I think, by God's blessing, the religious horizon of Ireland may ere long assume more hopeful aspects; God fearing too, having been so completely put out of all calculation in all that our rulers of late have done, that we may confidently expect that He will manifest His power on behalf of them who call upon Him, and acknowledge the glorious Godhead as the Sovereign of the world. If the late ministry had not been dismissed by the king, it appears that a plan was to have been brought forward for *withdrawing altogether* the Protestant clergyman from every parish where there were not a certain number of Protestant families, confiscating the revenues of the church in such parishes, and razing the Protestant places of worship! When this plan was suggested to the king, his answer was, "I will die first," and further he sent the ministers about their business. No ministry is yet formed, but Peel is to be Prime Minister and Lyndhurst Lord Chancellor; of the rest nothing yet is known, only all the newspapers with one or two exceptions are congratulating the country on having such a manly king, and there is every prospect that the return of the Conservatives to power, will be hailed by the nation as a blessing. [Seemingly unfinished.]

" Lady Osborne was very proud to reckon Dr. Arnott amongst her group of intimate friends, for possessing as he did in an eminent degree the qualities she especially valued, philanthropy and learning. He stands foremost amongst scientific stars as an intentional benefactor of the human race, and for his remarkable disinterestedness. She delighted in the study of his " Elements of Physics."

Bedford-square, 27th April, 1832.

My dear Lady Osborne,—As appears by the accompanying syllabus, Mr. Brande will begin his lectures on Electricity on Thursday, the 3rd of May.

When I left you the other day, I still doubted whether I had given you a correct idea of the nature of my chapter on " Religion," in the forthcoming book on " Education;" and as I value too much your good opinion I take the present opportunity to beg, that until I be able to present you with a copy of the work, you will merely recollect that my purpose has been to reclaim the sceptic on the one side, and the erring enthusiast like Mr. ——— on the other, and to be a peace maker between sects of Christians. The attempt I hope will meet approval, how imperfect soever the execution.

On thinking again on the scrap written in Miss Osborne's book, it appears to me that you might think it improved by the following addition—" He who did more than any other philosopher to remove all doubts from men's minds, as to the stupendous magnificence of the Universe, sketched in the preceding lines, was Sir Isaac Newton, than whom there never was a more sincere Christian."

I remain, my dear Lady Osborne,

Your faithful and obedient servant,

N. ARNOTT.

" The following letters are from the pen of a young man of extraordinary ability and brilliant genius, one who is considered by the best judges as amongst the greatest of English divines, one whose ambition as regarded this world was ' nil,' but was of that lofty character deeming that ' He builds too low, who builds beneath the skies.' Educated as a Roman Catholic, after he had attained manhood he joined the Church of England, and entering the ministry became one of its most shining lights. His sermons are exceeded by none in power and eloquence; his Theory of Development copes with Newman's Midway Passage to the Church of Rome, in a manner that clearly demonstrates that the stronghold of Romanism is not identity and antiquity, but its assumed power of development. Great as he was as an author, he was no less admirable as a parish clergyman, and caught the fever, of which he died in the prosecution of his ministerial duties. In the anticipation of an early death, his only regret was that he could not complete a book he had commenced upon the doctrine of Faith—a work that there is reason to hope may yet be given to the public, as far as he had completed it— under the auspices of the son of the person who had great influence in the direction of his mind on the subject of religion, namely, the Rev. Henry Woodward.

" The chair of Moral Philosophy in Trinity College, Dublin, was created that Mr. Butler might fill it, at an unprecedented early age."

" The first letter is striking in these days of reckless unscrupulosity as regards theological machinery (if I may use such a term), for it manifests such a sense of responsibility.

" The second points out the old desire of unity of tone of thought in church matters, more likely to be ever sought than attained."

Trinity College, Thursday, March, 1838.

My dear Lady Osborne,—I delayed to answer your very kind letter until I had an interview with Dr. Dickinson. You were not wrongly informed that my mind has often resumed its original preference for the profession of the Church. I had always turned habitually towards that profession as being the one in which peace and content of spirit might best be attained; and I have seen (even already) enough of this world of ours to have *nearly* learned to give up aiming at any higher or more marked happiness than such content can bring. These views were from a combination of circumstances, which I can scarcely describe to myself (is it not oftener a union of small motives than any single great one that governs us all?), suspended of late; and I had even resolved when I saw you last at Newtown to take the preliminary steps for the law, which accordingly on arriving in town I did take. I have, however, as you see, paused in my progress to the woolsack, and suffered my mind to flow in its old, and I believe happier, channel. Dr. Dickinson has kindly said that he would give me information of any clerical opportunities in this neighbourhood. To me there is, I confess it, something very overwhelming in the idea of undertaking this great responsible office; an idea which has often haunted me, and which has made the ministerial life always look to my imagination better at a distance and in future prospect than close at hand. As I begin to look at it now, I cannot conceal from myself that there is very much to be relinquished, and very much to be assumed, before I am what it demands; and I contemplate with a strange sense of terror *how far* I am at this moment from its requisitions.

A thousand levities of mind, that, small as they seem, show their real strength when we seek to conquer them; a thousand paltry ambitions, and a thousand worldlinesses, are at once in arms against its claims. I fear you would think but poorly of me if you knew what trifles have weight in the contest. I am truly glad, my dear Lady Osborne, that your school is as you would wish it. Whatever may be thought the general danger of a system that includes the Roman Catholic priesthood in a plan of religious education, there can assuredly be nothing but good effected in all those particular instances where the vigilant care of a Protestant superior constantly watches and works to secure substantial instruction to the pupils.

I feel very much your kind interference in this affair; and if it eventuates in furthering my religious happiness, I shall not easily forget your part in it.

Believe me to be,

My dear Lady Osborne,

Yours very sincerely,

WM. ARCHER BUTLER.

" Mr. Butler was but a school boy when he took by surprise the circle in which he moved, his own family included. He was invited to speak at a Church Missionary Meeting, and when he stood up, and, as if inspired, gave utterance to a flow of the most brilliant eloquence and the happiest epithets, such as denominating missionaries as " the chivalry of faith," then it was revealed that a star had risen to reflect radiance on his native land."

My DEAR LADY OSBORNE,—I think you have a fair right to receive a copy of a letter of mine in the present number of the " Irish Ecclesiastical Journal," which is making some commotion here, as it was written during the period of my last very agreeable stay at Newtown, and doubtless owed some of its merits to the " genus loci." The letter refers to an audacious attempt of mine to make peace between the parties now agitating the Church, by exhibiting the common ground upon which they can meet, an enterprize which seems to be received, as such attempts generally are, by very impartial abuse from both. I send you a number of the journal by post.

Believe me,
Dear Lady Osborne,
Most truly yours,
WM. ARCHER BUTLER.

" The following letter proves that the Rev. Theobald Mathew, ' not straining at a gnat and swallowing a camel,' but treating measures like characters, on the principle that ' He that is not against me is for me,' was willing, though each held his own religion to be the right one, to coalesce in the suppression of vice and the promotion of good. The Editor takes the opportunity of observing that the vice of drunkenness could in no wise be so successfully put down as by the establishment of cheap refreshment rooms in market towns, they being almost unknown in Ireland, and she regrets to add, much discouraged where efforts have been made to set them on foot."

DEAR LADY OSBORNE,—As you have taken such deep interest in the promotion of the great moral movement which has, with the Divine blessing, effected so much good, I take the liberty to inform you that the Very Rev. Dr. Burke has invited me to Clonmel to administer the total abstinence pledge.

Sunday, the 23rd, has been appointed for our meeting, and I hope, with God's assistance, to bring back to the fold of temperance such as have unhappily strayed into the paths of drunkenness.

If all whom the Lord has placed in high station exercised their influence to promote His glory and the happiness of His people as zealously and perseveringly as your ladyship has done, what a blessed change would be effected in our country.

I promise myself the honour of visiting your ladyship, but I must deny myself the privilege of being your guest, as it will be necessary for me to remain in Clonmel.

With fervent prayers to the Almighty that He may confer on your ladyship and Miss Osborne every spiritual and temporal blessing, I have the honour to be, with profound respect,

Your Ladyship's most devotedly,

THEOBALD MATHEW.

"The following letter, written by Mrs. Walker, wife of the Bishop of Edinburgh of that name, is given on account of the concluding paragraph, showing the wretched incomes of a Protestant Episcopal Church in a Protestant country. What then is to be expected in Ireland from the same system, where the clergy would be in a great degree dependent upon the caprice of individuals, those who required religious ministrations the most being least willing to contribute. Moreover, numbers are everything for voluntary payment, especially of a spiritual religion not dwelling upon externals; but it is well ascertained that the readiest way of making up large sums is through a multitude of small ones. Consequently the failure of funds in a poor country like Ireland would be no test of the sincerity of the followers of the church despoiled of her rightful inheritance."

Leckie, 27th October.

MY DEAR LADY OSBORNE,—So far from wondering at your silence, I marvel more that you should find time to write to me at all. It is a fortnight to-day since we came to this second home. My dear friend is very helpless in body, but with a wonderfully clear mind. Her will is God's will. All her afflictions, bodily and mental, are felt to be sent by the hand of a most merciful Father. She murmurs not, neither does she make a parade of resignation. It is the religion of the heart that sustains her; but as you do not know her, I need not bother you about her. To me the visit is generally a sad one; to my daughters one of great enjoyment, with their two young friends. Miss ——— is with us, but is now looking south; she and Madeline have just set off for Glasgow, to pay a short visit to some mutual friends there. Jeannie and I return home in two days, and they join us, I hope, on Saturday. I am anxious to get home that I may secure a cook, being still minus that useful auxiliary; and I shall not be sorry to be seated at my own fireside, pursuing our usual monotonous occupations, which have been so long set aside. Captain Walker is now in Edinburgh, has given up his comfortable lodgings, and gone a mile and a half from us. Old bachelors are very queer. Bishop Low occasionally corresponds with Madeline. I am glad you liked the good old man. I rather think to-morrow is the day Mr. ——— and Mr. ——— are to be consecrated,

two very different people. *You* would call Mr. —— a
Puseyite; *I* call him a pious churchman. He is the son of
Lord ——, a law lord, a humble-minded, self-denying Christian, who labours among the poor as their brother. He has
given a proof, and a strong one, of his love to the suffering
classes in Scotland, by giving up his living at Leeds, and all
hope of promotion in England, that he may labour in our
humble Zion. I hope I do not flout at Mr. ——. I only
fear he is not fitted for a bishop in a poor church, where
many of his clergy are simple good men, with very un-
polished minds and manners, but therefore better suited to
their flocks, and eighty pounds per annum. [Unfinished.]

" The Editor remembers Lord Bexley as a most kind and
hospitable host, when with Lady Osborne she paid a visit to
his beautiful place, Foot's Cray. He was a great lover and
patron of modern art. He was for some time Chancellor of
the Exchequer."

Great George Street, March 11th, 1834.

Dear Lady Osborne,—I feel much ashamed that your
letter should be so long unacknowledged, but as I am sure
you will consider truth as the best apology, I am bound to
confess that in removing to town it was somehow mislaid, and
I did not recollect your address. My sister has now fortunately hit upon the letter. I am sorry that I cannot give a
very favourable account of her health. We were for some
weeks in November at the sea-side, and she seemed to be
much refreshed by the air, but the benefit seems to have been
only of short continuance; I see, however, no actual cause for
alarm, but she is feeble and incapable of exertion. I hope both
your Ladyship and Miss Osborne find the air of Paris agree
with you. I am afraid I cannot give her any useful advice
respecting Decker's pictures. The late king had some pleas-

ing works of that master, and I think Miss O. might rely on the recommendation of her instructor. I am afraid we must not attempt in this country to rival the magnificence of the Louvre, but if Wilkins's design is carried into execution we shall have no reason to be ashamed of the British Picture Gallery, except that it will stand somewhat awkwardly with respect to the Portico of St. Martin's. I read Silvio Pellico's book with pain and disgust, though it is only reasonable to suspect some exaggeration in the statements; and it must be remembered, that the sufferers would in most countries of Europe have been punished with death at any time previous to the present century. It is however lamentable that the Austrian Government should expose itself to such imputations with any degree of foundation. It is very pleasing to see in a Roman Catholic the spirit of piety which prevails in the book. You must have heard of the heavy loss the friends of religion in general, and the Bible Society in particular, have suffered from the death of Lord Teignmouth; and it may have reached you that the Committee has pressed upon me to take his place. At my age it would better become me, and be far more agreeable to my feelings, to retire from a situation of exertion and responsibility, but being the only vice-president who has taken any active part in the detail of their business, I could not refuse such services as the Divine goodness, called for, I trust the united prayers of many sincere christians, may for a short period enable me to perform. My sister desires to return her thanks for your kind inquiries, and to send her kindest remembrances.

Believe me, my dear madam,
Yours faithfully,
BEXLEY.

I take the liberty of enclosing the minute of the Committee of the Bible Society on Lord Teignmouth's death.

DEAR LADY OSBORNE,—I am not a member of the Committee on Irish Education—the Government not having proposed my name, perhaps from thinking me prejudiced on the subject.   I must confess that I dislike the new system, as tending to suppress the Kildare Place Society, which appeared to me to be conducted with great ability and most beneficial effects.   I never, however, doubted that the new schools were capable of producing great good when conducted with perfect fairness, and under the superintendance of pious and judicious visitors; I have therefore no doubt that the schools under your care are very useful and indeed probably not distinguishable in practical effect from Kildare Place Schools, though in principle open to the great, and I think fatal, objection of a restricted use of the Scriptures.   But what I suspect is that in places not so carefully attended to, the ostensible rules of the system are disregarded, and that the schools are in fact conducted almost as Roman Catholic seminaries.   On this point I shall be anxious to see the evidence produced before the Committee, and it will give me great pleasure if I can see satisfactory reason to believe that my suspicions are unfounded.   How far any neglect of the rules is justly attributable to prejudiced opposition on the part of the Protestant Clergy is a very proper subject of inquiry before the Committee.   That any part of them should be placed in a state of collision with the Archbishop of Dublin is most deeply to be regretted, whatever may be the cause, and cannot fail to be injurious to the general interests of Protestantism.   I am not conscious of any prejudice against his Grace, but was rather prepossessed in his favour through some common friends; but I cannot say that I think the opposition to him unprovoked, though it has been carried to unjustifiable lengths.   In his theology, I know of nothing inconsistent with sound Christianity, though he is a bold speculator ; and in his character I believe him to be sincere and disinterested, though I am afraid dogmatical and imperious. With his duties, it is impossible he can attend to the details of the Education Board, which therefore must be left to subordinates perhaps less ingenuous than himself. He will of course take a leading part in the Education Committee, and between him and the Bishop of Exeter, I hope the truth will be brought out. I am afraid the enquiry will be a long one, and that we shall not have any report until late in the summer.

My nieces desire their kindest remembrances to your Ladyship and Miss Osborne; and they request you will have the kindness to inform them where Colonel and Mrs. Phipps are to be found.

Believe me, dear madam,

Very sincerely yours,

BEXLEY.

To a person superficially acquainted with Archbishop Whately, the Editor can understand his being supposed imperious and dogmatical, but Mrs. Hill understood his real nature.

."[The following letter was written by Bishop Walker, Bishop of Edinburgh.]"

Nunraw, near Haddington, 16th August, 1831.

MY DEAR LADY OSBORNE,—I feel both ashamed and sorry when I look at the date of your letter and recollect that it remains unanswered. The receipt of it gave me great pleasure, and my resolution was to answer it without delay. I have ever been a dilatory correspondent, but I often think of my friends and relatives, and many a time since your residence has been in Ireland, have I determined to renew my acquaintance with you. My locomotive powers, however, are much impaired; I am exceedingly bent and cramped by rheumatism, and since the 22nd of January last, to this painful complaint has been added a feebleness which is singularly distressing. This will account for my too long delay in answering your kind and most acceptable letter.

It would have afforded me much satisfaction if I could, in the course of the present summer, have paid my respects to you in Ireland, but I am quite unequal to such an exertion. From the 18th June we have been in a sweet rural retirement, where I have the advantage of getting out into the open air at all hours, from which I doubtless derive benefit, though my strength by no means returns.

On considering attentively your letter and the religious reflections which it contains, I am not aware that either in correspondence or conversation we should have any serious subject of dispute. I have never been satisfied, God help me, with my own attainments and efforts, either as a Christian or a minister; but my purpose has ever been to preach the Gospel and the whole Gospel as the Scripture gives it, and as our church faithfully receives and truly expounds it. I am no enemy, and never have been an enemy to the serious part of the clergy, so far as their seriousness is accompanied with sound kept sincerity. A clergyman without seriousness and sincerity in the principles and practices of his profession is a most pitiable object, while a sound faith is indispensably necessary towards a consistent Christian practice. What I dislike in the party called Evangelical is not their seriousness nor their doctrinal zeal, so far as their doctrine is sound; it is their want of charity, and the exclusive spirit which they so frequently display. I have in numerous instances found them mark with the zeal of their exclusion and therefore of their reprobation, men whose soundness, seriousness, and sincerity cannot in any circumstances be exceeded, merely because they rank not in their association. In this country these Evangelical men have within the last twenty years, gone through a course of changes not trifling but important and essential, while at each step they are peremptory, exclusive, and uncharitable; without learning caution or charity from the vast changes which they adopt. This singular infirmity has recently subsided into the most pitiable fanaticism or the most worthless deception. They work miracles forsooth; they have the gift of tongues—that is, they utter sounds which neither they themselves understand nor those who hear them. They announce the immediate advent of Messiah in language very shocking to Christian ears. They maintain the peccability of the Redeemer's human nature, and appear to place the poor fallen creature redeemed, on a par with the Redeemer, who can therefore be no longer divine. I have had a most distressing case of this kind before me in one of the clergy of this diocese; the consideration of which has been so far satisfactory in that all the rest of the clergy who were necessarily consulted in the discussion, have completely concurred in maintaining the doctrine of scripture, as that doctrine is expounded in the admirable articles of our church. In this concurrence I include one clergyman of the Evangelical class, who, about six years ago, drew me into a controversy on the subject of regeneration; the truth is that the clergy of this diocese generally though among the exclusives, they are not classed among the Evangelicals, are yet Evangelical in the truest and best sense of the word; and as we mix more together and know one another better than in time past, we all walk in the house of God as brethren and friends, and even my Evangelical opponent thinks very differently of my doctrine and principles from what he did

H 2

some six years ago, while he finds that I have not the slightest
objection to his Evangelical seriousness and zeal, so long as
they are combined with soundness, and discretion, and
charity. It were a hopeless task indeed to attempt to bring
all men to the same precise way of thinking. The leading
truths of the Gospel we must all maintain, because they are
essential; and while we apply these by the Grace of God in
the practice of the Christian life, charity will unite, as in the
blessed words of Christian fellowship with all faithful men,
however they may differ in some minor matters. If circumstances were to bring me into contact with your Evangelical
clergy, I should see no reason of estrangement—still less of
dispute—provided I should find them disposed to extend to
me (though not nominally of their class) the charity which
I willingly bear to them.

My little ones are getting on a pace. My eldest, Jane
Ramsay, was nine in February, and is remarkably clever.
She made astonishing progress last winter in music, and can
read French easily. My youngest, *Madeline*, was seven in
July, is clever in apprehension and in conversation, which
her sister is not, but she is deficient hitherto in application.
I have not determined and scarcely think I shall determine
to make them classical scholars; with my infirmities I am
not now equal to the task of teaching them myself, and
unless they were to show a decided bent that way I do not
see in their case the necessity. The case of your daughter
differs in the bent which she displays, and you are right to
yield to that bent which may be so usefully applied. My
two have taken, and will, if God spare them, continue to
take lessons in dancing; your views on that subject I will
not dispute, and would not combat even in conversation, for
a feeling of Christian duty firmly formed is always worthy
of respect. The world so far as it is a wicked world, and
this, alas, is lamentably far indeed, is one of our greatest and

most dangerous enemies. But in the world we must live and so use it by God's help as not abusing it. I would fortify the minds of my children by every Christian principle and by every godly motive. I would teach them what they are by nature, and what, if they would reach their heavenly inheritance, they must become by grace; but I would not lay upon them impositions nor urge on them prohibitions with respect to things innocent and indifferent, which might in after life become burdens or snares to the conscience. This in brief is my opinion on this subject, which I state, simply not to contest the point, but to account for my own conduct. My poor children have little to look for in this world of woe, for I have little to leave them; therefore so long as I *shall* be spared with them will it be my duty and my desire to bring them up in the nurture and admonition of the Lord, and may God of his infinite mercy grant me the ability and them the grace to profit by it. I could much wish were it to please God to restore my strength somewhat, to make an effort some summer day to pay you a running visit; I should have much satisfaction in renewing my personal acquaintance, and I am persuaded that we should easily understand one another on all the subjects which are most interesting and important to Christians.

I remain, my dear Lady Osborne,

Your faithful friend,

JAMES WALKER.

" Lady Osborne always took a lively interest in the varieties of schools of religious thought, and amongst them was occupied with that of the Wesleyan Methodists. The following extract with its luminous preface is written by a gentleman who at one time belonged to them, but subsequently entered the United Church of England and Ireland.

" The extract which follows relates to a subject which was always regarded with the deepest interest by its writer. To enter into its meaning we must have a just view of the opinions he held on the doctrine of sanctification. It is commonly understood that sanctification is the life's work of the Christian; that when a sinner has repented, his sanctification by the Holy Spirit begins and continues, if he is faithful to his life's end. But it has been held by many excellent men, especially among the followers of Wesley and Fletcher, and is now held by many in America and in England, that a *second* experience, similar in its mental accompaniments to the experience of conversion, is attainable by the Christian, and is to be regarded as the full accomplishment of his salvation. This work or experience has been designated technically by the terms sanctification, Christian perfection or full salvation, and of late years by that of *second conversion*, and is believed to be accomplished by a single act of faith, by which the soul, striving after full salvation, is at once admitted to the inestimable blessedness of a sinless state. This is the experience to the attainment of which Lady Osborne was exhorted by the writer of the following extract."

A topic formed the principal part of our conversation which always charms me, and truly delighted was I to witness the simplicity and ardent piety (which indeed instructed me) with which God has blessed you, and it will afford me the most gratifying heartfelt satisfaction to hear from you that you have found this pearl of great price.

Be not discouraged, dear madam; there is not a spiritual blessing which you are desirous of obtaining that God is not willing to bestow. " His love is as great as His power, and neither knows measure or end." But all His promises in their performance on His part are suspended on faith on ours. If we can once possess ourselves of this powerful and mighty engine (if I may so express myself), we may work out our own salvation, and make our calling sure at once. Faith is mighty, faith is omnipotent; it sees the promise, it smiles at impossibilities, and cries, "It shall be done." It is done; nothing can be more dishonourable to God than sin, nothing more lovely in His sight than holiness. Why should it seem a thing incredible with any that God should sanctify the soul? What He has promised to do, what He is able to do, what He is willing to do, must be accomplished if there be no hinderance in ourselves. To the single eye we say, "Now is the day of salvation;" and surely it is enough to say to you, madam, "The blood of Jesus Christ cleanseth from all sin." *Believe that doctrine.* Stumble not through unbelief, but believe the second time. It is mere voluntary humility to be exclaiming, "Who shall deliver me from the body of this death"? I reply, the Lord Jesus both can and will, and He desires it now. Yes, believe that His blood cleanseth you now from all sin, and as sure as you believe this saving truth it is done, and you will be able to sing with the sweet singer in Israel—

> " 'Tis done, Thou dost this moment save,
>   With full salvation bless ;
> Redemption through Thy blood I have,
>   And spotless love and peace."

Have you read the little works I took the liberty to recommend to your perusal? I can say they were really beneficial to me, and however simple the remedy, we value it if it has done us good. Permit me to add to the list Mrs. Lefroy's Letters; they are admirable. She was a saint of the very first order, as her lovely and most excellent letters (which she never expected would appear in print when she wrote them) fully and abundantly testify. But perhaps while I am thus writing, you have already entered into the

promised"land, and have taken possession of your rich inheritance. For it is indeed a rich inheritance, " Where pride and
unbelief expire, cast out by perfect love." Perhaps you are
even now rejoicing in the foretaste of that glory which is
to be revealed; your renewed mind with childlike simplicity
says—

> " Nor have I power from Thee to move,
> Thy nature and Thy name is love."

If this be your present happy experience, you will feel
the full force of those inspired words of the heavenly-
minded Apostle, " The anointing which ye have received of
Him abideth in you, and ye need not that any man teach
you, but as the same anointing teacheth you of all things and
is truth, and is no lie, and even as it hath taught you, ye shall
abide in *Him*." You are too well instructed of the Holy
Ghost to need that anyone should teach you that trials and
exercises and conflicts will come. We are still on earth, and
Satan roams to and fro, but he cannot hurt. Clothed with
panoply divine, you can now put to flight the armies of the
alien, for great is the Holy One of Israel in the mind of a
sanctified soul. Oh! how I shall be overjoyed to hear you
tell me that fear and doubt and unbelief have all yielded to
perfect love, and that you have no longer a temper or feeling that you could not take with you to heaven, and which
God does not now approve of.

" The Editor is not at liberty to put the name to this
extract."

" The readers of this work will probably be acquainted
with the Life of Stanley, Bishop of Norwich, the two next
letters are from him. The third is from Bishop Hinds formerly chaplain to Archbishop Whately."

Palace, Norwich, Nov. 22nd, 1838.

MY DEAR LADY OSBORNE,—I have forwarded your note by this post to my nephew, and shall be very glad to hear that he has the power of complying with your wishes; should he write to me on the subject, I will let you know the result; probably, however, he will communicate directly with you. I can assure you that few things would give me more pleasure than again visiting Ireland, in which your schools would unquestionably be an early and interesting object of attraction; but I fear my movements are for ever limited to journies from Norwich to London, with perhaps an occasional visit to my old parish in Cheshire, which I can never forget. On the whole I am making progress here, but the labour is immense, and the difficulties not few, considering that I have above 1,000 clergy, with near 900 benefices to look after, and that every word and deed, however well intentioned, are subject to the severest criticisms, and too often to the grossest misconstructions, for this diocese contains a concentrated essence of the highest Toryism. Believe me to be,

Yours truly,

E. NORWICH.

" Doubtless the pamphlet alluded to in the following letter by Bishop Stanley, referred to some convert to the National System of Education. He points out what was a marvel to the friends of the system as a method used for the promotion of the same.

The use of the word paradoxical shows the Bishop gave the Government credit for some deep right reason he could not fathom."

38, Lower Brooke Street, June 10th, 1844.

My dear Lady Osborne,—Many thanks for the pamphlet, but on a subject which has so long deeply interested me, I need scarcely say that I lost not a moment in procuring it, and for some days have had it in my possession. I was greatly disappointed with the earlier opinions expressed, but the latter portion from about page 26 and 27 to the end deeply repaid the perusal; and I venture to send you my own copy, with the passages I had marked as most congenial with my own feelings and views. A few such men in Ireland, and we might hope for better things, notwithstanding the fearful mass of prejudiced opposition, increased by the recent Church appointments to the higher situations, by a Government professing to be friendly to the National system. Such paradoxical proceedings are beyond my comprehension.

I remain, yours truly,

E. Norwich.

Norwich, 6th August, 1853.

My dear Lady Osborne,—I do not think that the Archbishop of Dublin intended to make any definite suggestion to you beyond signing the petition, and being prepared to join in any future movement which may take place in the same direction. The petition I presume, is that which is about to be presented to the two Houses of Parliament. I have not yet seen it, and indeed have only heard of it by a letter, which the second post of to-day brought, together with yours, requesting me to present it to the house of Lords. I am sorry to say that I am so engaged in my diocese during the remainder of the session as to be unable to do so.

I am, my dear Lady Osborne,

Yours very truly,

S. Norwich.

" From the address on Dr. Chalmers' letter the Editor concludes that Lady Osborne wrote to Dr. Chalmers for assistance in a controversy she had with a Socinian minister, who was a friend of hers. The Editor is not aware whether Dr. Chalmers' correspondence has been published or not; but in any case the important nature of the subject treated therein warrants the reproduction of these letters. Dr. Hanna's letters referring to Dr. Chalmers are put first."

Morningside, Edinburgh, 20th June, 1848.

DEAR LADY OSBORNE,—I have been given to understand that you are in possession of a valuable letter of my late revered father-in-law, Dr. Chalmers, which it might be desirable should be inserted in any collection of his correspondence which may hereafter be published. If it be so, I should be very much obliged by your ladyship transmitting to me a copy of that letter, and of any others you may have received from Dr. Chalmers.

I have the honor to be, madam,
Your ladyship's obedient servant,
WM. HANNA.

P. S.—My address is, Rev. W. Hanna,
Morningside, Edinburgh.

Edinburgh, 25th March, 1852.

DEAR MADAM,—I have to thank you for your kindness in sending the letter which, after having copied, I now return. I propose inserting it in a volume of Dr. Chalmers' correspondence to be published in the course of next autumn. But I have unfortunately forgotten the nature of the occasion which called forth this letter of Dr. Chalmers, or the kind of enquiry to which it was an answer. I might state generally, in inserting it, that it was in answer to an enquiry whether a Unitarian could properly be regarded as a Chris-

tian; but if there were any special circumstances which led
to the enquiry, which in a general and inoffensive manner
could be stated, it might give additional interest. Perhaps
also the year, if not the precise date, of the letter could be
ascertained.

I beg you will excuse my asking you to favour me with
any such information as you may possess on these points.

I have the honor to be, madam,

Your most obedient servant,

WM. HANNA.

Dr. Chalmer's Letter to Lady Osborne.

April 2, 1835.

MY LADY,—You must forgive me writing in another hand,
as I am very much overworked, and I hope to be further
excused if I do not go into the subject of your letter at any
great length.

It appears to me that there are two grounds upon which
an error in theology might be fatal. First, the error might
be so opposed to the clearest light of Scriptural evidence as
to imply the utmost moral unfairness in the examination of
Holy Writ, or a hard rejection of the Divine testimony.
With my views of what I hold to be the obvious sense of the
Word of God, I could not be an Arian without incurring
this delinquency. The second ground on which an error in
theology might be fatal is the great moral and practical
importance of the doctrine which is either violated or disowned. I could not renounce my opinion of the Divinity of
Christ without at the same time renouncing what I at present regard as the most essential and characteristic principles
of the Gospel. Exterminate this article of Christianity and
you, in the same proportion, exterminate other articles of the
faith no less vital and fundamental than itself; as the value
of the atonement, the depth of the enormity of the guilt that

calls for a Divine expiation, the need of a regenerating influence from on High, the unchangeableness and authority of
Heaven's law, and the dignity of moral government. These
are the great elements of the Christian system, but by
detaching the sentiment of Christ's Divinity we should take
all the force and the spirit from them. This doctrine
strengthens and impregnates the whole of practical Christianity; and whether it be the trust or the gratitude or the
obedience of the Gospel we are arguing, they can only be
urged with effect along with the belief that Jesus Christ, the
author and finisher of the faith, is absolutely, from eternity,
God.

The first chapter of the Revelation—the beginning of the
Gospel of St. John—Romans, ix. 5; 1 John, 20; Philippians,
ii. 5-8; chap. i. of Hebrews, appear to me the most decisive
passages of the New Testament in favour of the Godhead of
Christ; and the Old Testament appears to be the more
impressive and convincing the longer I attend to it. For
this let me refer you to the 6th of Isaiah, quoted in John's
Gospel, and applied by him to the Saviour; Isaiah, viii.
13, 14, quoted and applied in the same manner by Paul in
the Epistle to the Romans; Isaiah, ix. 5, 6; Jeremiah, xxiii.
5, 6 (where the " *Lord* our righteousness " is, in the original,
Jehovah)! Micah, i. 2; Zech. xiii. 7; Malachi, iii. 1.

I entreat you to excuse the brevity and the imperfection
of these hurried statements. The subject on which you
have called me to express myself is fitted for an elaborate
dissertation, and nothing like adequate justice can be done
to it within the compass of a letter written in great feebleness and manifold engagements.

I have the honor to be, my lady,

Your ladyship's most humble and obedient servant,

THOMAS CHALMERS.

Edinburgh, March 6, 1837.

DEAR LADY OSBORNE,—I think it better to refrain from
noticing the little publication of which you have apprized
me.   There was nothing wrong in your shewing my letter
to the person you mention, though it be somewhat unusual
in him to meet a letter addressed to an individual by a
pamphlet addressed to the public.   But I have a great deal·
too much on hand to do anything more in that matter.

Mrs. Chalmers and I feel greatly obliged by your kind
invitation.   We are both getting too far on in life to be
much from home.

I have the honor to be,
Dear Lady Osborne,
Yours most respectfully,
THOMAS CHALMERS.

" The rapid progress made in the regard of those who
became acquainted with Lady Osborne shows itself in the tone
of the following letters from Mr. Poulett Thomson, afterwards created Lord Sydenham and Governor of Canada.   At
the time of these letters he was President of the Board of
Trade.   He had the manners of the old school (now too
much gone out of fashion) and was remarkably agreeable."

Dromana, 19th August, 1837.

MADAM,—I had the honour of bearing a letter of introduction from Lord Duncannon at Newtown on Monday last;
when, finding out you were in England, I took the liberty of
visiting the school in your garden, from the inspection of
which I derived very great pleasure.   As I believe from Mr.
Villiers Stuart you are now returned, I must however beg to
offer my apologies for having used this freedom in your
absence.

As it is my intention also to pass through Clonmel again upon my return to Besborough (for from the circumstances of the election going on, I could not see what I wished there on Monday last) I would also venture to beg your assistance to enable me to see the schools in that town, in which I know you take a deep interest. If you are good enough to afford it, perhaps you will let me have a line to some one there who can go round with me, or I will do myself the honor of waiting on you at Newtown when I reach Clonmel. I leave this place on Monday for Killarney, and expect to return through Clonmel in about a week or ten days. My address will be at the Post Office, Killarney.

I must beg to apologize for this intrusion for which I have only to plead the assurance of Lord Lansdowne and Lord Duncannon that you would pardon me, and beg to remain, madam,

Your obedient servant,
C. POULETT THOMSON.

Mount Shannon, 28 August, 1837.

DEAR MADAM,—I thank you very much for your obliging letter which I found at Killarney, and which I had only deferred acknowledging until I could a little more definitely define my plan of route, which from the number of objects of interest I met to delay my progress, I have been obliged to vary.

I shall have the pleasure in availing myself of your kind proposal to spend a few days with you, and in profiting by your instructions to see what is most worth attention in your neighbourhood. I go from hence for a day or two to the neighbourhood of Tipperary, and on Thursday or Friday therefore I will take the advantage of your kindness to present myself at Newtown.

It is most gratifying to hear your opinion of the improving

condition of this country. I have always felt a deep interest
in it ; I had no idea of the extent of natural advantages
which I now see it to possess. Our object is to govern it so
as to allow of their full development, and if party spirit
from whatever side it come will only give us fair play, I am
sanguine enough to believe that it is impossible that we
should not succeed. Believe me, dear madam,

Your very faithful servant,

C. Poulett Thomson.

Phœnix Park, Dublin, 9th September, 1837.

Dear Lady Osborne,—I have settled with Mr. Blake
that our sceptical friend of Rathcormuck shall come to the
Normal School in Dublin, the nomination to which will
shortly take place. He has his address, and will send him
the necessary instructions as soon as the arrangements are
made. Colonel Brenton will likewise look at your Skib-
bereen homes at Glenpatrick, and I hope make the population there a little more orderly by depriving them of one
fertile source of disorder. So much for your business, which
I have had a melancholy kind of pleasure in attending to.
I must now tell you the extreme regret with which I quitted
Newtown, which was proportioned only to the very great
enjoyment I experienced there. I certainly had no such anti-
cipations when I accepted your kind offer of hospitality, thinking only to exchange a day at an inn at Clonmel for a more
agreeable private house. I little expected to exchange my
day into a week, or, instead of the possible acquaintance of a
few hours, to form a sincere and lasting friendship, such as
I most earnestly hope (and in this I count upon your promise) may long endure between us.

Most sincerely, indeed, do I regret that I could not follow
my own wishes, and have prolonged my stay; but I count
upon our meeting now, and I look forward with no little

pleasure to the time. It is true, as I remember you to have said, that the bustle of London is but a poor compensation for the quiet opportunities that the country affords for intimacy and knowledge of character; but still I, on my part, know that there will be opportunities even there for my enjoying your society, and I look forward with impatience for the time when I may embrace them.

In the meantime I shall trust to your good will for permitting the intercourse which is still open—that of correspondence. I found Mr. Nichols, the Poor Law Commissioner, here, and have been so busy in consequence with Poor Law matters that I have had no time for " Education." I mean, however, on Monday, when I return from Lord Mulgrave's, at Normanby Lodge, whither I go to-day, to go over the schools and attend the Board. Perhaps I may have something which I should like to communicate to you afterwards before I quit Dublin for the North. Deeply interested as I have long been in this subject, our conversations have rendered me still more so, and I feel that in some points they have given a new direction to my views.

By the bye, I must not close this without alluding which I had not the opportunity of doing before I left you, though I intended it, to the subject of your conversation to the last day of our meeting. I was then silent (which I think you remarked), because I have made a rule of never discussing controversial points of religion in a mixed conversation, or unless with those with whom I am on terms of real confidence and friendship; but it required all my powers of resistance to refrain or to avoid telling you how entirely I agreed with you, and how much I admired the admirable simplicity and truly Christian spirit you displayed. I have thought of it much since, as indeed I have of many of our conversations. But I should write more than your patience would bear, if I allowed myself to proceed with this topic. This one point, however, I could not avoid mentioning.

Adieu. Let me have the pleasure of hearing from you. My address will be the Castle, Dublin; and believe me that your suggestions will always weigh with me as coming from one to whom I feel proud in believing that I may subscribe myself, the sincere friend,

C. POULETT THOMSON.

Pray tell Miss Osborne that I expect a copy of the Kilmacthomas Gazette, with an account of her court at Bonmyhon. I am afraid I can't spell the name of the Principality!

Chillingham Castle, Belford, 23rd September, 1837.

MY DEAR LADY OSBORNE,—Your letter reached me only the day before I left Dublin, where I was so much hurried that I had not a moment to myself, and since that till my arrival here yesterday, I have been continually on the highways or high seas; so I have only now the opportunity of thanking you for it, or of telling you the extreme pleasure which it gave me. It is most grateful to me to feel, which I do from the whole tone and expression of your letters, that we understand each other, and that I have not been inspired with a sincere regard and esteem for you, without being able to believe that it is in some degree reciprocated. It is no part of my character to seek or bestow friendship lightly, perhaps the course of my life, and the career which I have run, would lead me to be over suspicious upon the matter, but one week's intimacy in the quiet of Newtown, equal to almost a life of ordinary intercourse in society, made me most anxious to obtain your regard, as I felt that you had acquired mine, and I value therefore the assurance you give me of having secured it most highly. You must remember however, that it is no part of friendship to flatter; and although I cannot but feel greatly gratified by what you say of myself, I must for the very reason that I am so anxious you should long think long well of me, caution you against thinking *too* well. I hope I may lay claim to the qualities of truth and mildness which you are good enough to ascribe to me, but I have many imperfections which a friend will feel, and a friend may likewise correct, and you will not therefore, find the duties of friendship altogether confined to the bright side. Indeed nothing more contributed to make me prize our intercourse (amongst the many qualities which I admired in you) than the candour and frankness with which you upon one occasion offered advice, and administered gentle reproof when you thought me wrong; and I have the utmost reliance upon your doing so in future upon more grounds than before. But if I ever could suppose that by intercourse with some of your Tory neighbours, I could have softened their prejudices, and brought them to the belief that we are not all of us the wild beasts which their press describe us to be, and their imaginations picture, I confess that I am too much of a man, and too little of a minister, to be sorry for the opportunity being lost. I do not think that our circle would have been improved by the addition, for in a crowd I could have hardly had the same means of really knowing you or Mr. ——, or your own belongings; and a few Tory converts would certainly not have been a compensation to me, or I had far rather trust to your own advocacy of my conduct and my principles. Thank you for the letter from Colonel Phipps. I have written to him to-day, and I hope that he will not think my wish to hear from him any suggestion he may be kind enough to make a mere compliment. He is a most valuable man to have in a country where party and religious (?) feeling disturb everything, and where truth is next to impossible to find. What a proof of this is the paragraph you send me in Miss H.'s

letter, which I return! and this too in even a London paper,
though furnished of course by some Irish correspondent. It
is indeed a lesson to us to give no credit to abettors' stories,
whether of Protestant clergyman or Catholic priest, of
laymen or lawyers, gathered from such sources. I
have read Mr. Woodward's two letters, which I suppose I
owe to your kindness, though you do not mention having
sent them. They are excellent, and written in the true
spirit of a Christian pastor. Had his recommendation been
followed in 1832, the date of the first, I believe that not
only would such a measure have been practicable, but that
all the contention which has since taken place upon tithe
and Church matters in Ireland would have been avoided;
now, it is alas! too late—both parties, but the Church most,
would regret such an arrangement.

I visited the schools in Dublin, and attended the Board as
I told you, and I hope did some good, for I found the latter
very much set against village schools, and anxious to devote
all their funds to a better class of schools in town—a plan
which I strongly objected to, and prevailed against. The
misfortune of the Dublin Board is that its members know
nothing of the country. They compose excellent books of
instruction, and have organized at their own schools, and at
some of those in the towns a good system of teaching; but
they do not know anything of the working of the schools in
the country districts, and therefore are quite ignorant of
the moral and social results which are to be expected from
them, and which are indeed already apparent there. I would
gladly improve the teachers, and I think the normal schools
will in time do much towards this, but there can be no comparison between a school with indifferent masters, and no
school at all; and it is besides of the last importance to induce the gentry, most of whom are Protestants, to join in
the National system, by which alone we can hope to give a

fair education to the Catholic poor. Funds indeed are wanting, and greatly wanting, both for the improvement of the system, and for its extension, and they must be had, partly I think from Parliament, and partly from the Proprietors themselves. It is surely no less a duty to educate, than to prevent starvation amongst the poor, and the proprietor ought to be made to contribute to the one as much as to the other. So that we must give if the system is to be made really effective, to that we must come. I went from Dublin into the North of Ireland, having appointed Captain Nicholl there to go over some of the towns which are interesting with reference to the Poor Law. I was pleased to find the schools there working upon the whole pretty well. In the towns at Belfast especially, far less jealousy upon the matter than I anticipated. Catholics, Presbyterians, and those of the Church of England attending together, where the instruction given is really good.

From the North of Ireland I came on here to pay an annual visit, and shall remain in this country, either here or at Howick (Lord Grey's) till I return to town the middle of next month. Our party would astonish some of *your* Irish neighbours, who think that different politics *must* make people enemies. My host is a Whig, his son the Tory member for the county; we have Lord and Lady Stanley representing the Dilly—Lord Fitzharris an ultra Tory and Orangeman—the Howicks and myself the government; yet we go on very harmoniously, talking a great deal of politics and laughing a good deal at each other. I find nothing, however, in this society, albeit composed of old acquaintances and friends, which pleases me as much as our quiet and rational conversations at Newtown, and I would willingly exchange it if I had the power, for the side of the car from Comragh, the pleasure of planning Irish improvements with you, or trying to make —— a Whig, instead of an

Orangewoman. But though the car will scarcely suit the meridian of St. James, the rest may all be attainable there, and I look forward with impatience to the time when it will be, and only hope that your arrangements may bring you to London early in the autumn. That more than any other time is the period when quiet society is practicable there,— before the full tide of what is called the London season sets in, and makes people, as Mme. de Stael said of them, pre-occupied with only one idea, how they can possibly be in two places at once. In the mean time you can give me no better proof of your kindness than by letting me hear from you, and grateful shall I be if you will bestow upon me some of those half hours of your morning study of which you speak. My address is for the present as I have dated this, or Godding, Northumberland.

I meant to have answered Miss Osborne's note, but I shall lose the post if I do. So pray have the goodness to give her the enclosed paragraph which I found in an Irish Newspaper, and which I deeply regret to find upsets all the flattering account of my reception at Stradbally which she sent me. I should like of course to believe hers rather than this sincere? but I fear this is *real truth*. Adieu, my dear friend. Believe me,

Most sincerely yours,

C. Poulett Thomson.

Castle Howard, 29th November, 1839.

I delayed writing to you, my dear friend, because I foolishly wished to send you at the same time the Bishop of Norwich's charge, which you ask for in your last letter. I had written to town for it, where it was *not* to be had, but it was promised me from Norwich; and at last it turns out that it is out of print, and we must wait for a new edition. I am provoked at having thus lost my time, and yet not done

your bidding. Another time I hope I shall be more success-
ful; and at all events I will not forego the pleasure of
writing to you, or the still greater one of hearing from you
whilst I look after any commission you may give me; apropos
of these smaller matters, I must beg of you not to push the
principle which you lay down in your letter as to larger ones
too far. You are right, certainly, in the answer you gave
your applying acquaintance, as a general principle, but you
would not be using the principle of friendship on any occasion
on which you feel a realinterest for the applicant, and
think that I can be any service in furthering *your* wishes, if
you do not tell me frankly how I may be of use. My power
is very limited, but as I should be certain that you will feel
that if I could *not* comply with what you wished, it was the
power, and not the will, which was wanting, I should not
hesitate to tell you so; and if I could I should have the great
pleasure of doing what was agreeable to you. I had, by the
bye, written as soon as I left Ireland, about that poor man
Sir E. Brydges, of whom you spoke. A few days afterwards
I saw his death mentioned in one of the newspapers, and
your benevolent intentions were frustrated. I was grieved
to see nearly at the same time the account of the death of
another person of whom you spoke in terms of regard,—the
ex-Queen of Holland—Hortense. It was singular that I
should be reminded of topics which we discoursed of together
so soon afterwards in so melancholy a manner.

There is much truth in your remark about the affair of
Colonel ——. This business gave me a good deal of uneasiness whilst it was going on, and when I was consulted about
it, which was whilst I was at Newtown, I entertained doubts
somewhat like your own. By taking notice of the foolish
and wicked toast of the Battle of the Diamond " there
was the risk of making the man a martyr with a certain
party; but the affair had already attracted so much attention

even before the Government took any steps, that it could not
sleep; and then the only question was, whether a magistrate
should be permitted with impunity to celebrate an outrage
against the law which he is sworn to administer, which must
have been admitted if no notice had been taken by the Lord
Lieutenant, or by adopting a vigorous but just course, to risk
the excitement of some feeling amongst the *very violent*.
Upon the whole, and under the choice of difficulties which
was all that remained, the step taken seemed and still seems
to me the best.   There is no one point of greater importance
in Ireland at the present time than to impress the people with
a conviction that the laws will be administered with impar-
tiality—that the law is their friend, and not their oppressor;
and how can they hope that this will be if they see one of
them charged with that duty triumphing in the violation of
it, attended too with the most revolting scenes of bloodshed
and cruelty upon an occasion where party feeling was concerned?   The best feature in the condition of Ireland which
I have seen, is the increased confidence, or I am afraid it can
still only be called the *diminished dislike* of the law, and it
is that feeling which, above all others, it is necessary to promote.   Persuade the people that the law is their friend—and
that can only be done by shewing them that it is impartially
executed—and they will cease to look to themselves and
their illegal proceedings alone for redress of their real or
supposed wrongs.   They will seek the law which is for the
protection of all, and they will learn to respect it.   For this
reason I would visit with severity, from whatever party it
may come, Orangeman or Catholic, any conduct which may
tend to check this growing feeling of confidence or impede
its progress.

   After I left Chillingham, where I was when your letter
reached me, I went to Howick (Lord Grey's), to Lowther,
and one or two other places, and am now here on my road

to town, and there is no flattery in what I told you of the first place, and of our party there, and there is none either in my repeating to you that in none of these visits I ceased to turn with recollections of superior enjoyment to our quiet days and evenings at Newtown. Nowhere, and with no one of my older acquaintances and associates whom I have met since we parted, have I found such community of sentiment or so much opportunity and desire for unreserved and frank communing, as then and with you. I attribute this, amongst other things, to the entire absence of selfishness which characterized all I heard from you,—a quality which I fear is little to be found amongst the circle in which I move. Polish, indeed, there is, and refinement, and that charm which arises from the absence of any attempt at display, which is the fruit of a long habit of society; but there is greater selfishness—little real desire to arrive at truth—and a sort of conventional dislike of serious subjects, which, although it leaves us amused, leaves us also uninstructed, There is nothing to *think* over afterwards. With how much pleasure I shall renew our conversations, of so different a character, when we meet and recur to the topics which at once amused and instructed me. There is nothing in a London life which can prevent this. Those, indeed, with whom I am now staying—Lord and Lady Carlisle—are less open to the general charge I have brought than any other of my friends, and I think you would, if you knew them, be of that opinion. Lord Morpeth is your *Vice-Governor*, too, and he is as deeply interested about Ireland, and all you feel so much for, as you or I. In two or three days my holidays expire, and I return to town. We—the unfortunate ministers —must assemble to look into our matters on the 1st November. I shall after that be, I suppose, a fixture in London till Parliament breaks up, some time in August next year. Your next letter will, therefore, I hope, bring me some

tidings of your plans. Tell Miss Osborne that the best singing and drawing masters are to be had in November, and
that it is before Christmas that London is quiet, and she can
expect to execute her plans. You cannot well execute
improvements during the winter, and, at least in your absence
from Newtown, you have a good substitute in ——. I am
delighted, indeed, to hear that you have set about improvements at Glenpatrick. The pigs in the houses, and the
dunghill outside it, are what Miss Ponsonby told me were
the " pons asinorum " of the Irish cottier, but at Besborough
they have vanquished this difficulty, and I doubt not if
Miss Osborne will offer a small premium for the neatest
garden and the most pigless cottage at Glenpatrick, it may
be achieved there. But I must not let my Irish instructions
run away with me.

I am sorry for your friend, Miss ——, whose letters gave
me a good opinion of her good sense and good feeling. Two
persons in the relation of husband and wife cannot differ in
so vital a point as their religious creed without great risk of
loss of happiness, and a foreigner, however agreeable as a
companion, must have tastes, feelings, and instincts, which
are hardly reconcileable upon the long run with those of
either Englishman or woman. I have seen two experiments
of this kind, unfortunately, even without difference of
religion, and both proved failures.

Adieu, my dear friend. Write to me to *London*. That
address will be sufficient.

Remember me to Miss O., and believe me,

Ever yours, most sincerely,

C. POULETT THOMSON.

Whitehall, 14th January, 1838.

A thousand thanks my dear friend for your letter, which made me more than ever regret the perpetual worries of business which has been the cause and the *sole* cause of my being so bad a correspondent. To receive your letters and to write to you are to me very great pleasure, but alas! pleasures of any kind have been rare with me since my return to town. Days in one's office, and nights in the House of Commons have left me but little time for them; and to this, not to any diminished regard, you justly impute my silence.

At the risk of your saying that you can only rouse me by a commission, I will first discharge myself of that which you give me in your last letter. . . .

I have been delighted by the account your letter gives of your occupations, gaieties they seem to be rather than pleasures. There is, however, a pleasure to be derived from seeing others amused and pleased, and by your mention of your society and the mode of spending their time, this must at least have been yours. I do not know the Tighes, though I do her family and his very well; but I have always heard them most highly spoken of, and he has the character of being one of the few Irish resident proprietors who really occupies himself sincerely about the welfare of the peasantry and tenants.*

I expected that the Ultra party would attack your evidence before the Lords, and you must have been prepared for it too; but such an attack is praise. To be willing to stand boldly forward in defence of the truth is the greatest crime in the eyes of the extremes of both parties, because their object is to conceal and disfigure it; they live upon lies.

* It must be remembered how long ago this was written, and even since then philanthropy has always been on the increase on their part.

To expose them is to take away their livelihood, and no wonder that they should be angry. But you have the consciousness of having done right, and the esteem and regard of all the right-thinking in return for your courage and disinterestedness, and certain reward both here and hereafter to support you against their attacks. Your archbishop, so much our friend upon this subject, has gone absolutely raving mad upon another—the Irish Poor Laws. He is denouncing our bill without mercy. . . . I expect to see him shaking hands with O'Connell, who, on his side too, is doing all the mischief he can to the plan. I am glad that the archbishop at least is out of Parliament this year on this question.

What do your Tory neighbours say to the exposure of all the lies which their press have been ringing the changes on for four months about Irish disturbances and Irish improvements? They had their own points of attack to choose, their own ground to select, and their own time; and yet, both in Lords and Commons, they have miserably failed in making out a single point, and Lord ——, in the one house and the two gallant Colonels —— and —— in the other, have been compelled to retract, unsupported even by their allies.

I send you Mulgrave's speech, which is an exposure of the attacks, and is worth reading. I have no fear, however, for your politics, but I hope my fair antagonist —— is whiging a little too. I see you have a good deal to do with Whig houses; the Stuarts, the Tighes, and the Powers, will do something towards her conversion, and London and the Court will, I hope complete it.

You will come shortly I earnestly hope—the session opening so much earlier than we expected, the 16th instead of the 3rd of February; you will find everybody come to town much earlier than usual, and you will not lack visitors. We the workers get little or no holiday. I shall go for a few days only to Lord Lansdowne's next week, and then return for good. May your next letter then tell me that you have fixed your plans and are actually preparing for the passage. I need not say, my dear friend, how happy I shall be to hear it, or how much more so to pay you my first visit.

Believe me, yours most sincerely,

C. POULETT THOMSON.

S. Audley-street, 24th February.

Our notes crossed yesterday, my dear friend, so I must both answer that and ' queries' of to-day at once.

I shall be always happy to meet anybody at your house whom you admit there; but I need not add that the party you mention, being most of them people I know well, will be more agreeable than strangers, and I thank you for your kind consideration in thinking of that. Sir —— is a gentle-man, and I believe thoroughly honest in his opinions, though rather changeable, since I remember him a violent advocate of O'Connell, when Dan was far more violent than now. He must be very weak to be swayed by a hypocritical adventurer like ——.

I sent for the book. The motion on Tuesday is not, then, the one I alluded to. It will be an ultra-Orange attack only, of the most violent, who will get a dressing for whatever they may say.

I am much better to-day, and look forward with hope to seeing you even before Wednesday, though my doctor will not answer for it. You forgot to return ——'s letter.

Ever yours most truly,

C. POULETT THOMSON.

MY DEAR LADY OSBORNE,—I am delighted to receive your remarks upon any subject; they are always valuable, and when our opinions may chance to differ, they are equally acceptable, because they show that between us there is no reserve. I suppose Sir G. alludes to what is to be done on Molesworth's motion, which stands for Tuesday next. I have no doubt that he and his followers will spit all their venom on that occasion, for none are so venomous as turn-coats. I shall be very glad to hear what their tactics are, however, if you hear anything to-day. I have been confined to my room since Monday with a bad cold and swelled face, and I am afraid that it will be many days before I get out again.

Ever yours, most truly,
C. POULETT THOMSON.

Chênes, Wednesday.

MY DEAR MADAM,—Most assuredly we do not forget our engagement to-morrow, nor am I very sorry you cannot come this evening, as my poor little party is so ill assorted; if you did, you would be discouraged from fulfilling your rash promise of every Wednesday. There is more danger of your wearying of your engagement than of our tiring of your company, in which we find such a rare union of talent and warm affection. We thank you cordially for our share in them.

Ever most truly your Ladyship's obliged,
J. S.

Chênes, 12th February, 1835.

My wife is out, my dear Lady, and you must excuse me for answering in her stead. I give to your servant the books, and to you many and many thanks for your kind anxiety. I have got no cold, and felt happy to see you some moments longer. Remember you promised to return on next Wednesday, when you will find us, I believe, quite by ourselves.

I am, with the highest regard,
Your most obedient humble servant,
J. C. L. DE SISMONDI.

Chênes, Octobre 25, 1835.

Votre lettre du **3** Octobre nous a trouvés encore ici chère
Lady Osborne et quelque arrêtés que fussent nos projets,
quelque désir que nous eussions de passer en Italie, quelque
besoin que ma pauvre nièce ait de nous depuis la perte de
sa mère et dans l'état de souffrance et de danger ou elle
se trouve, nous voyons bien que nous ne pourrons pas partir
avant quatre mois et nous nous estimons encore heureux si
dans les derniers jours de Février le choléra est absolument
fini en Piemont dans toute la rivière de Gênes et en Toscane,
si tous les cordons sont levés surtout par le Duc de Modène
et de Massa qui dans sa haine de la liberté est tout heureux
de faire exécuter les mesures sanitaires avec férocité, menace
de fair fusiller quiconque enfreindrait le moins du monde
les règles qu'il prend pour les quarantaines et ne connait
pas de meilleur moyen pour conserver la santé de son peuple,
que de multiplier les supplices ; nous sommes résolus à
passer derrière le choléra et de ne pas nous trouver sur sa
route et nous ne nous mettrons en chemin que lorsque
l'air sera purifié sur tout notre itinéraire par Turin, Nervi,
Génes Massa et Lucques. En attendant, nous vivons ici
à peu près comme vous nous avez laisses ; mais depuis
votre départ la société que vous avez rassemblée, me semble
avoir bien moins d'attrait, bien moins de mouvement Mr. de
St. Marsan est rentré en Piemont avec sa fille, Monsieur
d'Haussez et sa femme et sa fille avec lui et elles contri-
buent à le jeter dans une autre société que la nôtre. Mes-
dames Potoeka, Ossalynska, Gallitzin, nous ont presque
abandonnés les dames Stephenson sont venues s'établir de
notre côté mais nous ne les voyons pas ; en tout je crois
que nous devenons sauvages et si Miss Catherine a la
bonté de se souvenir avec reconnaissance du tems qu'elle
a passé, à Genève, au moins ce ne doit pas être avec regret

cette vie, et ce mouvement qu'elle y trouvait me semblent n'y être plus; mais sans doute ni elle ni vous chère my lady n'êtes troublées de regrets, nous sommes tous trois à Chênes vivement sensibles à votre affection, nous en sommes fiers, nous aimons à nous rappeler les heures si agréablement passés ensemble, mais nous sentons et votre lettre nous le montre plus clairement encore que vous êtes à present rentrées dans votre sphère de devoirs et de bienfaisance, que personne ne peut vous remplacer au milieu de vos domaines d'Irlande, que c'est là que votre activité peut s'exercer pour le bonheur de tout ce qui vous entoure, combien, j'ai été touché de votre réception si tendre et si enthousiaste qu'on vous a fait a votre retour dans vos terres, que ce sentiment d'affection d'espoir et de confiance de tous vos paysans devoit vous donner d'émotion ear il nous en donne ici. Sans doute après une si longue absence, c'etait moins pour le bien que vous leur aviez fait que pour celui qu'ils attendaient de vous, qu'ils exprimaient leur joie, ils sentaient et vous sentiez aussi que Dieu et les lois de votre pays vous les avaient donnés et que vous en etiez responsables. Tout ce que les pauvres paysans pourront connaitre jamais de bien être matériel et sécurité dans leurs maisons de proprieté et confiance dans l'avenir, d'ordre même, de nourriture salubre, c'est a vous qu'ils le devront. Dans aucun autre pays la richesse ne donne une influence si étendue, si directe sur le sort des pauvres, pour vous c'est une magistrature c'est presque une Principauté. Ces douze cents pauvres Irlandais qui se pressaient autour de votre voiture, qui la trainaient en remplaçant vos chevaux, qui remplissaient l'air de leurs cris de joie en vous voyant, si vous tenez la main, â ce que jamais le fermage la rente qu'ils paient pour la terre qu'ils tiennent de vous ne soient excessifs à ce qu'il leur reste pour récompense de leur travail, ce qui est le droit des laboureurs, une chaumière propre et saine, des

habits aussi grossiers que vous voudrez mais au moins chauds
et entiers, enfin, une nourriture en parti animale en parti
végétale, une nourriture qui ne se réduise pas à la seule
pomme de terre, mais ou le pain, le laitage et quelquefois
la viande entrent aussi, si en leur donnant des vaux d'une
certain durée (leases for many years) vous assurez l'avenir
aussi bien que le présent, vous ne les rendez pas seulement
heureux, vous les rendez moraux, ils vous aimeront, ils vous
révéreront et cet amour, ce respect sont le commencement
de toutes les vertus; Tandis que c'est un poison dans le
cœur des pauvres que la haine et la jalousie, et comment y
échapperait quand il voit que sur la terre qu'il arrose de ses
sueurs, aucune partie du blé qu'il récolte, du beurre qu'il
manufacture, des cochons qu'il nourrit, souvent au milieu
de ses enfans ne lui demeure pour son usage et que souvent
son maitre qui nage dans l'opulence lui dispute jusqu'à sa
misérable pittance de pommes de terres. Il faut le dire j'ai
eprouvé un redoublement d'émotion et d'attendrissement sur
le sort du paysan Irlandais par la lecture d'un voyage de
Mr. Inglis en Irlande, des Irlandais que nous avons eu ici
cet automne nous assurent que le tableau est d'une vérité par-
faite; mais il n'y a pas besoins de témoignages extérieurs pour
le faire croire. En lisant le récit de ce M. Inglis on sent qu'il
s'est mis consciencieusement à l'œuvre, qu'il a vu de ses
yeux, qu'il est entré dans toutes les cabanes, qu'il s'est assis
à toutes les tables, qu'il a causé avec toutes les classes
d'hommes, qu'il demeura étranger aux partis, que quoique
fortement anticatholique, sa charité, sa bienveillance, s'éten-
dait à toutes les opinions. En lisant ce livre en famille
nous avons douloureusement souffert à penser que les
sujets d'unpeuple chrétien et civilisé pourraient être réduits à
un si effroyable état de privation, mais presqu' aussitôt notre
pensée s'est reportée sur vous et nous nous sommes dit,
combien vous étiez heureuse d'être à portée de faire tant de

bien. Nous nous sommes dit qu' avec ce livre à la main, entrant dans les *cabines* questionnant, voulant tout voir par vous même vous seriez une providence bienfaisante, vous pourriez répandre plus de bonheur qu'il n'est donné à aucun mortel d'en faire.

Croyez chère Lady Osborne que ce bonheur que tous les bonheurs entrent toujours dans les vœux pour vous de tous les habitans de Chênes. Conservez leur je vous prie votre affection et celle de Mlle. votre fille,

J. C. L. DE SISMONDI.

Chênes, près Genève, 6 Juin, 1825.

Mille grâces chère my Lady, de la bonté, que vous avez eu de me donner de vos nouvelles de Paris, mille grâces, des expressions d'affection, de tendre souvenir que je trouve dans votre lettre et de l'espérance qu'elle me donne que nous vous reverrons ici. Ma femme et ma sœur n'y seront pas moins sensibles que moi ; tous ceux à qui vous me chargez de vous rappeler le seront sans doute également à mesure que je pourrois les voir mais depuis quelque tems nous avons vécu aux solitaires. Je n'ai vu je crois de vos amies depuis votre lettre que la Reine Hortense qui repartoit pour Arenenberg le jour même on je l'ai reçu et la Comtesse Potocka, toutes deux m'ont chargé de vous temoigner tout le prix qu'elles mettent à votre souvenir.

Je m'attendois chère Lady Osborne à ce que vous repondriez par lettres, le sujet de nos fréquentes discussions. Je crois que je vous ai fait peur d'y rentrer, en vous disant que je les craignois mais c'est seulement de vive voix que je m'y refuse sur des sujets qui tiennent de si fort au cœur, ou l'on confond si aisément la persuasion qu'on sent en soi et que l'on appelle foi, avec un vertu, un devoir, les opinions contraires aux nôtres vous froissent, vous provoquent souvent ; je sais qu' avec plusieurs, avec vous même peut être,

commençant par proférer la communion des sentimens religieux entre toutes les croyances, j'ai tout à coup passé a des
argumens hostiles presqu' a des personalités, parceque je
sentois de la part de l'antagoniste, non plus discussion mais
blâme.   Je saisis avec empressement cette occasion de
m'expliquer avec plus de calme.   Je le fais en Français
parcequ'on n'est jamais soi que dans sa propre langue et
pour cette raison même je vous demande de me répondre en
Anglais.   Je ne suis point de l'église de Genève comme
ayant des opinions communes avec son clergé; mes opinions
sont à moi seul, personne n'en est responsable, mais ce que
j'aime, ce que j'admire dans l'église de Genève, c'est sa
liberalité, c'est sa volonté ferme de ne jamais rechercher les
opinions et de ne demander aux croyans que l'accord des
sentimens d'adoration, de respect et d'amour pour Etre, des
Etres, c'est aussi que non seulement elle est grande déjà,
mais qu'elle est destinée à le devenir toujours plus à mésure
que l'humanite se fera des idées toujours plus pures toujours
plus relevées du Dieu et l'Univers.

Il faudrait être bien aveugle en effet pour ne pas recon-
nôitre que depuis l'origine du genre humain l'idée de Dieu
a grandi sans cesse, s'est épurée sans cesse, s'est approchée
toujours plus d'une verité que nous ne comprendrons jamais
entièrement parcequ' elle est trop sans mesure, pour l'intelligence humaine, Dieu a été compris par les premiers
hommes uniquement par instinct, par ce sentiment de respect
et d'amour pour l'inconnu qui les protège, sentiment im-
planté dans leur cœurs mais auquel leur intelligence ne
pouvoit pas se proportionner, parce qu'ils ne connoissoient
presque rien du monde visible, que celui se finissoit avec
leur horizon, aussi ils adorèrent Dieu dans le torrent qui
les menacoit, dans la foudre qui grondoit, dans le soleil qui
les eclairait, les echauffait et vivifiait la nature.   Le fétéchisme et l'idolatrie furent les premiers hommages du cœur

religieux, au créateur, et au bienfaiteur du monde, hommages cependant entassés d'erreur, aussi la première révélation vint elle ramener l'homme à son maitre, "Tu n'auras point d'autre Dieu devant ma face," elle est toute entière dans ces mots là, et cependant les mots mêmes sont proportionnés à la faiblesse humaine. *Point* d'autre Dieu, comme s'il pouvoit y avoir un autre! Dieu comme si l'être qui remplit et anime et protège l'univers, jusqu'à ces étoiles dont la lumière n'arrive à nous qu' apres des milliers d'années pouvoit être comparé a aucun autre être, pouvoit laisser place a aucun autre Dieu! Mais celui qui inspiroit Moïse vouloit avant tout, être compris de l'adorateur des fétiches· Il proportionnait son langage à l'intelligence des hommes, il l'a fait alors, il l'a fait depuis dans la seconde révélation adressée au genre humain plus avancé. mais bien loin cependant du tems de Jésus Christ, de connôitre comme aujourd-hui l'univers, de pouvoir comprendre comme aujourd' hui le Dieu de l'univers. De là dans les écrits des témoins qui ont recueillé ou rapporté par ouï dire les paroles de l'envoyé de Dieu une foule d'expressions empruntées au langage des polytheistes, au millieu desquels ils vivaient.

L'essence de la seconde révélation, c'est ordre de servir Dieu en esprit et en verité, c'est la spiritualization du culte. A ces deux révélations résistent, non pas seulement les impies, mais deux classes de personnes qui se croient religieuses, et qui de bonne foi en effet veulent se rapprocher de Dieu, mais qui l'attirent a elles au lieu de s'éléver a lui, qui le font a leur mesure et à leur passions au lieu d'épurer elles mêmes a son image. Ces deux classes sont les femmes animées de l'esprit du fétéchisme et les prêtres qui veulent de grandir par le sacrifice. Les femmes et une foule d'hommes qui sont femmes ne peuvent s'elever à l'être, esprit et vérité, elles ont besoin de se faire en Dieux qu'elles comprennent, qu'elles aiment personellement, qu'elles voient presque. Delà la renaissance dans le Christianisme du culte des saints, du culte des images et surtout et, toujours de l'antropomorphisme. Les prêtres ont fait métier du culte, ils ont vécu de l'autel et se faisant illusion sur leur importance, de bonne foi peut être, ils ont propitié Dieu, ils l'ont traité comme un tyran farouche qu'on ne satisfait que par le mal qu'on fait en son honneur. Ils lui ont offert le sacrifice de l'innocent pour le coupable, de là s'abord les victimes humaines puis les bêtes substituées aux hommes, dans le sacrifice, puis le sacrifice de la messe, puis le sacrifice de Dieu lui même à Dieu, voilà Sacerdoce qui se dit orthodoxe se défend aujourd' hui comme dans son dernier retranchement. Les uns et les autres s'efforcent à mes yeux de faire rétrograder le genre humain, de repousser d'anéantir le bienfait des deux révélations; mais ils le font de bonne foi: "Ne les jugeons point afin que nous ne soyons point jugés." Ma dissertation risqueroit d'être bien plus longue que mon papier mais je m'arrête en vous embrassant bien tendrement.

J. C. L. DE SISMONDI.

Crênes, 12 Juillet, 1835.

Je viens de recevoir votre lettre du 4 Juillet chère Lady Osborne, et je sens le besoin d'y répondre à l'instant même, je vois qu' elle vous a donné l'impression que, "I felt displeased with you when I wrote." J'en suis vivement chagriné, rien n'étoit plus loin de ma pensée ou de mon sentiment. Je ne veux pas laisser passer vingt quatre heures sans vous dire et ma reconnoissance de votre bienveillance et mon tendre attachement pour vous et l'assurance bien vraie que vous n'avez jamais rien fait, que vous n'avez jamais rien dit qui put le diminuer. C'est moi qui dois avoir été en faute pour vous donner cette impression et comme c'est sans le vouloir je cherche qu'elle en peut avoir été la cause. Il faut que ce

soit cette malheureuse controverse, je vous disois souvent et
à la Servette et a Chênes que je la redoutois de vive voix que
je la croyois toujours contraire à son but, contraire à la
charité, j'ai cru que la plume à la main lorsqu' on a tout le
tems de péser les expressione on serait plus maitre d'écarter,
de supprimer tout ce qu'elles ont d'hostile et je me suis
trompé. Ma règle de ne jamais attaquer les opinions religieuses d'autrui est donc encore plus générale que je ne la
faisois, je l'adoptois pour la conversation elle doit s'étendre
également à la correspondance. Sans doute toutes les fois
que l'occasion nous en est presentée, que nous pouvons le
faire sans avoir l'air de vouloir enseigner, sans nous arroger
aucune supériorité sur les autres, nous devons contribuer a
répandre, a fortifier les sentimens d'amour et de confiance
en Dieu; ils appartiennent à toutes les croyances et dans
toutes, ils sont également constans et édifians, mais nous nous
trompons nous mêmes, nous prenons notre préventions pour
un sentiment religieux, toutes les fois que nous travaillons
à détruire dans le coeur d'autrui une croyance pour sub-
stituer une antre. Nous faisons ainsi un mal religieux, car
nous avons bien plus d'influence pour ébranler la foi existant
que pour en fonder une nouvelle, nous faisons plus certaine-
ment en eux un mal moral car quelque mènagement que
nous y apportions, blessant les gens dans la partie la plus
sensible, nous faisons naître une irritation, un besoin de
combattre et de vaincre; souvent même, un désir de faire
sentir à notre tour notre aiguillon, qui sont les plus contraires de tous à la charité. C'est donc, de tout mon cœur
que je répète apres vous chère my Lady, "point de controverse
entre nous," pas plus par lettre que par conversation. Je
voudrois pouvoir engager tous ceux qui ont excité a Genève
des querelles religieueses a le sentir comme nous , et à dire
comme nous, "point de controverse !"

Depuis que vous nous avez quitté nous avons eprouvé un
grand chagrin, ma femme a reçu la nouvelle, de la mort tout

à fait imprévue d'une soeur Mrs. Drewe, qui 'etait l'objét de notre amour et de notre vénération à tous. Mes deux dames en ont éprouvé la plus vive douleur. Selon votre usage Anglais, qui me paroit au restefort raisonable, elles ne veulent voir absolument personne, mais je ne trouve point qu'elles réussissent comme je leur avois vu faire dans d'autres occasions à reprendre l'empire sur elles mêmes. Elles sont toujours également absorbées, je ne sais s'il ne seroit point sage de recourir a quelque consolation extèrieure, Vous savez que nous avons résolu un voyage en Italie et que nous comptions partir le 25 août. Je me demande aujourd'hui s'il ne seroit pas convenable d'avancer notre départ et de leur faire trouver cette seule distraction à laquelle l'âme affligée se prête, cette succession d'objets qui frappent la vue en voyage et qui renouvellent malgré vous vos idées; ce petit travail aussi de la vie materielle anquel il faut bien songer, quand on change chaque jour ses habitudes, ce doute, cette incertitude sur le lieu où nous serons dans un mois, font que je ne saurois guère à prèsent vous donner d'adresse pour me répondre. Notre domicile final sera cependant toujours Chénes, c'est là que j'espère que nous reviendrons plus calmes, là que je me flatte chère Lady que nous vous reverrons. Je crois que vous ne vous considérez point comme liée a une demeure fixe, que vous mettez en délibeation où vous passerez l'hiver, que vous hesitez entre les trois royaumes. Vous aimez la Suisse et je ne doute point alors que vous n'y reveniez. Jamais il me semble elle n'a été plus belle que cette année. La saison a éte ravissante, les chaleurs ni la sécheresse n'ont point été excessives et la verdure est éclatante comme au printems, en même tems que toutes les récoltes sont abondantes, et qu'on voit la prospérité dans tous les ménages de Paysans . . . Ma femme vous remercie tendrement du soin que vous avez pris de sa chaine et du sage parti auquel

vous vous êtes arrêtée Recevez aussi l'expression de mon
bien vif attachement presentez mes vieux hommages à
Mdlle. Votre fille, je sais bien qu'elle ne les recevra qu'en
attendant mieux et conservez moi votre amitié.

J. C. L. De Sismondi.

Pescia en Toscane, 4 Avril, 1836.

C'est ici chère my Lady que votre lettre du 23 Fevrier
m'a été renvoyée, c'est ici que je vous prie de m'écrire encore
car nous y séjournerons probablement jusqu' à la fin de
l'automne et après vous avoir fait en hiver un voyage dans
l'Italie meridionale probablement nous reviendrons passer
encore quelques tems à Pescia au printems prochain.   Cette
petite ville sur la route de Lucques a Florence est à 10
milles de la première ville a 34 de la seconde, a 14 de Pistora
à l'endroit où une rivière nommée aussi Pescia sort des
Apennins et fertilize par des eaux abondantes le pied des
collines et les magnifiques plaines qui s'étendent jusqu'a
l'Arno La petite maison que j'y possède est sur la pente
d'une colline toute couverte d'oliviers, le petit bassin qui
contient toute ma proprieté est planté d'oliviers, de vignes de
figuiers, d'arbres fruitiers de tout genre tous en fleur à
présent et dans les haies, le laurier le grenadier, le myrthe,
l'arboussier, presentent l'image du midi sauvage tandis que
le jardin est rempli d'orangers, et orné d'un gigantesque
palmier et d'une mimosa d'Egypte, notre maison est très
petite, pauvrement meublée, mais il est impossible de voir
une situation plus riante; des petis sentiers en terrasses qui
parcourent toutes ces collines, nous ouvrent des prome-
nades infiniment variées et dont chacune, présente à son
tour, des points de vue ravissans.   Ce n'est point ici que ma
famille avoit autrefois des possessions, elles etaient sur
l'autre versant des Monts de Pise qui bornait notre horizon,
mais il y a quatre cent trente ans que mes ancêtres furent

exilés de ce pays et que toutes leurs propriétés furent con-
fisqués. Nous sommes partis de Chênes le 11 Fevrier, nous
nous sommes arrêtés quelques jours à Turin et à Gênes et
cependant nous étions ici avant la fin du mois. Depuis
quelques jours nous sentons un retour de l'hiver, des vents
très froids, des pluies et la neige sur les montagnes mais
nous n'en eprouvons pas moins une jouissance continuelle
dans le spectacle que nous offre la nature; il semble que
comme nous vieillissons la société perd pour nous de son
charme, l'homme nous occupe moins, tandis que la magnificence de la nature nous parlent un langage plus vivement
senti et ramènent plus constamment nos pensées et nos cœurs
vers le grand bienfaiteur, le Père commun qui a semé à
pleines mains sur la terre, les élémens du bonheur pour tous
les hommes. Au contraire les institutions humaines sont
faute de presque touses les souffrances et presque tous les
malheurs, et à côté des infortunés qu'on fait, les mauvaises
lois et les mauvais gouvernemens, se place le mauvais prêtre,
qu' s'est fait un Dieu à son image, un Dieu exclusif et cruel
un Dieu qui condamne tous ceux qui n'ont pas compris son
essence incompréhensible et qui punit comme hérétiques,
tous ceux qui ne pensent pas comme ce prêtre. Oh! comme
la nature est belle! et comme elle tourne les coeurs vers la
piété et comme l'homme refroidit ces doux sentimens!
l'homme surtout qui a usurpé le pouvoir et qui se dit le
representant de Dieu, l'homme encore qui vent diriger les
consciences, et qui se dit l'interprête de Dieu, qui se dit
orthodoxe et qui se dit Saint. Nous avons quitté Genève
dans un mouvent où des calamités domestiques sembloient
frapper de toutes parts nos amis et nos connoissances. Il y
a peu de familles qui n'ait pas perdu quelques uns de ses
membres; quelques uns de nos amis et une cousine qui
m'etait bien chère, (la parente que j'aimois le plus), sont
mortes encore après notre départ. Ici aussi je trouve de

nouveaux sujets ou de deuil ou d'inquiétude, je suis sur le point de perdre un neveu de 23 ans un jeune homme de grande espérance mais qui je n'avois pas vu depuis son enfance. J'ai en même tems une nièce que j'aime tendrement et pour laquelle nous sommes venus ici dont la vie est menacée par des maladies violentes. Il y a donc de tous les côtés de la tristesse et de la crainte. Cependant il y a encore bien du bonheur dans l'état intérieur de notre famille. Il y en a aussi dans le travail; j'en avois pent être abusé à Genève depuis votre départ je n'ai je crois publié pas moins de trois volumes, un quatrième doit avoir paru au commencement de ce mois à Paris sous le titre, " Etudes sur les constitutions des peuples libres." Je désire fort que vous vous le procuriez et que vous me disiez quel jugement on en porte autour de vous. C'est un envoi de paix, de reconciliation que j'ai voulu faire, et il pourrait fort bien arriver qu'avec cette prétention je provoque également tous les partis contre moi. Ici je vais préparer un ou deux autres volumes sur l'économie politique qui feront suite a celui là et je traiterai en particulier la question des agriculteurs en Irelande, et les moyens de les ramener à l'indépendance qui leur est due. Car votre lettre, de même que toutes les informations que je reçois; montre clairement que leur état actuel est un opprobre pour un peuple chrétien civilisé et libre mais depuis que je suis ici des distractions continuelles ne me permettent de faire que fort peu d'ouvrage.

Ma femme et ma belle sœur jouissent comme moi de l'Italie cependant il semble qu'il leur faut un peu de *seasoning* avant de s'accoutumer a un nouveau climat, elles ont beaucoup maigri, elles ont perdu leurs couleurs et sans être malades elles me donne de l'anxiété. Ma femme me charge de vous dire combien elle est sensible a votre souvenir, combien votre amitié lui est precieuse et combien elle accepteroit avec empressement l'hospitalité que vous nous offrez,

si des liens de famille ne nous retenoient, ne nous en-
trainoient sans cesse dans un sens opposé. Elle et moi nous
vous prions aussi de nous rappeler avec affection a Miss
Catherine, Chère Lady Osborne conservez nous à tous votre
amitié et soyez assurée que c'est un souvenir bien doux pour
nous que celui du tems on vous nous avez l'accordée.
Adieu.

J. C. L. De Sismondi.

Rome, 8 Avril, 1837.

C'est à Rome chère Lady Osborne que j'ai reçu votre
lettre du 23 Janvier. Ne croyez point encore que j'ai tardé
près de six semaines à y repondre, que je n'ai pas été vivement sensible à l'amitié qu'elle me témoigne, qu'elle n'ait pas
éveillé en même tems toute ma curiosité et tout mon interêt
mais j'avois beau me sentir impatient de vous remercier de
vous parler de mon sincère attachement, de vous dire en
même tems avec combien de plaisir je voyais la nouvelle
direction que vous donniez à vos efforts, combien je voyais
de sagesse et de vraie religion dans votre réunion, avec ceux
of *the Board* qui s'efforcent de réformer l'education par un
systéme de concessions réciproques et non pas la violence.
Je me trouve ici moins mâitre de mon tems que nulle part.
Je ne fais rien, je n'apprens rien, je n'enseigne rien et
cependant je m'aperçois que toutes ma correspondance est
arrière. Votre amitié me semble exiger que je vous dise
d'abord quelques mots de notre histoire, puisqu' il y a tout
juste, une année que je vous ai' écrit la dernière fois. Alors
nous étions établis dans notre charmante solitude de Valchiuso
près de Pescia, enchantés des fleurs, du paysage, du climat,
mais n'attendant absolument rien de la société. Les enfans
de ma sœur dont nous nous étions rapproachés nous causaient
beaucoup de chagrin, un des fils étant mort tout récemment,
un autre était bien malade et ne tarda pas à mourir, la fille

ainée semblait dans ún état desespéré de chagrin.   .   .   .   .
Sa santé s'est admirablement rétablie et elle est à prêsent
aussi heureuse qu'elle avait été, longtems infortunée. Bientôt
après nous vinmes à Florence ma femme Mdme. Surtees et
moi, et nous y avons passé deux mois dans cette société
cosmopolite qu'on retrouve toujours la même dans toutes
les grandes villes qui se compose d'Anglais, d'Americains,
de Russes, d'Allemands, avec chacun desquels on se trouve
tout étonnés d'avoir eu par avance quelque point de contact
qui vous amuse, qui vous intéresse, qui vous exerce l'esprit
mais qui ne laisse pas de vous faire sentir sa profonde frivolité,
de vous inspirer un remords, de n'avoir pas un but plus
sérieux dans la vie que le succès d'une soirée, et le brillant
d'une conversation.   Rien ne fait plus plus sentir la maladie
universelle de nos societés modernes ; tous les rangs supérieurs
n'appartiennment plus à aucune nation, ils ne sont plus citoyens
que des salons.   Ils tirent bien leurs revenus de l'Angleterre
ou de la Russie, ils conservent bien quelques préjugés
nationaux qui les empêchent de s'unir franchement et de
cœur avec leurs semblables d'une autre race, mais ils ont
quitté leurs foyers sans se soucier des progrès de leurs com-
patriotes, sans se rappler qu'ils n'ont droit à leurs revenus
que pour réveiller l'industrie de leurs voisins et contribuer a
leur aisance.   On s'ètonne à la chûte des influences aristo-
cratiques, c'est l'aristocratie elle même qui les a détruites,
les ancêtres de ces Lords de ces Princes que je vois tour à
tour dans les salons de Florence et de Rome vivaient dans
leurs chàteaux entourés de leurs vassaux qu'ils commandaient
à la guerre, qu'ils soignaient dans leurs adversités qu'ils con-
naissoient tous par leur, nom et auxquels ils inspiroient
aisément leurs idées et leur sentimens, mais quel lien reste
t'il à cette noblesse cosmopolite avec les provinciaux qui font
naître ses rentes et qui les lui payent? aucun que ce paye-
ment même, est il étrange que ceux qui payent désirent le

voir finir. Le 9 Fevrier nous nous revinmes en route a Florence pour Rome; une autre sœur de ma femme Miss Allen est venue nous y réjoindre avec son neveu, nous sommes ici pour huit jours seulement encore, fort désireux d'aller à Naples mais résolus à ne point y entrer que les cordons sanitaires ne soient levés l'espérance de les voir supprimer me semble diminuer lous les jours. Alors nous retournerons à Pescia où nous serons dans un mois et où nous passerons encore une année, j'ai dans cette intervalle publié un second volume de mes études sur les sciences sociales et peut être l'été prochain en publierai-je un troisième, j'espère que leur caractère sera de plus en plus tolérant; plus j'étudie ceux qui ne pensent pas comme moi et plus j'arrive a comprendre que leur manierè de penser et d'agir a aussi des motifs et des avantages. Cette intelligence ne diminue point mon zèle pour ce que je crois la verité, mais elle me confirme qu' on y arrive par plusieurs voies diverses et elle augmente je l'espére, ma sympathie pour ceux qui diffèrent d'avec moi. Je ne saurois plus dire, my lady, avec combien de plaisir je vous ai vu entrer dans un sentiment semblable pour ce qui concerne l'éducation des catholiques en Irelande, et combien j'ai trouvé de raison et de justice dans les motifs que vous me donnez pour votre union avec des hommes dont vous n'admettez pas toutes les opinions. Vous avez la bonté de me promettre deux livres. The Dublin University Magazine, and A. B. Whately, Pol. Econ. Il n'est pas façile de les faire arriver si loin et les frais pourraient être exorbitans mais si vous pouvez le faire, voudriez vous les faire remettre à Paris à Messrs. Trentel et Werth, mes libraires en les priant de les faire passer pour moi' a M. Viesseux Gabinnetto leterario a Florence, si vous trouvez quelque difficulté attendez cependant que je me sois rapproché de vous, car Dieu sait encore si vos livres ne seront pas arrétés a leur entrée en Italie.

Mrs. Otis, m. 'a. interrompu, elle aussi etait venu voir
Florence et Rome; elle repart incessament pour Naples où
elle s'embarquera pour Marseille, elle me demande de la
rappeler a votre souvenir. Je ne pense plus que nous ayons
vu aucune autre de nos connaisances communes. Ma femme
me charge de vous dire tout son attachement.

Daignez aussi recevoir l'assurance d'une affection bien
sincerè et bien vive comme de mon respect.

J. C. L. De Sismondi.

Rappelez nous les uns et les autres a Miss Catherine.

Chênes, October 1, 1841.

Thank you warmly, my dear Lady Osborne, for the most
agreeable way in which you could have awakened our love
of you, if that had been necessary, by sending your friends
to us, and with so kind a letter ; they could not have been
but welcome, even without the aid of their own merits.
They have made only an apparition, and are already about
to depart, which we regret ; but you promise to come yourself next summer. Shall we be here to profit of it ? It is a
question I put to myself with some anxiety. Sismondi is
labouring so indefatigably to be ready to go into his dear
Italy that I have my fears. He is now writing the 27th
vol. of his history of the French ; he is already in the reign
of Louis XV., and he draws up at the Revolution. I have
never seen him work with such pertinacious vigour ; he does
not quit his desk for an hour in the day. It seems as if his
whole existence was there ; yet he has a sort of malady that
from its persistence might well make me uneasy if I perceived
it affected his health ; this sounds somewhat of a riddle, but
there it is. Ever since our visit to England he has been
afflicted with what he calls a hiccup, but which is in truth a
sort of ebullition of gas that seems to work in his stomach

like a bottle of eau de seltz, and which talking almost immediately produces. It began with pain in the stomach, but that has ceased ; and independent of this strange symptom of disorder I should say he was remarkably well ; his appetite, sleep, and strength are undiminished ; but as he takes no exercise whatever he is become very fat. I am in constant dread this sort of life must end in mischief, but the physicians assure me not. May God grant it! It has now lasted 18 months. It cuts us off from all enjoyment ; that of society we have no more, for he dreads a visit which of half an hour will bring on a hiccup of many hours ; and beside that we have lost and are losing by death almost all our old associates. This year the grave has closed over Madame Neckar, Monsieur de Candolle, Monsieur de Chateauroux, almost the last of his set, and the two friends he best loved. We are left almost alone, and, alas! too bereaved to stand firm. I am become so deaf I am more an ennui to bear with, than a companion to cheer him ; but I am well and strong, and could still exquisitely enjoy the beauty of this sublime land this lovely autumn if I could but prevail on Sismondi to take a little excursion among its mountains for 8 days or so, and try its effect on himself before we shut up for the winter. The season is delicious ; there never was such an opening of October. While I take my solitary turn round the field I envy every one that can spread their wings and take flight. My very soul longs for the mountains, and I almost cried the other day in seeing the swallows making their short joyous flights, and wheeling in the air preparative to being off. Dear Lady Osborne, I wish we could pass again the happy year that you were here ; we have had none so pleasant since. We have your little landscape in our little salon as a fond memorial of it. If you return here I am afraid you will be far from finding what you left. And I am so delighted with your impression of Geneva I should be

sorry to have it effaced. Nevertheless " come," only temper
your expectation to what we are, not were. If " our way
of life has fallen into the sere and yellow leaf," there are
other of your friends that you will find still young and
prosperous. The Meuniers, for instance. She has made great
progress in her art, and her husband in his mind, for all
clever people do; he has been giving conferences that I hope
he will publish. Talking of mind, I greatly admire the
activity of yours, and envy the progress you have made in
the German language. I have this moment put down a translation of scraps from a variety of the best authors, with
an enthusiastic feeling of admiration for its literature, and
an ardent desire that I could read it in its own dress.

Pray remember me most affectionately to Miss Osborne.

.   .   .   .

Je prens la plume des mains de ma femme car je veux une
place dans cette lettre chère Lady Osborne. Je me demandois
souvent comment notre correspondance avait cessé. Je
sentais bien que ce n'etait pas de ma part manque d'une
tendre attachement et de l'interêt le plus vif dans tout ce
qui vous concerne. Mais nous avons sans cesse changé de
place l'un et l'autre et nous avions de la peine à savoir où
nous retrouver je suis flatté et reconnoissant de ce que pen-
dant notre silence mutuel vous aviez trouvé moyen de con-
tinuer notre échange de pensées en lisant mes études sur les
sciences sociales. Hélas, il y a dans les nations qui passent
pour prospérantes une se grande masse de souffrances que
je désire ardemment attirer l'attention vers ces études qui
seules peuvent y porter quelque remède. Il me semble à mon
tour que jentrais un peu dans votre societé en m'occupant
des écrits de votre ami l'Evêque Whately. Je voudrais
pouvoir vous envoyer une petite brochure qu'il m'a fait
écrire sur les colonies pénales. Mais je ferai mieux, j'esperè
si je vis pouvoir vous la remettre ici l'année prochaine. Ce
sera une grande joie je vous assure pour tous deux de vous

revoir et quoique ma femme ait raison de vous dire que
nous avous bien vielli que nous avons bien perdu de nos
pouvoirs pour la société, que nous sommes souvent bien
tristes, il nous reste pourtant un coeur chaud qui se sentira
rajeuni en se retrouvant près de vous.

J. C. L. DE SISMONDI.

Chénes, Dec. 9, 1841.

By this time you are settled in Vienna for the winter, and
I feel impatient to thank you, my dear Lady Osborne, for
the kindest letter that was ever penned ; for the tender
solicitude with which you prescribe for us ; for your fervent
memory of the past in which we had our share ; in short,
for all the contents of your sweet letter. It was a great
comfort and pleasure to us in circumstances still more dis-
astrous than when I wrote. Perhaps you have seen something of our political troubles in the newspapers, but where
you are perhaps the word "revolution" must not be pro-
nounced. But I may tell you that ours has been completed
in a manner the most disgraceful on one hand, and the most
humiliating on the other, that can be imagined. The mildest,
most paternal government of the happiest and most prosperous people has been wantonly overturned in one moment
without a single person's knowing why. It is too long a
story to begin from the beginning, and living so apart from
the world as we do, we are not, perhaps, sufficiently well-
informed, as you may imagine, when I tell you that the first
intimation we had of any revolutionary disturbance was
from some compatriots of yours ; but to give you some idea
I will sketch a little of my imperfect knowledge.

On the 3rd of last March an association was formed of the
malcontents of the Canton, distinquishing themselves by the
title of "Convocation du 3 Mai." Government paid little
attention to them, and they amused themselves with meetings,

talkings, and a bad newspaper employing the disgusting fudge of the French papers to excite the people. Suddenly they gained sufficient strength to summon the Council, with much insolence of tone to advance the usual session and give them a constituent assembly to new model the Constitution. The Government which at first answered with dignity on investigating the state of the public mind found they must yield, and it was accordingly done on the 22nd. The Council met, but the day before a mob assembled some say in addition to the refuse of the people ; here there were also the dregs of Gex, Ferney, and Savoy; attacked the Maison de Ville where " le petit conseil" were sitting to prepare the law they demanded, and remained all night in riot on the Traille and round the maison de ville. On Monday the 22nd they still continued only in greater numbers, and with vociferations interrupting the debate. The Militia, instead of obeying the Government, grounded their arms, many seduced and disorganized by their own officers. There was nothing to be done but to grant them their frivolous desires. The Government was not quick enough to please them and they marched off to attack St. Pierre, in order to open it for a National Assembly. In short, to quiet the tumult the " Constituante" was hastily voted by a third of the members and a new mode of election has been adopted to form the " Constituante," at this moment the Republic is busy on all sides with the preparatory work for an election of members; on one side for those who will preserve what they can from the ruins of the old constitution, on the other for those who will destroy all. Sismondi, who was twice prevented from speaking by his own party, embodied in a little brochure what he meant to say; I shall put aside a copy for you when we meet. I acknowledge to you I thought it excellent, but its success has surpasssed my warmest expectations. I believe no pamphlet has ever had more effect, it has brought back many and enchanted them already with him, eight editions are already exhausted, and it appeared only last Friday, he wrote it in a few hours on Thursday morning, so that with all his long sufferings the vigour of his mind and fervour of feeling remain undiminished; he received letters of thanks from every one, and no one has met him since without a grateful wring of the hand for the service he has rendered his country. All this is consolatory, but it cannot do away his sorrow, his humiliation, his regret for what is destroyed, and accordingly his malady has been greatly aggravated since. Dear Lady Osborne we had often tried the simple remedies you recommended—magnesia, rhubarb, soda, &c.—but without effect, and as half his complaint is nervous on a very nervous habit we find that all remedies are bad, and he is better when none are in operation and so his medical men tell him that his malady is only to be cured by care of general health and severe diet.

If I gave you a melancholy impression of Geneva in my last letter, I have one far more so to give you now; you can conceive nothing more melancholy than the appearance of the town and the countenance of every one you meet. Trade already suffers, nothing is bought, not a dinner or soirée even has been given since the political agitation; no public entertainment except the theatre, where the Marseillaise is sung and to which the gamins only go; never was there in a small place more bitter dissension, more strong hatred. In the association are two or three of our friends who are lost to us in a worse way than by death, which has already taken so many. As you know so much of Geneva I may give you the names; ——— a Federal Colonel is one of the most active and most mischievous members; ——— another but he has been silenced by an awful blow from heaven itself, his daughter, his only child, the only thing he loved on earth, and she was the idol of his soul as he was of hers

died of terror the day after the 22nd, occasioned by the
mob of his own exciting, and organized by his cousin ———,
a man who merits —— more than many now in these lenient
times condemned to it. —— is another member, but we
have reason to think a repentant one. I believe this is the
whole of their aristocracy—the rest are a few doctors, a few
régents de l'école and tradespeople. How glad I shall be if
we can meet and pass a little time together this summer,
that is the coming one! S—— says that if he finishes his
work he should be tempted to leave the place now so painful,
and try, perhaps, some of the German baths before he goes
into Italy, which he seems determined to do in the autumn;
but if he is elected in the Constituante, of which I think
there can be little doubt, it must necessarily retard his
historical task; he so desponds of doing any good that he
heartily wishes to escape. It will be laborious and painful,
for every effort of his will be hotly combatted by active,
younger, and wicked men, but he must gird himself to the
strife. It is hard on him after fifty years, after having been
twice ruined and five times under imprisonment in his youth,
to find himself again in his old age retracing the same painful
steps, and perhaps again an exile; for if the association de 3
Mars gain the victory, he, probably with many others, will
leave Geneva to their misgovernment.

Dear Lady Osborne, farewell, do not give way to any
discouraging feeling in your literary efforts; we exercise
and improve no one faculty of the mind without raising the
whole moral being, the understanding is necessary to the
perfection of the soul. How many are, from defect of
judgment or want of thought, perhaps more than from the
heart; God has granted us time and means for the cultivation of both. We know not what thoughts, feelings, and
faculties are exercised and called forth even in the learning
of a language we may never be called upon to use. Go on

then in those labours for which I so much admire you and which bring them the " cui bono." Pray remember me affectionately to Miss Osborne. I should have great pleasure to see her once more. I leave the remainder of my paper to Sismondi who wishes to say a word for himself, and am ever, my dear Lady Osborne,

Affectionately and obliged,

J. Sismondi.

" Monsieur de Sismondi's prevision regarding the future of the present French Emperor should add weight to his warning about the demolition of time-honoured institutions."

Chère Lady Osborne,—Je ne veux point que cette lettre parte sans que j'y mette deux mots de tendresse et de reconnaissance et d'autre part je suis si découragé que je crois bien que ce ne sera que deux mots. Ma femme vous a écrit nos malheurs mieux que je n'aurois su le faire mais toutes sortes de douleurs se comblent dans celle que j,éprouve. C'est ma patrie et vous savez qu'on l'aime peut étre d'autant plus qu'elle est plus petite, qu'on l'embrasse mieux d'un regard, qu'on la saisit par les yeux du corps et non pas seulement par ceux de l'imagination, et surtout quand elle est si belle. Ce sont les institutions de nos pères qui sont tombées auxquelles nous attachions tous nos pieux souvenirs, tous les honneurs de notre race, ce dont aussi sous plusieurs rapports les résultats de mes propres efforts et ceux de mes amis. Et ce que nous mettions à la place cette constitution à laquelle je devais travailler moi même sans espoir, sans courage la pensée m'en est insupportable. Et puis la bêtise de la race humaine me fait rougir, cette précipitation de gens heureux dans l'inconnu par fatigue du bien être, elle me fait peur pour tout le monde, elle me fait peur pour vousmêmes en Angleterre je vois un parti toujours nombreux à Oxford, abandonner l'une après l'autre toutes les conquêtes de la Réforme, pour se rejeter dans l'Eglise Romaine. Votre letter est si tendre chère Lady Osborne, qu'elle a redoublé notre desir de vous revoir, qu'elle nous a fait sentir que notre amitié n'était point de celles que crée le voisinage et que l'absence détruit. Nous nous sommes au contraire unis davantage encore depuis votre départ, nos idées se sont rapprochés, nos désirs s'harmonisent, nous avons désormais des amis communs, et la famille Whately forme un nouveau lien entre nous. Puisse ce désir croissant de nous revoir surmonter tous les obstacles et nous rapprocher en effet. Puissiez vous ensuite trouver le repos que vous désirez en Irlande et moi en Toscane et puis, près ou loin, soyez bien sûre que notre tendre affection et nos vœux vous suivront partout.

J. C. L. DE SISMONDI.

Cresselly, November 26, 1842.

MY DEAR LADY OSBORNE,—I was sad enough when I wrote my last letter to you, but most blessed in comparison of what I have been since and am now. When I was complaining to you of the losses we had sustained at Geneva, how little I anticipated the one great one that hung over me, and which would render every future one light: " One sorrow that throws its dark shade" and for ever over me; you knew and loved him, dearest Lady Osborne, so warmly that you must be for ever dear to me. Your last tender letters did him good, and seeing you again at Geneva were among the last pleasures he anticipated, even in the fatal month of June we talked together of seeing you, but let me leave my own sorrow a moment . . .

Thank you warmly for your most friendly invitation, but dear Lady Osborne I am no longer presentable anywhere, my sorrow has not apparently destroyed my health, but it has fixed its fangs on my heart, the circulation of the blood is troubled and occasions such an astounding noise in my head, as not only to make me completely deaf, but to render me almost stupid. I seem to speak myself against a storm and therefore know not well how to modulate my voice; it seems also to confuse my understanding, so that I am slow of comprehension. This, added to dejection, renders me extremely unfit for society, even of those who love me. I am now with a beloved brother and sister, but I see no other than such near relations, and in a week or two shall remove to Tenby, to Mrs. Surtees, only who has tenderness and patience enough to bear with me, and love sufficient to make her task dear to her.

We wrote you a joint letter the 10th of May ever so late, "the day after his last birthday," directed to Vienna; we found you would not get it, but knew not where else to direct it. We were nearly sure you had left it, for you did not seem to enjoy it much as a residence, but we trusted you would have ordered your letters to be forwarded. I remain in England over the next year, but if I live longer I hope to return to my dear Chênes and its churchyard, where lie all that is left of his earthly existence; I have purchased my place near him; would I could as easily secure the immortal one in heaven—when that is accomplished I have nothing more to do on earth. I will not further prolong this sad return for your kind letter, than to beg my most affectionate remembrance to your dear Catherine, and fervent wishes for her happiness—hers will secure yours. Ever most gratefully your ladyship's

Obliged and affectionate,

J. De Sismondi.

My dear Madam,—I have been with my son at his living in Hampshire, which has caused this delay in my answer to your friendly letter, and in expressing to your ladyship how much I was pleased and honoured by such a communication; but let me just assure you that you mistake Mr. Woodward if you do not think that in him you have not only a steadfast friend, but also a warm panegyrist, as it was his report which so disposed me to fall in love with your ladyship at first sight. You will readily excuse this playful expression from an old gentleman like me, with his old wife to boot, and put it down for what it means—a lively pleasure in your society, a deep interest in your spiritual estate, and a hearty wish to contribute in any degree to your well being. And while I thus acknowledge your power, you will not be disposed to abridge my Christian liberty in the full and free expression of my sentiments, even where they may differ essentially from your own.

You seemed to think in our last conversation that I wished to draw you too much to a contemplative life. No, my good lady, for this in your circumstances would be a sullenness against Providence, which by its gifts of large means of usefulness, and by investing you with such various social graces, points out to you your calling. And indeed after reading your enumeration of the large sources of happiness which indulgent Heaven has placed in your reach, and finding all this followed by the expression, "Yet I am not happy," I could not but think there must be somewhat of the undisciplined will of our first mother in Paradise; and if the object of this restless desire be the tree of knowledge, the likeness is the stronger. But to speak more seriously, if we have faith in the Christian religion, ought not such glorious truths to make the favoured mortal happy—to whom they are revealed; and if they do not so, may we not suspect that our faith is weakened, our mental vision dimmed by a latent worldliness, and ought we not with the whole regulation of our course of life to adopt those rules which may best contribute to restore our awakened minds to clearer vision, or elevate us above the smoke and stir of this dim spot. And this it is which makes me distrust the system of your friend ———; that it does not make him happy, that he seems scarcely to imagine a state of that sacred and homefelt delight, that calm certainty of waking bliss, which I think every chapter of the Bible speaks of as the privilege of Christians, that which the Psalmist so sweetly describes— " Thou shalt hide them privily by thine own presence from the provoking of all men; Thou shalt keep them secretly in thy pavilion from the strife of tongues."

I speak to you in confidence. Though I know the high talent of ———, and respect his integrity and admire his manly and generous sentiments, yet it does appear to me that he apprehends religion too logically. He has worked out for himself the problem of the truth of Christianity, and would go to death in testimony of his convictions; but he does not seem to me to have gotten those new tastes and affections which denote the new birth, and enable us instinctively to lay hold on God, and to see with the mind's eye the adorable perfections of the Father, and the spiritual beauty of our Lord Jesus Christ, the Holy One and the Just, which at once decides the soul for ever, which now devotes itself without hesitation, and solemnly adopts the sentiment, " Whom have I in heaven but Thee, and there is none on earth that I desire in comparison of Thee." . . .

I fear that some of the friends to whom you were so acceptable have but a feeble hold of Christianity, and feel inward scorn of its pure and lowly disciples; but how am I trespassing on your patience? Do you not already repent of your inviting such a correspondent? Truly I should be sorry for this, as I do most gladly accept of your proffered friendship, and am ready to profess myself your true knight against all gainsayers.　But in sober earnest I do assure you that few things have given me more pleasure than the prospect of improving that friendship which you so graciously offer, and it will be a strong inducement to visit Ireland that I may hope to have freer and fuller discourse with you on the best and happiest subjects.　This letter I feel is no answer to yours, but I would not defer, even for a day, to assure you how gratefully and sincerely I receive your kindness.

Yours truly,

J. DUNN.

17, Chester Terrace.

MY DEAR LADY OSBORNE,—I am very sorry that I am not equal to the very agreeable engagement I had made for this evening, but indeed I am not well, and was unable to go to church yesterday morning.　Will you please to give the enclosed note to Mrs. Benson.　I hope you will let me know when you move into your house, as my lady wishes much for the honour of being presented to you, and you must soon fix a day, when we can have a conference from six o'clock till ten.　There is a good and very able man now in London, Mr. Thomas Erskine, author of several valuable tracts, whom I think you would like dearly, and I would get him to meet you.

I remain, my dear Lady Osborne,

Yours truly and affectionately,

JAS. DUNN.

17, Chester Terrace, March 19.

MY DEAR LADY OSBORNE,—I have been in close attendance
at the death bed of an uncle of mine, who closed his mortal
career on Friday, and has left a widow and large family,
who needed all the consolation I could minister, otherwise I
should have called on you before this to inquire how you get
on in this wicked city. My lady has eloped from me for a week.
I have been greatly troubled with rheumatism in my head. I
think I have scarcely recovered the effects of my dissipation at
the Colosseum, so I must be on my guard how I follow where-
ever your ladyship may lead, to which I am a little too prone.

Yours, my dear Madam, very truly,

J. DUNN.

June 19.

MY DEAR LADY OSBORNE,—You complained, and justly,
that I puzzled you with my metaphysics, but remember it
was at the unpropitious hour before dinner when Dr. Johnson
himself was stupid and cross, and if he were so, "non ego
homunculus;" and now this fine morning, when I have slept
off the effects of your feast, and my eyes are no longer dazzled
with the golden embroidery of cabinet ministers, I must try to
incense you as to Coleridge's distinction between thoughts and
ideas, not that I defend his use of the word, which he borrowed from one of the peculiarities of Plato's doctrine, but
only to unfold his meaning, by giving an example as you
required. Thus, a single rose or a leaf in your hand suggests
a "thought," something that stands alone without connection or consequence; but a seed which you are going to
plant affords "an idea," because it leads on the mind to
growth and expansion as containing a principle within it,
which is to work out its own development, and will go on,
if it gets fair play, to bring forth its proper leaf and flower,

full of beauty and fragrance. So when Coleridge speaks of the *idea* of the constitution, he means some seminal principle which is at work throughout it, and is continually producing fruit of public freedom, security, and prosperity. This which is called the heart of a country is to be discovered, and is itself dependent on a large number of particulars, by extensive acquaintance with its history, knowledge of its social relations and habits, its popular customs and traditions, its literature, and innumerable other agencies, which it requires a comprehensive, a candid, and sagacious mind fully to embrace; and so must be formed our *idea* or leading principle of Christianity, that vital truth or truths which, received into the heart, grows up and expands into all the blessed fruits of a holy life. This our Lord refers to when He says, " One thing is needful." And again, " God is a spirit, and to be worshipped in spirit and in truth;" " make the tree good;" and when St. Paul says, " The law of the life of the spirit has set me free from law of sin." All these passages refer to some great principle, which by its vital working is to produce in us all the fruits of holiness, and its end everlasting life. Now, to apply this, a man may make laws, but if he does not know what is the heart of the country they will prove finally inoperative ; so casuists may heap up rules and make distinctions, but if they do not cherish the vital principle of action, their rules will prove a dead letter. So particular acts or offences suggest " a thought," but every passion is an *idea*, because it works inwardly and unseen to produce its own fruits of good or evil.

Now, my good lady, I beg of you to receive all this as from the Pope, as infallible wisdom; though after all you cannot see it to be quite so clear as I seem to think it, but positively I can say nothing more upon the subject, and therefore will be very glad to get Mr. Babbage's book, which you can send to me by that very convenient system (whether a thought

or an idea) called the Parcels Delivery Company. I like your
friend Mrs. Congreve exceedingly ; and my day was a
happy one, though I retreated so early from your circle of
fashionables, as they do not at all fall in with my *idea* of
social life.

Believe me always, my dear lady,

Yours very truly,

Jas. Dunn.

June 25th.

My dear Lady Osborne,—I am obliged to go and see a
sick friend in Kent for a day or two, which will prevent my
calling on you with Mr. Babbage's book which I therefore
return, and hope when I next see you to talk over some of
his notions. He is a very clever man, and his illustrations of
the System of Providence from his calculating machine are
just and natural, and only follow up the argument of Paley
as to the mechanism of the watch. Many of his observations
I could not follow, not being a mathematician; but as to his
notion of the everlasting continuance of sounds, surely all
the motions of elastic fluids may counteract and extinguish
one another, and so this multiplicity of sounds must be
diminishing every day by their mutual action and reaction.
But I have many other observations to make on it, and
therefore shall have the pleasure of calling on your ladyship
as soon as I return, and have a talk about that and other
things.

Believe me, yours very truly,

J. Dunn.

My dear Lady Osborne,—Many thanks for your kind
visit of yesterday. I only went to see a dying friend at the
urgent solicitation of his wife, and I must assume an
obstinacy which you are not accustomed to from any one,

much less from me; but for the whole of this week I must refuse going out in the evening, but any day in the next week I shall be happy to wait on you at the tea table. I give up all dinner parties until after Easter—do not be surprised at this unsocial rule of mine, but verily I have attained for the last year to such health of body and of mind from this management of myself some of my friends abuse me. " At mihi plaudo ipse domi, &c." I hope to call on you between one and two to-morrow.

Yours, my dear madam, very truly,
J. DUNN.

I wish to speak to you on behalf of an old friend and curate of mine, Mr. Carr of Ross.

17, Chester-terrace.

MY DEAR LADY OSBORNE,—Can you dine with us on Wednesday next the 20th? Miss Catherine expressed a wish to know Mr. Carlyle, and she will meet him here on that day, and one or two other interesting persons. I am still much of an invalid.

Yours, my dear Lady O., very truly,
J. DUNN.

[These little notes are given for their vein of playful courtesy, which is becoming rare.]

February 19.

MY DEAR LADY OSBORNE,—I find I must defer my expeditions with you until the weather is more friendly to my crazy constitution, for even from my short flight to-day I have caught cold. I hope, however, that this pleasure will not be long deferred, and that under kindlier skies I shall prove a better squire of dames. I was glad to see you fairly

planted in a house which promises that I may often pay my
visits there until you get tired of me, which I can tell you
may be sooner than you think. With kind compliments to
your daughter,

Believe me, yours very sincerely,

JAS. DUNN.

I hope you may sometimes see your landlord. I feel an
interest of late in Mr. Bulwer.

MY DEAR LADY OSBORNE,—I do not call on you because I
despair of meeting you at home. Could you do such a thing
as breakfast with us on Saturday morning at half-past nine
or ten? And you will meet one or two very good and clever
men; and if Miss Catherine could bring her beautiful
Arabian and allow me the honour of escorting her in another
ride, I should be duly grateful, as would become an old rusty
parson to be for such an honour. Believe me, my dear Lady
Osborne,

Yours most truly,

J. DUNN.

July 24.

MY DEAR LADY OSBORNE,—I should fee you instead of the
doctor as you really did me great good by the pleasant drive
and still pleasanter chat of yesterday. I hope to go to-
morrow to Cheltenham, and my address there will be at Mrs.
Crofton's, 12, Priory-street; and I hope you will write to me.
I very much regret leaving London at this time when you
would be so much more at leisure for receiving a friendly
visit, and I also regret very much having lost the opportunity
of improving your brother's acquaintance. Since my indisposition I have asked no company to my house, and in
London it is an affront to ask a man to your family party;

but I forget that your brother is no "Lunnuner," and that
probably I might have enjoyed some days in that way with
so very amiable and intelligent a companion, for which, in
the unusual depression of my spirits, I often sighed. But I
do not despair of finding you all here on my return. How
do I lose opportunities of pleasure and improvement, while
this wool-gathering pate of mine is occupied in far-fetched
reflections, instead of what is under my eyes.

  Yours, my dear lady, truly and affectionately,

          J. DUNN.

MY DEAR LADY OSBORNE,—I have been so very weak since
I left London that I have scarcely opened a book, and they
also tell me that while drinking the waters I must write as
little as possible, but one or two lines I must send you to express the pleasure I found in your last most friendly, though
too flattering letter, which I will answer at full length the
first day that I find myself equal to cope with such an accomplished correspondent. Indeed my dear lady I feel your
partial kindness as quite a cheer to me in my pilgrimage.
Pray write to me whenever you can spare an hour and consider it is as it were a visit of mercy; and though I can
make no return, being stupid and old, yet this gives new
merit to your work. My kind remembrance to your daughter
and also to Mrs. Riall. I regretted much that I could not
cultivate her acquaintance. I think myself better, but for a
time I was convinced that you must elect another Pope, as
you seem to go upon the policy of the Cardinals, to choose
the most infirm of all the doctors that they might get rid of
him the sooner. You see I have a little fun still left in me,
but what will always remain with me is the warm and affectionate friendship with which I am always yours.

          J. DUNN.

17, Chester-terrace, August 5th, 1837.

My dear Madam,—I was on a visit to my friends the Thorntons, at Clapham, or I should have answered your kind letter sooner, and allow me to return my very cordial thanks for its gracious communication ; and I hope that when you come to London, you will let me know by a line that I may have the pleasure of a little conversation with you, which is better than epistolary greeting. I am sorry to say that I can get no information about the Bristol and Waterford Packets ; my son, whom I despatched immediately to make enquiries, called at three offices in Regent-street, and one in Haymarket, but at all he received for answer that they knew nothing of the times of the Bristol Packet sailing, and this I have to regret that your first commission to me should have been so unsuccessfully executed. I hope at all times that you will employ me, and I can promise the utmost diligence in your service. I shall certainly get the archbishop's sermons and read them attentively, and shall then venture to give you my opinion. Do not suppose that I condemn the exercise of intellect in religion, for man has thoughts as well as feelings, and those must be engaged as well as the latter, and when they are so on religion they endear it and familiarize it to us by the pleasurable exercise of our faculties, but we must not mistake this for the primary faculty by which we allow the saving knowledge of God as He is manifested in Christ. But by a higher faculty which is called in Scripture the Spirit, which is the breath of God in man, and is alone receptive of, and must be filled with, that divine influence which is as necessary to our *spiritual* life as the atmosphere we breathe is to our natural ; and when this is once established then under its governance all the minor faculties and tastes are usefully employed. But all this you know, and I must conclude my letter, which I delayed in hopes of getting the intelligence you wished for, until the bell-man warns me to close it. But believe me, my dear Lady Osborne,

Yours most sincerely and affectionately,

J. DUNN.

MY DEAR LADY,—I rather wish that what I said to you about Mr. —— should not be mentioned again, for reasons I will tell you again. I do not think you had reason to be angry with the letter you read part of to me this morning. I assure you I receive letters from my own sister, who belongs to a religious party, that would make a stranger think I was an infidel, yet no one can love another more partially than she does me. Pray, my good lady, is it not a just and a good rule not to require sympathy from those to whom you do not give it? this would limit and legalize our love of popularity or general sympathy. It is equally unreasonable and injurious to our happiness, to demand sympathy, but in proportion as we feel it to another, and pray as I do most fervently, that God would cleanse our hearts that we may perfectly love Him, which can only be when self-love is well nigh extinguished in us; in short, my dear lady, to be a Christian is a very sublime and arduous undertaking, i. e., not to be a Christian, for this is peace, joy, and love, not to become one; for this we must cut off right hand and pluck out right eye.

Ever, truly and affectionately yours,

JAS. DUNN.

I delivered Miss Warde's note with my own hand.

MY DEAR LADY OSBORNE,—I am very sorry that I cannot join your breakfast table to-morrow. I have been obliged this day to relinquish an engagement from finding myself too unwell. I must apply Horace's advice to his friend, " Loose the aged courser in good time from the car, lest he break down at last." I return you ———'s letter, which is clear and forcible, as is everything that comes from his pen. He has indeed a masterly intellect, and fully deserves the character of " sincerity;" though he does not seem to me to have reached that beautiful quality described by Fénélon, which he calls " simplicity," the total absence of all self regard in what we do, either as to praise from others, or complacency in our own talents. There are side long glances to our reputation or our consciousness of power, which are found out at length by an irritable sense of the least slight, and a magnifying of all men who agree with us. ——— finely reasons from the agency of the Holy Spirit as the height of moral greatness to which we may attain; and I would further conclude that the operation of such a divine agent would at length raise us into a state of holy serenity, and a noble indifference to the opinions of men concerning us, always attentive not to offend them, and also to do them all good, but like the stream from the fountains of living waters, always clear at its source; and when subject to calumny or opposition, which, like dirt thrown in, may muddy it for a moment, yet it soon, as it runs on, grows clear and pure, and can reflect each happy object on its banks, and also the heavens above. I have a little book of yours, by the Archbishop, on money matters, which is a very happy specimen of the mode of introducing knowledge to the young mind. I shall bring it with me; and truly this good man is very highly gifted in various ways.

Believe me, my dear Lady Osborne,
Your affectionate friend,
JAS. DUNN.

M 2

August 12.

My dear Lady Osborne,—As I do not go to Shooter's Hill to-morrow, which, besides being a breach of duty, would be also beyond my strength, which will be tried to the utmost by preaching in such weather, I therefore cannot let you leave this country without a few words from me of most cordial greeting, and very grateful acknowledgement of your unusual kindness; and believe me, my good lady, that your friendship has been very pleasant to me, and helped to cheer me on my pilgrimage. It is true that I feel a strong conviction that you have sadly miscalculated both my wisdom and piety, so remember that I warned you of this, and do not therefore, when you discover the truth, allow me to fall as much below the mark as you have now raised me above it, but give me Sancho Panza's mark, neither black nor white, but good brown ochre. However, I confess even your undue estimate has a sweetness in it; and as I am persuaded that where there is true principle there must be a growth, so I hope yet to reach to the point at which you have placed me, and I hope you will help me to that by the free censure of all my faults as they may come to light.

Believe me your Ladyship's obliged and affectionate friend,

JAMES DUNN.

17, Chester Terrace, August 16, 1837.

My dear Lady Osborne,—I really am vexed, or rather let me say I ought to be so, by the extravagance of your praise, which is given in larger measure than I have ever before received from any of my fellow mortals. And I can only picture myself as a traveller, who having been ship-wrecked on a distant shore, where the inhabitants were looking out for some great but unknown prince, mistakes him for the expected visitor, and insisted on paying him all the honours of royalty. How do you think he would feel upon such an occasion? Even so do I when Lady Osborne, influenced by her own ardent desire to find the good, and guided by a bright imagination and an affectionate heart, has mistaken me for one of those who are kings and priests unto God.

You have clothed me, my dear lady, in a gorgeous robe all of your own needlework, dipped in the colours of a rich fancy, and a hearty intense desire to realize the image of good. I wish I could say I was really angry with you for such an error, but alas! corrupt nature relishes but too keenly the sweet poison, and I must feel myself under penance for having felt so much pleasure from your praise, for this is one of my many faults, which will yet develop themselves to your eyes, and dissipate the mirage which your intense desire to realize Christian goodness has conjured up. This indeed is the source of much that the world miscalls my virtues, an extreme desire to please, joined with a quick sensibility to the feelings of others; this which is the basis of my old nature gives a grace to many parts of my character, and finally imitates true charity, while it really feeds the self central life, and is as far as the poles are asunder from the Christian character, which is renewed after the image of God in righteousness and true holiness. Pray read Fénélon's beautiful comment on St. Paul's description of charity in Cor. xiii., and then Leighton's Life by Mr. Pearson as the best exemplification of it.

One of the secrets of my popularity has been, that I early withdrew from the chase and the strife for this world's honors and emoluments, partly on principle and partly from taste, and therefore I stood in no man's way, so they had no longer any motive to refuse me their good word as they passed me by, giving me the praise of goodness, and thinking me a fool for being content with it.

Here is a letter all about self, while I seem to disclaim it, and therefore soberly, my dear and too kind friend, you must no longer praise me.   To enjoy your cordial and Christian friendship has become a prominent wish of my heart, but let it prompt us in all sincerity to help each other to escape from the snare of an evil world, and to lay aside every weight which may impede us in running the race set before us.

Let me now answer your kind enquiry after my health; such enquiries are enough to make anyone well.   I suffered a good deal from my sermons, chiefly in headache.   This of late has been very troublesome, and it often makes me a bad correspondent, but you may be sure I shall always do my utmost to encourage you to favour me with a letter, who write so sweetly and so well.   I hope that if it please God to spare us until your return to London, that I may be allowed to enjoy many hours of your conversation, and I hope it will not be without edification, as I am sure it will ever be attended with a very lively interest.

Believe me to be, very sincerely,

Your affectionate friend,

J. Dunn.

17, Chester Terrace, Regent's Park,
September 20, 1837.

My dear Madam,—I have been a sad invalid since I last had the pleasure of writing to you, having been confined for near a fortnight to my room, which has interrupted all my plans, and obliges me now, by medical order, to go for some weeks to Brighton to brace me after so much confinement. I write now partly to explain my change of plan, and also to enquire if you received a letter at Bath, in answer to your most kind one; for as your ladyship did not mark your direction there, I was obliged to direct mine to the post-office, Bath, and I hope it has reached you. It is the fear that this has not been the case that makes me trouble you at present, when I am little fitted to write to so agreeable a correspondent, for I have been forbidden to write or read much, as I have been much affected with headache. I hope my head will not go wrong, for it is that must give its best direction and worthy exercise to the intellect.

I have met of late with three admirable men, who, I think, have seized on the very vital principle of the Gospel, and whose conversation has deepened the sense I was beginning to entertain of the glorious privilege of being a Christian, and unto what a blessed state of liberty and light and love it does, even at the present, introduce the faithful follower of Christ, and how prepared we should be to sell all to serve such a Master. How faint is language to express the deep-toned feelings of the heart, to which God has manifested Himself in His adorable perfections, as exemplified in our Lord and Saviour Christ, and how should the heart be pure and vigilant and devoted which seeks to invite the habitation of God in it by His spirit. I hope Mr. Woodward is well, and that you see him often. He is the man amongst the religious world, as it is improperly called, that I esteem the most, and I think whose conversation never fails to impart pleasure and edification. Give my affectionate remembrance to him and to Miss Darby. If you favour me at any time with a few lines it will be a great favour, and received with all gratitude

By your obliged friend,
JAMES DUNN.

Brighton, October 9th, 1837.

MY DEAR LADY OSBORNE,—The enclosed came to me a few days ago, and I now send it to you though little worth the carriage, except as a proof that I was not insensible to the great kindness of your letter to me. I do look forward with great pleasure to holding some conferences with you on the most important interests, for I am sure you will be a candid disputant, and, what is more, a sincere lover of the truth. My late indisposition has given a deeper interest to every question connected in any degree with our salvation, and there are some on which I eagerly seek discussion with everyone whom I think in earnest. I came here for change of air, and I feel somewhat recruited by it. I sometimes wish for a little more strength that I may be enabled to finish some essays on the epistles of S. Paul, upon which I have laboured for some years past ; but this is but the dictates of self love which prompts the thought that I could be of use to the Church when the All-wise Disposer thinks otherwise by denying that health to me. I hope you will write to me when you are at leisure, and believe me, my dear madam,

Your obliged and grateful friend,

JAMES DUNN.

17, Chester Terrace, November 17, 1837.

MY DEAR LADY OSBORNE,—I have been kept very busy for this fortnight past making sermons to preach for a sick friend, and this is now by disuse become so heavy a task that I could not sooner answer your most kind letter. But I need not apologise, for you cannot suppose it could be from neglect. If there was nothing left in me but self-love that alone must strongly incline me to cultivate so accomplished and so flattering a correspondent. Not, my good Lady, that I expect to hold very long the same place in your estimation

that I do at present. It seems to me that your besetting sin
is the idolatry of talent and of strong and decisive characters, to none of which qualities have I any claim. You have
told me that you never can be brought to the contemplative
life ; but let me ask do you include in this daily examination
in order to watch the state of your affections, thoughts, and
hopes. You would not condemn what the Psalmist recommends so often, "commune with thine own heart in thy
chamber and be still." I would say that you do not seem to
me sufficiently aware of the corruption of human nature, and
how fatally this would minister to that which the Gospel is
intended to destroy, our *self love.* You are, therefore, not
aware of the delusive mists which it casts around the finest
understanding—giving false colours and forms to things
which we once saw in a very different light. You will,
therefore, soon tire of my repetition of a few simple truths
on which I live. You will mix freely with the wise and
prudent in this world's wisdom, and must grow to distaste
the simple truth which is known to babes and sucklings.
Did you ever read the admirable letter sent to Fénélon when
he was appointed tutor to the French Princess, from his old
friend who was himself in high esteem with all the eminent
personages of his time. Yet to this devoted and most humble
of Bishops he writes:—" A more than ordinary degree of
grace, and an uncommon portion of faith, is necessary to
resist the strong and seducing temptations you will meet
with. The dark mists which cloud the moral atmosphere of
a court are capable of obscuring the plainest and most evident
truths. It is not necessary to remain there long before we
learn to consider as unnatural and excessive those very truths
which had been so often felt and so often acknowledged
when they had been meditated at the foot of the cross. The
most established duties of life become gradually doubtful ;
a thousand occasions will occur in which prudence and even

benevolence will seem to dictate that something must be
conceded to the world.　Truly, sir, your post is a dangerous one.　Confess that it will be a difficult task, and require
a consummate virtue to resist such temptation.　If ever the
study and meditation of the sacred witness have been needful to you, they are so now in an especial manner." You
will not regret these admonitions which were thought needful
even for a Fénélon.　I do not wonder you were captivated
by ——, he is so unaffected with all his cleverness, and so
playful with all his knowledge.　I assure you when I com-
pare my knowledge with his I seem like a little cock boat
beside a man-of-war.　But still allow me in the confidence
of friendship to speak the whole truth.　I do not think him
a wise man either as to temporal or spiritual wisdom.　The
morning I met him at your rooms, he seemed to me to in-
dulge in unchristian bitterness against those who are called
the religious world, among whom are all my friends, and
whom I know to be honest, and amiable, and pious men,
though they have often dealt very hard measure to me ;
yet I considered it was always, and must ever be, that men
will think the truth they hold as the very essence of salvation, and of course condemn those who differ too severely ;
but we should look on all this as one who inhabits the
" Sapientum templa Serena ;" and he openly speaks his
opinion against establishments in a way which I think
scarcely consistent . . . .　Therefore I fear if I were
at his dinners I should not support many of his sentiments.
But I admit that he is an honest and assuredly a highly
gifted man, and probably of personal piety though he would
object to my notion of Christian devotion.　I am sorry to
say I have not yet read the sermons, for this long illness
sadly interrupted me ; but I shall do so before I write to
you again, for I feel that without doing so I am not qualified
to form a judgment. . . .　I must conclude at present,

though I had many things to say about Ireland ; but of this
I hope to talk with you when you come to London. I have
never been at Woolwich since I had the pleasure of seeing
you there, and you must when you come introduce me there
again. I assure you it is seldom I meet with such a cordial
reception as from that excellent family ; and now, my good
lady, please to pardon my freedom, and be assured that I
am your truly obliged,

And affectionate friend,

J. DUNN.

Pray remember me affectionately to the Woodwards.

MY DEAR LADY OSBORNE,—I hoped to have paid my respects to you this day, but I have a sore throat which made
me fearful of such a drizzling day.

I wish you could come to Mr. Scott's lecture to-morrow
at 3 o'clock, at Exeter Hall. It is on a noble subject, on
the various ways of God's revealing himself to his creatures;
which I have no doubt he will treat in a most Catholic spirit.
I had a long and very gracious visit from Mr. Bulwer to-day,
and I must say he is a very interesting personage, and seems
able and willing to discuss all subjects with freedom and
fairness. You may suppose one of the subjects discussed
was your Ladyship. His countenance denoted great sensibility, and his voice is sweet and expressive, altogether I
liked his visit exceedingly. You must never expect of me
to do any one any good, for I never know how to set about
it. Is it not better that I should be willing to see and to
receive all good from any who possess it.

Yours, my dear Lady Osborne,

Very truly,

JAMES DUNN.

12 Priory Street, August 13th, 1838.

My very dear Friend,—I must put you to the expense of postage, though for a few lines to tell you why I cannot write more. Believe me that I feel I return your friendship with a cordiality and an intensity I have seldom felt for any one, and certainly I never felt so deep an interest for any one on the same acquaintance. But I am positively forbidden to write, and to tell you the whole truth I have been going down hill ever since I came here. Dr. Barrow, our chief doctor here, wishes me now to consult other physicians in London, and therefore I shall leave this on Wednesday morning, and hope to reach London by Thursday night, and perhaps you may not have left it before that. What a pleasure and what a cheer to me to hold a little further converse with you, to which my present circumstances would add much of interest. My own view of my case is that I shall not recover, for the Doctor assures me disease must have been growing for at least a year, and this under the most temperate diet, and regular exercise. So that I do not see how it can be removed without such severe remedies as I am little fitted to bear. But oh! my dear friend would that I could express to you the feelings of confidence, the entire peace I now feel, not from my own deservings, but from the unspeakable, inexhaustible love and mercy of my Heavenly Father, whose adorable perfections it has been my delight to contemplate, and that my happiest hours have been in my latter years, those in which I drew nigh unto Him in prayer. If I do not see you, you will I know not fail to write and when at home I can get an amanuensis to help out my writing.

You have my prayers and my blessings, my very dear friend for you and yours.

J. Dunn.

My dear Lady Osborne,—I am afraid I shall not be able to join your party at Shooters Hill on Friday, for in fact my side is so sore from all the leeches applied to it yesterday, and my doctor further insists I must undergo his prescriptions for this whole week, that I suppose I must stay at home as long as he pleases to annoy me. I suppose you will be ready to say, well we have escaped a sermon by this. I assure you however, that I never mean to lecture in our conversations, but only to discuss. The questions you have to decide as to your path in your Christian pilgrimage, are very difficult ones, and I am not a master in Israel to know these things. I suspect your present life does not elevate you, but then it is better far, than being at the head of a religious sect where you

> " Like Cato give your little Senate laws,
> And sit attentive to your own applause."

I have just been reading to the servants, John viii. 31–36. These verses are worth considering. The case of the servant is where all our tastes are one way, but from duty and the hope of reward we do his word, but the freedom with which the son makes free is the congeniality of our tastes with his by the extinction of the opposite tastes, and the feeling that we are now in our own element, and in the region of ever-lastingness. Do not let the world or the devil persuade you that this is unattainable here below, for if so then the pillared firmament is rottenness, and earth's base built on stubble, all mental and moral excellence is only working its way painfully into chaos and darkness; but if there be any such thing as truth in the world, if we are not to renounce the common hope of all good men, then am I convinced that all are wrong, fatally wrong, who do not make their relation to

the Father of all, and the fountain of all good, and the duty
and affection which belong to him, the primary object and
pursuit, and the subject of daily, serious and anxious enquiry
and effort, and in this I am confirmed, not by the opinions
of Christian devotees, but by the free confession of every
moral and metaphysical writer, and even by the judgment of
Mr. Hume himself. Excuse this being so like a sermon, and
make your utmost allowance for one who is

Your truly attached friend,

JAMES DUNN.

17, Chester Terrace, Regent's Park, 1838.

MY VERY DEAR FRIEND,—It seems to me that my strength
declines daily, and pray for me that my passage may be
smoothed by the comforts of grace and entire resignation of
spirit; and believe me, my dear friend, that I pray for you
heartily that you may be kept from the delusions of this evil
world. Watch and pray yourself that you may not be en-
tangled in its spirit, but that you may be enlightened to see
its real evil that makes its enmity with God, and that He
will by His grace and providence lead you even through
severe trials to be purified from all its evil and brought
under the full and sweet influences of heavenly love. Cling
to that Saviour who came to seek and to save us, that you
may plead His promise, that " whoso cometh unto Him He
will in no wise cast out," for this is now my hope and my
comfort. I am not able to say much to-day, but believe me
you have the fervent blessing of a dying friend that Christ
may lead you amongst His flock, and bring you into eternity
in His own likeness; nor is your dear daughter forgotten in
the prayer of your ever affectionate friend,

JAMES DUNN.

" The following letter is inserted to point out how remark-

ably well-behaved a vast assembly of Irish may be when
the circumstances of the occasion do not lend themselves to
the designs of agitators, and the thorough way in which
Lady Osborne identified herself with the honour of her
adopted country, and thought of others rather than of herself.
She would often mention with delight that when repairs
were going on at her residence, ladders were left by which
at any hour of the night the house might have been entered
and yet 'no one dreamed of fear.'

Bishop Sandes makes one mistake; the crowd was composed of all classes and not of one only, though he speaks as
if such were the case.

The fact is, the Irish are a most courteous, amiable,
delightful people, when not subjected to almost irresistible
bad influences, and practised upon by selfish agitators. The
entertainments provided after an eighteen years' minority
were a dance, called in the language of the country a
' long dance,' which was in costume, a dinner to the tenants,
their wives, and a son and daughter of each to the number
of 1,165 persons, in a huge tent, and at night fireworks."

Waterford, 11th July, 1839.

MY DEAR LADY OSBORNE,—I have written to the Ecclesiastical Commissioners about the churchyard of Killaloan,
and urged them to adopt the judicious advice of your ladyship and Miss Osborne.

You must be delighted, as I am, at this wet weather, for
enhancing by contrast the sunny days by which you were
last week favoured.

You are not pleased at the newspapers praising the givers
of your fête more than they do the guests. Perhaps the
editors felt that landlords more stand in need of being
stimulated to benevolence than the tenantry to gratitude, by
holding out to them good examples for their imitation; but

no newspaper accounts could add importance to the unprecedented fact of thirty thousand peasants assembled at a merry making, full of gaiety, and ranging uncontrolled through flower-gardens and drawing-rooms without exhibiting any breach of decorum, and without so much as trampling on a flower.

I do not understand my exact position here, and whether I shall have occasion for a school mistress, but I am much obliged by your letting me know where to get one.

Mrs. Sandes and my daughters look forward with much expectation to the honour of being known to you and Miss Osborne.

I remain, your obliged faithful servant,

STEPHEN CASHEL.

"The subject of National Education was one that was taken up by Lady Osborne with all the energy and perseverance that were amongst her characteristics, and the following letter from Lord Lansdowne, alludes to that as well as the subject of the foregoing letter. Lord Lansdowne points out the truth, that the National system of education, while giving an excellent secular education, does not interfere with the religion the parents and their delegates choose to impart to their children."

London, July 18th.

DEAR LADY OSBORNE,—I had, before receiving your kind letter, read with great pleasure in the newspapers some account of the proceedings on an occasion which must have been so deeply interesting to you, as the celebration of your daughter's birthday and majority. The vice of the Irish is certainly not ingratitude for benefits of which they are made duly sensible; and I was delighted to observe the genuine warmth of heart which appears to have been displayed on this occasion, and which must have more than repaid you for the exertions of many years. I wish that such an interchange of sentiment between the upper and lower classes—between those who own and those who cultivate the soil was more frequent, and their mutual welfare felt to be what it certainly is, an object equally desirable to all.

You will perceive that I have been engaged in a new battle on the subject of National Education on English ground. We have been able to accomplish very little for the present, but little is the end of the wedge which will drive at last; and I have reason to hope another year will convince most churchmen that our proceedings are as safe in a religious as they are beneficial in any other point of view.

I got a glimpse of the Archbishop of Dublin on his way through London, and shall be anxious to hear the report of his proceedings as a traveller—a calling quite new to him I believe hitherto—as well as to his family, who seemed enchanted with the prospect. Believe me, dear Lady Osborne,

Ever, your sincere and faithful servant,

LANSDOWNE.

Let me beg you to present my best regards and congratulations to your daughter.

" The following letter arose from the Lord Lieutenant of that time being struck by the tone of earnestness with which Lady Osborne vindicated the reputation of some tenants which had been assailed by a portion of the press. Lord Ebrington's letter led to an acquaintance with Lady Osborne, and a visit to her while travelling in the south of Ireland; his second letter again proves how much she cared for the impression made by others in their own favour.

" On the occasion of the visit of His Excellency, instead of the vehement manifestation of party feelings evidenced against Lord Normanby, his predecessor, the gentry who did so having forgotten that he represented the Queen, they all, without distinction of political opinions, met Lord Ebrington with the greatest alacrity to testify their respect for his office and extreme personal worth. The particular circumstance referred to in the second letter not being detailed is not remembered."

Phœnix Park, August 23rd, 1839.

MADAM,—Mr. Drummond has shown me your ladyship's letter of the 17th, and I cannot help expressing with my own pen the gratification afforded me, as well by your refutation of the charge made by a portion of the press against Miss Osborne's tenantry, with reference to the murder of ————, as to the valuable testimony borne by one so well qualified to judge as yourself, to the general improvement both of the state of the country and the habits of the people in your neighbourhood.

I fear that I shall have left Dublin before your ladyship is likely to be passing through on your way to the Continent, but I hope at no very distant time to have the pleasure of assuring you in person of the respect and esteem with which I beg to subscribe myself

Your Ladyship's faithful and obedient servant,

EBRINGTON.

Lady Osborne.

Castle Hill, October 17, 1839.

MY DEAR MADAM,—I am very sorry to find from your letter to Captain Romilly that you have felt any annoyance from what took place respecting the Clonmel addresses, as I can truly assure you that there is nothing in that or any matter connected with my visit to Newtown Anner that has been other than a source of gratification to me. Indeed I

must be very unreasonable if it were not so, as whilst I had
the good fortune of receiving an unexpected tribute of respect from political opponents, and have in the end and on a
fair consideration of the circumstances had full justice done
to my conduct by those to whom, as the tried and staunch
supporter of Government, I should have been truly sorry to
have given anything like an appearance of slight.

Your ladyship's indulgence will, I trust, pardon me for
troubling you with this; and I cannot do so without availing
myself of the opportunity which it affords me of renewing
my thanks to yourself and Miss Osborne for your most
agreeable hospitality.

I am, with much respect and esteem, your ladyship's very
faithful and obedient,

EBRINGTON.

Lady Osborne.

" Lord Lytton has very kindly permitted the insertion of
two of his notes, as they contain in one a most beautiful
tribute to the nature of maternal love, and in the other a
compliment to Lady Osborne as true as it is gracefully put."

Charles-street, Sunday.

DEAR LADY OSBORNE,—I am extremely sorry to hear you
are likely to suffer so severe a loss. All that I have met in
the world of sympathy, generosity, and faithful friendship,
is identified with the name of mother; and the thought of
that loss seems to me like the taking away of the candle
from a child, who is terrified in the dark. It is a protection
and a safety gone.

A dreary solitude commenced, and all we have left is to
wish the night well gone, and the morrow come.

But you, I know, have other friends and ties, and I trust

N 2

that a thousand hopes will console you if doomed to the one privation.

I am much flattered by Mr. Dunn's kind opinion, and I am already strongly impressed with the charm of his character.

Believe me, my dear Lady Osborne, ever yours,

E. L. BULWER.

(*Another.*)

Pardon me if I remind you, that in order to show us the perfection of modesty, you forgot what no one else ever will do, the name of Catherine Osborne.

" It is well worthy of consideration in these latter days, that the intellectual giant who wrote the foregoing beautiful little message of condolence, between thirty and forty years ago, startled ' the upper ten thousand' with the trumpet tones, ' the schoolmaster is abroad.'

" In a work on England, he went on to say that the classes below them were treading on their heels with a speed and vigour that threatened to leave them behind nowhere, and that unless every nerve were strained they could not keep ahead. In those days he belonged to the so-called Liberals, but now he has quitted the ' Destructives,' and joined the ranks of those whose very designation bespeaks an approximation to that state attained at the goal to which all are hastening, no less a one than eternity.

" If by the term ' Liberal,' a perpetual overthrow of every institution be meant, this implies unmixed evil in the gradual arrangements of Providence ; argues a most restless and uncomfortable introduction into an existence of rest, and is unsuited to the dignity that should accompany advancing years; besides, advancing into chaos is not progress, but retrogression; a ministerial reputation such as that of the Huns and Vandals is not to be desired."

" The following letter was written by Dr. Dickinson, afterwards Bishop of Meath, the valued friend of Archbishop Whately."

Friday.

MADAM,—I was prevented, partly by illness, and partly by Easter occupations, from seeing Mr. Butler as speedily as I wished, but I have now had a long interview with him, and feel your ladyship only did him justice in the high praise you gave him.   There can be no doubt of his talents, and I think there ought to be as little of his candour and good sense; indeed I have conversed with few whom, on a short acquaintance, I have taken such a fancy to.   I told him I should be most happy to see him whenever he called, and that I should do everything in my power to facilitate his ordination.   My curate seems now recovering, contrary to my expectations, therefore I could say nothing upon that matter.   I hope, however, I have given him assistance in a far superior way.

I had occasion to call on the Provost to-day.   I found him deliberating about the appointment of a professor of moral philosophy, to which the college would attach a salary, and also a small parish, now vacant.   He spoke highly of Mr. Butler, when I joined him *most warmly*.   He said his not being ordained was an obstacle.   I promised to endeavour to have this removed, and I wrote off to the Archbishop instantly on the subject.   I think I have shewn his Grace that it may be done without any objectionable irregularity.

To-morrow a Board will be held in college to decide.   I have gone to the Senior Fellows, whom I felt I might influence, to state my impression of Mr. Butler. I should not have felt myself warranted in doing this on my short acquaintance with Mr. Butler, however favourable my impression of him, but your ladyship's testimony in his favour I feel justified me fully. I shall regret that I have no prospect of him as a curate, but I shall rejoice if he is taken away to so much better a purpose, and indeed from the promises made to me I anticipate his appointment. I am sure the good Archbishop will be pleased by the arrangement. I shall take the liberty of sending your ladyship, in a day or two, a copy of the Archbishop's answer to the lay remonstrants, which I dare say you will admire as much as I do. As a bishop, he could not but express censure of the mode in which signatures were attached to that document. If Christianity be true, or supposing it false, if the Archbishop thinks it true, he is bound to object to irreverent and thoughtless proceedings in so solemn a matter as prayer. The remonstrants published their letter to the Archbishop before it was sent to his Grace. They apologized for this (or one of them did), but they have now had the Archbishop's answer in their hands for three weeks, and this they have not published. This is very unintelligible. I suppose I shall escape this time, as the Archbishop happens to be in England; but indeed I am uncertain, considering what insincerity has been exercised. Not that I care for this; for when I act conscientiously I must not fear censure; and when my conscience is in agreement with such a heart and such a soul as are possessed by the Archbishop, I feel tolerable confidence that my conscience cannot be very desperately astray.

I am, madam,

Your obedient humble servant,

CHARLES DICKINSON.

The Lady Osborne.

May 22nd.

Madam,— The Archbishop has enclosed to me to forward to your ladyship the letters which I now send.

In a letter lately from his Grace, he writes that one of the witnesses examined before the Education Committee said the schools had all diseases (the Roman Catholic, the plague; the Protestant Church, the lethargy; the Presbyterians, the jaundice; and the Arians, the palsy). He adds, "There is much truth in this; and the same may be said of all human communities and assemblies. In Parliament, for instance, the Tories have a putrid fever, the Whigs a tertian ague, and the Radicals a brain fever. But it is providentially ordered that different diseases check one another, and so the world goes on. Our schools are hospitals, in which there is one additional advantage above literal hospitals, that they have a panacea suited to all diseases alike, a knowledge of Gospel history, and general mental cultivation. If in proportion as these extend, Romanism gains ground, that I must admit will be a strong presumption that it is true."

I think both parts of what is implied in this sentence are quite true. It seems to be by a system of evils counteracting each other that the world of human beings has been chiefly managed, and this ought to make us bear with greater patience those evils which we discern in others. The quiet-minded and the energetic have each their advantages, while each counteracts the disadvantages belonging to the other. The latter part of the Archbishop's sentence has been opposed by many of the witnesses, more especially I believe ————, who is afraid of mental cultivation. If I thought this unfriendly to the Christian religion, I should be full of suspicion that this religion was not true, for surely mental cultivation cannot be unfriendly to the promotion of truth.

It is astonishing to me upon what minute points prejudice

can fix its gaze, while the great fact is wholly overlooked
that the country is sunk in the depths of ignorance and superstition.   To withhold all instruction, because there is some
ignorance which you have not the power to remove, is like
refusing to apply salves to some wretched Lazarus, because
he has some internal disease which at present he will not
accept a cure of.

Woodward now admits that if the system should continue,
the Protestant clergy ought to take a part in it.   I do not at
all despair of his ultimately coming round.

Has your ladyship seen Baptist Noel's " Tour in Ireland"?
It contains a controversy, evidently with Mr. Daly, on the
subject of the National System, well and rationally managed.
The book contains a good deal worth perusal, though he is
certainly mistaken as to many facts.   I do not know whether you have yet seen the account of an expedition to New
Holland, edited by Lady Mary Fox.   It will richly repay
your perusal.

I am, madam,

Your Ladyship's humble and obedient servant,

CHARLES DICKINSON.

" The following letter was written by a son of the Rev.
Henry Woodward.   He was well known as the English
Chaplain at Rome.   His views were very High Church,
unlike those of his father.   The estimation in which he was
held was very great indeed.   His brother, the Dean of Down,
authorized its publication."

11, Kildare-street, May 9th, 1837.

MY DEAR LADY OSBORNE,—Having heard that you were
angry with me for my evidence before the Committee on
Education, I feel a strong temptation to write to you on the
subject.   I should feel much obliged by your letting me

know anything that struck you as particularly objectionable. The examination which rigidly confines one to answering questions, is not always the best way of eliciting one's whole views on any subject. In my own case I feel sadly hampered by such a restriction. I wished for an opportunity of speaking more fully than I did on several points, and can easily imagine that several of my answers may seem to require explanation; such explanations I should be most happy to give you, if you thought it worth your while to wish for it. In the meantime allow me to submit to your consideration some of my objections to the whole system, as drawn out in the course of my examination.

· The principal ones were these two. First, that the system gives a legal establishment to Popery, Unitarianism, and in fact any religious error that may happen to prevail: secondly, that it has a tendency, I think a strong one, to promote infidelity.

1. That the National Board is, in the strict sense of the word, an establishment of the various forms of religious error that may be in the country, I affirm, because it is a State provision for the teaching of them; one of the two objects of the institution, as recommended by the Committee of 1828, and expressed in Lord Stanley's letter, is to afford such separate religious education as may accord with the tenets of the different denominations. The institution is maintained at the expense of the State, and to give religious instruction at the expense of the State appears to me plainly to involve the principle of an establishment. It is true the teachers are not paid, but the proper question is as to the fact and purpose of the endowment, and not the precise mode in which the money is applied. Building churches at the public expense is as complete a recognition of the principle of an establishment as the payment of the clergy. I know it is said that the system does nothing more than pro-

vide for the fair exercise of liberty of conscience. The assertion is not true. Liberty of conscience would be effectually provided for by securing that the children should not be compelled to receive religious instruction which they did not approve. But more is done than this; direct provision is made for their receiving such instructions as they or their parents do approve. A school will not be founded or supported by the Board unless this object is secured. It is "*required*" as one of the conditions on which aid and patronage is granted, and you could not to-morrow obtain assistance towards establishing a school without entering into an express stipulation, not merely that you would not interfere with the religious principles of the children, but that you would give your school-house at stated times to the priest for the avowed purpose of teaching Popery, or (if you lived in certain districts, and large ones too, of the north of Ireland) to the Unitarian minister for the avowed purpose of teaching the children to deny the Lord that bought them. If all this is not in principle an establishment of Popery and Unitarianism, that is, a State provision for the teaching of them, I know not what could be so denominated; and if so, allow me to ask whether the system can be right, should you enter into the letter of the stipulation that I have mentioned?

2. The system is calculated to produce infidelity, for this reason, that it places all forms of religion on an equal footing. Unitarianism is treated as if equally true with Christianity, Popery with Protestantism ; equal privileges are allowed to the ministers of each, equal facilities afforded to their respective ministrations. But the main point is not the fact of this being done, but the grounds on which this is done. It is not done on the ground of irresistible necessity. Necessity will justify anything; and persons who fancied themselves compelled to teach what was false, might at the same time bear their testimony to the truth, and lament the

circumstances that prevented its full course. No such plea is set up by the National Board or its founders.

The arrangement that I am objecting to are adopted on the express grounds of the *importance of religion*. They are the measures provided by Lord Stanley by which the " interests of religion" are to be secured. They are appealed to by the Commissioners as a proof that they afford the " benefits of religious instruction" (First Report) to the children, and that they are alive to the importance of religion as an " essential part of education" (Third Report). Not the slightest intimation is given that one form of religion is better than another. Equal solicitude is shown for the teaching of all ; equal " care is taken that the ministers of God's word"!!! (First Report) should have access to the schools. Unitarianism is a " benefit" to be as sedulously provided as Christianity, and the teaching of it as effectually guards the interests of religion, " and as fully attests a sense of its importance." Now all this appears to me sheer infidelity. I do not mean that everyone is an infidel who takes part in the proceedings of the Board, but I cannot the least comprehend such views except as held by an infidel. I can see no meaning or common sense in them otherwise, for they imply that all forms of religion are equally true (that is, equally untrue), or at least that the differences between them are of no importance, and I would ask what effect such a system can have on the mass of the population among whom it is in operation? I mean, what is its natural and intrinsic tendency? for its effects may be warded off by the priests converting it into an engine of Popery. Is it not a promulgation on the part of the Legislature, that the differences between the different sects are points not worth contending about, and that what alone is of importance in religion is held by all? And what can be the effect of such a principle so sanctioned, and that not merely as an abstract speculation, but acted on and exhibited in practical operation, except to make the people equally indifferent, and thus bring all religion into contempt?

To this charge which I bring of infidelity against the whole principle of the National Board, I have heard only one answer, and that since I returned from London. It is this, that religion in the documents to which I have referred is spoken of as opposed to Atheism, and consequently that no undervaluing of the differences among professing Christians is implied, since any form of religion must be considered a "benefit" when compared with it. Admitting this reply for a moment, the system is still liable to my first objection, that of directly taking a part in the teaching of awful religious error. It would be better to leave the people to their chance of becoming Atheists than to do this. But really the reply cannot stand an instant, for the people are not Atheists, nor will any sane man say that they are in such danger of becoming Atheists that it is a "benefit" to secure their being Unitarians, or that there is a call on the Government to make them Unitarians; or, to speak with strict fairness, to take measures that they shall be so brought up. These are my principal objections to the National System of Education. I have others, but I dwell on these, because they seem to me too much lost sight of by many of the opponents of the system. They think (or most of them) that everything is gained if the Bible is introduced into the schools.

With a vast deal that is said on this subject I by no means concur. Much of it is extravagant and unreasonable, and much of it (to me) perfectly unintelligible. You will not, therefore, class me with those who think it a duty to give the children free access to the *whole Bible at all times,* and yet without allowing this unrestricted liberty to interfere with the proper quantum or orderly conducting of their instruction in other things. This principle has been propunded by able men as a " sine qua non" in any system of education that Protestants could in conscience accept. In my humble apprehension it is downright absolute nonsense, and I am convinced that from the commencement the Protestant party took up a wrong and a weak position in resting their oppotion so exclusively as they have done on the conduct of the Government and of the Board in regard of the use of the Scriptures, not that I do not think that bad enough. But I think that if the Scriptures were placed in the hands of every child in Ireland, still on the grounds I have stated the whole system would be one of horrible impiety. I will suppose the case of a school in which the system is in full operation, with a clergyman of the Church of England teaching Christianity, a priest teaching idolatry, and a Unitarian minister teaching blasphemy, and I will ask whether anyone who loved Christ and loved souls, and thought the Bible was not a fable, could look on such an exhibition with any feelings but those of unmingled pain. What then must be the state of that person who can look on it with pleasure, and actually boast of it as effected by him from his anxiety about religion? I will not pronounce judgment upon others whose minds may be differently constructed from my own, or whose clearness of apprehension may be dimmed by party prejudices. But in my own case I will say that such a state of feeling would be separated by a very narrow interval from infidelity. I trust that you will excuse the freedom with which I have expressed myself, and that you will believe me

Most truly yours,

F. B. WOODWARD.

" The arrangement of Archbishop Whately's letters was
extremely difficult, so the plan adopted has been to put first
the notes that must have been the earliest, then the imperfect
ones and the extracts, and those dated last. Before Lady
Osborne's correspondence began she had met his Grace at
the house of a relation of hers and held an argument with
him that disinclined her to appreciate him, but later and on
more perfect acquaintance, no one held him in greater
reverence for his goodness and masterly powers of mind. The
imperfect letters are supposed to be the remnants of those
published in Miss Whately's life of her father."

" The Blue Book containing the evidence given before a
Committee of the House of Lords as the result of the follow-
ing communications, bears ample testimony to the praise
Lady Osborne received for giving it being well merited.

The National system of education never had a warmer
friend to it on the ground of its being the best that was
feasible in Ireland than she was, nor one that devoted more
care and valuable time to the working thereof; and as a proof
how open to conviction she was, she had at first been
strongly against it, and was brought round to it by the
arguments she had listened to against it at a monster meeting held in Exeter Hall to oppose the system."

Committee Rooms, 1st June, 1839.

MY DEAR MADAM,—I have heard from Colonel Phipps that
he does not wish to be examined, and Mr. Archdall, though I
have never seen him, appears to be of the same mind. Lord
Lansdowne is expressing great regret to lose such valuable
testimony as that concerning your schools. " Could not,"
said he, Lady O. come and give the evidence herself ? At
least if she cannot, name anyone who can and will do so,
thoroughly and fairly. Of course, said he, we would not

Yrs truly
R. Dublin

press her if it did violence to her feelings, but if *she would
consent it would be very desirable.* So I consented at his
and Lord Duncannon's earnest desire to write and beg your
consent. Excuse haste, and believe me,

Very truly yours,

RD. DUBLIN.

Monday.

MY DEAR MADAM,—I am just come from Southend, to
which I shall return in two days to bring back my wife and
children, who are much the better for the sea.

I am glad to see in your letter that you would rather have
been glad of finding it a *duty* to the public to come to
London; for I think you will now perceive from my last that
you are placed in that predicament now.

What you say about having the advantage of having ladies
to speak for one, is very true and very much to the purpose
of your being examined before the Committee.

In great haste, yours very truly,

RD. DUBLIN.

Monday, Park House.

MY DEAR MADAM,—Your letter which I received yesterday
(I do not know how) and that of to-day are just what I would
have wished a sister of my own to write. It was wholly
Lord Lansdowne's suggestion that you should come, but on
his applying to me it had my *fullest* approval.

Colonel Phipps writes me word that there are agents
going about to collect evidence *against* the schools, and he
presumes we have counter-agents, but we have not, only our
own regular inspectors. We disdain sending out people to
collect all they can on one side, suppressing all on the other.
Your evidence will be very valuable, so is Mr. Noel's and
that of some other unbiased persons; but I would not leave

the decision to be drawn wholly from the adverse witnesses; their bigotry, unfairness, and absurdity are enough to ruin any but a very good cause. One of them, however, gave fair and very favourable testimony as to many of the schools, to the great displeasure of his employer—" I called thee to curse mine enemies."

I presume you will receive regular notice to attend, and probably also a private letter from Lord Lansdowne. I suppose you know that all witnesses summoned may claim their expenses. Ever, my dear madam, in great haste,

Yours, very truly,
R. D.

P.S.—I have ordered to have sent to your ladyship a letter from Mr. Senior, whose authority was (seemingly) appealed to in the House of Commons, as approving of the Poor Law Bill; you will see in the first sentence that the reverse is the fact, and it may be as well to insert part of it in the papers.

Friday Night.

My dear Madam,—I believe I omitted in my hurried note of yesterday to add that I did not give any hint of sending for you, but it was wholly Lord Lansdowne's own idea, backed by Lord Duncannon, who observed on the almost impossibility of summoning to any good purpose either Colonel Phipps, or Mr. Archdall, or Mr. Butler; and Lord Lansdowne spoke of the evidence, which, judging from your letters, he felt assured you could give, as that it would be important to have, and to have *well* given, as he thought you could give it.

Mr. B. Noel was examined to-day and was a model of mild intrepidity, candour, and good sense.

To-morrow morning I go to Southend for two days where my family are, to the great benefit, I can thankfully say, of their health. Ever, my dear madam,

Yours very sincerely,

RD. DUBLIN.

Park House, Brompton.

MY DEAR MADAM,—Dr. Cooke, of Belfast, is expected to be before the Lords' Committee next Tuesday; and it has been thought important that he should be immediately followed by two or three witnesses who are prepared to prove him as honest a man as any on the cards when all the kings are out; that is the reason of your summons not being immediate. On Thursday, 22nd instant, Mrs. Whately will go to Rugby to our friends the Arnolds, and I shall follow in a day or two to hold a confirmation of the boys there the Tuesday or Wednesday following. We shall return, and I shall try to contrive that your examination may come on on the 29th or 30th.

Lord Lansdowne, and what is perhaps more, Mrs. Whately were as much pleased with the tone of your letters as you or I could have wished. I would give two male friends to the cause (though a scarce commodity) for another such female.

I have been revising the evidence I gave last week before the Commons' Committee. in which Serjeant —— came off decidedly second best in his attacks on me; but I have so little of the organ of combativeness, that even when sophistry is the most triumphantly refuted, the feeling of disgust gives me more pain than the triumph pleasure. Ever, my dear madam,

Very truly yours,

RD. DUBLIN.

Have you yet seen Mrs. Whately's edition of Mrs. Richard Trench's little book on education (Parker, Strand.)

MY DEAR MADAM,—The paper you last sent me over from
Mr. ——— has *very greatly* interested Lord Lansdowne,
and he wishes to know whether it would not be better to
send for Mr. ———, or for the gentleman (un-named) who
he says can attest all that he says, or for both, or for any
other gentleman well acquainted with the working of the
system in that district. Pray let me know which of these
you think right to come, and they will be regularly moved
for.

Yours, dear madam very truly,
Rd. DUBLIN.

P. S.—Many thanks for the paper just received.

MY DEAR MADAM,—You must not object to my sometimes
commissioning Dr. Dickinson to convey a message to you;
if you knew how many letters I have to read and write
(sometimes as many as sixteen in a day) you would not
wonder at any expedient resorted to to save time. But I
do not show your ladyship's letters to him, I only *tell him* to
say so and so. At the same time I must remark that if there
were any need for it, I should not scruple to expose *your*
mind (I do not say everybody's) unveiled to such a candid
judge as he is. I am sure he will always view with the same
eyes that I do all the working's of an ingenuous mind. The
more you are known to each other the better you will agree.
I will look after Lord Bexley.

Mr. ——— is a well meaning man but (between ourselves)
not very discreet. I never answer attacks on myself, nor
engage in any controversy, but I do not profess to throw any

impediment or raise any objection to others doing so. I only beg them (if they consult me about it) to be cool and cautious lest they do harm instead of good to the cause.

Ever, my dear madam, yours most truly,

RD. DUBLIN.

I almost forgot to say that I shall be very glad to see your ladyship, and really think you may do good to the public as as well as give gratification to us.

Park-avenue, Bromptom, Tuesday.

MY DEAR MADAM,—I have seen Lord Bexley, but he has not yet paid a visit to our Committee. There is indeed but dull work there at present, but next week I trust we shall have something more profitable.

I have called on Colonel Phipps, but found him not within. If you knew Mr. Jessop as well as I do you would sympathize with my anxiety, and all but despair about him. There seems to be now a gleam of hope that he may recover. I never ordained a man who gave greater, if so great, promise of being a most exemplary and faithful fellow labourer. Could you not get the Tipperary papers to notice the " Strictures?" It is no party question. If due exertion and vigilance is used a little longer I have great hopes the ruin that was impending will blow over. In haste, my dear madam,

Yours very truly,

RD. DUBLIN.

Friday, half-past 3.

MY DEAR MADAM,—I have had the copy taken which I enclose. This is the first moment's leisure I have had since I rose; and I must not go to work again at other business till night.

Seen so little of me indeed! when you come to have some

o 2

faint conception of what a life of London business is, you
will be much surprised at having seen so *much* of me, more
in a week than my own relations and oldest friends in town
have in a month, except on indispensable business; and all
because of your being a stranger from such a remote region.

In haste, yours very truly,

RD. DUBLIN.

17th June.

MY DEAR MADAM,—I think you have good ground for
saying what you do of your own independence of party; at
any rate you have shown that you can dare to act for
yourself.

Pray let your bookseller in "the fifth town in Ireland"
get some copies of the Digest of Evidence. The Education
Board has a supply to dispose of at 2s.

I forget whether you ever saw that book of " Extracts from
the Archbishop of Dublin," which was published here last
winter. I found by chance, through a third person, the
author's name, almost a stranger to me personally. I understand he is in poor circumstances, so that if you could get it
known in London by ordering it, the sale of a few copies
would be a benefit to him.

Ever, my dear madam, yours very truly,

RD. DUBLIN.

P. S.—You are at liberty to shew the annexed postscript
at your discretion.

It is shameful no addresses on Queen Victoria's coming of
age came from Ireland! Could not some (from Protestants)
be got up in your parts.

" The above remark is curious, inasmuch as the fact speaks
volumes as to the Queen not having earned for herself
any want of loyalty."

" A postscript, to which letter the Editor knows not."

P. S.—That dissenter probably may have meant that he agreed with the High Churchmen in holding that we are *bound* to conform in every particular of Church government to whatever shall appear to have been the *practice of the earliest churches, &c.*, which the one party consider to have been Episcopacy, and the other Presbyterianism. According to the one therefore, it is *unchristian* to have Bishops; according to the other not to have them. I disagree with both, as I have said in my last volume. What do you say to Dr. Dodsworth's notions of fasting; I have been lately preaching on the subject.

A scrap with no reference.

This will do very well, and if sent along with a private note to the Editor, containing the real name and description it is not unlikely to be inserted.

The thing is just what the Poor Inquiry Commissioners recommended many years ago. " *Irish* landlords could support an indefinite number of paupers."

DEAR MISS OSBORNE,—I suspect that by asking for a passage out of my own works, you had a sly design of ascertaining *which I valued most ;* as some persons in making choice of one puppy out of a litter, take them all away, and then watch which one the mother first brings back.

However, I have thought it best to extract a passage *not yet published,* from a volume which, when it does appear, you are not so likely to read as some other of my works.

I have added a riddle (what is a lady's album without one ?) which deserves a place if any one ever did.

1. It makes all the difference whether you pursue a certain course *because* you judge it right, or judge it to be right *because you pursue it ;* whether you follow your

conscience as one follows a *guide*, or, *as one follows the horses* in a carriage, while he himself guides them according to his will.—*Elements of Logic*, Appendix No. 1, seventh edition.

2. What is that which was to-morrow and will be yesterday?

MY DEAR MADAM,—Thank you for your letter and enclosures, which I have no doubt we shall find a use for.

I think it likely that within half a year Mrs. Hill (and others) will wonder at herself for having listened to such an objection as you allude to, and will perceive that a person who could reconcile image-worship with the commandments as we have printed them would never be much at a loss to explain away *any* thing.

How strange it is that such confusion of thought and misapprehension should still prevail relative to books sanctioned by the Board ! Once for all, the *Board never* sanctions *any* book at all for the separate religious instruction of any denomination of children. It sanctions only such books as are employed in the joint-common education of the children of all denominations. The regulations only forbid the employment in separate religious instruction of any books *that* are not the recognized standard books of each respective Church or Sect, without the permission of *those members* of the Board who are of the same persuasion with the children for whom such books are designed. If, for instance, a clergyman of the Established Church wished to employ (no such case has occurred) any tract in the religious instruction of children of his own persuasion, he must obtain the permission of Dr. Sadlier and me. But the Bible, and the Prayer Book, and Catechism being authorized works of our Church we could not, if we wished it, restrict him from using. And so with the rest. But the *collective body* of Commissioners—the Board—have nothing at all to do with the matter. As I was looking over, preparatory to a new edition, my second series of Essays, I was forcibly struck with a passage (p. 20, l. 17, 3rd edit.) as coinciding with what Lord Bexley says of " my boldness."

I understand that the only obstacle now to Mr. ——'s taking duty in my diocese, indeed becoming curate of ——, is the state of his health, which I fear is likely to be at present an insuperable one. But were it otherwise, you could not surely, my dear madam, expect or wish that I should deal out a different measure of justice to the son of an influential man from what I would to the humblest curate ; and write to him spontaneously to announce that I had made a special retractation in his favor. If I were conscious of having annoyed —— (or his footman) I would instantly write to him to apologize and to offer compensation ; but as it is I imagine he would think much the worse of me. I am sure I should think much the worse of myself if I could stoop to make any such advances. I am almost sure you must have cast a hurried glance at the subject or else you do not yet understand.

Your very sincere friend,

RD. DUBLIN.

Thursday.

MY DEAR MADAM,—I was at the Board to-day and learned that an application had been made by you some time ago, which had been acceded to ; and that there is not now any communication of yours unanswered. If, however, there is any dispute about the appointment of a master in any school, that is a point in which the Board leaves the patron to decide, and does not interfere unless there is some violation of their rules. I will engage that you will always find applications from you favourably listened to.

There is a strong effort made to prejudice the court of Rome against the National schools ; but I have good hopes it will not succeed. I had some conversation on the subject at Brussels with the Pope's nuncio! Objections have been raised, among other things, to the little tract on evidences.

The Pope does not know, I suppose, of the infidel tracts (including *newspapers*) now so current in Ireland. And if so he is not so foolish as those Protestants (supposing them to be really believers) who cry out against men's shifting the grounds of *their belief from faith to reason, &c.*

My daughter, I am happy to say, derived benefit from the excursion. I could myself, perhaps, find pleasure or at least refreshment from going abroad, if the affairs of the diocese would stand still in the interim ; but I know that instead of that the reverse takes place, and my adversaries watch the opportunity of my absence to devise fresh plots, as has been most especially the case during my last absence.

I am as you see in Parliament, but I do not intend to go over: I have found by experience that it is mere loss of time. There is no good to be effected in a single Session. Is there any hope of your coming to Dublin soon ? On the third of October I shall hold my visitation (in Dublin only) ; and about the middle of the month a Confirmation, also for Dublin alone.

Believe me, my dear madam,

Very truly yours,

RD. DUBLIN.

Saturday.

MY DEAR MADAM,—I remember your mentioning in a former letter Mr. —— calling me a Whig, an Ultra-Whig I think it was: and now he tells you I can do so and so through "my Whig friends." I do not wonder at the common run of Dublin people supposing me of course a political partizan, because (judging by themselves) they conclude ministers would not have appointed anyone who was not. Nor do they always, I believe, mean it as an affront, though to call me a Whig or a Tory is to call me a liar (since I have always strenuously professed my independence of all parties) ; because their notions of truth are so low. But I should have expected Mr. —— to be every way above such nonsense. Ministers would, I believe, have respected me less, but would have been likely to allow me more influence, if I had allowed myself to enter the partizan ranks. As it is, there is a poor man with a large family, my excellent curate in Suffolk, who has long been soliciting a small living among the many Government livings in his own country, backing his application with my *testimony* (for I never go beyond that) to his desert ; but he is always passed by, though he has some peculiar claims of his own to boot. Then I have been laboring above three years to obtain the king's signature to a charter enabling me to appropriate some of *my own* revenue to the foundation of a divinity college: but the Primate has hitherto succeeded in baffling me. And again, there is an old lady in Dublin who has lost all her five sons in the service of their country by wounds or climate, and is left at above four score to subsist with her three daughters, one of them bed-ridden, on the produce of needlework. One would think it required no great stretch of influence to obtain a hearing for her claims to a pension: it surpasses mine however, for I have been trying what I can do for her above a year in vain. So much for my influence at present, with those I do know personally connected with the Navy. I have not the slightest acquaintance with any official person. My strenuous opposition to the ministerial measure of Irish Poor Law would perhaps diminish my influence if it were capable of diminution. Yet about half of my old acquaintance are mortally offended with me (joy go with them !) for

not going to the Premier and insisting on his providing for
them. If I answer that I have not the power to do so, they
resolutely disbelieve me. If I add that supposing I could do
so I would not lay myself under an obligation to a minister;
this they do believe, and are shocked at my unnatural conduct. Nor do I say it is natural (χυχαων) but if not nature
I hope it is grace.

I chanced to meet yesterday a young man, Lieut. ——, a
great favorite of mine, to whom I showed as a matter of
curiosity that portion of your letter; he took a mem. and
wrote off straight to a friend of his, a naval captain, who he
thought was one of the very few persons likely to be able to
accomplish the very difficult object of obtaining a mid.'s berth
if for a very promising lad, as all proceeds on what you have
said. If he should succeed and not turn out something more
than well, your credit will greatly suffer. Lieut. —— is
going on an exploring expedition to New Holland, (whether
to inspect the civilized nation said to have been found) lately
in the interior by the expedition of which the curious account
has been published by Lady Mary Fox, there is no saying,
and if you know of anybody at any of the settlements, or
can offer any suggestions as to the benefitting of either
aborigines or others, they cannot be put into better hands.
I found a little boy, nephew of a friend's wife where I was
residing in Cheltenham, whose father fell at Waterloo, and
his mother being married again quite neglected him, and his
aunt, though kind, was a gay gad-about lady not fitted to
look after a boy of eleven. No boy could well have had a
worse chance; but there are some that *will* do well. I found
him so very intelligent, amiable and well-disposed, that I
made him the constant and sole companion of my walks in
the country; and he now says it was my notice and conversation that first gave him an ardour for improvement. The
fact is he was a combustible only waiting for a spark to set

it alight; and I happened to be that spark that happened to come in his way. He has gone on ever since gaining unmixed esteem and admiration, and in one word, I should be glad and proud to think my son would be just such another. This is Lieut. ——. I am more grieved than surprised at what you say of poor ——. Having been long at death's door, when his wife died he dropped down insensible, and on being revived was found to be in a state of fatuity. I collect from what you say that his disease has now taken another turn. What I admired most in him, besides good ability and good principles, was a *sober* and quiet energy. *That* is his natural character.

Mr. Archdall has called, but I have not seen him. It was this day week I had that glimpse of Colonel Phipps; I have not seen or heard of him since.

If you or somebody else will get articles into the *Tory* papers exposing the tendency of the poor law bill to subvert Protestantism in Ireland, it will do more good than any other argument. I have tried it with success on Lord ——, and Mr. —— and others. And it is really a sound argument though not more *sound* than some others which they cannot or will not take in. For though no friend to what some call Protestant ascendancy, no more am I to Romish ascendancy. Now the Protestants have most of the *property*, the Roman Catholics an immense preponderance of *numbers;* then when the property of the one million is confiscated (for such as O'Connell confesses is the tendency of the measure) and made over to the six millions, the Protestants must be utterly crushed, and will have nothing for it but to fly the country, which they had better do while they can carry something however small with them. Some may suppose that if this *were* the tendency of the bill, O'Connell would support it; and so perhaps he would if the *real* benefit of the six millions could be promoted by the total ruin of the one

million. But he knows that *they* would be ultimately reduced to still greater misery, and, like the blind giant, would
only reap the harvest of revenge, and be crushed in the
same ruin with their enemies. Ever, my dear madam,

Yours, much fatigued and hurried,

RD. DUBLIN.

Tunbridge Wells, Wednesday.

MY DEAR MADAM,—Many thanks for your communications,
which will be used in some way or other.

Mr. J.'s letter is highly interesting, but the stone masons
remind me of Mr. Puff in the critic vindicating the right, *in
a free country*, of all the commonalty to use as big words as
lords and ladies; which very same joke, by the bye (nothing
new under the sun) occurs almost in the same words in the
frogs of Aristophanes Τημοτικον γαρ τουτο, &c.

A man who through jealousy of another's friendship resorts
to slander and deceit, is as base in his means though not in
his end as if actuated by sordid self-interest. But the existence of that jealousy as a demon, unperceived by the possessed
person, is a very common human infirmity, so that the suspicion of it is natural enough. This reminds me of one
rare merit in Dr. Dickinson, who has not merely the *con-
tradictory* but the *contrary* of jealousy: *i. e.*, he is so anxious
to introduce me to all such men as are likely to attract my
regard (not merely his juniors but his equals and seniors)
that of all the clergy in the diocese from Dr. Wilson down
to the junior curates, all the very best are men who have in
fact been specially recommended to me by him. And if there
is no better among them than himself I am convinced that it
is not his fault. It is one of his high-minded traits of character.

Do any of your neighbours take in the *Saturday Magazine?*
It is now entirely the property of Parker (West Strand), the
publisher; and the series beginning with the present year is

better than ever. Being only a groat a month it would furnish reading for some of the poor.

I suppose you know the "lessons on money matters" (which, by the bye, are now gone to China as well as Ceylon to be translated) appeared there originally. Of the separate little volume Parker told me the other day he had sold between 8000 and 9000, and it has been translated into German and Dutch. In haste, my dear madam.

RD. DUBLIN.

P. S.—What is Mr. Butler ?

I forgot to say that since you have thought fit to make me your Father Confessor, I suppose I am bound to prescribe a penance.

I prescribe therefore that you should read the latter part of Essays on the Kingdom of Christ and note A in the Appendix. Also repeat seven times over the portion of the Sermon on the Mount, about doing good to those that persecute you: reflecting the while how much the disciples when they came to apply these precepts to individual cases, must have found their "feelings" enlisted on the other side, though their "reason" assured them that the precepts were of divine authority.

Brunswick Hotel, Hanover Square,
Monday 5, March.

MY DEAR MADAM,—In two respects your letters are rather troublesome to me : Firstly, they are in such pale ink that it tires my sight, which is not so strong as it was; and, secondly, they tempt me to answer them, which I have not much leisure for.

You are often brought to my recollection now by the Committee on Irish Education, now sitting, of which I am a member. I expect it will bring to light a great deal of truth where the public had been much deluded, and on that ground

I warmly supported it. You will have seen in the papers, perhaps, a curious hash of my speech; but though I cannot speak slowly enough for the reporters (who piece together the beginning of one sentence with the end of the next) I was well heard and favourably received.

You are quite right in the view you seem to have taken of my circular on prayer-meetings. I heard of the article in the *Examiner*, but never read it. I do not take it in and seldom see it. Dr. ———, the professor, is the author of the late attacks on me in that work; whether of all of them, or of a part only, I am not sure. Being a man of ability, I fear he will always succeed in poisoning against me the minds of . . . The only provocation he ever received from me is, that I made advances to him, as holding that office in the College, and several times invited him to clerical dinners, which he always declined. I dare say your ladyship has lived long enough in the world to be prepared to meet with dislike from any one who has rejected proffered kindness. From all that I have heard of his original good qualities, I am disposed to grieve over him. His heart seems to have been no barren soil, but one in which " thorns spring up," not pleasures and riches, but that most overgrowing weed . . .

I have often had occasion to remark what a loose notion of moral character many people have in England, and certainly not less in Ireland. They judge of each separate *action* as good or bad, and seem to have a very imperfect idea of *character*. I greatly startled many persons, I believe, by saying in a charge, that virtuous and vicious are terms not strictly applicable to any *action*, but to the *agent*, and his *disposition* and design, of which the acts are only the indication. Now those who gave you the account you received of Dr. Dickinson's conduct on that occasion, seem evidently to have entertained, and endeavoured to convey the belief, that he designedly misrepresented the young man's sentiments and language, and conveyed to me an untrue impression of them, with a design to prevent his being ordained; and yet it probably never occurred to these very persons to set down Dr. Dickinson in their own minds as an utterly base and unprincipled character. They were probably accustomed to look to each separate portion of conduct insulated. Now, I happen to know, that he always had a high opinion, which he has often expressed to me, of young ——, but had it been otherwise, had he been guilty of such an act of treachery in respect of any of these persons, of whom he does think unfavourably, I should set him [Imperfect].

Brunswick Hotel,
Hanover Square, London.

My dear Madam,—You most not suppose that any communication you may be so good as to make, respecting schools, or other matters in which we have a common interest, are indifferent to me, from not receiving answers, as this may perhaps be the last letter I shall have time to write, except on indispensable business, for a good while to come. Your last and the preceding were very interesting and satisfactory, I only regret want of leisure to answer them more fully than I can. Before I had the pleasure of renewing my acquaintance with you, I had often thought of our first interview at Tunbridge Wells; and though I never anticipated so much agreement of views as has since taken place, and thought you probably enthralled for ever by a party which I knew but too well. I always gave you credit for that ingenuousness, which I have in them so often found wanting.

On all matters connected with schools you may safely write confidentially to Rev. J. Carlisle, at the Education Board. You may, perhaps, find him blunt and unceremonious, but I have good reason to think him one of the most frank, single-hearted, honest men you will meet with any-

where; he is also discreet, and of his intelligence you can
judge from the pamphlet of his I sent you, and which you
did me the honour to mistake for mine.

Mr. —— is the only one of the few (for they have been
very few) that have been refused ordination by me whom I
had any cause to regret. Dr. Dickinson, who it seems is
promoted to the important office of Blame-bearer, thinks
very highly of the young man, and of . . . . and of
his lady, though she is known to be much under the influence
of persons who are apt to abuse it by falsehood and misrepresentation; two, especially, neither of whom have much
scruple in saying *any* thing that may serve their party
objects; one, who is of a fervid temperament, generally, I
believe, succeeds in convincing himself of the truth of whatever he thinks fit to say; and the other, though I believe
he does not do this, is not the less skilful in convincing his
neighbours.

The account you received of the case of young Mr. ——
was, perhaps, as near correctness as could be expected, considering it was a report of a report. Some circumstances,
indeed, that were not immaterial, were omitted, and others
so far altered as to give a different complexion to the transaction; and it is not unlikely that he may also himself have
in some degree misunderstood Dr. Dickinson. But the
main fallacy which has warped the judgment of so many
well-meaning persons who have had it impressed upon them,
is the crafty use that has been made of the word " test," the
truth being, that I had never introduced any test at all. I
am bound to ascertain as well as I can a man's fitness for his
office, not only in point of knowledge, but also of moral and
religious disposition; and this must be with reference to the
dangers to be apprehended in each respective time and place:
for instance, suppose there was a considerable number of the
clergy, who judged it not inconsistent with their functions to

be members of a jockey club or boxers, &c., I might then think it requisite to ascertain a candidate's views and intentions with respect to such matters, and then this might be called "imposing a test." Now, if you will look at the ordination service you will see a solemn vow to promote "*peace and quietness* among all Christian people, and especially those who shall be committed to your charge," if then there is a considerable portion of the clergy who think it consistent with this vow to desert those who are committed to their charge, and go about as missionaries in another diocese, in defiance of the prohibition of the Diocesan, I feel bound to ascertain a man's intentions in respect of this matter, before I ordain him. And this is called imposing an unauthorized test. But now, mark the dishonesty of my adversaries: the late Bishop of Ferns exacted a promise from candidates not to preach extempore. I myself think he was very injudicious in doing so; but the very persons who are assailing me, never uttered a word of complaint against *him*, but are subscribing to a monument to him as an exemplary bishop!

I find the excuse now made for me by the most moderate is, that I am misinformed as to [imperfect].

When the inestimable Bishop Dickinson was appointed almost all the clergy of this diocese, except a small number of the most thorough-going, drew up (quite unknown to him and me), and signed an address of congratulation, expressing a joint sense of the great service he had rendered in this, and was likely to render, in his own diocese; together with their obligations for the unwearied and unparalleled kindness with which they had always been treated. In addition to the party bigots above alluded to ———— was one who refused his signature, on the ground that Bishop Dickinson having (in concurrence with me) supported such and such principles and measures, which he conceived ren-

dered him an unfit person for the office. Now, if ——
had not had great *simplicity* of *heart* he would (as I dare say
some did) have disguised or suppressed his real sentiments; and
if he had not had great *simplicity of head* he would have not
failed (considering what ample opportunities he has had of
being enlightened) to entertain quite different sentiments.
Voila l' homme! I respect him much up to a certain point,
because I do not think he would lend his weight to a party
he did not approve, for the sake of the weight lent to him
by them, in respect of things he did approve.

You see, by the bye, a description on this last point in
one of my Essays on the "Dangers," under the head of
"party spirit." Perhaps I never told you that portion of
the Essays is an expansion of a conversation respecting *yourself*, which I held with a person who was lamenting to me
your secession from the "evangelical party." I took down
the heads of our conversation immediately, considering it to
involve important principles, and afterwards (omitting, of
course, all *personal* allusions) I brought forward the substance of it as a charge. One main question debated was,
whether it be consistent with the character of an honest
man to co-operate with a party, and allow himself to be
reckoned a member of it, when several of their principles
and acts (to which of course he lends, by the circumstance of
his belonging to the party, his own weight) are such as he
inwardly disapproves, but thus connives at and favours in return for the increased weight which their influence gives him.

There is a great storm raging on the other side of the
Atlantic, which I expect will reach us before long. The Protestant Episcopal Church in America has taken a step, which
if not recalled will amount, in my judgment, to a *self depo-
sition* of all its bishops and ministers. I have written for
explanations, and to set forth my own views, to some members of it; and shall write also to Dr. M'Ilwaine, Bishop of

Ohio. His last Charge has been reprinted (Seely's) in England; and if you have a curiosity to see what is going on you should get it.

Ever yours truly,

RD. DUBLIN.

Dublin, Saturday, 16th September.

MY DEAR MADAM,—I have been meditating and contriving how to pay you my respects at Newtown Anner for a good while past, but lo! the fine weather is gone by; I have not been able to get a week or half a week free from engagements, nor can at all tell when I shall. At the worst, I shall necessarily be on the move for the visitation next spring, and then I may, perhaps, bring Mrs. W. with me, as far as to your country, of which this autumn there would be no chance, as she is so glad to be settled at home after such a long absence, nothing but imperative duty would take her away again for some time.

One of my impending engagements is the examination and ordination of some candidates; and I shall also probably have to examine some candidates for curates' licenses. Some ordained men come before me (including men sent out by the *Home Mission* to lighten the darkness of the parish ministers!) so grossly ignorant that a child of ten years old in your school would put them to shame!

Your young friend Mr. —— is, I expect, to come before me, as nominated by one of the two conductors of what you call the Anti-Christian Examiner. Mr. ——, his father, acknowledges that nothing really required by me of candidates is at all unreasonable; but he adds that my requisitions having been so much and so successfully *mis*-represented, his son would be exposed to obloquy by compliance, as having complied not with what is, but what is represented and believed to be required, and so he would **be**

for yielding to the storm, and avoiding by concealment of
real sentiments, the threatened persecution.   How many are
ready to say Lord, Lord! who would willingly bear the cross
but for its being heavy and galling their shoulders, and
would fain come to Jesus by night for fear of the Jews!   I
am anxious about the young man from all I have heard of
him; for the trial is whether he will fear God or man most.
It is a sore trial for a young person to be exposed to the
persecution of the most merciless—the most unscrupulous—
active and unrelenting bigots, that ever fired a faggot.   And
these very circumstances, which must make these the more
disgusting as associates to a man of any moral taste—make
them at the same time more formidable as enemies.   He
must have seen that the whole course of their persecution
against me has been based on misrepresentation and carried
on by every kind of intrigue, trick, and subterfuge.   He
may not know, and probably does not, the worst; but he
must know enough of the leaders of the party to disgust any
man of pure principles.   He probably does not know how
worldly, sordid, and shabby some of them are.   One who is
much put forward by the rest as ——— will not pay his
debts, but suffers his own child to be a burden on a poor
curate!   But he must know by what a paltry quibble they
distort what they must know to be the designed sense of the
Ordination Service.   Satisfied to make out that the words
may be so construed as to bear a different sense, though one
which none but an idiot could for a moment suppose to have
been their intended sense.   There is many a man I conceive
who has taken more false oaths than he could count, for
Custom-house business, that would shudder at the impiety of
thus tampering and quibbling with vows before God, made
in a sacred matter!   In haste,

Yours very truly,

RD. DUBLIN.

" From this note it would appear that Lady Osborne was instrumental in the establishment of the first-rate Model School now flourishing in Clonmel, of which Mr. Terence Smith is master."

Friday.

My dear Madam,—I will see what can be done about Mr. J.'s letter. Anything you wish to propose about a Model School at Clonmel had better be in a letter (enclosed to me) to Mr. Kelly, the Secretary, or to Mr. Carlisle as resident Commissioner; and then it will be brought regularly before the Board, which I will see shall give it due attention.

I trust you will have received a copy of my reply to the Lay Memorial. In haste,

Yours very truly,
Rd. Dublin.

Tuesday Evening.

My dear Madam,—I find we answered each other's notes to-day after the Irish fashion. Receive my assurance again that I am never displeased with anyone for conscientiously differing from me in opinion and frankly avowing it. Let each but think for himself without tying himself to a party, and again, let him not act on different motives from what he professes, looking one way and rowing another. Those who do this I am ready to forgive, but the others have no need to be forgiven. In the present instance, however, I am more and more convinced that if you are fully in possession of the facts which many of those around you know, or might know, but do not choose to communicate, you would find that you differ from me little or nothing. For instance, most of them probably know—all of them might know—that what you propose as a modification of my (so-called) test would be, and would always have been perfectly satisfactory to me. I ask every man to explain for himself in his *own* language what his designs and intentions are in respect of preaching in other dioceses, and if it appears he has no design of countenancing those irregular and schismatical proceedings which you allude to, I make no objection to licence or ordain him; but the fact is the leaders of the Party which is assailing me are mystifying you and others by pretending that they would be satisfied with this or that, when in truth they are only seeking a pretext, for which, if it were removed, they would instantly substitute another. I do not ask you to believe this on my assertion; you may yourself make the trial in this way: say before those who have signed or are about to sign the various memorials, &c., that have lately been got up, the proposal contained in your last note to me, bewailing at the same time my obstinacy in refusing to accede to it (this will not be a lie any more than Nathan's parable to David when he had the true explanation of it just ready to follow) you will find I dare say many of them declaring that this would fully satisfy them. Then tell them that I do accede to it, and I am greatly mistaken if you do not find that as soon as they find it will satisfy me, they will draw back and refuse it.—"Mark now, I pray you, and see how this man seeketh mischief," (see 1 Kings xx.)

Here is one proof among many that the above conjecture is not thrown out rashly. A clergyman who applied to me for a licence, and who appeared to have no inclination himself to any turbulent proceedings, but to stand in awe of some members of a Party, had several conferences with me on the subject of the injunction, and at length wrote a letter expressing what his views and intentions were, which letter, as I subsequently learned from himself, was *dictated to him by a member of the Home Mission*, in the expectation as I am led to conclude by what afterwards occurred, that I should refuse him the licence. The letter, however, was perfectly satisfactory to me, and he did receive a licence. Now this *you* would probably imagine would have settled the dispute at once and for ever! But no. As soon as ever it appeared that I would accept the terms they were immediately withdrawn! The very letter was shown to subsequent applicants and it was proposed to them to make a similar declaration; but this it seems they were not permitted to do, "lest they should be cast out of the synagogue." The truth is, my dear madam, you and I might weary ourselves in vain, like the lamb in the fable, in exposing one pretext after another that the wolf set up. The main roots of all the clamour are political hostility towards the ministry under which I was appointed, and a desire to usurp the episcopal power, and last, but not least the Education Board.

There are other less widely extended motives coming in aid of these which operate on some, such as "odium theologicum," personal jealousy, national jealousy, and others. One of the leaders of the Lay memorialists I remember some time ago called on me when a living was vacant to beg for it for his son; the young man bears, I understand, a respectable character, but as he was only just ordained deacon I did not think it right to put him over the heads of aged and tried labourers in the diocese, and I refused the application. Not long after the father proclaimed me as of unsound religious opinions, and it has so happened, that from that time to this, no steps that I have taken in the diocese has given him any satisfaction.

I think you know now if you did not before, one way by which one may escape charges of heterodoxy. And I may add that I have no doubt I should have been easily forgiven for providing for all my own *relations*. The family of the most unblushing nepotist must be gorged at last; a bishop's own family cannot hold *every* thing; and those who have wealth, party interest, and other such recommendations, hope to come in for their share in time. But when they see quiet, and modest, and humble worth made the sole title to preferment, they naturally lose all patience from foreseeing that there will be (thank heaven!) no end of men possessing this qualification. With thanks for your kind wishes, believe me to be, dear madam,

Yours very faithfully,

RD. DUBLIN.

MY DEAR MADAM,—I have sent to the Board the books, &c., which I received from you. . . . The Secretary received a gentle admonition for showing you the Inspector's report without an order from the Board; it is against our rule and a most wholesome rule.

—— perhaps describes Trinity College as a perfect theological school in reference to himself; considering that if men are sent forth *nearly* as good divines as one who is presented as a "goodly and well-learned man to be consecrated a bishop," *a fortiori* they must be fit for the humbler branches of the ministry. According to that standard I believe he is right; but if your ladyship were to take him in hand to examine him in the Greek Testament, I doubt whether he would give you a very high idea of Trinity College as a school for divinity. It is, however, greatly improved of late years (chiefly through the means of that very system which I have been, though imperfectly, carrying on. I can shew you some articles in the *Christian Examiner* three or four years before I came here (when that work was conducted by Dr. Singer) reflecting severely on the deficiency of theological studies, which is not wonderful as the examination for Fellowships contains no allusion to anything of the kind. Of late they have as I said, much [imperfect].

[Beginning of this letter missing.]

I, on the contrary, will call that gold or silver which yet has five or ten per cent. of base metal; and I find that most lead has 2 or 3 per cent. of silver.

And hence it is that by a great part of mankind I am regarded as one of the most inconsistent of mortals; merely because I recognize defects where I approve and acknowledge good qualities, even where I disapprove. It is as in the fable of the clouds,

> The man his party deem a hero,
> His foes a Judas or a Nero ;
> Patriot of superhuman worth,
> Or vilest wretch that cumbers earth;
> Derives his bright or murky hues,
> From distant and from party views;
> Seen close, nor bright nor black are they,
> But every one a sober grey.

Mr. ——, however, seems to me (and to several other competent judges) to have more striking inequalities than most men. Hardly anything that he has written is there that does not contain things which very few men could have equalled; and again, here and there, things below the level of an ordinary man.

His pamphlet on National Education, for instance (though I am far from thinking it equal to his best things) contains much that is very forcible and well put; and some things that are absolutely weak. I was reminded when reading it of the opening of Ovid's Metamorphoses. " Corpore in uno Moblia cum duris sine pondere habentia pondus." That most of the arguments he used had been urged on him in vain, about twelve years before, in a correspondence between us, he had probably forgotten. But I could not so easily excuse his saying that the opponents of the system were incomparably better men than its supporters. He could not have *known* this, and no one can know what is not true, and I hardly can conceive how he could have failed to know the contrary.

There are of course good, bad and indifferent on both sides, but it is my belief that if some impartial judges were to go through Ireland, and select fifty of the wisest and best men they could find, the result would be that—vast as is the numerical superiority of the opponents, there would be found a majority of the fifty, supporters of the system. Why to go no further than Dr. Dickinson, Mr. —— did not probably know above half his qualifications, moral and intellectual, but *that half* was enough to set him far above any of the opponents of the system. As for that conversation with me which I alluded to, I can assure you that nothing could be more *calm* than our discussion was, on both sides, indeed I never was aware of his being subject to imitation. He certainly showed none then, and I admired (though unconvinced) the ingenuity with which he maintained his position, else indeed I should *not* have thought it worth while immediately on going home, to commit to paper the whole conversation and afterwards to embody it in a charge, omitting of course, the reference to you individually. I felt it to be a matter not only of importance, but of some nicety, to set forth clearly all that could be said on the question, especially because *political* partizanship, though a thing most perilous and full of shoals on which many have been lost, I do not consider as *in itself* unjustifiable. Whether he really thought at the time and ever since exactly what he said, I have no means of deciding; but of what he did say, I have given a most faithful report. I sympathize deeply with the affliction —— must feel on account of his son; but if that son has (as I understand) adopted for a good while the Romish doctrines and practices, it is surely more for his credit, and for the good of the Church also, that he should openly join that communion, and make a sacrifice in doing so, than go on in dissimulation as so many do. And surely you could not really wish that he should stifle his convictions, and profess what he does not think out of regard to his father, however dutifully he may feel towards that father. I should be sorry any son of mine should do so.

Ever yours truly,
Rd. Dublin.

Friday.

My dear Madam,—Mr. Kennedy and Mr. Carlisle had a disagreement or two between themselves, and the upshot is that *both* have withdrawn. Mr. C. is about to proclaim publicly that he is as friendly to the system as ever. He is succeeded by another Presbyterian clergyman of high character, but will continue in office till the end of March. So there is reason for your friends to fear that I shall be able to save them in spite of themselves from the total ruin they are struggling for. Strange! that persons living in Ireland and not totally without intellect should be so blinded by passion as not to perceive that if they and Archbishop M'Hale succeed in overthrowing the National system, there *must* be immediately a *separate* grant to the Roman Catholics, which is what he wants, and that under that system the rising generation will grow up in such a state of mutual animosity as must within 20 or more likely 10 years, break out in a civil war, of which our great grandchildren will not be likely to see the end.

I have sent a man of your school to the Board. I have been very hard fagged with the business of our ordination. In great haste,

Yours very truly,
Rd. Dublin.

Tuesday.

My dear Madam,—Pray keep the enclosed. Mr. —— is
not always very accurate in his statements, as he views events,
books, persons, facts, everything, through the medium of
strong feelings.   Look at the " Christian Examiner" and the
papers signed .   . . will own that this is the most
charitable view.

I ordained thirteen gentlemen yesterday, and they presented to me a request, to which they even dared to sign
their names, for the printing of the sermon I delivered, as
likely to be instructive to the clergy as well as laity in these
critical times.   If you had seen it you would see why I use
the word "dared." There certainly is an apparent beginning
of a strong reaction.

I suspect that if your letter did influence Mr. —— not
to accept the curacy, it was by raising scruples in his mind
as to the propriety of taking the " test," for a test there is,
proposed not by *me*, but by the very cabal who stigmatize
me as having imposed one! There is a certain set who have
agreed not to accept as curate, but to send to coventry, any
clergyman who shall express his intention of not obtruding
himself into another diocese or parish against the will of
the bishop or rector.   But there are symptoms of a break-up
among them.   The whole conspiracy is based on falsehood,
and time brings truth to light. Yesterday's ceremonial asto-
nished and undeceived many who had been actually brought
to believe that I could not find any respectable men to accept orders!

Mrs. W—— still poorly; if she gets better I am still in
hopes of visiting you this week.   By the bye, an Irish lady
(anonymous) has presented £400 to what she calls the
Whately Schools.   She (I suppose it was the same) had
before given £100 in 1833. Shall you petition for a share?

The assistant curate of St. Anne's is dead. It is Dr. Dickinson's parish. He has a most excellent curate in Dr. West, one of the best men in the diocese, but he must have a second. It would be a great advantage to a man of the right sort to be trained under such a curate as Mr. West.

Ever, my dear madam,

Very truly yours,

RD. DUBLIN.

P.S.—The evidence before the Lords' Committee is published, with an index, and can be bought, 2 vols. folio,

Dublin, Wednesday, 23rd May, 1838.

MY DEAR MADAM,—I sent for you about ten days ago that memorandum of the conversation with a friend of yours; but I had mislaid your direction (unluckily you do not give it me again in your last), so I enclosed it to Senior, thinking he knew or would find it out. He is at Kensington Gore, or at Southampton Buildings, Lincoln's Inn; you can send for it to him, or if by any chance it should be lost, I have a copy here. I am to be sworn in Lord Justice to-day, so am an unlimited franker during the Lord Lieutenant's absence.

Very truly yours,

RD. DUBLIN.

[The conversation is in the Appendix.]

Education Board.

MY DEAR MADAM,—Your application shall be attended to as soon as any, but we have much business and little money.

I am excessively busy, as it is ordination week, and Mrs. W. is ill, but is, I trust, recovering.

How should I get to your place from Clonmel, supposing me to be able to get down by coach next week?

From your letter I had the first information of Mr. ——
having given up the idea of Mr. ——'s curacy, for Mr. ——
did not think proper to answer the letter of assent he received. He said (as I since heard) at a clerical meeting that
you had prevented Mr. —— from taking the curacy.

There is much in what you say of the course pursued by
the other bishops, but what is to *me* the main thing, you do
not notice. I should be very glad that any evil should be
prevented or lessened; but the chief question for *me* is
whether it is to be imputable to *me ;* the greatest fault of
the other bishops is of less consequence to me than a smaller
fault of my own.

No man must have it to say that *I* have sanctioned,
expressly or impliedly, anything I have no right to sanction.

                    In great haste,
                              Yours most truly,
                                        RD. DUBLIN.

                                        31st October.

MY DEAR MADAM,—Mr. Drummond has been to England,
and is now returned. Perhaps he has by this time forwarded
that letter to you; Lord Morpeth promised me last night to
inquire for it. I contrived to keep awake *most* part of the
evening. To-day I feel a little tired.

. I hope you and Mrs. Hill went to bed, and had, if not a
good night, at least a good morning. I feel most compassion
for *her*, because she may, perhaps, be of Sir Andrew Ague-
cheek's opinion, that " to be up late is to be up late," and yet
could not very well refuse to keep you company in your
frolic.*

---

* The frolic alluded to was this:—The Archbishop was going away very early
by the coach, and to avoid missing seeing him in the morning, Lady Osborne
and Mrs. Hill sate up talking to one another after the Archbishop retired to
rest, and remained up till they saw him off.

There is no one I met at your house that I should better like to meet again. There is something very prepossessing about her. I am not sure whether I left with you a sufficient answer to Mr. Archdall, as for a requisition signed by a number of the parishioners. I explained to you the other day my view of the unsatisfactoriness of such applications; but pray tell Mr. A. that I have found *single* sermons never had much circulation (unless they are connected with some popular controversy); and even where they do circulate, are soon overlaid like other pamphlets, but if I should publish a *volume*, I will remember his recommendation.

In haste, yours very truly,

RD. DUBLIN.

Friday.

MY DEAR MADAM,—I am just thinking of writing, to ask whether you could furnish any information that might be useful to the Committee. You have long and earnestly been engaged in promoting education under various systems, and have long been surrounded with persons prejudiced against ours. You have heard various complaints against it, and have learned how far they are well or ill founded, and what right or wrong influence they have exercised over people's minds; and you can point out what alterations or substitutes have been suggested, and on what grounds hopes and fears are entertained by any as to the ulterior progress and effects. If you were to write me a letter (attested, perhaps, by other persons) to that effect, it would certainly be of service in some way, whether produced in evidence or shown privately. I believe you have been misled in one respect as to ———'s curacy. I had nothing to do with the application to young ———; it was made entirely without my knowledge (except after it was done), from Dr. Dickinson's confidence as to my good opinion of the man, which I had

derived entirely from his account of him. Let anyone but
lay aside *prejudice* against Dr. D., and judge of him from
personal inspection, and I feel certain that all right-minded
people will value him the more the better they know him.
I do not pretend to any great *quickness* in discerning character, and am accordingly very slow in forming a decided
judgment; but when I do form one, though I still keep
myself open to conviction, I have lived fifty years in this
world, and have never found myself mistaken yet. Nor is
this from "laying their characters on the shelf," as Cecil
said, and shutting my eyes against evidence; for in fact I
have had occasion to mourn over two or three friends who
have turned out quite different from what I had hoped; but
still I found no ground for convicting myself of having been
mistaken, for the cases were of men whom all who knew
them agreed to have totally *changed* their character, apparently through the influence of bodily disease, in other words,
from partial derangement.

I wondered a good deal at what you said of the High
Church Tories; not that it is not quite correct in itself. but
as distinguishing them from the Low Church, it is quite
against my experience. The worst portion of each of the
two parties always have reminded me of the celebrated anti-
thesis of Archbishop Magee applied to the Presbyterians and
Romanists. The Low Church have religion (not very good
of the kind, by-the-bye) without a church, and the other
a church without religion. The latter are a degree less
inconsistent and hypocritical in their glossing over the vice
and irreligion of any who will but support an *establishment*
and a *party* and *temporalities*, because these things are what
they almost avowedly care most for; they are the seculars,
properly so called, the Hophni and Phinehas' school, who
carry for their arms the flesh-hook with three teeth. The
others make high puritanical professions, and have, like the

Maccabees soldiers, idols hidden under their garments. They always spoke of Bishop Elrington (who, after all, was a better man, with all his faults, than most of them) while living as one who did not " know the Gospel," and after his death they eulogize and monument him, whom they well knew to have gone far beyond me in the very points for which they abuse me.

There is a Mr. Larken, curate of Cowbit, in Lincolnshire, personally a stranger to me, who has been so mad as to dedicate a little volume of sermons to me. I hear from those who have read them (which I have not yet) that they are sane and rational, and I am told he is a most amiable and conscientious man. His publisher, in case you have any curiosity to see them, is Pelham Richardson, Cornhill; but Milliken has it.

Your remarks on spiritual pride are almost verbatim those of a sermon of mine!

I am surprised at what you and some others in Ireland say of the reports of my speech. To me and to all who heard it there seems such a miserable hash, that I almost wonder how you could make head or tail of it. I am too rapid for the reporter. Lord Plunket repeats, and the Bishop of Exeter speaks very slowly, but I find those who were present at the debate repeating faithfully the substance and almost the very words of every argument and remark. There is in the *Dublin Morning Register* and *Evening Post* a letter from a private correspondent about it, which diverted Mrs. W. and me.

Ever, my dear madam,
Yours very truly,
RD. DUBLIN

Pray circulate the enclosed pamphlet.

"This letter is inserted because it has long ceased to be a secret who wrote the book mentioned."

Dublin, 1st May, 1838.

MY DEAR MADAM,—I shall write to you, if I can find leisure, a long account of a conversation I lately had with a friend of yours, which I think will interest you.

I have forwarded the application for books for your schools. Pray keep on your table and mention as you have opportunity those two pamphlets on Irish Poor Law, Remarks on Nicholls, and abstract of the reports. If the Bill should pass in anything like its present state—of which there is still some fear—notwithstanding the numerous petitions pouring in against it; all efforts to benefit Ireland in any other way are thrown away. Your estate will be, in a few years, swallowed up, and the people you are labouring to civilize hopelessly demoralised and every way ruined.

If you enquire of Parker, West Strand, you can get the "Easy Lessons on Christian Evidences" separate. Do not hint any suspicion you may have of the author, as that might check its circulation. I have been before the Transportation Committee *by letter*; if you have a curiosity to see my evidence, any M. P., can get it for you—it is fit for a lady's perusal, which is more than can be said of most of the evidence; but the subject is not an agreeable one.

I am, dear madam, in haste,
Yours very truly,
RD. DUBLIN.

12th October, 1839.

MY DEAR MADAM,—No; I did not send that paper, but I should recommend most emigrants to South Australia and New Zealand, to each of which labourers well recommended can get a free passage; any enquiries I can forward to the respective agents and send back their answers; there are little books in Dublin giving particulars respecting each colony.

I do not know where Lord Ebrington's popularity is to end. Of course it cannot continue in its present state any longer than till he is called on to take some decisive steps one way or the other, and a decisive step that will satisfy both Whigs and Tories, especially in respect of Ireland, is not on the cards. He wishes it to be known, and I suppose it is known, that the appointment of Bishop Plunket was entirely his (Lord E's.) spontaneous act; but very likely the party who call themselves the friends of the Church would more readily forgive a purely political appointment than that of a more efficient man not of their own party. A man of no party, religious or political, who exerts himself to secure the Church by raising its character and increasing its utility, meets with no favour from either party. The more I see of political and politico-religious parties, the more and the more equally I loathe them. The clergy, generally, except those who are enslaved to a party (a large proportion I am sorry to say) are most of them not really opposed to my *real* plans, because *they do not know what they are*, but have been brought to credit representations the very opposite of the truth. Some of them, perhaps, would be opposed if they did know, because it is natural for men to be jealous of increased learning in others when they themselves are deficient in it.. . . .

In my own diocese an insolent protest has been got up by ——— and signed by a large proportion of the *Incumbents*, mark you, not *Curates*. The fact is I am the *Curate's friend* and if I had suffered ——— to continue leaving his *Curates unpaid*, the case would have been I suspect very different; yet I treated him as tenderly as I could consistently with the obligations of justice.. . . . " But if when ye do well and suffer for it ye take it patiently, this is acceptable."

I know not of any acquaintance of mine at Naples or Rome. When do you start?

I am in Parliament but shall not attend this session, nor probably ever any more. I find there is no good to be done in a single session, especially when one does not act with a party; it is only at best getting a crop into the ground to be ploughed up before harvest.

Mrs. W. has set up a girls' school-house within the grounds which I hope you will come and see when you are next in Dublin. There is also a boy's school-house building in the village. The Protestant Rector is a terrible firebrand, and preaches against them with all his might, and is so insolent and abusive to the R. Catholics, that I am in daily dread of his being knocked on the head, and thus canonized as a martyr—it would soon be done if the Priest encouraged them, as some would do; but fortunately for all parties he is a peaceable man.

Ever, yours very truly,

Rd. Dublin.

Tunbridge Wells, 8 April.

My dear Madam,—Many thanks for your letter and the enclosure, which I expect to find a use for.

I do not lose a moment in assuring you that I am not, and was not, angry with what you said, though I thought, and still think you will, on consideration, perceive that it would be not only stooping but stooping over a precipice to volunteer such a letter as you suggested to any but a very intimate and confidential friend.

If an application came from Mr. —— to me I should probably answer, that the only way to avoid most invidious and galling distinctions is to require exactly the same engagements from the least and most trustworthy. I myself should have no scruple in declaring my intention of abstaining from any irregularity or absurdity however gross, or of performing any duty however obvious, PROVIDED the same engagements were required of all alike; for then (and then only) no injurious suspicion would be implied. In fact, if you look at the Ordination Service you will see that I *have* already, in common with every clergyman, promised many things, in which it would be very affronting to doubt me. In the present case, however, more especially, it would be most insidious to declare open war against the Home Mission, by accepting a man on the avowed ground of his expressing disapprobation of them, when I have been carrying on a negotiation with them, which however unlikely to come to a favourable termination, shall never be broken off by *my* means for the purpose of bringing about an agreement with them, or at least with such a society as shall have in view the objects they *profess* to seek.

Sound Church discipline, however hopeless, shall never be overthrown by *me*. You ought to have received before now a copy of a reply from me to a certain lady's memorial (in which I saw as plainly as the king of Babylon, " the footsteps of men, women, and children"), which reply, after a month's delay the framers of it mean to print, with their own rejoinder, in the papers. I shall not, however, enter into a paper pleading against those who have no jurisdiction before a tribunal, that of newspaper readers, which has no jurisdiction either.

Poor Mr. —— has been examined. He has done no harm to the system, but, I fear, some to himself, in having his declarations taken down by the short-hand writers, who sit ready to " write me down an ass." That he is for giving *no* education to those who are not to be brought up strictly in the principles of the Established Church; and that he has excluded the school-teachers from his religious instruction, for fear they should so profit by it, as to be a benefit to the system!

I shall return on Monday to the Brunswick Hotel, Hanover Square.

Ever, my dear madam,

Very truly yours,

Rd. Dublin.

P. S.—If you will order from your bookseller, Mrs. R. Trench's " Thoughts on Education," edited by Mrs. W., published by Parker, West Strand; it will probably be out by the time the order arrives.

Tunbridge Wells, Tuesday.

My dear Madam,—I often ask the question which clowns do of one who enquires his way, "Where did you come from?" and with reference to that question Mr. ——'s letter is very satisfactory; looking at it *in the abstract* I see a man who (in common with many worthy people) has missed one of the most fundamental principles of Protestantism, and (consequently) of Christianity; viz., that all men should be left free, as far as secular coercion and civil government are concerned, to worship (or not to worship) God according to the dictates of their own conscience; and to obtain for themselves and their children such religious instruction, good or bad, as they choose. We have no right to advise or urge them to receive what we think bad instruction as *such*, but we are bound to allow them to receive what instruction they think good. This principle has in fact been long since recognized in practice, though people are so silly as to imagine, or so dishonest as to pretend that it is a novelty introduced by the Education Board. We do not deserve the credit of having introduced this great principle of toleration. The Board leaves the people *two* days in the week, who already had *seven* days in the week to give their children what religious instruction they thought fit; but Mr. A. has begun to leave error behind him, and I think he will attain right *principles* in the way that people usually do (and as I hope the Roman Catholic's will), by beginning with right *practice*—" If any man is willing to do the will of my Father," &c.

I had some communication with Lord Bexley some years ago relative to the Jews Bill, so that there is an opening for co-operation between us in that quarter also. Suppose you were to ask him whether he has seen my volume of charges and tracts, in which I have reprinted my speech on the Jews Bill, with additional remarks. By the bye, has Mr. A. read that? If any one is not a convert to my views of toleration, from what I have there said, he is beyond the reach of any arguments *I* can devise. I should not like to be Pope or Dictator in Ireland; not because I should not pursue such a course as I am convinced would be beneficial, but because I should have a *successor;* but what I want is, to have a *government* for the Church such as the American Episcopalians have, and such as was hinted at in the petition of the Kildare clergy, which is in that volume of charges. If you and Mr. Woodward could get up a petition in the same spirit, signed by people of respectability about you, you would do a real service to the Church, in the only way in which, I believe, it *can* be effectually served. By the bye, that pamphlet I sent you is not by me, nor do I know the author, but I thought it likely to be useful. There is another in the press, which I expect will be still better.

I have just been talking about your ladyship with Pope, whom you remember here, and who always, I find, even when there was much difference in your opinions, gave you credit for that ingenuousness, which I had always observed, and to which I am now indebted for the benefit of your alliance, as far as I can judge. Yesterday I went with Mr. Bishop and looked over the Union Workhouse, which is a good building, and in good order, *nearly* strong enough (with twenty or thirty soldiers) to confine Irish paupers. It cost about £4,000, and would hold (tight stowed) near 400, including children. Workhouses, therefore, for 80,000 Irish would cost £800,000 for building, but this is only one-tenth of what others propose. The food and clothing, &c., costs 2s. 6d. per week, or £12 10s. per annum—call it for Ireland only £10, and that for only half the year; this makes, for the 800,000 paupers, an annual expense of four millions,

Ever, my dear madam,

Yours, most truly,

Rd. Dublin.

Extracts.

7th November.

There is a party at Oxford associated for the purpose of publishing what they call, " Tracts for the Times, who are disseminating principles far more Popish than are *necessarily* held by those professedly *Roman Catholics*, or than *are* actually taught at this very time by many of them. If your ladyship were to look at the ingenious little pamphlet which has made *some* noise of *late*, under the title of a Pastoral Epistle from the Pope to some members of the University of Oxford, you will see convincing specimens how far the principles of a religion may co-operate while the empty name is scrupulously retained.

It would be strange, indeed, if there were not some resemblance of style between Dr. Dickinson and myself, considering what loads of letters and other documents have been written by each of us, and for the most part looked over together by us both.

If whenever you write to Mrs. Whately you drop in a word in favour of the National Schools, you will do a great service. Mr. ——, and the rest who talk of our Popish Catechism are but ill read in Scripture, for they would find in John vi. 55 the very words they censure."

Scraps from Letters.

I am happy to say No. 8 of the Cautions is printed, and will be out in a day or two. I like Mr. Fitzgerald's writing better and better. I send him some bricks and timber and he makes them into a neat house. The sale continues to improve, though not rapidly.

I understand there are many in the neighbourhood of your ladyship's residence who speak chiefly Irish. I should be glad to know your opinion on the much-debated question, as to the expediency of teaching them to read Irish.

I congratulate you on the lies told about you. It is a high compliment, showing, first, that the adversaries are afraid of you; second, that they can find nothing *true* to found complaints on.

If you and I had full credit from men for all our toils and public spirit, it would turn our heads.

Dublin, 25th February.

MY DEAR LADY OSBORNE,—I think the publication of that correspondence in which Mr. —— is quite triumphant is likely to do great good. We shall go to England some time this year; but whether I shall appear in the House is doubtful—not unless for some special matter in which *my* presence may be particularly called for. I have ascertained by experience that a regular attendance for a session by one who is only there for one session at a time is wholly useless. As for a vindication of the system of National Education, it would be worse than useless for me to take that out of the hands of the ministers. If the present Lord Lieutenant had been sent over at *first*, I do believe ministers would have almost entirely escaped a most distressing series of troubles and opposition, which they will now have to struggle against with very partial success, as long as they remain in power.

I cannot find that Mr. W. has done them any good, any that is considerable, which I think he *might* if he had come forward frankly owning *himself* to have been in error. I have good hopes that the Board will at length be incorporated by Charter, which is what we so long urged in vain on the Whigs; this will be a step towards better things that will still be wanting.

Have you seen the new Reading Book (with prints) supplement to No. 3 ? I hope you will have time to look in at our Model School as you pass through, and that you will find it still improved.

Very truly yours,
RD. DUBLIN.

Palace.

MY DEAR LADY OSBORNE,—I sent last week a pamphlet for Senior to forward, after reading it, to you. I cannot account for its not having reached you. I asked in the note which accompanied it, what you thought of Mr. W's. pamphlet, now you ask *me*. It certainly shows much ability and is likely (as I lately told him in a letter) to do important service; this I can say with a safe conscience, and I think I had better say no more, as you are evidently wishing to see only the golden side of the shield. There are many things that might be censured by the opponents, and many by the supporters of the system; but I do not know that those defects will diminish or will not even increase the service done to the cause. Do not take up the notion that I think ill of Mr. W., or am on an unfriendly footing with him. We are very good friends, but I am not one of those (though a most numerous class) who are either all *for* or all *against* a man, and will see either no defect or no goodness in him. I have received an invitation to his house, and he to mine for next Wednesday. In haste,

Yours truly,

RD. DUBLIN.

Dublin, 20th March, 1844.

MY DEAR LADY OSBORNE,—I was amused at your former letter complaining of the different tone Mr. ——— had assumed at the Palace and with you over night; I think I can explain it. You brought Mr. ——— *along with him*, and that forced him to be on his good behaviour, and not speak out, lest the other in the simplicity of his head and heart should *peach*. Your last letter was highly instructive. We ought to copy whatever recommendations any new party introduce with a view to gain converts, as far as we innocently may. None of those recommendatory circumstances really belong to any particular party in itself, but are to be found almost in every one at its origin. They each look well *in the bloom of youth*. The gross profligacy, the profaneness, the secularity, the ignorance, and the absurd superstitions which the Church of Rome displayed just before the Reformation, would, if displayed in the time of the first advances of the Romish system, have killed it in the bud; and Tractism is merely one form of the revival of that system, with its natural tendencies concealed from the vulgar, and bedecked with the ornaments which do not properly constitute any part of it; "Positis novus exuviis, nitidusque juventa," *i. e.*, the snake which Virgil describes is most dangerous when it has just cast its slough and put on a bright new skin.

The Evangelical party has just now rather passed its prime. Those who had long been preaching Antinomianism —many of them without knowing it—are succeeded in many instances by men who practice as well as preach it; on the average there are many admirable exceptions. As a general rule it is more needful to be on your guard in any money transactions with men of high profession in that school than with the common run of worldly men; yet at first *every* party is rather distinguished by what is called moral purity and freedom from *vice*; I mean those vices to which Satan alone will allow that name to be given, because they are not *his*. Since, as old Isack Walton says, " he is not a glutton, neither can be drunk, and yet is he still a devil;" but as for evil-speaking, lying, and slandering, envy, hatred, malice, and all uncharitableness, these he will not permit us to call " vices." Then in process of time, as a party gains strength, more and more scamps join it, by way of white-washing themselves, or of gaining some consideration in the world which they could otherwise have no chance of. " Rubbish and mud portend a flow;" when the stream of party is swelling it gets fouler and fouler, and you will find this the case before long (it is beginning already) with the Tractites.

Mr. ——'s friend Mr. ——, if he has good testimonials and passes a good examination will have his fair chance like other candidates. I will use as much influence on his behalf as if he were my own son, viz., none at all. The story about his having obtained promises of votes I do not believe, but shall enquire about it. Mr. —— does not at all know me, nor could, I apprehend, if he were to live with me for a twelvemonth, because hardly any one *can* understand any one's acting on a purer system than himself. The plan *we* go on is to look out for the very fittest person we can find for each office, without any personal considerations. But I should despair of making Mr. —— believe this—

> " Non vivitur istic
> Quo tu vere modo; domus hæc
> Nec purior ulla est
> Nec magistris aliena matis."

With kind regards to Miss O., believe me to be,
Very truly yours,
Rd. Dublin.

P. S.—I do not know whether you are a reader of Horace, but it is almost worth while to learn Latin for the sake of enjoying that satire of " Ibam forte via Sacra," where he meets with a modest and disinterested Irishman.

P. S.—Do you know my excellent friend Bishop Stanley?

Dublin, 30th March.

My dear Lady Osborne,—I have made one of my girls write out from my common-place book the thoughts on fasting, which I developed into two sermons lately. It is only brief heads put down for my own use, but may, perhaps, suggest to you what I meant.

Mrs. W. is gone to Oxford to tend her son, who is laid up with rheumatic fever. She was forced to leave me, though herself not stout, to take care of my eldest, who was not yet able to travel. We mean to start on Monday for Cheltenham, where my daughter is ordered the waters.

That *discovery* you allude to of pressure for cancer I remember being in great vogue between thirty and forty years ago, when it was said to have given relief to several patients, but I am sorry to say that none of them recovered.

I had seen those ballads last summer. There is a good deal of ability in them, for even the parts that are nonsense, are such nonsense as will *take* with the people they are designed for. On the whole, the vulgar and profane phrase of " devilish good " will apply well to them. They are truly satanical.

Yours, very truly,

RD. DUBLIN.

" The thoughts on fasting will be found in the appendix."

Dublin, 16 June, '44.

MY DEAR LADY OSBORNE,—I send you a pamphlet of " Notices," reprinted from sundry loose papers, that have been sent me from time to time, and which I have thought it right to distribute in the course of my visitation.

I am just returned from it, and am " pretty considerably used up," as the Yankees say. The triennial visitation will begin on the 27th of July, and will keep me out about three weeks.

I should like to know what you think of Mr. Woodward's very important pamphlet on the Education Board. It is, I am told, selling very fast.

My family are at the sea side, among the rocks of Dalkey, to mitigate, as far as possible, the annual attacks of hay fever, with which my eldest two, are always visited. Of course my son's convalescence is retarded by this superaddition of new disease.

Have you seen the Memoir of Dr. Arnold? I find there is a new edition of it already called for.

Yours, very truly,

Rd. Dublin.

5th July, '44.

My dear Lady Osborne,—That pamphlet I did not *publish*, but only reprinted it for distribution in my tour. It may be published by any one who should think it worth while; which in London I think it might, as I have found it excite great interest. Suppose you try.

One thing which may have diminished the estimation in London of Mr. Woodward's pamphlet is, that people may wonder why that should produce any effect *now*, which has been said (though he certainly has put some of the arguments very well) in substance, again and again, for the last twelve years, and to which the majority of the Protestant clergy, including himself, had so long turned a deaf ear. Many men think it unreasonable that the same arguments coming from one man should go for nothing, and from another have great weight; though, perhaps, they themselves, in some other cases, evince the same unreasonable prejudice.

Perhaps, also, some may remark (as I have heard some do here) that he does not write like a *convert*, nor take any particle of blame to himself for having (though in a quiet way) favoured and sanctioned the refusal to listen to evidence, and to adopt a reasonable course, for which he censures the rest of the clergy. He did not, indeed, *join* them in their violent attacks; he only, as it were, "kept the raiment," without throwing stones himself. But it has been thought not only unjust but impolitic to cast blame on others, and take no share of it to himself. Perhaps it is as a compensation for this that he flatters the opponents of the National Education, at the expense of the supporters, who it seems (see page 2) are incomparably inferior to them. I wonder

whether he is serious or jesting when he speaks (in preface) of the willingness that his bishop should make free use
of his name.

Very truly yours,
RD. DUBLIN.

P. S.—Thank you for your enquiries. The hay fever is
nearly over.

Dublin, 26th January, 1847.

MY DEAR LADY OSBORNE,—I know a good deal of the
case of that school—more, I apprehend, than Mrs. —— did
when she communicated with you. She has now been written
to, I am nearly certain, by the Secretary of the Board, on the
subject. The patronship of the school was *not* vacant.
The priest, who was the original patron, on leaving the
parish handed over at once to his successor that office, and
this was acceded to by the Board, who are now called on to
oust the present patron, and substitute another. Now, the
best way to judge is, to put one's self in another's place.
Suppose the priest of your parish had been a disciple of
M'Hale, and had done his best from the first to keep children
from your school at Newtown; and at last, finding it still
prosper, and having got possession of a better house, had, on
the occasion of your handing over the patronship to your
daughter, sent to the Board to propose transferring the
school and appointing him patron; and supposing this
had been acceded to, and that he had shortly afterwards
dismissed your master, and put in a Roman Catholic, a creature of his own; and had endeavoured, as far as the rules of
the Board would allow, to make it a kind of " priest's
school," would you not feel that you had been " jockied?"

Now this is just the sort of thing that is, and doubtless
will be, attempted in various places.

The opponents of National Schools, when they find their opposition ineffectual, come forward at the eleventh hour to try and get them into their own hands.

N.B.—The labourers who were hired at the eleventh hour are not mentioned as having been invited before, in vain; much less as having reviled and pelted those who went to work in the vineyard.

If Mrs. —— will be so public spirited as to give a better house for the school, she will, without being the regular patron, have enough control to see that the rules of the Board are strictly adhered to; that the master does his duty well (else the Board will have him dismissed), and that the children accordingly receive as good an education as in the best conducted National Schools.

If their benefit be her object this is what she will do. Should she set up a rival school, under a rival society, that though I shall regret the ill blood that will thence be generated in the parish, will be sufficient proof that she was actuated by party spirit, and would consequently have been a very undesirable person for patron.

For aught I know the priest may be an undesirable patron. But Mrs. —— could easily keep him by a little judicious superintendence from doing any serious hurt. Should however, the Board supersede him as patron, he will be very likely to vent his indignation at the grievance, by raising a great deal of jealousy in the parish, and probably keeping up a rival and hostile school.

As for the famine, I have long lamented, what I find even the ministry now hardly attempt to justify, the long *delay* of the measures for removing the duty, admitting corn in *foreign vessels*, and allowing *sugar in the breweries*. But it has ever been the curse of this wretched country, that remedies for its evils, when they *are* applied, are *too late*.

The combined baseness and *folly* of those who try to bribe a starving population to change their religion is worthy of all scorn and detestation. A slight effort has been made in that direction here, but I believe it is quite quashed. Is it decidedly going on in your parts? Believe me to be,

Yours, very truly,

RD. DUBLIN.

Dublin, 30 September, 1847.

MY DEAR LADY OSBORNE,—I supposed you had known that ———— *has* been offered a living, and declined; it was very small, as almost all are here about; and I believe would have involved more cost than it would have repaid. I have full confidence in his conversion, as I have in all he says; when he *was* an opponent he plainly owned it. Do you not remember bringing him and Archer Butler together to the palace some years ago? I should be very glad to pay you a visit, but it is next to impossible to get away without some evil result. It is not the quantity of business, but the distribution of it, one thing to be done one day and another next day; and something may arise the day after, and so on. With kind regards to Mrs. O.

In haste,

Yours, very truly,

RD. DUBLIN.

November 26th, 1847.

DEAR LADY OSBORNE,—I will set on foot an inquiry about that school. I have always regretted that there should be so little inspection, but we are kept short by Government. If the Protestants did but know their own interest, they would look after the schools in their neighbourhood, but party spirit swallows up all. I quite agree with what you say about Radicals, they will be regarded as apostates unless they " go the whole hog." I believe the Lord Lieutenant is ready and willing to take effectual measures for putting down outrage. But there never was a more difficult problem to solve. I will take care not to let out your name.

Very truly yours,

RD. DUBLIN.

Dublin, 18th December, 1847.

MY DEAR LADY OSBORNE,—I conclude you will like to hear what I think of Mr. Thomas Woodward's pamphlet.

The Searcher of hearts can alone decide who is really honest, but Mr. T. W. writes like an honest man. He does not, like too many of the deserters from the ranks of our opponents, either shirk all mention or allusion to his former opposition, or back out of it by pretending that the system of the Board is changed, &c., but confesses frankly that he was in error as to facts. Now, I shall always be ready to admit that, as far as I can see, an honest man could have done no more than he has.

By the bye, in page 18 I think he mistakes in saying that our Lord *rebuked* the ruler. He only represented that two things must go together, and that consequently both must be denied or affirmed.

In my " Thoughts on the Evangelical Alliance," when I spoke of their rejecting Quakers as not " evangelical," though they confessed them to be " Christians," what I said might, with a slight alteration of the words only, have been expressed thus:—" Why do you call these men Christians; none is a Christian who is not evangelical"?

The Coercion Bill is, I find, the most stringent that could have been *speedily* passed; and those who declared that they would have opposed anything more stringent, have declared also that if this fails, they will be prepared to vest greater

R 2

powers in Government. I think Lord Clarendon will try fully and fairly what can be done with this Bill.

Ever yours truly,
Rd. Dublin.

P.S.—What a blow to the Church have these bishops inflicted by their address to Lord J. R——, and how well he has answered them!

Dublin, 3rd January, 1848.

Dear Lady Osborne,—I send you a paper containing the best account I have seen of the Hampden persecution. Please to return it, unless you can get the article copied into some provincial papers.

There is something in what you say of the Roman Catholic population. No doubt that religion is far less favourable to civilization than Protestantism, as may be seen best in some of the Swiss cantons, because they are on equal terms in all other respects; and yet the contrast is striking between the Roman Catholic and the Protestant cantons. But to try what could be done for the deterioration of Protestantism, you must suppose England again conquered by the Normans or some foreign people of a different religion, who seize on all the land, and take all the church endowments for their own church, leaving the mass of the population all poor—to maintain their own minister on the *voluntary system*, and especially if this had been done 300 years ago, when the English were far less civilized than now, what would they be at this day? Till the priests are paid there is no hope of civilization for Ireland, and so thought Lord Grenville. I have taken steps to have the Bonmahon schoolmaster surprised.

Yours very truly,
Rd. Dublin.

P.S.—In the lectures on a " Future State" (Millennium), I

have said all that I think Scripture authorizes us to say on the prophecies relative to the Jews. A man may form his own conjecture (not contrary to Scripture), but he must not put forth as Scripture doctrine what is not clearly revealed.

Dublin, 11th August, 1848.

MY DEAR LADY OSBORNE,—It is very seldom that I have time to read any debates. If the speaker be ever so eloquent and trustworthy, and the subject ever so important, still unless there is strong reason for supposing that *something will come of it*, that he will practically be more attended to than ever I have been, I do not undertake the task of reading the speech. I have not seen either of those you mention. My views on the subject may be seen as concocted between Dr. Dickinson and myself several years ago (and brought forward as the Baring clauses) in the volume of his remains.

I am sincerely glad to hear that Mrs. B. O. is doing well. I send you a copy of a tract which Parker has now printed separate, and will supply, I presume, if wanted for distribution at a very low rate.

Very truly yours,

RD. DUBLIN.

26th August, 1848.

MY DEAR LADY OSBORNE,—Were I in the place of *either* of the contending parties, I should feel bound to yield at once, because *either* arrangement shuts out all possibility of improper interference, except any that the Commissioners could and would at once remedy. But although I think both parties wrong, I do not think them both *equally* in the wrong. The priest may naturally, though not reasonably, imagine that the determination to shut him out from all share in the patronage of a school would be originally set on foot, implies some unfair design, and the case of that other priest does not apply.

First, because, if one priest has done wrong to take for granted that any other will do the same, would justify the same mode of judging of *Protestants;* and secondly, because a *joint* patron could not appoint or retain an unfit master, since, in the event of a division between the patrons the Board would decide. But both of the parties will have on their heads the blood of hundreds of innocent children sacrificed to their paltry jealousy. If these are brought up in ignorance, vice, and degradation, what will those say who have to face them at the day of judgment? I would not incur such a responsibility for all beneath the moon. As for the Commissioners, they can do no other than they have done. Many persons who opposed the system for fifteen years, now that they find it will succeed, are for mounting the winning horse, and ousting the —— from all that they —in spite of timely warning—have allowed him to get into his hands. What would be said of us, and justly, if we should make ourselves a party to this? Not so; you must buy the one Sybilline book at the price for which you might have had the three.

Very truly yours,
Rd. Dublin.

13th September, 1849.

My dear Lady Osborne,—A copy of my charge has been sent you. Did you see the sequel to the tract on " Evidence" (on the history of religious worship), parts one and two, and have you seen "Lessons on Paul's Epistles" (another hand, for the use of young people)? It is very well done. Poor Dr. Taylor has been carried off by the cholera. There is one honest man the less in the world!

You will have seen the death of my valued friend the Bishop of Norwich; he is a great loss both public and private. I hope Mrs. Osborne and her lovely children are well.

Very truly yours,

RD. DUBLIN.

9th April, 1850.

MY DEAR LADY OSBORNE,—Most of the bishops have benefices in their gift, double in number and quadruple in value of mine. And this, many do not know and many do not consider; but, were the reverse the case, still many respectable men must be left unprovided for, and I should still have to expect that each of these would be reckoned by himself and his friends as aggrieved; and this the more from the *principle* on which I am understood to bestow preferment. If I provided for my own relatives and connections, and for persons who would befriend these, in return, many even who would rail at Nepotism; would hug themselves with the thought, " *if it went by merit,*" I, or my friend such-a-one would be the man," and *I* was, on my own appointment, exposed to much more envy than if I had been a personal or political friend of Lord Grey. But he who is appointed without any such recommendation, merely from his supposed qualifications, is exposed to the indignation of all who think their own or their friends' qualifications greater. He has robbed them not only of the *advantage*, but the credit of the preference, winning not only the trick, but the " honours.

As for Mr. ——, if you meet with any more persons who ask whether " I have any objection to him," and have " laid him on the shelf," you will do him a service by saying that if it were so I should not have recommended him, as I did, for a living (which it did not suit him to take), and again for a chaplaincy, for which I was asked to recommend, but which was given to another; nor should I have given him the introduction I did to the Bishop of London—" Deliver me from my friends, &c." His friends do not consider how they injure his character by insinuating that I think unfavourably of him. As for promises, I have sometimes promised a man the offer of *some particular living*, for which I have thought him especially suited, but never of the *first that may chance* to fall vacant, because it might happen to be one for which another was better suited. I am not sure how far —— is suited for M——, or he fit for it; but I never *advised* him on the subject. I only gave him a letter to the Bishop of London when I found he meant to apply. I am not sure what his views are as to the Catholic Universal Church; but certainly there are some men—as safe from themselves becoming Romanists as I am—whose doctrines would lead many of their hearers, in Italy especially, Romewards. I mean those who speak of the Church Universal as *one community on earth*, and of its offices, its ordinances, decisions, &c., as claiming our obedience. A person of rather more clearness of head and consistency than the preacher, sets himself to find out *where* this Church is, and who are its organs. One of *our* bishops is a bishop, indeed, *in* the Universal Church; but he is not a bishop of the Universal Church any more than our Queen, who is a European Queen, is Queen of Europe. Our bishops have no power beyond the pale of our own church. The result is, that after groping about for a long time and asking everybody where *the* church is, he at last finds his way to Rome, which at least sets up a *claim*, though a groundless one, to *be* that Church. This man, though wrong, is consistent. His teacher, if keeping aloof from Rome while he talks of the *power* and the *decisions* of the Universal Church, is inconsistent.

Ever yours, very truly,

R. Dublin.

P.S.—Many thanks for your inquiries. Our last accounts of my son and daughter are much better.

6th December, 1850.

DEAR LADY OSBORNE,—I have not time for writing, but if you wish to know my thoughts on the late Romish movement, Mrs. Hill can give you a sketch of them. I am trying hard to keep my clergy from making any stir about it, which would be most mischievous, and in that Bishop Daly and I are agreed. As for my opinion on free trade your cousin may be referred to the "Lessons on Money Matters."

Yours truly,

RD. D.

Dublin, 15th Feb., 1851.

MY DEAR LADY OSBORNE,—I hope you have received the *printed* answers to your letters which I have sent from time to time. I have been too busy to write, and am not much less so now. Besides an unusual pressure of other business, I have just been bringing out a little volume of "Lectures by a Country Pastor," and have another in the press.

I am afraid you do not approve the "cautions" written at my suggestion, and under my superintendence; but you know you may freely speak your mind. I do not think but that we shall ultimately agree. The Atlantic and the Mediterranean are at the same level *on the* whole, and in the long run, though the one has *tides*, and the other none. You have had sundry ebbs and flows since I first had the pleasure of meeting you at Tunbridge Wells, a quarter of a century ago; but, on the whole, you have not been very far from the same level with me.

Have you seen Archbishop Cullen's letter to his clergy, and the answer to ditto, by a priest of Dublin Diocese? They are very well worth reading. So is also "Historic Certainties," a little pamphlet which some people father on me, though it is not mine. If you do approve of the Cautions, pray do your best to bring the publication into notice, since so cheap a one cannot go on unless it have a very wide circulation.

Yours very truly,

Rd. Dublin.

" Mr. Gladstone having stated that Archbishop Whately agreed with him in the cry on which he canvassed South Lancashire, part of the following letter was published in both an Irish and Manchester paper, which is a direct contradiction, as direct as any retrospective letter could be in its bearing upon a crisis that had not then arisen. Great was the surprise therefore of the Editor to see in his published and corrected Lancashire speeches, his Grace again brought forward as sharing in his views with regard to Ireland. From the allusion to Mr. Gladstone in his life, it does not appear that there was the slightest mental sympathy between them, over and above the especial difference upon the subject of Ireland. The Archbishop had a logical, practical and consistent mind."

Dublin, 8th March, 1851.

My dear Lady Osborne,—I signed, and indeed had a large share in framing those Addresses; simply with the object professed of guarding a'gainst the design which I knew was entertained (as you may see it advocated in the Times), of *separate* legislation for England and Ireland. I took care to have clauses inserted deprecating all interference with liberty of conscience. Whether any legislation can be contrived that shall *not* so interfere, I was not nor am, prepared to determine. And though I do not myself see any objectionable course, I could not presume to say that no one else could. But supposing I had fully decided (which I had not) against *any* legislation, and that I could have induced (which would have been impossible) the other Irish

Bishops to adopt that view, and to embody it in an address, the result would have been to defeat the very object we had at heart. For those who are disposed, even as it is, to legislate separately for what they call " the Church of England," would have said " You see the English Bishops ask for legislative interference, and the Irish deprecate it; therefore let us do for each what they ask. And thus we should have helped on a piece of the most unjust and mischievous, and foolish legislation that ever was perpetrated; a measure fraught with danger as well as disgrace, not only to the Church, but to the Empire. For what could more encourage the advocates of Repeal, than to see the British nation deliberately and spontaneously violating the Act of Union? I did not sign the addresses for the *purpose* of embarassing Government. I always endeavour to support when I can with a safe conscience, every Government, no matter whether Whig or Tory, but when they are pursuing an unjust or mischievous course, *I wish* to put what impediments I can in their way.

In the case of the poor law, and in that of transportation, I did my little best to impede their progress ; and though my efforts were of course vain, I have the satisfaction of feeling that for the enormous evils inflicted *I* am not responsible. Instead of my last letter, you might as well if you think it worth while put before Mr. W. what I said and published in a Charge, and afterwards in the " Essays on the Dangers," Essay ii. § 3; which was drawn up *from a memorandum taken at the time* of a conversation on the subject with him; in which he had been urging that you and the *generality* of Christians—all but a few very eminent ones, ought to belong to a religious party. In that publication will be seen not merely a description of the course advocated, but a fair statement, to the best of my knowledge and belief, taken down immediately after the conversation of the *arguments* on both sides that were adduced.

I have looked over the proof of No. IV. of the Cautions and it will I trust be published on Monday.

Very truly yours,

Rd. Dublin.

16th March, 1851.

My dear Lady Osborne,—I have just time to tell you that Cautions IV. is out, but I do not send it, because it will become the more known by your ordering it of a book-seller.

I think *my writer* is doing his work well; though of course our sentiments will not be acceptable to all.

If when your *tide* slackens a little, you will look over again my last letter, you will see that it does not at all relate (as you seem to suppose) to questions about religious liberty, but reprobates the folly as well as iniquity of legislating for Ireland and for England separately.

Mr. —— whom you speak of as the most unlikely person to turn Romanist you *describe* as the very person of whom I should expect it. A calm thinking reasoning person, who has become impressed with religious sentiments will be most unlikely—of all religions—to embrace Romanism. Most of the conversions are of those whose *imagination* had been allowed to predominate or whose *feelings* were stronger than their reason, or who had been altogether frivolous and mere creatures of *impulse*. And when these became impressed with a sense of religion they will snap at something gaudy, like a salmon at a peacock's feather.

Yours truly,

Rd. Dublin.

12th April, 1851.

My dear Lady Osborne,—Pray order the new edition of " Paddy's Meditations," it has some considerable additions which are admirable.

You can now get six numbers of the Cautions, viz. No. V. Parts 1 & 2.

I have desired Parker to communicate, *direct*, with Mr. Gardiner, as the shortest and most effectual course.

There is a new edition—an improved translation—of the *Evidences* in Italian brought out at Florence, by a Roman Catholic Priest, with the sanction of his Archbishop! If you have occasion for copies, for any friend, they are to be had at Parker's.

By the bye, Bishop —— at a late meeting of the Church Education Society, adverted very fully to Archbishop Cullen's published censure of the tract on *Evidences*, and suggested that this was likely to alter my views as to National Schools! The men of that party are strange reasoners!

To find that a bigoted Roman Catholic disapproves of this Tract is likely it seems, to disgust me with an Institution which *circulates the very Tract* by thousands, under the sanction of the Roman Catholic Archbishop Murray!

Yours very truly,
Rd. DUBLIN.

26th April, 1851.

MY DEAR LADY OSBORNE,—I direct this at a venture, as your direction was so obscurely written, that neither I nor Dr. West could with certainty decipher it.

We purpose sailing next Tuesday, and my direction will be Merton Lodge, near Slough.

I have left Mr. ——'s verses in the hands of our Professor Sullivan, to see whether there is anything exceptionable; if there is not, what is it that is proposed to be done with it? It would be rather below the dignity of the Board to publish it ourselves, though we might sanction the use of it if published by himself.

What you said about my giving up the Board put me upon enquiring, and I then learned that reports (which I suppose had reached you) have been industriously spread of my having such a design but you must not give credence to such reports now. The opponents, chiefly the Evangelical party, have always been most unscrupulous in propagating idle words to serve the purpose of their opposition. It was one of them (now ——), who reported a good many years ago, at a public meeting, that I had been endeavouring to persuade a school-master to place his school under the Board; the charge was received with shouts of indignation against me, and when afterwards he acknowledged in a letter that it was un-founded, and was urged openly to contradict it in public, he said *that* was a matter of opinion and that he did not feel bound to do so! and his letter, saying this, I *could* have produced before the Commons' Committee, of which he was one! but I spared him. Another of the party, ———, declared on oath that I had accepted the Archbishopric on condition of supporting the National Schools; and when this was proved to be false, and he was brought to *confess* that the person he had referred to as having told him this, never had told him any such thing, he publicly repeated this falsehood the other day; and I might fill a quire of paper with an enumeration even of the falsehoods which have come under my own knowledge, and the other unscrupulous feats of the members of that party. Why, one of the leaders of them, ———, of some note, sent directions to the *Evening Mail*, to attack and decry me (before I had set foot in Ireland) in every possible way, though he was a total stranger to me, only I was appointed by a ministry to which he was hostile!

There are some good and some tolerable men in that party as in every other; but take them as they come, and I must say I have found them not at all more scrupulously moral than the Tractites, or than the avowedly irreligious; so pray do not let the tide carry you to them by "mistaking reverse of wrong for right." It was a reaction from *their* errors that I am convinced had a large share in generating Tractites; just as a reaction from these is now generating infidelity.

No. VI. of the Cautions is out or just coming out, and No. VII. is nearly finished.

Very truly yours,

RD. DUBLIN.

P.S. — I have had occasion to say lately what I often said before, that if the Commissioners should (which I do not anticipate) depart from *fundamental principles*, or break faith with the public, either by prohibiting the use of any book we have sanctioned and placed on our list, or otherwise, I must resign.

Dublin, 9th Sept., 1851.

MY DEAR LADY OSBORNE,—In reference to that pamphlet edited by Dr. Elliotson, on "Mesmerism," I have found it necessary to protest for the benefit of puzzle-headed people (who are, I fear, the majority), that I am not to be regarded as *approving* of *everything* in a work which I recommend as *worth reading*. Pray keep this in mind, in your behalf as well as mine—No. X. of the "Cautions" is just out. I think dear Mrs. Hill enjoyed her visit to us. Certainly we did. I think it right to let you know that the clergyman, about whom you are so kindly interested, has resigned his curacy, and in such a way as to make me far from inconsolable for the loss. He has acted like some Irish outgoing tenant who takes leave of the house and ricks, by leaving a lighted turf in them as a token of remembrance, and sends a farewell present of a bullet to his successor, or to the landlord or agent. He has written a letter of *advice* to the new rector as to his conduct in the parish (by the bye, the Spanish proverb says, " There is a fig at Rome for one who gives his advice unasked." Now he can easily apply for his fig), and he very plainly insinuates that the said rector and his diocesan are unsound members of the Church, and threatens that great discontent will arise in the parish if his dictations are not complied with—if anything is introduced contrary to the doctrine and discipline of the Church of St. ——, as by —— established; and lest he should be found a false prophet (which I am happy to say I feel confident he will) he privately circulates a copy of this letter among the parishioners. I have always found the Tractites the most active in creating schisms and rebelling against lawful authorities.

Very truly yours,

Rd. Dublin.

Dublin, April, 1852.

My dear Lady Osborne,—Of Bishop Hampden's alleged high-churchism I cannot speak from my own knowledge; but you may remember my telling you long ago, that the high-churchmen who *led* the persecution, were in reality urged to it by his having advocated the admission of Dissenters to the University, and had not, really, any quarrel with him on doctrinal points, though they put forward the charge of heterodoxy with success to mystify their credulous dupes. This is not an *opinion* of mine, but a *fact*, which is proved by their not only taking no steps for the censure of the Bishop's Lectures for two years after their publication, but highly praising them. Among other witnesses of this, a friend of mine *was present* when Bishop —— loaded Dr. A.

with the most fulsome compliments on his admirable work!

On the subject of Baptismal regeneration, I never had any conversation with Bishop ——, but I cannot doubt that if he has used expressions just such as are to be found in our formularies on the subject, he would be loudly condemned by many members of our church (a Mr. ——) a clergyman of our church printed and circulated tracts condemnatory of our formularies; he was sentenced to *two years' suspension!!* They used the word in a different sense from that of our Reformers; it is hard to denounce them for this, and still more hard that *they* should denounce all who do not agree with them.

I endeavoured in my charge of 1850, to point out how much of the controversy was *verbal,* but in so doing I gave far less satisfaction to many persons than if I had thrown myself fully into one or the other of the contending parties; " the ridder gets, aye, the worst stroke in the fray." They seemed to say it is a very pretty quarrel as it stands, and explanation will only spoil it. The same sort of feeling which makes the vulgar delight in a cock fight or a boxing match, is found to operate in a different but analogous way on the higher classes.

You should read Mr. Spurrell's Rejoinder, and also Miss ——'s pamphlet against Miss ——; any one who can read carefully all that is now published (though there is a great deal more behind) and approve morally of Miss S., must have strange moral notions. But many are misled by hearing so much of her charities, under the belief that nothing was done for the poor in that district before her time. Supposing this had been so, the beneficence which was merely the *bait* to hide the *hook* of covert Romanism, would not be deserving of very high praise; but it is utterly untrue. There are in that very district *eighty* ladies and a proportionate number of gentlemen, devoted to works of charity—schools, dispensaries, asylums, &c., and this systematically, though without wearing crosses or in any way blowing a trumpet before them; and they had been and are doing five times as much as Miss S. & Co., at half the expense, because they do not lay out money on costly decorations; giving for instance seven pounds for flowers (?) for the adornment of a chapel for the admission of a sister!

Yours truly,

RD. DUBLIN.

Dublin, 3rd April, 1852.

DEAR LADY OSBORNE,—You need not fear that any alterations in the system will take place while I am a commissioner. And I believe by this time ministers are aware that they must not expect me to be a party to anything of the kind. The Lord Lieutenant has visited our schools, and seems really interested; but I find the hostile party are complaining bitterly of the "exclusion" they were placed under by the late Government in respect of patronage. They would have Government remain *impartial* as to that point, giving preferment to supporters and opponents indifferently. If this suggestion is acted on it will amount to this—that by opposing the schools a man *may* gain, and cannot lose; and, by supporting them, he may lose, and cannot gain. For the bishops that are hostile exercise the strictest "exclusion" against all who even do not *actively* oppose; and the chief patronage is in their hands.

If the present ministry, like Sir R. Peel's, appoint hostile bishops, and then support the system, they will, like them, be building a wall to run their own heads against.

What would have been thought of a Governor of the Cape who should himself have supplied the Caffres with powder and guns?

I hope you continue to like the Cautions. No. XVI. came out about three weeks ago, and No. XVII. is begun. Give my love to your charming grandchildren. Mine are, I think, as lovely. They can hardly be more so.

Very truly yours,

Rd. Dublin.

Dublin, 13th April, 1852.

My dear Lady Osborne,—Your informant has misled you, though I cannot tell to what extent. There is not, nor ever has been in my time, any clergyman in the diocese of the name of Graham, or anything like it. This may serve you as a warning that some besides Tractites are inattentive to accuracy as to facts.

At Stephen's Chapel there are two curates—one who was there before and one newly appointed; but the Archdeacon will himself officiate there from time to time when it is opened for service. It has been under repair ever since it came under his care. If any curate there or elsewhere can be convicted of improper proceeding you may be assured he will be removed; but it will not do to trust to vague reports, especially just now, when the high-fliers of the Evangelical party are so ready to raise the cry of Puseyism against any one, (*myself* for instance among others) who refuses to fall into their ranks; they used to charge us with being Socinians, &c., now they have added the charge of Puseyism.

There is a clergyman in a diocese, not a thousand miles from you, who, as far as I have been able to learn, is quite free from any such taint, and who professes his hearty concurrence in the "Cautions" which he is endeavouring to circulate, but who is most cruelly persecuted by having had a house in his parish licensed and a minister placed

s 2

there . . . . . avowedly for the purpose of opposing him, for no fault as I can learn except that he is
not a high Calvinist, and that he was presented to the living.
. . . And while these reports are spread by malignant
partizans, others, who have no evil intention, but are simply
frightened out of their wits, give credit to them. For the pressure of an alarming danger, while it makes prudent people
doubly cautious, makes the imprudent doubly incautious
—Scylla frightens them into Charybdis. And sometimes
they are like the deer which are scared within reach of the
hunters through dread of some bunches of white and red
feathers; we shall notice this kind of danger in one of the
Cautions.

I took the liberty of assuming there was no danger of Mrs.
Osborne's forgetting me, or imagining that I had forgotten
her, and of writing as if to her and you jointly; but as for
the little ones, I could not but feel doubtful whether they
would retain any recollection of me.

I will remember your Welsh friend when the case comes
before me.

Very truly yours,

RD. DUBLIN.

Palace, 1st June, 1852.

DEAR LADY OSBORNE,—I am excessively busy, and not at
all well, so you must excuse a hurried note as better than
none.

As far as I can collect, the impression you received from
Miss —— was (in substance, without regarding the exact
words) just what she intended to convey, viz., that Dr.
West, while disposed to suspect —— of a leaning towards
Tractism, yet continued in office another curate who went

rather farther; and that consequently he must have been guilty of imprudence, or else injustice. If this were *not* the impression she meant to convey, it is hard to understand why she should have spoken to you at all on the subject. You conveyed this to Dr. West, that he might either exculpate himself or confess, and as far as he could remedy the error. For this Miss —— censures you as guilty of a breach of confidence.

I am for holding most sacred all confidential communications, *provided* they relate *merely to what concerns the parties themselves* who communicate. But I must protest against the principle of keeping secret in all cases that which concerns *other* parties. Suppose I were to go to this, that, and the other acquaintance, saying that you (or that Miss ——) had misconducted yourself in some instance, adding, "but pray let this be a profound secret—do not let it come to her ears;" and exclaiming against breach of confidence if any one brought it to your knowledge that you might clear your character, would you not say that this was making it a point of honour to allow a person's reputation to be whispered away. I think, therefore, that you are not only justified in letting Archdeacon West know what you had heard, but that you would have acted unfairly had you concealed it.

Yours very truly,

Rd. Dublin.

27th July, 1852.

My Dear Lady Osborne,—Be assured you are quite mistaken in supposing that any of the books of the Board were made *compulsory*, or were ever generally supposed to be so. For every one who made even the slightest inquiry learnt at once that it was quite against

" fundamental principle." In fact that was the rock on which the Kildare Place Society split, which differed from our Board *only* in making the reading of Scripture imperative; and though this was resented as an affront by the Roman Catholics, it still did not *injure* at all those who were against the reading of Scripture. For it was their delight and triumph to *nullify* the order by having two or three verses of the Bible (the same every day) read in the schools, without the least attention being paid; and so it would have been with the Scripture Extracts, where the patrons are unfavourable; so we should have excited disgust, alarm and resentment, without effecting any good. There are hundreds of schools in *Ulster* whose patrons would never have joined the Board if the Extracts (which they most unreasonably objected to) had been compulsory. They have the authorized version read every day by those children whose parents allow them.

It is also a mistake to suppose that the Extracts were ever *universally* used. I do believe, however, that a somewhat larger *proportion* (though a smaller number than now) of the schools did formerly read them—[not finished].

19th August, 1852.

My Dear Lady O.,—What you say about N. Schools is quite true, but it is sending coals to Newcastle to say it to *me.* If you would make similar representations to *my wife and daughters* you might be doing much good, not that it is at all different from what they have often heard from *me;* but every additional witness known to be unbiassed and trustworthy, is an aid to the cause.

I have directed Mr. Trench's (of Cloughjordan) pamphlet to be sent to you. It is one of the very best that has appeared. He is not known to me personally, but I believe him to be a man who has sacrificed and borne much in the cause of what he regards as duty.

Yours very truly,

Rd. Dublin.

Many thanks for thinking of plants for me. I shall have a scarlet elder tree for you this autumn. You can get my Charge by the time this reaches you. It is just coming out.

Dublin, 27th January, 1853.

My Dear Lady Osborne,—If you have this pamphlet already you can send it to some one else. It is very ably written. The Norwich paper which I send contains two speeches of B. C. Hinds, and also an interesting article on the Madiai, though not likely to be accordant with the views of *some* of the sympathisers. You may send the paper also, perhaps to some friend whom it may interest.

Have you seen Caution No. XXIII., and can you guess the authorship of each portion? Have you seen a tract called " The WrittenWord the Interpreter of Tradition?" (Parker). It is well worth reading. So are also the little tracts by "Hopeful" (Oldham, Dublin), of which No. 4 is just out. There is a little tale which I have been reading with great interest ("Early Experiences," Grant and Griffith, Paternoster Row), which gives a vivid picture of Tractism, and also some phases of Irish life which have not been before exhibited.

Yours very truly,

Rd. Dublin.

13th February, 1853.

Dear Lady Osborne,—I enclose you a copy of a note of mine to the Lord-Lieutenant relative to a matter which I think you ought to be made aware of. I fear a Norwich

paper which I sent you about ten days ago, begging you to
forward it to Mrs. Hill, did not reach you. Whether this
will find at once, or follow you, I know not.

Very truly yours,

RD. DUBLIN.

31st October, 1847.

Have you seen Dr. Elrington's pamphlet? and Dr. Taylor's?
and Dr. Miller's? You should read all three. What a low
morality is shown in the *Christian Examiner* as well as in
Dr. Miller's in advocating the trick—for I can call it nothing
else—of alluring children by making a solemn engagement,
and then "keeping the word of promise to the ear and
breaking it to the hope." I send you the little tract on self-
examination, which the Christian Knowledge Society have
published, and which I have, I trust, improved by subjoining
a note at the end. They printed 8000 copies in May, and it
is now out of print. I hope your little grandchild is well,
and as lovely as ever. With kind regards to Mrs. O.,

Believe me, yours very truly,

RD. DUBLIN.

P. S.—Mr. Woodward's dread of the majority swallowing
up the minority is in itself rational, and I was not wholly
without it fifteen years ago. But during the whole of that
period not one proselyte has been made on either side; and
to any one who knows this, as everyone does who chances
to inquire, the objection surely loses all its force.

" The Editor inserts the following letter, as it relates—
though not addressed to Lady Osborne—to a subject about
which both his Grace and Lady Osborne were deeply interested, and which is likely to create fresh controversy.
Moreover, it shows the lofty and independent nature of the
man."

Dublin, 8th March, 1854.

DEAR MRS. OSBORNE,—I had not heard of your dear mother's illness. I need not say how glad I shall be to hear of her complete recovery. I thought you had known that I never ask Government for anything, for myself or anyone else. When *consulted* by ministers I have sometimes given my advice as a matter of favour to *them.* But to volunteer a recommendation of any one, is set down as a request for a personal favour. And if I were to accept any and should afterwards be asked to vote on some question, I should feel very awkward either in complying or refusing. Hence, if I could have had for asking an archbishopric for myself, and bishopric for all my best friends, I should not have asked though the alternative had been to break stones on the road.

I am just starting for London to be examined before the Lords' Committee—a thing of which Lady O. has experience, but I fear it will be all labour lost. Ministers, I expect, will resort to the plan of *separate* grants, which the most vehement of *both* parties are calling for, and both will be dissatisfied when they have got it.

Yours very truly,

RD. DUBLIN.

APPENDIX.

APPENDIX.

No one, I believe, has lived a certain time without having remarked that whenever a person starts some project or method he deems the first of the sort, he immediately discovers that it has just at that very time been anticipated. Thus, the Editor finds that the mode in which she intended to develope the life and character of Lady Osborne through the medium of her own letters has been used by the biographer of Miss Mitford, a lady whom she once had the privilege of meeting in her house at Three-Mile-Cross, where she kindly read to her and Lady Osborne and their hostess (in her marvellously musical voice) her own " Inez de Castro," and she possesses a note of hers in which she speaks of Lady Osborne as her " delightful guest."

The sequence of the letters from Lady Osborne are, in almost every case, chronologically disposed, except in a very few instances, some of the later ones. The dates, however, manifestly correct the mistakes, and the errors are of no importance.

The Editor is much indebted to Mr. Woodward's devoted and highly esteemed friend, the Rev. John Hiffernan, for the loan of the plate which has preserved the heavenly expression of his features. To Dr. Hemphill she has to return thanks for the power of perpetuating photographs of scenes once brightened by the presence of Lady Osborne, and adorned by her taste and generosity.

The Protestant bias of Lady Osborne's letters is strongly marked, and the compiler, fully participating therein, deems that these are no days for withholding it when Protestantism has been betrayed from within its fold, and trampled on from without; when a poor country has £70,000 a-year hitherto coming into it in the shape of grants from the consolidated fund now paid out of Irish money; when a council is sitting at Rome to confer or refuse personal infallibility to the Pontiff who claims to be the representative of the Almighty upon earth. Doubtless, assuming the attitude he does, the assertion is only a consistency, but wherefore does he seek his power and title from below?

While many of the educated and thinking of the Romish Church take refuge in unavowed infidelity, doubtless there are many believing Roman Catholics who practice many unimpeachable virtues, but none that are not equally demanded by Protestantism on higher grounds.

These are no days to shrink from proclaiming belief in the divine right of orthodox Protestantism, exhibiting as it does, the true spirit and freedom of the Gospel. This is an age of revived memories, and no Protestant country or town can be pointed out, as is the case in the Pope's palace at Avignon, possessing the savage curiosity of a room shaped like an extinguisher, the ceiling of which is blackened by the smoke of those who were burned therein for their faith. These volumes disclose various phases of religious thought in the school of Protestantism, but not one that would not shudder at such a mode of purification.

The foregoing observations, and, indeed, the whole of the Appendix, had been written, when a letter from an "English Catholic," printed in a supplement of the *Times* of January 24th, 1870, came under the notice of the Editor, and it is such an important testimony in favor of them that the Editor thinks it deserves to be printed in a more accessible shape than that of a pile of old *Times*, and accordingly inserts it as follows:—

PAPAL INFALLIBILITY AND PERSECUTION.

The following statement, drawn up by an English Catholic, has been forwarded to us for publication.

" The controversy, whether the Pope is or is not infallible in his decrees upon faith or morals involves many more and harder questions than is generally supposed. It is a question for the conscience of every Catholic, for he may suddenly find himself required to approve principles and practices which he has been taught to consider contrary to morality, and only excusable in an age of barbarism, when passions were strong and reason defective. If the Pope is the infallible teacher of morals, it is impossible that precepts which he has commanded to be observed under pain of excommunication, and which he has declared to be valid for the whole Church and for all time, can be immoral.

" But the whole principle and code of persecution and the means taken by the Popes for the extirpation of heretics have long been disowned and repudiated, by English Catholics at least, as abhorrent from justice and Christian equity. The dogma of the Pope's infallibility would make this repudiation impossible; and the Catholic would have once more to acquiesce in a system which is now condemned by the conscience of Christendom, and has been obsolete for more than a century. Nay, he would have to find a place for the principles of that system in his abstract theories of morals and politics, to make it his ideal, and declare it to be consonant with the social and political perfection to which Christianity continually tends. Whether he can do so or not can more easily be determined after reading the following:—

"In the early part of 1559, when the unity of Western Christendom had already been irretrievably broken, and half separated itself from Rome, Paul IV. published, after 'mature deliberation,' and with the full assent of his Council of Cardinals, the Bull *ex Apostolatus officio*, wherein he does by his Apostolic authority approve and renew all and singular sentences, censures, and penalties of excommunication, suspension, interdict, deprival, or any other whatever that had been, at any time and in any manner, decreed or promulgated by any Pope, or person esteemed at the time to be Pope, or by any Council or decree of the Fathers, or by any canon or Apostolic Constitution or ordinance, against heretics and schismatics. And he further defined and decreed that all these decrees ought (*debere*) to be perpetually observed, and replaced wherever they have grown obsolete, and ever after kept in vigorous (*viridi*) and fresh observance.

" The first laws against heretics, on which all subsequent ones were founded, did not originate from the Popes; they were promulgated by the Emperor Frederic II., partly in 1220, and more completely at Pavia, in February, 1224. As they had been dictated by the reigning Pope, so they were instantaneously adopted by him, and confirmed over and over again by his successor. Honorius III. in 1230 promulgated them as his own:—' These laws, published by our dearest son, Frederic, Emperor of the Romans, for the utility of all Christians, we praise and approve so as to be valid for all time. And if any one by temerarious audacity, at the persuasion of the enemy of the human race, shall in any way attempt to infringe them, let him know that he will incur the wrath of Almighty God, and the blessed Apostles, Peter and Paul.' The revised and enlarged code of laws, solemnly approved by Innocent IV. in 1243, Alexander IV.

in 1258, and Clement IV. in 1265, who, as well as Urban IV. in 1262, when commanding the inviolable observation of ·all the Apostolical constitutions and Imperial laws promulgated at Padua against heretics by Frederic, takes care to assert of him that he was at that time persisting in devotion to the Roman Church. These laws are for the 'extermination' of heretics. Heresy they declare to be a public crime, worse than treason, and one which attaints the persons, the goods, and the memory of heretics.

"As for the persons of heretics, they are all, without appeal or possibility of pardon, to be 'burnt alive in the sight of men, being committed to the ordeal of the flames.' They are to be branded with perpetual infamy; all their goods are to be confiscated, and never to be restored to their families. Their children and grandchildren are disinherited, and rendered for ever incapable of receiving benefices or serving in public offices. An exception, however, is made in favour of the orthodox son who shall inform against the secret heresy of his father. Heretics may be captured in any place, even in the sanctuary. Persons who are only suspected of heresy, unless they can clear themselves, are to be under ban, and after a year and a day, unless they clear themselves, are to be adjudged heretics and put to death as such. Repentant heretics to be imprisoned for life; if they relapse, to be put to death.

"All believers in, defenders, and favourers of heretics are put under ban, lose all their goods, are made infamous, incapable of holding any public office, or taking part in any election to such office; their testimony is not to be received; they are incapable of making a will, or of succeeding to any inheritance. They cannot sue any one in a court of justice, but they may be sued by any one. If they be Judges, their sentences are to be invalid, and causes are not to be carried before them; if advocates, their pleas are not to be received; if they are notaries, all deeds which they have drawn up are to be rejected as of no moment. Their children and grand-children are to be disinherited and incapacitated, and after due admonition they are themselves to be put to death as heretics. But any such favourer of heretics may at any time be restored to his pristine rights if he denounces a heretic, and gives evidence to bring him to the stake Moreover, all houses in which heretics may be found are to be razed to the ground and never built up again, as likewise all contiguous houses which belong to the same owner; all the goods therein are to be abandoned to pillage, and the owner to be branded with perpetual infamy and fined. The same is to be done to any house which is closed against the hue and cry for heretics, and the township is to be fined unless it produces the person or persons who closed the house. Again, persons not heretics, but allowing themselves to be captured as such, in order to allow the real heretics to escape, are to forfeit all their goods and to be put under ban. A special prison is to be provided, in which heretics are to be kept apart. Within fifteen days all heretics taken are to be sent to the bishop or ordinary, and by them, after condem-nation, delivered over to the secular power for punishment. The secular power is to carry out the sentence within five days, and in the meantime is bound, by the use of torture extending to the diminution of a limb or the danger of death, to force the heretics expressly to confess their errors, to accuse other heretics, to declare what goods they have, and to indicate their believers, receivers, and favourers.

" All magistrates, under pain of excommunication and interdict, are to recieve these laws, and to make oath that they will *bonâ fide* exterminate all heretics from their lands. In default, they are rendered incapable of acting as magis-trates, and all their acts are null and void. The magistrates are to arrest all persons indicated to them as heretics by the Inquisitors or other Catholics, and are everywhere to protect the Inquisitors against popular outrage. They are also to keep a register of all the children of heretics, to make sure that no such be ever admitted to any public office. The magistrate who refuses to swear to execute these laws is to be deprived of his office; all subjects are to be released from any oath of obedience to him; he is to be noted as a perjurer, to be perpetually infamous, to be fined, to be reckoned a favourer of heretics, and suspected in faith, and made incapable of all civil employments.

" The population in general, together with the military and police, are bound, whenever required, to assist with information, counsel, and force in the capture, spoliation, and inquisition of heretics under pain of ban and fine. Every one who knows of heretics, or of persons who meet in private conventicles, is bound to reveal it to his confessor, or to some one through whom it may come to the knowledge of the authorities, under pain of excommunication. Judges, advocates, and notaries are to give no official assistance to persons accused or suspected of heresy, under pain of perpetual deprivation of their office. Clergymen are not to give them the sacraments nor receive their oblations or alms. Those who give burial to a heretic are excommunicated without absolution until, with their own hands, they dig up the accursed corpse and throw it away. The grave where the corpse has laid is never afterwards to be used for burial. Any temporal lord refusing to exterminate heresy from his dominions is to be admonished, and, after a year's contumacy, his lands are to be assigned over to some other Catholic, who may seize them, and, after exterminating the heretics, may keep them as his own; where there is a lord paramount, his rights are to be respected in case he puts no obstacle in the way; otherwise not. No condemnation or penalty for heresy is ever to be relaxed by any means or for any reason, whether the demand of the people, or of the council or anything else,

T 2

and all statutes to the contrary are to be repealed and abolished. Innocent IV. in 1254 abolished the distinction between heretics and believers in the heretics, and adjudged them both to the same torments. He also founded a confraternity of Crusaders expressly to defend the Inquisitors against the effects of popular indignation. Urban IV. in 1262 further provided that to prevent scandal the testimony of the witnesses against heretics was not to be taken in the presence of the accused nor their names divulged to them. Also that the processes were to be conducted without formality or the 'row' *(strepitus)* of ordinary courts where the pleading of advocates was permitted. Clement IV., in 1265, added a provision that any one might take a heretic, and seize his goods to his own use. Nicholas III., in 1280, added a sentence of excommunication against any layman who, either in public or in private, disputed on the Catholic faith, and decreed that if after the emancipation of any person from serfdom his father should become a heretic, the emancipation should be void, and the son should become a serf again. When, in 1486, the magistrates of Brixen refused to burn heretics, on the ground that heresy was only an ecclesiastical offence, Innocent VIII. excommunicated them unless they carried out the sentences of the Inquisitors, without appeal, within six days. Finally, in order not to prolong indefinitely this catalogue, Leo X., in 1520, condemned the proposition '*Hereticos comburi est contra voluntatem spiritus.*' 'It is against the will of the Holy Ghost to burn heretics alive. If Popes are infallible, Catholics are bound to believe that it is not against the will of the Holy Ghost to burn heretics.

"Further, in 1535, Paul III. wrote a Bull against Henry VIII., which he promulgated in 1538, and which contains some new measures against the accomplices of heretics. In the 12th section all the faithful are admonished, under pain of excommunication, to avoid and cause others to avoid all the adherents of the king, and to have no commerce, conversation, or communication with the same, nor with the citizens, inhabitants, householders, subjects or vassals of the said king, his cities, dominions, lands, castles, counties, towns, or forts, by buying, selling, exchanging, or exercising any merchandise or chaffer, and to abstain from bringing or conducting, or causing to be brought or conducted, wine, grain, salt, or other victual, arms, clothes, wares or other merchandise or things, either by sea in ships, triremes, or other vessels, or by land on mules or other animals, and to refuse to receive such things when brought by them, and to refuse all assistance, counsel, or favour to those who presume to hold such traffic with them, directly or indirectly, secretly or openly. All this under penalty of excommunication, nullity of contracts, and forfeiture of all such merchandise, which is to become the property of the captors thereof.

" The 16th section requires and commands, in virtue of holy obedience, all rulers and persons having armed forces under them to set upon King Henry and his adherents, and to compel them to return to the unity of the Church, and obedience to the Holy See, and to capture them and all their subjects or vassals who even *de facto* recognize the said King as their Sovereign, or presume to obey him, or refuse to aid in expelling him,—to capture them with all their goods, movable or immovable, merchandize, moneys, ships, deposits on trust, things, and cattle, wherever they may be found, within or without the territories of the said king.

" And the 17th section declares that the Pope, acting with full authority, knowledge and power, gives such captors full licence, authority, and faculty to convert to their own uses the goods, merchandise, moneys, ships, things, and cattle so taken, and decrees that they belong of legal title to the persons who take them. Moreover, that all persons born in the dominions of the king, or domiciled there, or inhabiting there in any manner, who do not obey the clauses of this Bull, shall become the slaves of their captors, wherever they may be taken; and that this clause shall apply to all men, of whatsoever dignity, degree, state, order or condition, who shall presume to furnish Henry and his adherents with victuals, arms, or moneys, or hold commerce with them, or afford them help, counsel, or favour.

" If the Pope is infallible, it is clear that we must accept as principles of morals, the principles upon which this legislation is founded. They are such as these:—

" 1. No man has a right to his life or property who even secretly disbelieves any one article of the Catholic Creed.

" 2. No Christian Government ought to assure to any such man the enjoyment of his life or property.

" 3. Christian Governments are bound to put such men to death by burning them alive, and to confiscate their goods.

" 4. Children and friends are bound to inquire into the secret belief of their parents and companions, and denounce them if heretical.

" 5. Though moral turpitude does not affect dominion, yet error in faith at once renders a man incapable of all dominion over either persons or things.

" 6. That it is consistent with Christian civilization to proclaim that the goods and lands of any heretic, or collection of heretics, or adherents of heretics, no longer belong to the reputed owners, but are the property of the man who first takes them.

" 7. That a heretic is an outlaw; that he has no claim to justice; that all contracts with him are null and void; that no debts to him are to be paid, no oaths made to him are to be kept; and that his incapacity taints all his acts, renders his children incapacitated like himself, and makes all his deeds, judgments, and contracts void, even though the avoidance of the same should be injurious to a true believer.

" 8. That the slave trade and slavery, are institutions which should to be kept up, provided that the slaves are either heretics or favourers of heretics, or persons who have held commerce and communication with them.

" The question is not whether these principles can be reconciled with Christian morals, but whether government or civilization could exist one whole day if these principles were *bond fide* put into universal practice. Some of the most enormous injustices of history, such as the Irish Penal Laws, or the French Revolution, have only been faint and feeble attempts to apply partially and in a very circumscribed manner some of the less shocking of these laws. Pope Pius IX., if he would but read these laws, would be the first to shudder at them and abjure them, instead of making the claim of infallibility for their authors and promulgators. Even those who are most agog for declaring that the Papal authority is supreme, and, therefore, free from error, and that its decrees are final and irreformable, would shrink to acknowledge these principles to be real and practical doctrines of morals. They would find some subterfuge, some subtle distinction, to prove that these decrees were not formal, lacked something necessary to give them infallible weight, or, with Dr. Manning, they might say that an appeal to history is treason; that the Pope's authority is for the moment, and that the duty of reasonable men is to suppress the faculty which looks before and after, and to receive on each occasion the decision of the moment as supremely wise and entirely virtuous, though another century may discover it to have been fantastically foolish and ineffably wicked."

" As a proof how long the Editor has wished to raise up a literary memorial of her beloved mother, she adds a note received from Archbishop Whately in answer to an offer she made him of returning Lady Osborne's letters unless he allowed her to keep them with a view to the present undertaking "—

Dublin, 12th Feb., 1857.

MY DEAR MRS. OSBORNE,—You are welcome to keep any of my letters to Lady O. that you may think worth it. I had not supposed that there were any that were of sufficient consequence to be saved from the fire; but they were at least a proof of my regard for her; and as a memorial of that, some of them may be kindly valued by you.

Yours very truly,

RD. DUBLIN.

" The Editor considers the following letter, though it has already appeared in a pamphlet, worthy of reproduction here, as a correct statement of Archbishop Whately's views concerning the Church in Ireland, misrepresented as he often has been."

MISS WHATELY ON THE IRISH CHURCH.

The following letter, written by the daughter of the late Archbishop of Dublin to a friend, clearly shows, says *Saunders' News-Letter*, that Dr. Whately did not approve of the " disestablishment and disendowment " policy:—

Monterey, Vaud,
Switzerland, August 10, 1868.

MY DEAR MRS. OSBORNE,—I am surprised how any one could read my father's life and think that he entertained the impression that the Irish Church ought to be destroyed. The answer to such suggestion is sufficiently given in the circumstance not only of his remaining a dignitary of that Church, but of his having exerted all his powers throughout his life to save it from the impending danger, as his whole political life bears testimony. I have not, unfortunately, the memoirs by me at present, so can only refer from memory to the passage, I think in the appendix, in which his opinion is shown most plainly. There he mentions that he considers the mistake was calling it the Church of Ireland, instead of a branch of the Church of England in Ireland, as is the case with India, Australia, Canada, &c. But I know that when he first came to Ireland he was not fully and clearly aware of the real state of the case with regard to the Irish Church —*i. e.*, that it was not introduced as a novelty, but the original Church reformed, owing to its leaders having left the Romish Church. Some of his early expressions would have been modified had he entirely understood this as he afterwards did.

Believe me, &c.,

E. J. WHATELY.

(A fragment in Mrs. Hill's handwriting.)

As God in his Godhead is a simple essence known only to Himself, so also hath the soul an inherent divine essence which none can analyse. This simple essence of the soul we call spirit. It is in this which we can no more define than we can the great Incomprehensible himself. It is in this that the soul most nearly approaches its divine original. This is the inmost sanctuary of that temple of the living God which man was created to be. It is the holy of holies into which none but our Great High Priest can enter, the sacred and unapproachable shrine of the divinity in which alone is known the full and blessed import of the incommunicable name, "I am that I am." Draw not nigh thither until thou hast put off from thee all to which aught of the dust of human motive and human action may cleave, for this is indeed holy ground.

" The following extract from a letter to a young girl is a proof of Lady Osborne's natural love of the theatre, though with the self-denial for which she was conspicuous, she entirely gave it up for years, and only went to them to accompany her daughter."

You are right, my dear Margaret. I have been quite gay since my abode in this place. Two dinner parties, a play, and a ball. I need not tell you which I enjoyed most. You know how often we have decided that a good play is the greatest enjoyment in life. I saw your favorite, and the public favorite, Mr. Kean, in the character of Macbeth. I was delighted with his action and his manner, and wished much that you could all enjoy his representation with me, as you have seen him. I shall not deliver a long account of my admiration of his genius, but simply observe that I admire him as much as you do—need I say more!

She goes on—this house is charmingly situated in the midst of a large paddock. I feel amazingly disposed to favour you with a description of it, but I recollect having assented to the justice of Miss Edgeworth's remark that nothing is so dull as a picture on paper, and therefore resist the inclination, only observing that were you here you would never suppose yourself within six miles of London.

Mrs. Meyer delights in roving about the farm-yard in search of eggs and in admiring her cackling brood. Now you know that this is the part of a country for which I have no taste, as I never had any penchant for geese except when they are on the table. Do not suspect that I meant any play on the word geese. You may remember my dislike to trite witticisms. I only alluded to my terror of the gander's furious protection of his wife's offspring whenever I chanced to pass near.

"The following extract is from a pamphlet published by Mr. Grattan in the year 1800, is in reply to a speech of Lord Clare in favour of a legislative union. A graphical sketch of some of the friends with whom he had acted, speaks thus of the father of Sir Thomas Osborne. Having spoken of others, he goes on thus:—

Mr. Brownlow and Sir William Osborne, I wish we had more of these criminals. The former seconded the address of 1782; and in the latter, and in both, there was a stature of mind that would have become the proudest senate in Europe.

" As Lord Sydenham's Life may be a book not universally known, the Editor transcribes an anecdote from it that she thinks interesting."

On one occasion the king being on the pier head, about to embark in the Royal Yacht on one of his sailing trips, and having the child in his arms, turned round to Mr. Pitt who was in attendance at his elbow, (having probably hurried down from London for an audience on important business) and exclaimed, " Is not this a fine boy, Pitt? Fine boy is not he? Take him in your arms, Pitt: take him in your arms; charming child is not he?" Then suiting the action to the word he made the stiff and solemn Premier—weighed down as he seemed to be with cares of State—dandle and kiss the pretty boy, and carry him some minutes in his arms albeit strange and unused to such a burden. The circumstance though trivial, had so comical an effect, from the awkwardness and apparent reluctance with which the formal minister performed his compelled part of nurse, as to make an impression on the writer who stood by, though but seven years old himself, which time has never effaced. Pitt, although no doubt fretted by his master's childish fancy, which exposed him to the ill-suppressed titter of the circle around, including several of the younger branches of the Royal family, to whom the scene afforded great amusement, put the best countenance he could on the matter, but little thought, no doubt, that the infant he was required to nurse would at no very distant time, have the offer of the same high official post which he then occupied, the chancellorship of the Exchequer, and would be quoted as perhaps *next to himself* the most remarkable instance in modern times of the early attainment of great public eminence by the force of talent alone; equally purchased, alas! by premature extinction at the zenith of a brilliant career.

" The Editor is under great obligations to the brother of Lord Sydenham, for most kindly sending her the following gratifying mention of Lady Osborne in his private journal; and Mr. Poulett Scroope speaking of her own letters of which he says, ' I found them the unreserved outpourings of a highly refined and religious mind.' He very considerately added, ' I ought perhaps to have returned them to her daughter,' but not having the honour of her acquaintance, I destroyed them."

Extract from a Journal kept by Mr. Poulett Thomson, September 6th, 1837.

I have now spent six days in Lady Osborne's society, during the greater part of which we have conversed most unreservedly. She is decidedly one of the most agreeable and interesting persons I have ever met with. What influence a woman of superior mind may gain?

" The following notice of the Rev. Henry Woodward is

given from the letter of a lady who stayed at Newtown
Anner, because it alludes to a striking feature in Mr. Woodward's character in real life, though not appearing either in
his letters or works, and that is 'his sense of the ridiculous'
which was very strong."

I have seen the celebrated Mr. Woodward several times.
He is a totally different person to what I expected the first
time. He had just learned . . . and he conversed little;
after we met under livelier auspices, and had some good
humoured sparring. I made him laugh in spite of himself,
and that was all I wished. He is, you know fond of a jest.

Mrs. Young, mentioned in Lady Osborne's letters, wrote the
" Life and Times of Paleario," a book of which Dean Hook
speaks thus in his Life of Cardinal Pole, one of the Arch-
bishops of Canterbury: " Mrs. Young's interesting Life of
Arnio Paleario, a work of considerable research, and great
fairness." The word Papist is used throughout this book
not in a spirit of disrespect to the members of the Romish
Church, but as the word Royalist; adherents of the Pope,
like adherents of the king.

" Most of the notes were written before the sacrilegious
Church Bill had passed the Houses of Parliament, a measure
meant to gratify the enemies of Protestantism, but really
dealing an awful blow at the civilization of this poverty-
stricken country."

" An extract from a Juvenile Journal of the Editor may not
be wholly uninteresting to those who care to know the
external lineaments and peculiarities of a writer."

Monsieur de Sismondi is short and fat, with very shaggy
eyebrows, intelligent dark eyes, a turned-up nose, and brown

hair, thickly sprinkled with grey. The expression of his countenance is extreme benevolence, which he seems to feel for everybody. He is perfectly free from the airs that many persons give themselves from a consciousness of superiority of intellect, and in conversation expresses himself with a force and clearness that cannot fail to keep up his listener's attention. Madame de Sismondi being English, her drawing-room is arranged "à l'Anglaise." They are extremely hospitable; every Wednesday evening they receive company, they have a great passion for seeing at their house remarkable people, and I believe that a person of any note whatever leaving Geneva without being invited to Chênes is a thing that never occurs.

At present there are seventeen or nineteen volumes (I am not sure which) of his history of France, and he has only got to Francis I. He has written a history of the Italian Republics, and a work called " Literature du midi de l'Europe." He speaks English very well. Monsieur S. has also written " The Decline of the Roman Empire."

He had a great peculiarity of vision—the red ray disappeared out of every color, so that one evening when Lady Osborne told him the color of her cloak, which he went to get for her, he said " you need not tell me the colour for what appears so-and-so to you seems so-and-so to me."

" While revising these letters the Editor has received one from a relation containing an application of a character given by a third party of another lady so singularly appropriate that she cannot refrain from copying as such."

I quite agree with you that your mother's was a very beautiful character, and a very loveable one in its sweetness and unselfishness. It reminds me of what Lady Combermere wrote of my friend, Mrs. Aldis, to her really inconsolable husband after her death:—" I never knew any one more admirably endowed with the finest qualities of heart and mind. Her fine and even prodigious memory was an addition, not a substitute, for original thought, and the stores of her mind, instead of fostering the sense of her own superiority, only gave an additional charm to her courteous manner and ready appreciation of the merits of her associates. All these fine qualities were but the exponents of the high religious sentiment which was the basis of her character."

It is quite true that Lady Osborne had a prodigious memory in connection with other faculties—well versed in history, theology, the classics in the original, " belles lettres," and, to a certain extent, science. She had mastered seven languages, so that a friend wishing to give her a suitable present, procured a Polyglot bible in eight languages—English, German, French, Italian, Spanish, Greek, Latin, and Hebrew; and at one time she knew by heart the whole Gospel of St. Luke in Greek. Always able to seize the point and principle of a subject, as far as she went in the field of science she made it completely her own, and thus was fitted for further enterprise therein. She had the keenest enjoyment and appreciation of art in all its branches. So much for her powers of mind. Her meekness, frankness, large-mindedness, unselfishness, generosity, and sympathy, can only be understood by those who knew her, for they felt their exercise upon themselves. Thinking of her is like gazing on a lake which, when at rest, reflects the blue and smiling heavens.

" The following extract is copied from the *Clonmel Chronicle* as the concluding notice of her, (to whom the foregoing letters were addressed), on the occasion of her burial:"

The Rev. Henry Woodward of Fethard, one of the most

attached friends of Lady Osborne, officiated inside the church, and delivered a deeply impressive address, which was listened to with the profoundest attention. The touching beauty of the character of Lady Osborne, as depicted by her venerated friend, found an echo in the heart of every one who had the privilege of her ladyship's acquaintance.

" The following is the substance of Mr. Woodward's address:"

I have been requested, as having been honored for so many years with the friendship of her whose loss we all deplore as a public calamity, to say a few words to this congregation now assembled to pay the last tribute to her mortal remains, and I do so the more readily as this wish finds an echo in the deepest emotions of my own heart.

In St. Paul's Cathedral there is a simple memorial of the illustrious architect by whom that stupendous edifice was reared, and this monument is but the signpost pointing to another. The inscription on it consists of four Latin words, which in English signify " If you seek a monument look around—survey this splendid pile, the offspring of his genius and product of his skill." And so, in raising a memorial to Lady Osborne, I would say, " look around." Go, in the first place to that house she has left this morning, never, alas! to return, unless, as some have said, the spirits of the just are permitted to visit, and love to hover round the scenes which were dear to them on earth. Ask the domestics of that household, from the highest to the lowest, whether Lady Osborne had any proud looks, and whether her language to them was not that rather of a mother and friend than of a superior and a mistress. Travel next the whole circle of this neighbourhood and ask of those who, from their station in life, formed what is termed her acquaintance, ask them what

Lady Osborne was. For my own part, if those words of Job ever applied to human character, they applied, I say, to her—"When the ear heard me, then it blessed me; and when the eye saw me, it gave witness to me; because I delivered the poor that cried, and the fatherless, and him that had none to help him. The blessing of him that was ready to perish came upon me, and I caused the widow's heart to sing for joy." Let those who followed her during the course of that tedious, trying illness that brought her to her grave; let them declare whether they ever witnessed more lamb-like patience, more gentle submission, more perfect resignation, a firmer reliance upon Christ, more perfect trust in God? Yes, it was that reliance and that trust which led her daughter to desire that I should address you on this occasion; and it was that trust which makes me desire to do so, and to tell you that I never witnessed a more entire renunciation of self, and all dependence upon self, upon any supposed merits or righteousness of her own. No, it was simply a desire, as a sinner lost and undone, to cast herself upon the all-prevailing sacrifice and righteousness of her Redeemer.

During her last days, when all was coming to a close, it was her solace and delight to hear those which I might call her favorite hymns. One of those I shall repeat, and leave it to that hymn to explain what Lady Osborne's leading views of religion were. I would direct your attention particularly to the last verse which she continued repeating until utterance failed her—

> " There is a fountain filled with blood
>   Drawn from Emmanuel's veins,
> And sinners plunged beneath that flood
>   Lose all their guilty stains.
>
> The dying thief rejoiced to see
>   That fountain in his day;
> And there may I, as vile as he,
>   Wash all my sins away.

Dear dying Lamb, Thy precious blood
   Shall never lose its power
Till all the ransomed Church of God
   Be saved to sin no more.

E'er since, by faith, I saw the stream
   The flowing wounds supply,
Redeeming love has been my theme,
   And shall be till I die.

Then in a nobler, sweeter song,
   I'll sing thy power to save,
When this poor lisping, stamm'ring tongue
   Lies silent in the grave."

And now, my brethren, to conclude, there lies the body of that much-loved friend; but where is her soul? I humbly trust singing the song of Moses and of the Lamb. But where will our souls be in a few fleeting years? It rests with us to determine now; it rests with us to determine what will present itself to our view when we first look on that country in which we are to live for ever. Will it be ours to stumble on the dark mountains where there is neither sun, nor moon, nor stars? or will it be ours, with that friend whose remains are now before us, and with all those who have departed this life in God's faith and fear, to turn out on those green pastures in which the good shepherd of the sheep will lead, and feed his flock for ever.

The funeral was one of the largest, if not the very largest, we have ever witnessed.

The hymn Lady Osborne preferred to all others was that exquisite one of Mr. Charles Grant's, beginning

   " When gathering clouds around I view."

and on her dying bed she desired those around her to commit to memory the one of which the first and last lines are these—

   " Nearer, my God, to Thee, nearer to Thee."

" These remarks of Archbishop Whately's on " Fasting" the Editor considers well worth reproducing for preservation."

" *Fasting.*"

We should first determine whether fasting comes under the head of *moral duties* or *positive ordinances;* if, for instance, we confuse it with temperance, we place it under *moral duties* for which *we have no positive precepts.* But Fasting comes under the head of *positive ordinances.* We should therefore expect positive precepts and commands if it were intended to be observed. We have such for prayer, though it had always been practised by the Jews; but we have none such for fasting, as may be shown by an explanation of those very passages in which our Lord is supposed by precept or example to enforce it.

That Jesus did not *forbid* private fasting to his countrymen, as he does not appear to have interfered with the habits or customs of his nation on ordinary occasions, may be inferred by several passages: " When ye fast be not as the hypocrites, &c." But he neither recognized it (as recorded) in his own practice, *nor in conjunction with his disciples;* neither does he sanction it in any way as connected with his religion. The forty days fasting in the wilderness has been erroneously appealed to, but the whole of that mysterious transaction being, in its literal sense, entirely unconnected with our conduct, it forms no example for us. In our sense of the word our Lord did not *fast;* we are expressly told that it was not till " after he had fasted forty days and forty nights that he was an hungered." Which hunger appears to have been appointed for a particular purpose connected with his temptation. But the mistake about fasting seems to have arisen chiefly from a misrepresentation of our Lord's words, as recorded by Matthew, Luke, and Mark. Matt. ix. 15: "And Jesus said unto them, shall the children of the bridechamber mourn as long as the Bridegroom is with them? but the days will come when the Bridegroom shall be taken away from them, and then shall they fast."

St. Luke attributes this question to which our Lord is here replying, to the Pharisees, Matthew to the disciples of John; they had both probably been offended at the omission. Here then our Lord seems absolutely to forbid the practice of fasting (as an ordinance of his religion) to his disciples *while he remained with them*, but he adds: "The days will come when the Bridegroom shall be taken from them, and then shall they fast:" viz. as a *natural expression of mourning*. This period of the Bridegroom's absence, was, that in which he lay in the grave, and the time which passed between his ascension and the day of Pentecost; while the disciples were awaiting in Jerusalem "The promise of the Father." On that day our Lord returned to them, according to his promise, not in bodily form but as their "*Comforter to abide with them for ever.*" This period of his return he calls a period of *joy*. "Ye now have sorrow," in the prospect of his going away, "but I will see you again, and your joy no *man taketh* from you." On this subject of his return and abiding with his disciples for ever it is only necessary to refer to his last conversations as recorded by St. John.

It appears then that this practice of fasting, which had been a customary sign of mourning and contrition among the Jews was not to be used by Christ's disciples while he abode with them whether in the flesh or by his spirit; under which last dispensation, a higher and more joyful one (since our Lord is no longer a prisoner of earth but exalted to glory) we live. But there is a passage in Mark's Gospel which is supposed to enforce the duty of fasting. When our Lord's disciples having failed in working a miracle, enquire why could we not cast him out? He replies "this kind can come forth by nothing but prayer and fasting." Now whatever this passage may mean, it could not be intended to reproach the disciples with *not fasting*, since a little farther back the same writer after mentioning that the disciples of John and the Pharisees used to fast, relates the reproach made to our Lord that his disciples fast not, and his justification of them in the passage above quoted about the Bridegroom. Probably our Lord simply meant by this expression *earnest prayer*, since it seems to have been customary among the Jews, to use fasting in conjunction with prayer on remarkable occasions, and the disciples might have found some difficulty in disjoining them. But whatever the interpretation of this passage may be, it does not evidently concern us, since whatever might have been the habits of the Apostles themselves *as Jews* they certainly do not enforce or even recommend fasting to their heathen converts, which they would surely have done had they understood such to have been the purpose of their Master's injunction. With respect to fasting as an ordinance of the Church, it does not appear that she has made it an ordinance. Her Collect for the first Sunday in Lent recommends such abstinence as shall subdue the flesh to the spirit, which should mean abstaining *habitually* from excess; for the abstaining from food or particular kinds of food, on certain days or parts of days, appears to have no such tendency, but as we see in the Roman Catholic Church a contrary one, it is as an external sign of mourning and contrition in commemorating our Lord's death and sufferings—for instance, it might be suitably employed as a mourning dress might be, but this it should be remembered would be very different from the fasting practised by the Pharisees and John's disciples, which our Lord in reference to their views declares should have been done secretly, so that they appear not unto men to fast. Now no *public* ordinance can ever be so kept.

" Nothing can be clearer or more rational and scriptural than these observations of Archbishop Whately on the two Sacraments."

Tendency in men to regard the two Sacraments both erroneously, but with opposite feelings; the one with a superstitious and mistaken kind of desire: the other with an equally mistaken dread and an awe mixed with repugnance. Baptism they are anxious not to *omit* : but are culpably careless as to the solemnity of the administration and the things implied in it. The Eucharist they respect as something even too solemn for ordinary Christians, but the necessity of it, they are apt to overlook. Hence they have in fact made Christianity *two* religions; that of communicants and non-communicants, &c. Baptism on the contrary they are anxious never to omit, but are apt to look on the outward visible sign as a kind of charm, and to think little of what is suitable to an ordinance conveying an inward spiritual grace. Sponsors, in particular, they often select with very little reference to the Sacrament of Baptism regarded as a religious rite.

They would not choose as *guardian* to take care (in the event of orphanhood) of the *temporal property* of their children, any person whom they knew or believed to be utterly unfit for such a charge. But they sometimes choose as sponsors, who are to be solemnly charged to " see that this child be religiously brought up" as a sincere and regular member of our Church, persons whom they know to be not even such themselves, (*e. g.*, persons who never attend the Lord's table, which yet no one denies to be an essential point of conformity to the regulations of our Church as well as to the command of our Divine Master). And the unnecessary resorts to private baptism often by choice and as a kind of domestic festival with an avoidance as far as possible of all that connects it with the congregation into which it admits the persons baptized (that being its very purport), is another instance of the mistaken feelings with which this Sacrament is regarded.

These causes tend to give an undue plausibility to the arguments by which Anabaptists support their own peculiar view. The scrupulous eagerness with which the baptism of an infant is sought and the unscrupulous carelessness with which the administration of the rite is too often connected, helps the opponents of all infant baptism to represent it as a weak and irrational superstition. This is greatly aided by the total neglect, in some, of the rite of Confirmation (which is in fact the sequel and completion of Baptism) and by the thoughtless carelessness with which others are apt to bring forward their children to receive it. It should be represented as being and should be made the connecting link between the two Sacraments; the completion of the one and the introduction to the other.

Notes of a Conversation.

Mr. —— began by expressing his regret that you had withdrawn from the party you had long been connected with; I could not, I said, participate in that regret, it being always my advice to every one to keep clear of the shackles of every party. He said he conceived me to be prejudiced against the party in question, on account of the very unjustifiable treatment I had received from some particular members of it.

I strongly protested against the charge of "prejudice" in the strict sense, viz., as a præ-judicium, a judgment formed antecedently to knowledge. Having lived so many years in various situations in the midst of men of various parties, personally intimate with many individuals of each, aloof from all parties as parties, and a watchful by-stander, it was imputing to me the most perverse kindness to say that I judged not by evidence, but by prejudice. He said he did not mean prejudice in the strict sense; but only that the ill conduct of some members of the party made me think the more unfavorably of others.

I dislike all parties as parties; but as for the *individuals* composing them, I make great allowance for a party-man's acting in a way that would be execrable if he were un-shackled. Having enlisted, and marching in the ranks of a party, his conduct when urged on him by his associates is, though not excused, yet palliated, and is entitled to some degree of pity (not unmixed with contempt) if it be such as he would if left to himself abhor. But then, on the other hand, he is in a great degree responsible for all that is done by the rest of his party, in the cause and in the matters wherein they are associated; even when he has no personal share, he is affording them his countenance, comforting, aiding and abetting.

Mr. —— said that you were of a disposition to need and wish for the support of a party, and could not well do without it. I replied that though some may be more in-clined than others to join a party, I had advised you as I do all persons, to keep clear of all. And that holding as I do, that this is the *duty* of all, I could not doubt that it was *possible*, though more difficult for some than others.

He said he had felt convinced that he could effect some highly important objects much better by enrolling himself in a party than by standing single, and that he had therefore done so, though he disapproved of much that was done by his party.

I said it was perfectly justifiable and right to join with any person or any party or association (ἐπὶ ῥητοῖς) for some *specified, definite* object or objects; but not to enroll your-self as a supporter—*indefinitely and generally*—of the general views and practices of those whom you do not throughout approve of. It is quite right for instance to join in some charitable association with men of various religions and political sentiments; the nature and objects of the association being *distinctly stated*, you are pledged to nothing else; the members are not pledged to each other's religious or political creeds, they are responsible each for himself alone, in all matters not pertaining to that particular charity. So also if I join with certain members of Parliament to oppose or to forward some specific legislative measure, I am not responsible for the rest of their public, any more than of their private, conduct. So also as an Education Commissioner I act with Roman Catholics and Dissenters on a specified plan, for a definite object. But if I allow myself to be reckoned as one of the High Church or the Low Church *party*, or any such party, as is characterized not by aiming at some one or more *specified measure*, but by the general tendency of their religious principles and views, everything which comes before the world (in reference to those principles) and which I do not distinctly and publicly disavow, becomes to a certain degree my act. Though not distinctly done by me, the agents derive from me (as well as from each of the other individuals of the party) some of that countenance and support which I in return receive from them in furthering such measures as *I* seek to promote. In fact, this is proved by the very reason Mr. —— assigned for acting with a party; viz., the support and countenance of a party enabled him to accomplish the better what he reckoned desirable objects. Now it would be absurd, and indeed unfair to think of obtaining himself this aid towards his own views from others, if they were to derive none from him towards *theirs*. Now this makes you, said I, responsible to a certain degree, for much that you admit to be most unjustifiable conduct. Are you not therefore, even more to be blamed (instead of being thereby excused) in consequence of the disapprobation you feel of that which you nevertheles so far sanction.

No doubt one may as a member of a party, effect many good objects more fully than he could otherwise. So he might by turning Roman Catholic, or Mahometan, or Hindoo, he might convey some good moral lessons and check some faults among those who could not otherwise be brought to listen to him. But would he be justified in becoming on that ground, a member of a church or sect which he believed taught much that is false, and sanctions much that is vicious? This is clearly a case of doing evil that good may come. And it clearly makes no difference in principle whether the error be one or another, whether greater or smaller, whether there be two, or three, or fifty errors thus sanctioned.

If you have no right, for the sake of effecting some good object, to become a Mahometan, you have no right to become the member of an orthodox or an Evangelical *party* if they inculcate or practice as a *party* anything you disapprove; unless you distinctly and *publicly protest* against every such act or tenet of theirs.

By the bye, it is curious to observe how Mr. ——, and other members of his, and of other parties, are themselves actually doing the very thing for which they censure, without any real foundation, the Education Commissioners.

You hear much clamour about our *combining* with Roman Catholics, compromising principles, and all that ; and I am made accountable for Dens' Theology, and for all the Roman Catholic errors ; as Archbishop Murray is, by "John Tuam," for all that I have written *against* Romish errors, as if we were members of a *party*; for all which there is no ground whatever, because we are acting together (ἐπὶ ῥητοῖς) for a specific object, the diffusion of a certain kind and degree of instruction to the poor, and on a system of which the rules are all written, and printed, and published. It is just so that the members of the Dublin Mendicity Institution are acting together for the relief of a certain class of poor ; and that the Irish landlords, Whig and Tory, are uniting to concert means of altering a certain portion of the Poor Law Bill. If, indeed, the object of the Education Board be a bad one—if it be better that the poor Roman Catholics should be left totally ignorant, unless they will consent to be educated as Protestants, on *that* ground let us be censured ; but it is mere folly, or something worse, to represent us as responsible for each other's acts and tenets; as Commissioners we are responsible only for what is regularly resolved on and ordered by the Board. But it would be otherwise if, *like the very persons who censure us*, we allowed ourselves to be considered as members of a party formed not merely for certain specified and definite objects in particular, but for the advancement generally, of certain religious views and practises ; and if we allowed, without protesting against them, certain views to be promulgated, and practises recommended, and measures adopted by members of that party, and understood as coming from the party, while we secretly disapproved of them. This is what we do *not* do, but which those persons do who, at the same time, impute to us the very fault they are guilty of. They think, forsooth, they can effect, as members of a party, some good which they could not otherwise. I think that, as an Education Commissioner, I can effect good objects which would otherwise be unattainable ; but *that* consideration would not justify me if I purchased this advantage by giving my sanction to something which I thought wrong or erroneous- And why am I *not* giving my sanction to some error, for instance, of Dr. Murray ; *not* because I tell you, or Mr. ——, in a *private conversation* that I disapprove of Dr. Murray's views, but because I am not one of the same *Party* with him ! not combined with him at all except in the specified *work* of carrying into effect a certain distinct plan, drawn out by Lord Stanley, for a precise object

But to return to my narrative, Mr. —— said it was very well for such a person as myself to resolve to stand aloof from all parties; that I was able and worthy to stand single; but that from more humble individuals like him, it would be too presumptuous, &c.

I said I had not been thought much of early in life, but that I had very early formed the resolution to tie myself to no man or party, but to listen to reason from every quarter, to " prove all things, and to hold fast that which is right," according to the best judgment I am able to form. And this plan I laid down for myself, not because I thought myself an eminent man, but because I thought it a Christian duty. I have faults enough of my own to answer for. I cannot afford to answer for other people's. And yet, that I must do if I act at the bidding of others, or if I give my implied sanction to the acts of a party. It is in vain for me to throw off my free agency. I *can not* throw off my responsibility; whether the light of reason that God has given me be strong or weak He does not authorise me to shut my eyes and be led blindfold by any human party or rabbi. Accordingly, I never did, said I, even when I was a person of no note or expectation, enrol myself as a partizan; and what is more, I added, if I had, I should *now* have been a party *leader*.

It was not, I said, from disdaining to occupy an *inferior place* in the ranks of a party, that I kept aloof, but from objecting to *party*—especially religious party—as contrary to the words and spirit of the Apostle's admonitions, when he censures as " carnal " those who said, " I am of Paul, and I of Apollos, and I of Cephas, and I of Christ," he does not make any exception in favor of some humbler class of Christians—he does not say " you, that are great and eminent men ought not to be carnal, but ordinary Christians may," nor again when he says, " Are ye not carnal and walk as men," he does not say that such conduct is carnal in *some* persons and not in others ; but he censures and forbids parties in the Corinthian Church generally. I must conclude therefore, said I, that he meant to extend this to all Christians (till I see some reason given me for an exception) and not merely to great and eminent men. It may be said, to be sure, that there is something of moral greatness of character in resolving not to follow a leader and to show *due* respect and kindness indeed to all men, but to " call no man master upon earth."

Aye, said he, that is just what I mean when I speak of a great man being such a one as can, and should, keep clear of party: it is not so much intellectual as *moral* greatness that is wanted for acting such a part. True, I replied, but it is precisely this moral greatness that is *required* of every Christian and which he is *enabled* to manifest. If this be a *duty* (as Paul distinctly declares it to be) it must be something *possible*. What is the Gospel given for? What mean the promises of Divine grace ? Is the Christian religion *not* designed to elevate our nature? and if so, and *intellectual* capacity or superhuman *knowledge* are not to be looked for by all Christians, what is the elevation of our nature to consist in, if it be not that *moral* greatness which you speak of as being a thing not to be thought of but by one in a thousand? Are the rest—the mass of Christians—to claim by virtue of their being God's people, the privilege of being allowed to continue carnal? Are these to show their humility not by submitting to *God*, but by submitting to a party of men? " Be not deceived : God is not thus mocked."

Extracts from Lady Osborne's Letters, omitted in the first volume.

Palace, St. Stephen's Green.

In the evening I had some conversation with Lord and Lady Clarendon, with both of whom I was charmed. Miss Campbell is staying here—a nice, pretty little girl who, at my request, read the Historic Doubts aloud to me. They are very amusing—his Grace has given the work to me. Mrs. Pakenham spoke to me of Mrs. Congreve—she has heard of me from her. You ask how I like Lady Monck. I am perfectly delighted with her, and I think Lord Monck the model of a country gentleman. He is, besides, very intelligent, and truly liberal. " Since those days Lord Monck, as Governor-General of Canada, to the humbler character of 'a model country gentleman,' has added fresh laurels as the agent who accomplished the confederation of the British Provinces in North America."

With regard to ——, I think him a fearful mischief-maker. He was preordained to represent all the landlords as the cause of Ireland's miseries, and the priests the sheet anchor of salvation.

Sir Thomas Osborne though he spent the greater part of his life in Ireland went to Christ Church, Oxford, for his university education. As he has often been misrepresented the Editor inserts a passage from a letter to Lady Osborne written by his brother-in-law, the Earl of Carysfort, though it does not state the nature of the causes that led to his remarkable dislike of general society.

" I am greatly rejoiced by the wish your ladyship so kindly expresses of introducing your children to their relations. Exclusive of my near connexion with the Osborne family by my first marriage I am related to them by blood and friendship in a very high degree. The mother of the late Sir William Osborne was my father's aunt. The two young men were educated together and had the strongest mutual regard for each other which terminated only with their lives. My intimacy with Sir Thomas began, therefore, at a very early age, and was never, I hope interrupted. I lamented extremely some unfortunate circumstances which led him to contract a singularity of character which prevented his worth being known and appreciated as it ought to have been, and at last, I fear, disgusted him with the world. Your ladyship will forgive my saying that I was most anxiously interested for your happiness, though as I never heard again from Sir Thomas, and had, soon after I was last in Ireland, the misfortune (I have experienced no severer blow) of losing Judge Osborne, and as I received no intimation by your ladyship's direction of Sir Thomas' death, I could not presume to obtrude myself upon you.

"All these recollections cannot but make me delighted at finding by your ladyship's letter the disposition you are in to resume a friendly intercourse with the family, now much reduced in number; I am sure that you will find yourself greeted by them with all possible affection. I shall be most impatient to see the representative of a family I have loved so much." He goes on to say, "I am no longer worth any one's notice, I am now in my 71st year, and though not infirm and without any strength of the vital principle, yet I suffer continually, almost without any respite, from very troublesome disorders, of which asthma is the worst, but I bless the goodness of God who has given many great comforts and very tolerable spirits."

Lord Carysfort made a translation of the poet Camoens.

Note on vol. 1, p. 238.

"In one of Lady Osborne's letters from Scotland, the possibility of the prefix of "reptile" to the revered name of William Wilberforce, may seem unbearable impertinence, but can easily be explained. Captain Walker (described as a character) evidently classed men under two heads: reptiles and geniuses. He was under a mistaken impression that Mr. Wilberforce had not done justice to the Rev. Mr. Ramsay as instigator of his interest in the cause of the slaves; whereas Clarkson was the appropriator of the credit due to him, but being thus misinformed, Captain Walker would naturally put the great Wilberforce in a wrong category.

The reader who has reflected properly upon the characters of the writers of these letters, the Editor thinks, might address three classes of individuals thus:—To the *infidel* he might say, 'You think the *strength* of your intellect places you beyond the reach of superstition; but this is not the case. Your *weakness* withholds you from acknowledging as inevitable, though incomprehensible, the superiority of the code of belief to which you owe devotion. You are a self-seeker, beginning and ending with self.'

To the *political destructive* he might observe, " You profess to love liberty and hate oppression, and like to sneer at the oft-quoted lines—

'Let laws and learning, arts and commerce die,' &c.

But take care that you are not turning the engine of oppression against the truth 'which maketh free,' and those who are providentially appointed to foster 'laws and learning, arts and commerce.'

To the *superstitious* he might thus address himself: " You think want of faith a terrible crime—so it is in those who have the means of arriving at it ; but there is infidelity in not holding the negative truth, a sort of unbelief that caused Galileo to be cast into a dungeon because he asserted the sun did not move round the earth.

The Editor takes this opportunity of giving to the public some most beautiful lines sent to her by Mrs. Hill, in 1839, that they may become known, and also with a faint hope that some one may perhaps be aware of their authorship, for she has never met with them in any collection of poems."

HOPE.

Again, again she comes ! methinks I hear
    Her wild sweet singing and her rushing wings !
My heart goes forth to meet her with a tear,
    And welcome sends from all its broken strings.

It was not thus—not thus we met of yore,
　　When my plumed soul went halfway to the sky
To greet her, and the joyous song she bore
　　Was scarce more tuneful than its glad reply.
The wings are fettered with the weight of years,
　　And grief has spoilt the music with her tears!

She comes! I know her by her starry eyes,
　　I know her by the rainbow in her hair—
Her vesture of the light of summer skies.
　　But gone the girdle which she used to wear
Of summer roses, and the sandal flowers
　　That hung enamoured round her fairy feet,
When in her youth she haunted earthly bowers,
　　And culled from all their beautiful and sweet.
No more she mocks me with her voice of mirth,
　　Nor offers now the garland of the earth!

Come back, come back! thou hast been absent long,
　　Oh! welcome back the sybil of the soul,
Who comes and comes again with pleading strong,
　　To offer to the heart her mystic scroll;
Though every year she wears a sadder look,
　　And sings a sadder song—and every year
Some further leaves are torn from out her book,
　　And fewer what she brings and far more dear.
As once she came oh might she come again
　　With all the perished volumes offered then?

But come! thy coming is a gladness yet—
　　Light from the future o'er the present cast
That makes the present bright. But oh! regret
　　Is present sorrow while it mourns the past,

And memory speaks as speaks the curfew bell
    To tell the daylight of the heart is done.
Come, like the seer of old and with thy spell
    Put back the shadow of that setting sun
On my soul's dial; and with new-born light
    Hush the wild tolling of that voice of night!

Bright spirit come! the mystic rod is thine
    That shows the hidden fountains of the heart
And turns with point unerring to divine
    The places where its buried treasures rest,
The hoards of thought and feeling: at that spell
    Methinks I feel its long lost wealth revealed
And ancient springs within my spirit swell,
    That grief had choked and ruins had concealed
And sweetly spreading where their waters play
    The tint and freshness of its early day.

She comes! she comes! her voice is in mine ear,
    Her wild sweet voice that sings and sings for ever,
Whose stream of song sweet thoughts awake to hear,
    Like flowers that haunt the margin of a river.
She comes! I know her by her radiant eyes,
    Before whose smile the long dim cloud departs,
And if a deeper shade be on her brow,
    And if her tones be sadder than of yore,
And if she sings more solemn music now,
    And bears another harp than erst she bore,
And if around her form no longer glow
    The earthly flowers that in her youth she wore
That look is holier and that song more sweet,
    And heaven's flowers, the stars, are at her feet.

THE END.

www.ingramcontent.com/pod-product-compliance
Lightning Source LLC
Chambersburg PA
CBHW060516030726
47498CB00004B/971